HE WASN'T FAST ENOUGH

With his eyes closed and the music filling the car's interior, Brenton did not notice the figures slowly emerging from the mist.

For a moment they stood at the edge of the swamp. Then they parted and began to encircle the car, the yellow light of the emergency flashers illuminating the fog and casting a firelike glow across their hideous faces.

The jolt to the car awakened Brenton. He shook his head a moment and then stared through the windshield.

At that instant, the monster on the hood slammed into the windshield, the impact spreading a network of cracks across the glass.

Brenton kicked about, trying to quickly lock all the car doors.

He wasn't fast enough.

BLOOD HUNTER

SIDNEY WILLIAMS

PINNACLE BOOKS
WINDSOR PUBLISHING CORP.

PINNACLE BOOKS

are published by

Windsor Publishing Corp.
475 Park Avenue South
New York, NY 10016

First Printing: November, 1990

Printed in the United States of America

To David,
my buddy.

Acknowledgments

Once again I've made a foray into the fictional world of Aimsley, Louisiana.

As on previous trips, I did not travel alone. While all of the people and places in Riverland Parish are the product of my imagination, I have had some help with the real things, especially weaponry.

I express thanks to Jack Harp of *The Alexandria Daily Town Talk* for his assistance with the research on domestic weapons mentioned in this book. Any errors in that realm are mine and not his.

Special thanks also to Dan Nance of the U.S. Army Post at Fort Polk, Louisiana, for the fact sheets he provided on weaponry.

Cruelty has a human heart,
And Jealousy a human face;
Terror the human form divine,
And Secrecy the human dress.
                    —William Blake

Prologue

On the morning of the day they died, Cody Jackson and Mark Turner were told they were being transferred from the Aimsley City Jail because of overcrowding.

The two had been cellmates for two days in the dank second-floor lockup, and the prospect of getting bumped over to a parish work farm was appealing. At least they would have some opportunity for fresh air.

Cody was awaiting trial on an armed robbery charge, although he had a rap sheet long enough to get him declared a habitual offender, a ticket to longer jail time. He was a massive black man with shoulders that stretched against the seams of the blue prison work shirt he had been issued. The length of his hair sometimes led people to wonder if he was a Rastafarian.

With the scraggly beard that covered his chin and the scar which stretched from the scalp line down across his forehead and through his left eyebrow in a jagged pink trail, he created a threatening presence. He was the kind of guy cops hated to deal with, and they were careful to keep him shackled wrist and ankle anytime he was out of his cell.

Turner was less formidable by size. He was only about five feet eleven inches and weighed one hundred fifty pounds. Still, wearing the faded jeans, tee shirt and denim jacket in which he had been arrested, he was a perfect example of the kind of person motorists didn't pick up hitchhiking.

His long black hair and beard were what made him frightening; they gave him a resemblance to Charles Manson. When they'd hauled him into the police station on a charge of vagrancy, one of the officers had muttered, "I bet you he's no saint."

He had been passing through Aimsley, Louisiana, drifting toward Houston for no particular reason, when they had nailed him.

It wasn't the first time he had been in jail on a "no visible means of support" rap. More than a few times in the six months he'd been drifting through the South, he'd been accommodated on bunks in jail cells in small towns and in some cities.

He didn't really mind, because he had no place in particular to be. Turner had been concentrating on losing himself since his girlfriend's death in a car wreck. He had dropped out of medical school in Florida and begun to thumb along the Gulf Coast, taking jobs once in a while but more often then anything devoting himself to oblivion.

He drank, picked up drugs in the nooks and crannies where he could find them and kept his head in a stupor that usually helped ease the pain.

He had been deeply in love with the girl, expecting to marry her some day. They had met in a bookstore near campus and been smitten with each other immediately.

She was just out of college, working as a computer programmer. She had become a breath of fresh air for him, a refuge from the grueling pace of school and work. He had to work because both of his parents were dead.

In a way, Lois had filled a void that their loss had left inside him long before.

He had not realized how much she meant to him until word arrived that she was dead. Someone had run a red light and slammed into her car, a Toyota, which had been demolished by the force of the collision.

He had gone numb at first; then the tears had begun. After the funeral he had tried to return to the routine of his life, but every time he turned a corner, there was some reminder of her: a shop where they'd had coffee, a bench where they had rested, a thousand other reminders.

Running had been his only alternative, his only hope to escape his pain, and so he had bundled a few things together and fled with his thumb extended.

A cold wind hit him, bringing him back to the present as they guided him out of the police station behind Cody. It was November and unusually cold for late autumn in Louisiana. Normally autumn was little different from the last days of summer.

10

With his hands shackled, he had difficulty adjusting his jacket. Cody remained stoic as the guard motioned them toward the rear of a blue police wagon.

Once his feet were released, Cody stepped up into the rear of the vehicle and sat down on one of the cold metal benches that stretched along the inner wall.

"Got a cigarette?" Turner asked the guard.

Without changing expression, the man gave him a slight shove.

"Moving, moving," Turner said and followed his cellmate into the van.

Once he was seated, the doors slammed shut, and the sound of the lock being set slipped through them.

A moment later the van was moving, rocking slightly as it bounced out of the parking lot.

They rode in silence for a long time. Cody rested his head back against the wall, his dark eyes rolling up toward the ceiling. He didn't talk much, and his expression was grim.

Turner read some of the graffiti that had been scratched on the gray metal walls until he noticed some that showed love messages. That made him think of Lois, so he turned his gaze toward the rear window. For a moment he could see her face reflected there. He forced himself to look beyond it.

The glass was lined with protective wire, and the only view it afforded was the ribbon of highway that stretched out behind them.

He could see that the morning was a drab gray color, maybe a better morning for sleeping than anything else. If the rain that was threatening appeared, it would be a cold drizzle, enough to make any other activity miserable.

"What's it like at the sheriff's penal colony?" Turner asked to break the monotony.

"Ain't never been there," Cody replied.

Turner shrugged. "Maybe it won't be too bad."

"Long as we got a roof over our heads."

"I'm sure I've been in worse places than we're facing here," Turner said. "There are some smelly, shitty places to lock people up in the world."

"Been in a few of those myself" was Cody's reply.

Turner only nodded back. He didn't want to get into an argument about who'd had the worse incarcerations. He saw no reason to stir up trouble with Cody. He kind of liked the guy, and he figured he needed all the friends he could get.

He'd learned it was good to have tough friends in the lock-ups. They kept bad things from happening.

His eyes trailed back to the window again, and he stared out at the roadway. It had narrowed. The van had made some twists and turns to which he had paid little attention. Somewhere along the way they had left the main highway.

"Where is this place located anyway?" Turner asked.

"Edge of the parish," Cody said.

Turner stared out at what he could see of the roadside. "Is it in a swamp?"

"It's a work farm. Why would it be in a friggin' swamp?" Cody asked.

"Just judging by our surroundings," Turner said.

Cody frowned and looked out the rear window himself to see the narrow road which was heavily shrouded by the tree branches that stretched out from the roadside.

He shook his head. "Somethin's wrong," he said. "The farm is on Route 1. There's easier ways to get there from downtown."

The van clattered over a pothole which jolted them both about.

"Maybe it's a shortcut," Turner said.

"I don't think so," Cody said. "I think we're in trouble."

"Come on, settle down. We're prisoners. There's a limit to what they can do to us. Remember the Geneva convention?"

Cody shook his head. He was visibly nervous. It was the first emotion of any kind he'd shown since Turner had known him.

"Easy," Turner said, beginning to grow a little uneasy himself. If the big man was scared, there might really be something wrong.

They hit another pothole which once again jostled them about, almost spilling Cody off his seat.

"I'm sure it's going to be all right," Turner said.

"You don't know the stories," Cody hissed. "You ain't from here. You ain't heard."

"Heard what?"

"Rumor, fact, who knows? In the jails they always talk about people who got released, only nobody ever heard of them again on the outside. It's like they let 'em go from the jail, and they just disappeared from the face of the Earth."

"What are you saying?"

12

"Nobody knows what happened to those people," Cody said. "But everybody has suspicions." He pulled against his handcuffs in a futile effort to free his hands.

"They couldn't get away with that sort of thing," Turner protested. "I've been in lots of jails all over the place. Things are regulated. The state or even the federal people would catch on to it."

"They got other things to worry about," Cody protested. "We ain't nothin' but scum where they're concerned."

"What do you think we're in for?"

"We needs a plan," Cody said.

He started to get up and move toward the rear doors. When the van lurched to a stop, Turner had to catch him to keep him from falling backward.

An instant later the doors were yanked open.

The guard was standing there, but he was not alone. Beside him were a couple of men in jeans and work shirts with heavy, sheepskin jackets. Each held a rifle cradled in his arms, and cowboy hats tilted down over their eyes.

"Climb on out, boys," one of them said. He was a tall, heavy man with long sideburns. A thin brown cigar was clenched in his teeth.

Turner followed Cody through the door. He could feel his heartbeat quickening, and he studied each of the men without finding any indication of who they might be.

As the guard herded them around the side of the van, Turner and Cody found themselves in front of several other men who were on horseback. The horses pawed the ground nervously, wisps of white puffing from their nostrils in the chill air.

One of the mounted men reached into a saddlebag and pulled out a computer printout.

"What we have here are a couple of habitual offenders," said the dark-haired man. He wore a black baseball cap instead of a cowboy hat, and he had cold blue eyes that offered no sign of mercy.

A thick black beard covered the lower portion of his face like a mask, making him seem even more sinister.

Like the others, he wore jeans and a thick vest that left his arms free, but they did not look like the kind of clothes he would usually wear. There was an elegance about him. In a way he seemed like a younger, slightly heavier version of Vincent Price. He was in his late forties, but he had aged

13

well. Only a few touches of silver-gray were visible at his temples.

"Gentlemen. Cody Johnson." The man's voice was soft and his words precise. His breath also turned to smoke in the November air. "He's in jail for robbery now. He will probably be set free because there is not an accurate description of him from the convenience store clerk he pistol whipped."

Johnson stood silently, listening to the charges.

"Prior to that Mr. Johnson was before the judge for aggravated assault, theft, battery, attempted murder and on and on. We can't prove he killed his girlfriend's brother last summer, but we have a pretty good idea he did so, over some money. That's why he's joining us this morning."

Cody didn't bother to move. He had regained his stoic expression. Turner guessed it was the same look he would have assumed if he had been facing a judge.

The dark-haired man flipped the sheet up and looked at Turner. "Mr. Turner here has several aliases. He has ridden with the Lucifer's Disciples motorcycle group, sold drugs in three states and committed assault on numerous people including several elderly gentlemen in Jackson, Mississippi."

The words rattled Turner. "What the hell are you talking about?" he asked. "You're making a mistake." One of the men jabbed him in the side with a rifle barrel to silence him.

"Mr. Turner has four aliases that we know of, so who can tell what kind of crimes he's committed besides these on his list."

"You're making a mistake!" Turner shouted. "I haven't ever been picked up for anything worse than vagrancy."

"The guilty man speaks loudly," the man replied. He stuffed the papers back into his saddle-bag and nodded toward the guard, who unlatched the handcuffs on both men.

"You have never done society any good," said the dark-haired man. "Never contributed anything. You've slipped through the fingers of the law. Now you're going to be hunted like the scum you are. It would only be a matter of time until you killed somebody else or did some other damage. So now you are ours. Judgment had been rendered."

He pointed toward the edge of the forest. "Run. There is your only chance of refuge, but don't get your hopes up. You will be shown all the mercy you gave to your victims. We'll be after you, and who knows what lurks in those woods?"

Turner and Cody looked at each other for a brief instant.

Fear filled their eyes.

With little choice they turned and sprinted toward the edge of the forest, seeking to disappear as they burst into the trees.

Branches quickly began to slap at them, and their legs ached as they moved across the rough ground. The cold air burned in their lungs, and their hearts thundered, filling their ears with the sound of rushing blood.

Dodging smaller trees, the two men tried to find some kind of refuge within the forest. Their legs kicked high as they ran, and they gasped through their mouths. The air made their faces numb and brought tears to their eyes.

When they reached a small creek, they paused, heaving for air as they looked back.

"We're in it deep," Cody said. "We got to do somethin'."

"What the hell can we do?"

"Get some weapons, somethin'."

"Are those cops?"

"Could be. Some of them. Hasta be."

"That man, their leader. Who the hell is he?"

"Don't know," Cody said, shaking his head. He leaned against a tree for support as he tried to catch his breath.

An instant later the sound of hoofbeats carried through the trees. It was like thunder, loud and coarse.

"We can't outrun those horses," said Turner.

"If we don't, we're gonna be dead men," Cody responded.

They splashed through the icy water of the creek and climbed up the opposite bank in a frenzy of movement. The water soaked their pants and made the material heavy as they continued to run. In moments the wind had chilled them.

Their muscles began to shudder.

On top of everything else, Turner realized hypothermia was going to become a threat, but as the shouts of their pursuers echoed through the trees, he decided illness was the least of his worries.

Stumbling along, Cody discovered a heavy oak limb on the ground. Seizing it, he tucked it under his arm.

"We'll get you somethin' too," he told Turner. "We both gonna have to fight if we're gonna get out of this, and I'm gonna need your help."

Turner only nodded. His head was a flurry of confusion. He had never dealt with a situation in which his own life was in danger.

He couldn't understand the charges they had read against

15

him either. Somehow they had made a mistake, confused him with somebody else. He had made no contribution to society, but he hadn't done what they had accused him of either.

For the first time since Lois had died, he longed to be back in school, going through the rigorous but familiar routine of classes and work. What was he doing in the Louisiana swamps, being chased by a group of madmen?

He stepped on a root without realizing it until it was too late. His foot hung on the snag, and the pain drove up through his leg. Dropping to one knee, he groaned at the ache in his ankle.

He tried to rise again immediately but was unable to stand due to the pain.

Cody stopped beside him. "Can you move?"

"It's twisted bad."

"Shit."

He tried to help Turner stand. When it proved impossible he cursed again.

"We've got to keep moving," he said.

Turner could only shake his head. His face was wet with perspiration that quickly congealed, and his throat was tight and dry. "Go on," he said. "I'll find somewhere to hide."

Cody gave a quick look around to see if there was anything amid the pine trees that would offer shelter. Their surroundings were barren. The leaves had fallen, and the ground was matted down with a damp blanket of brown.

He failed to look upward, so he did not see the movement in the branches. It probably wouldn't have done him any good to know what was coming anyway.

With his stick in hand, he got to his feet and started to take a step. The hoofbeats were not far away now; flight was his only chance.

Turner tried to get onto his knees so that he could move or at least do something to find safety.

When the tree branch above them bounced and rattled, they both turned their gazes to the sky — too late.

What they saw was no more than a grimy blur.

At first it appeared to be an animal, then a man, and then it didn't matter anymore because it was upon Cody, sitting on his shoulders with its arms around his neck as its teeth began ripping at his throat.

He clubbed at it with the oak branch, but he could not reach behind him far enough to affect it. He was forced to the ground. Struggling against his attacker, he rolled, kicking and punching. His blows had little effect, and when something cut into his jugular, he stopped struggling. In moments his eyes glazed over, and he stared sightlessly at the forest sky.

Turner tried to move toward him, unsure how he could offer help against the creature. When he saw no sign of movement from the black man, he hesitated.

The attacker spun around then, its movements quick and erratic. Turner thought for a moment he was hallucinating as a flap of Cody's flesh fell from its teeth.

He still did not know what he was seeing, and the terror that swept over him was so immense his mind stopped processing data altogether.

He screamed and began to thrash backward, dragging his injured leg. He was still looking toward the ruins of Cody's body, so he didn't see the second creature as it moved in on him, grasping his head to mash it until his skull crushed.

He died almost instantly; so he didn't feel anything as his flesh was devoured, and he never formulated the thought that might have come: *jailhouse rumors weren't all just rumors after all.*

Chapter 1

Jag listened to the soft buzz of the phone, the sound that was supposed to indicate it was ringing at the other end. He'd lost count at a dozen, but he didn't place the handset back into its cradle. He didn't want to give up. Somehow he believed if he could just get an answer, if she would just pick up the phone so that he could hear her voice, everything would be all right.

He drummed the fingers of his left hand across his desktop, waiting. She was supposed to be there by now. He suspected she was and that she had unplugged the cord again to avoid his call. If what he suspected was true, she wouldn't want his call.

Tomorrow maybe, but not tonight. Tonight it would be an inconvenience.

He chewed his lower lip, realizing he felt like crying. He could feel the pressure behind his eyes as a long stretch of sadness curled up through his abdomen and settled in his throat.

And the tone clicked again, and again, and again. . . .

"Jag."

The voice startled him. He jerked around, realizing it had not come from the receiver.

It was a nasal voice from across the newsroom, a voice belonging to Norman Breech, assistant city room editor for the *Aimsley Daily Clarion.*

"Are the obits finished yet?"

Jag reluctantly slipped the phone down and picked up the stack of printed death notices piled beside his computer terminal.

"Almost," he said calling up a page and beginning to type.

He'd been at the paper six months, and all they gave him to do were rewrites and obituaries. He filled his days chronicling deaths and business meetings.

Breech was hell to work for too. He was a thin, smart-assed

guy with a tendency to make printouts of Jag's copy and bloody them with a red felt-tipped marker.

It didn't matter that half of the things he corrected were arbitrary and a matter of personal preference rather than errors. They went into the file anyway and reminded Jag anew he wasn't particularly cut out to be a reporter.

Adjusting his glasses, he hammered in the obits and dispatched them with a keystroke.

It was coming close to deadline, meaning he would be able to get out of the office soon, barring some major broadcast over the police scanner. That suited him fine.

Except that he knew he wouldn't have any peace when he got out of the office. His emotions weren't going to let him rest.

He'd been dating Caroline Martin for four of the months he'd been at the *Clarion,* and there had been little peace during that period.

She was a cute, little blond girl with a bubbly personality. He'd met her in the supermarket. She had approached him, actually, asking a man's opinion on something about plumbing. They were on the hardware aisle, and he'd wound up suggesting duct tape for her problem. They had hit it off almost at once.

She occupied his thoughts most of the time, at first in a pleasant way. Later the turmoil had set in, when he'd realized there were strange things about her. She had a tendency to take trips without telling him where she was going. She got phone calls she didn't want to explain, but she kept telling him there wasn't anyone else. Their relationship was too perfect, she claimed.

He wanted to believe her, wanted to badly, but the circumstantial evidence kept pointing the other way.

Tonight was no exception. She was supposed to have been back from visiting friends by six p.m. the hour he'd started calling. Either she was four hours late, or something was wrong.

Slipping off his wire-rimmed glasses—when people teased him, they said they were yuppie glasses—he began to run his hands through his hair. It was starting to get a little long, but the style fit with the rest of his ensemble.

He'd taken to wearing his tie loose and rolling up his sleeves. At twenty-two he was learning the real world was not the same as J school had been.

He'd had one good story about a family who had received a delayed letter from their son's friend years after the boy's death in Viet Nam; but the rest of the time Jag had been stuffed in the newsroom, trying to please the plethora of editors, and that was no easy task.

They all had different preferences, and all seemed to be having second thoughts about hiring him. He'd been an acquisition of convenience, handy to have around while other reporters were vacationing.

But summer was gone.

Now he was losing his allure for the editors it seemed. He couldn't help but wonder what he'd let himself in for.

"Jag." Breech again.

He got up from his chair and smoothed out his khakis before walking across the room. He was tall with broad enough shoulders, although he'd never qualify for any football teams, and his build made him look thin. They told him the Man Upstairs didn't like the length of his hair, a fact he tried not to let concern him.

"Look at this, Jag," Breech said when he reached the corner of the cluster of editors' desks.

Jag was a nickname that had been with him since high school when he'd wanted to own a Jaguar. All of his notebooks had sported stickers or drawings of the sports cars, and the name had caught on.

His real name, the one they used in his infrequent bylines, was Everett Walker.

He peered down at the screen's green-on-black display and studied it. He couldn't spot anything wrong.

"This doesn't conform to AP style," Breech said. "The state abbreviations are wrong, you're using commas where you should have semi-colons and you didn't put a dateline."

Excuse the hell out of me.

He held his initial response and only nodded as Breech gave him verbal corrections.

His mind was more on Caroline than anything else, trying not to conjure images of her in someone else's arms.

Sometimes that was difficult. He could imagine her lying back as some unknown man made love to her. The lover was always older, somewhere in his thirties with dark-brown hair and a lean, muscled body.

The man sighed heavily as he filled her body, performing tirelessly, and she moaned with an ecstasy that drove needles

21

into Jag's heart.

Finally Breech entered the command that sent the obits off to be typeset and leaned back in his chair, curling his hands behind his head where his light-blond hair was starting to thin.

With his suspenders and mustache, he looked like a typical stereotype of a newspaper editor, maybe a little behind the computerized world the *Clarion* had become over the last few years.

"I guess you can go before something happens," Breech said, his voice growing a little kinder. He had a streak of decency in him he kept hidden most of the time.

There were a couple of other reporters in the newsroom. Jag moved past them and got his overcoat from the chair across from his desk. It was a London Fog his father had given him one Christmas. Now it had grown a bit faded around the edges.

At least it still kept him warm. They teased him about that too, another yuppie icon.

He shrugged it on and paused long enough to tap out Caroline's number on his desk phone one last time before giving up.

It rang, rang, rang, and he hung up, walking from the newsroom with his hands in his pockets.

At the back door a blast of wind hit him in the face. Its edge was bitter cold, colder than it should have been, even for January.

The security guard passed him in the parking lot, wearing a long black coat. For a moment he looked like the Grim Reaper stalking through the shadows among the cars.

Jag spoke to him before moving to his own car, a battered red Mustang that had seen better days. He quickly fired up the engine to get the heat going, but he didn't immediately shove it into gear.

He wasn't sure where he wanted to go. If he went home, he would only pace around his apartment with futile agony as he wondered where Caroline had gone or what she was doing. Or who was screwing her.

Perhaps she was at home, just not answering her phone. She got into moods where she didn't want to see anybody.

He slipped his fingers over the steering wheel. Why should he spend the hours in pain? He could end them with a quick trip by her apartment. That would at least give him some satisfaction.

A few minutes checking and all would be well.

The tires crunched in the gravel as Debra Blane eased her Volvo onto the shoulder of the road, letting the windshield wipers keep up their labors as the car pulled to a stop.

The rain showered down on the roof, and wind whipped around the car, creating a loud roar even as the vehicle sat still.

In the beams of the headlights the slashes of rain remained visible like streaks of silver in the white light.

Reaching up to the ceiling light, she flicked it on as she fought with the road map she'd been given by the state police in Lafayette. The dim light poured down onto the map in a dull puddle.

Somewhere she'd made a wrong turn and was now in the middle of some kind of farm country in south central Louisiana. All the roads were alike.

From the looks of things, the swamps weren't far away. The last thing she needed to do was drive into a bottomless hole somewhere and disappear.

Earlier she'd seen a sign for Bunkie, but she didn't know if she still headed that way or not. She'd wound through a couple of fields since then, passed signs warning that she was traveling on a substandard surface (weren't they all in Louisiana?) and clattered along one path that changed from black-top to gravel and back again.

She prayed it was not all a lost cause. She wasn't familiar with Louisiana, but Bunkie was a visible point on the map. She could find her way if she could just reach Bunkie, because a major highway passed through it. Even if she screwed up, she'd end up in Alexandria, not the best place in the world, but not the end of the world either.

If she could make Bunkie, she could survive. A service station attendant had told her the town's name came from one of the children of one of its old families. The child had been given a stuffed monkey, but she couldn't say monkey. Her pronounciation had become the name of the town.

In spite of all she was up against, Debra was able to pick up tourist trivia without thinking about it.

She was on a tight schedule. She'd already been gone longer than she'd intended from her job in Atlanta, so being lost in

23

the middle of nowhere didn't fit into her plans.

Being slowed down by a rainstorm didn't help either. The clouds had burst open a few miles back, dumping their contents on her in what seemed like waves.

If she made it to Riverland Parish by dawn, she would be lucky, and that wouldn't really give her much time to get a hotel room. There were several stops she needed to make in Aimsley, and if she learned there that she had to keep travelling, she would need to be back on the road quickly.

The travelling was beginning to take its toll on her. At twenty-five she was learning that some of the things she had taken for granted a few years earlier—like skipping meals and staying awake for long periods of time—didn't come easily any more.

The cherubic quality of her features—her rounded cheeks and dimples and the large brown eyes—kept her looking young in spite of her recent strain, but she was feeling very old. And she was developing hollow caverns under her eyes where dark circles had formed.

Her long brown hair was wound into a tangled bun behind her head, and her clothes—pullover white turtleneck that fit loosely enough to keep her figure a mystery and jeans that hugged her hips after shrinking in spite of her efforts to buy a size larger—were feeling gritty and clammy.

Raising a hand to her forehead, she fought back tears. She was tired and frustrated, and there was no end in sight.

She'd thrown herself on her boss's mercy at the small production company where she worked in Atlanta, pleading for some time off. She'd had no choice but to go on her own on her little mission. She couldn't get any police help, and a private detective was out of the question on her subsistence wages.

Writing scripts for commercials and occasional documentaries provided some creative fulfillment, but the firm was not successful enough to make her rich for her talents.

Opening her eyes again, she put on her glasses and studied the map once more as the rain hammered down on the car and splashed across the windshield.

Tracing a blue line on the map from the last point she had recognized, she realized where she could reconnect with the main road. It would curl up through the southern portion of Riverland, finally taking her to Aimsley.

A new flash of lightning slashed down through the black sky across the field with a loud roar of thunder following to let her know the storm was not going to be kind to her progress.

She shoved the Volvo into gear and guided it gingerly back onto the roadway. The clutter from her days on the road rattled on the floorboards. A paper cup rolled against her feet, and a wadded taco wrapper bounced about, reminding her there was a reason that her stomach was a little queasy.

Holding the car between the ditches was a challenge. She began to wonder how long it had been since she'd had the tires changed. Two years? Three?

The Volvo was eight years old. She'd never planned on subjecting it to such a grueling trip, but it was important that she find her brother.

He was all she had, really. And she was all he had. Somehow she sensed he needed her. She didn't let the other feeling, that of dread, sink over her. She couldn't. She had to have hope. It was the only thing to keep her going.

A streak of lightning cut a bright path through the storm-shrouded sky, igniting the scene before Jag's eyes as he steered along the roadway. He was half hunched over the wheel, gripping it tightly as he navigated the slick road.

A Paul Simon tune played faintly on the radio, but the music did not affect him. He was lost in his thoughts, unable to think about anything but Caroline.

She could be wonderful at times, bright and witty, versed in many topics. She could talk about so many things, and engage others with her knowledge.

The confusing thing was that she could turn that off just as easily, becoming cold and distant.

Jag found that almost unbearable, that she could seem so bubbly one moment and the next be almost cruel in her indifference.

With the anxieties of the job and the agony of the relationship, he was beginning to wonder if he had a place in the world. He didn't fit in as a journalist, but that didn't matter. Jag had never fit in anywhere.

As a child he had always been in fights, defending himself against the schoolyard bullies who did not like his quiet demeanor.

Nowadays he still preferred to avoid conflict. Even as a reporter, he was not good at dealing with cops or anybody else he encountered in his job, and he was not much better at personal relationships.

He knew he had handled things badly with Caroline. She resented his insecurities, resented his reactions to her secretiveness and berated him if he grew suspicious.

She would be angry if he showed up on her doorstep now, if she was indeed at home. His explanations would be hasty and unbelievable, and that would lead to friction. A day or two of coldness or worse. Perhaps another long talk would be in order—conflict.

He didn't let the fear of that dissuade him from his destination. He kept his hand tightly on the wheel until the sign for her apartment complex came into view. It blurred in the rainfall on the windshield, but the bright yellow letters still glowed in the beams of his headlights.

He hit the turn signal and twisted the wheel hard to the right, losing control for the first time when he gave the car too much gas. It fishtailed slightly as he skidded into the asphalt parking lot, but he was able to guide it to a stop before hitting anything.

He climbed out quickly. The rain pelted down on him, soaking his hair and beading on his glasses, but he didn't wipe them as he scanned the lot. He could see Caroline's Datsun parked in its usual slot. As the rain bounced off its blue surface, he walked over to it. Peering in the window, he could see a wadded McDonald's sack and a package of her cigarettes on the front seat. They gave no answers.

Moving past the car, he stepped along the slick sidewalk which led up to her door.

The porch light was off, and everything inside appeared silent. He brushed his wet hair out of his eyes, then curled his hand into a fist and knocked.

Nothing stirred. No one came to the door, and with the roar of the storm, he could not be sure if there was any sound of movement inside or not.

Turning back to the parking lot, he stared through the raindrops on his lenses. The lot was bathed in white light from a nearby dusk-to-dawn lamp. The light made the rain seem to glow as well, and it reflected up like an orb off the slick black asphalt.

Two slots down from Caroline's car, he could see a small Ford pickup with Texas plates. He searched his mind, trying to remember if he'd ever seen it there before. Memory would not serve. He'd never paid any attention. It had never been

26

important before who parked on the same side of the lot.

Turning back to the door, he hammered his fist against it again, calling out this time. "Caroline?"

He thought of the old Harry Chapin song called "Caroline" when the word escaped his lips. He had listened to that song a dozen times when he had first met her. Although the message of the song had little to do with his own relationship, it struck a chord somehow, seemed a special way of thinking about his Caroline as he was driving or sitting in the living room of his apartment.

Now he did not feel like singing. He hammered on the door a third time, and he was almost certain he heard movement.

"Caroline, dammit, open the door."

He hammered again, then listened. He couldn't hear anything this time because of the clap of thunder that came. He took a step back from the door, a chill wind whipping at the tail of his coat as he moved. He ignored it, ignored the rain that it swept against him. His hair was soaked, and cold water ran unnoticed down his cheeks.

She was in there, and someone was with her; and she had lied to him about it.

Taking still another step backward, he charged at the door, slipping slightly on the concrete so that his shoulder struck it with less force than he had anticipated.

The door rattled but did not give. He stepped back again, his mind shutting out the pain that shot through his shoulder.

Placing his steps more carefully this time, he hit the door with his full weight. The wood budged slightly, the facing cracking around the latch, yet still it held.

He knocked again, screaming her name this time. Tears mingled with the rain on his face, and his shoulder throbbed.

He choked and rubbed his arm, waiting. The wind continued its onslaught. All else was the same.

Drawing a deep breath, he lifted his foot and stomped it against the door. His heel struck near the knob, finishing the job of splintering the facing.

The door crashed inward, flying back against the interior wall. He could see the light was dim inside, candles. A pile of pillows and sheets were amassed near the couch.

Caroline was there, her face streaked with perspiration, her hair tousled. She was naked, pulling at the tangled sheet in an effort to cover her breasts.

Jag walked through the ruined doorway with his hand still

27

clutching his shoulder. He was stunned. His expression was a mirror of the hurt he was feeling, and his lower lip trembled.

He spoke her name again, a soft whisper that came out like a croak or even a death rattle.

She looked up at him. Her eyes were on fire. He could see that even in the dim light.

"You had no right," she seethed. "No fucking right in the world."

Just then the cat struck him, its claws cutting into the back of his neck where it was not protected by his coat.

Its loud screech startled him, and he couldn't stifle a moan. It screeched again as he twisted around in an effort to dislodge the animal.

When he finally found its collar, he yanked quickly, but one of its paws managed to steal a piece of his flesh before he tossed the feline onto the sofa.

As he touched the wound, he realized the other man was standing there in the corner.

Wearing only a pair of jeans, his upper body appeared ghostlike in the candlelight. He was tall, his shoulders broad and firm. Perspiration gleamed on his skin.

He was in his mid-thirties and appeared to be the type who took his health a little fanatically. He probably ate all the right foods and — from the look of his torso — lifted weights, Jag mused.

His hair had a touch of gray, and his face was rugged. He was not what Jag had pictured.

"You can get the hell out of here," the man said. He stepped out of the corner, keeping his arms loose at his sides. He was aware that he was tough.

"Not without an explanation," Jag said.

"You don't have any business here!" Caroline shouted.

"No?"

The man tensed his muscles now, trying to be intimidating. He was doing a fairly good job of it, but Jag was still functioning on adrenaline.

He planted his feet, shutting out the pain in his shoulder once again. He let his arms dangle at his sides, positioning himself with his back to the sofa.

"The lady asked you to leave," the man said softly. "You've ruined the door, so you obviously know where it is." He reached forward, preparing to take hold of Jag's coat.

Jag ducked the way he had on the playground when Hal

28

Cooper had reached out to grab him one winter. Hal had always hated him, had always served as his tormentor, and with Hal's coaching, others had joined in.

He'd had to learn survival skills to live through recess.

Dropping below the man's grasp, Jag pulled a pillow from the sofa and raised upward, stuffing it into the man's face.

With his arms flailing, the man tried to push it away. Jag let it go and drove a knee into the guy's groin.

No ground rules had been set for this altercation, so he saw no need to fight fair.

Chapter 2

The old man staggered along the alleyway as rain showered down off the eaves of the bordering buildings like waterfalls, pouring down onto his raincoat and soaking into the stocking cap that was pulled over his thinning gray hair which he wore in a crew cut. He was unaware of the onslaught.

The alcohol kept all of that away. His mind was as numb as his body. He could not really think. The things that swirled through his head were like ghost images of thoughts, reminding him faintly of things he did not want to recall and feelings he did not want to awaken.

His bottle was empty or he would have taken another swallow to drown the images. He did not want to remember the way his daughter had spoken to him the last time he had seen her, and he did not want to think about the death of his wife.

Willis Carpeter's life had never been a pleasant thing, so repeating parts of it was not at all desirable.

He was forty-five and looked sixty. He was a big man, his shoulders broad and his chest thick like an oak tree. His head almost had a square shape thanks to his massive jaw.

He stood almost six feet five inches.

Beneath the coat, he wore a faded blue suit that had once looked good on him. Once a long, long time ago during one of his forays into respectability.

He'd been put in jail the first time at nineteen. He'd been back on minor offenses frequently.

Mostly he did stints for public drunkenness. They'd had him at the detox unit at the mental institution in Penn's Ferry a time or two, but the treatments never seemed to last.

No matter what, he just couldn't rid his mind of the night his wife had died in a fire. She had been home alone. Their daughter had been visiting friends, and he had been out with the boys—and some girls too for that matter.

Some kind of electrical problem had caused the blaze, but that didn't really matter. The truth was she'd been trapped in the place because she'd been upstairs taking Valium to ease the pain of their marital problems and his police record.

For all intents and purposes he was responsible.

He could never forget that, never.

Life with her had looked like it might work once upon a time. They had operated rental houses together, earned decent money, and even joined a church and attended Sunday services regularly for a while. That had all faded quicker than he could have dreamed. Friends from his past had called on him, asked favors, and dragged him out for a while, until he didn't have to be dragged anymore. Leaning back against one wall, he realized he was remembering again. He looked at his empty bottle in his left hand and cursed at it. It was doing him no good. It was useless.

He pitched it across the alley, where it hit the opposite wall, and shattered in a spray of brown glass.

That prompted a dog to bark, and someone nearby shouted. He shouted back before staggering up the alley and onto the street.

He was in a decaying part of the city where shops had closed and the windows were either boarded or filled with dust and grime.

He didn't know where he was going. He had no money for more liquor, nor did he have anywhere to go.

Turning his collar up against the rain, he staggered along the street, blinking his eyes as he tried to clear his vision. He noticed now it was raining, but he couldn't bring himself to care.

Somebody in one of the old bars along Fifth Street would do him a favor. He knew they would.

He rounded a corner, singing without realizing it, some sad ballad he had heard sometime in the past.

Things had a way of popping into his head from the past lately, not just images of his wife, Joline, but other events as well.

He remembered people, and he remembered events, phone numbers and other junkyard items of the mind. He couldn't help himself.

He relived the razor-strap beatings his stepfather had administered, and he thought about Betty Sue Honermeyer's blue party dress from his sixteenth summer. Emotions he couldn't explain flooded him in ways worse than the rain.

He started to stagger about, running from the ghosts of the past because he hated the way he felt when they pursued him.

Cold chills gripped him. He lived a nightmare. Regrets, the most hideous monsters of all, assaulted him.

It had been a while since they had been this bad. He began to cry out. He saw his wife's face as it was consumed by flames. Then he heard his daughter's curses. She shouted terrible things.

What had he done to his life? What had led him to this mess he was in?

Rain poured down on him, splattering on his face. He shouted at the top of his voice. "Leave me alone. Leave me alone." He began to curse, profanities showering from his lips.

He stumbled back against one of the storefronts and dropped to one knee.

He didn't see the patrol car when it approached.

The blue-and-white cruised up to the curve without flashing its lights, and two uniformed officers climbed out, pulling on their yellow slickers as they walked toward him.

He was crying when they moved in on him, but he looked up an instant before they reached him.

A new fear struck him, and he tried to pick himself up to run.

"Easy does it there, Pop," one of the officers, a tall guy in his late twenties, said. His nametag read Elliot.

His partner, nametag Phillips, had curly black hair, a mustache, and less patience. He slipped his billy club from its strap with an arm that resembled a gorilla's.

Screaming, Willis tried to swing at Elliot, and Phillips clipped him behind the knees. Because of his size, they were taking no chances.

That sent Willis down onto the concrete. He rolled through the accumulated rain, swatting at the air and screaming.

Elliot moved to his side, trying to calm him, but the old man kept tossing his arms from side to side.

"Damn it all to hell. Let me get away," Willis begged.

Both cops leaned over him, catching his arms and pinning him to the concrete.

He grunted and swung his arms upward with all his strength, sprawling both officers backward with the force of a wrestler.

Phillips landed in a sitting position and felt water soaking through the seat of his pants. He swore as he pulled himself back to his feet.

"Get away!" Willis screamed.

Elliot was on his feet again already. His uniform was wet also, but he was ignoring it as he watched Willis get up.

"You can't take me!" the old man screamed. "Blue bastards. Blue bastards. Won't take me."

He charged at Elliot, screaming. Before the cop could get out of the way, Willis slammed into him, hitting Elliot like a freight train.

The cop reeled backward, dazed.

Willis tried to turn and run, but Phillips dived for him, catching his shoulders and dragging him down. The old man struggled beneath him, but Phillips threw his weight on top of him, holding him while he got the cuffs ready.

He got a bracelet around the old man's left wrist first and tugged it behind the man's back to meet the other hand. With it cuffed, he pulled up on one arm, forcing the old man to his feet.

Elliot was recovered enough now to offer some help. He grabbed the old man's other arm.

As they tossed him into the back seat, he began to scream again.

"He's scared of cops," Elliot said, wincing at the screeches from the old man.

"Don't pay any attention," Phillips replied. "He's drunk out of his mind."

"Don't take me away!" Willis screamed. "Don't take me to the bad place. I don't want to die. I don't want to die. I don't want to be taken to the swamp."

"We'll take him to the parish lockup," Phillips said. "They can put him in their drunk tank there and let him dry out."

Debra stepped out of the storm, into the musty lobby of the Aimsley Police Department. The heat made the air thick

33

and hard to breath, and the smell of the place had a sickening quality.

As she tugged her scarf off her head, a few droplets of rain remained in her hair like small pearls. She didn't bother to wipe them away as she draped the scarf around her shoulders and adjusted her tweed jacket. She didn't feel a great need to attempt the impossible by trying to create an appearance of composure.

She walked across the tiled lobby, her footsteps echoing through the room as she made her way to the complaint desk. It was behind a wall of glass, and the floor on the far side of the wall was elevated, making the desk sergeant's chair higher. It offered a point of intimidation.

The man at the desk now sat as if he were on a throne. He was a rugged-looking fellow with sandy hair and a chiseled jaw. If he hadn't been wearing a blue uniform, he would have looked like a thug.

Deb guessed him to be in his late thirties or early forties, and the look in his gray eyes seemed to indicate he'd earned every year the hard way.

He looked through his glass shield as if he were peering at a criminal.

"Can I help you?" The nametag read LaFleur, but he had no hint of a Cajun accent. He was pure redneck.

She drew a quick breath and offered the speech she'd had a lot of practice with the last few weeks. "My name is Debra Blane. I'm looking for my brother, Mark Turner, and I thought he might have been through Aimsley. I need to see if you have an arrest record on him or anything. He has a tendency to get picked up for vagrancy."

"Little early in the morning for this kind of query, isn't it?"

"I've been driving all night. I thought I'd make a stop here before getting a motel."

"That's kind of a hard thing to check," LeFleur grumbled. "It'd be easier if you came back later when the captain was around."

Deb lifted one hand to her eyes, massaging them slightly as she drew in a slow breath through her lips. "The jail records are public domain. I have a right to check them as long as they're not in use. I see a computer bank there, so I assume they're on that. It should take you about three keystrokes."

LaFleur almost seemed to snarl. "I'm not sure what's public record and what's not. I'm going to have to have authorization from my superiors before I can do anything."

"Sir, I've travelled a long way. It's very important that I find my brother. He's in a very bad condition."

"I can't do it without authorization."

"Can you call someone?"

"If you can call my chief and get him to call me and tell me it's all right, I'll do the check," LaFleur said. He raised a stubby index finger and jabbed it toward the door. "There's a pay phone across the street." His voice was cold and hard.

Deb looked back over her shoulder. "It's pouring down rain."

"This line here is just for police calls. If you want the check run, that's the best I can do."

There was no sympathy in his voice, not a sign of compassion. He just peered at her with his gruff expression and remained silent.

With a sigh, Debra took a notebook from her purse. "Can you give me the number I need to call?"

"That'd be Chief White."

It surprised her that he was willing to give the number out. She took it down and put her pad into her purse again. Then reluctantly she pulled her scarf around her hair once more and walked back to the door, looking at the heavy rain pouring down outside. Bracing herself, she pushed the door open and ran.

Water splattered down on her, soaking through the tweed into her sweater. She felt the dampness against her skin and shuddered. She almost slipped on the concrete as she moved toward the post that supported the small blue bubble that housed the pay phone.

At the edge of the street, water roaring along the gutter splashed over her boots before she could step up on the curb.

She was clenching her teeth as she reached the phone and dropped a quarter into its slot. Her anger was boiling, but she didn't want it to consume her. She was going to have to play the cops' game. They had the information.

She'd run into red tape frequently, but the attitude of this LaFleur seemed to make things worse. It was almost as if he was purposely abrasive.

With a trembling finger, she tapped out the chief's number and waited. Water continued to pour down on her, soaking through her scarf. Her teeth started to chatter, and raindrops

35

stung her eyes.

"Hello" came a woman's voice through the receiver.

"May I speak to Chief White please?"

"Can I ask who's calling? He's getting ready for work."

"My name is Debra Blane, and I'm at the police station; that is I'm outside the police station in the rain, and I need to talk to the chief." She was struggling to control her voice.

A moment later a voice with a slow, Southern twang came on the line.

"Can I help you?"

"My name is Debra Blane. I was told to call you. I have a problem."

As concisely as possible she outlined her situation. "It's a matter of public records," she said, trying to keep her voice soft. "Since it is such a little thing, I was hoping it could be taken care of."

"It's a simple thing but a little unusual," White agreed with a chuckle. "LaFleur is just a little cautious. Don't want to give the wrong thing out do we? Might set a criminal free on a technicality or something. Just go back over there and I'll give him a call, darlin'."

It was hard not to respond to the condescending tone. "Thank you, Chief."

She hung up and hurried back across the street, stomped into the station and moved up to the desk, yanking the scarf off again.

LeFleur was on the phone. He nodded a time or two and hung up.

"Okay," he said without emotion. "The chief said it will be all right to help you."

He turned around to his computer terminal and tapped a few keys, bringing it to life.

"What's your brother's name again?"

"Turner. Mark Turner. T-U-R-N-E-R."

LaFleur typed in the name and popped the enter key.

The screen want blank except for the cursor which remained in the upper corner, blinking as the machine searched its memory.

LaFleur stared at the blank screen coldly as Debra leaned against the window. He drummed his fingers impatiently until the cursor stopped flashing and some words crawled onto the screen.

"This shows that we never had him," LaFleur said. "Never

booked." He looked back at her without changing expression. "Sorry."

"Thank you," Debra said. "I appreciate your courtesy."

She was soaked to the skin and ready to explode, all for another dead end. She walked from the station and climbed into her car, closing the Volvo's door before she screamed.

She did not weep, although she felt like it. She had to remain strong. There were other places to check, like the newspaper to see if there were any obituaries or reports of unidentified accident victims.

The dogs barked when Tim Gunter pulled his old pickup truck up to the house trailer nestled in the woods south of Aimsley. He was sharing it with Bess Jackson, a girl he'd met at a lounge called the Alibi.

She'd started feeding the dogs in the neighborhood, so they hung around outside the trailer.

He climbed out of the truck and kicked one of the mutts out of the way, stepping into a puddle of rainwater as he moved toward the door. He swore and kicked at the mutt again, then bounced up the small flight of steps that led to the front door.

Bess was waiting for him when he stepped into the narrow living room. She didn't look as good without her makeup as she had the night he'd met her. This morning her hair was kind of oily looking and limp, and she was wearing a bathrobe that was faded.

A cigarette dangled from the corner of her lips. "Out all night," she said. "What were you doing? Out with some of those little sluts that hang out at the pool hall?"

Gunter snarled and shook his head. "I was with my friends. That's all."

He dropped onto the lumpy sofa beside the end table which was piled high with women's magazines. She had so many of the damned things, he could never find his Zane Grey paperbacks anymore, and it wasn't like the makeup tips did her any good these days. She didn't even try them lately.

"Who is it? Is it that little brunette that works at the Clairmont?"

He couldn't think of any little brunette, and he never went near the Clairmont. The place was too fancy for his tastes.

"There's nobody. I was out with the boys." He pulled his

long black hair back from his face and scratched his head. His thoughts were a little fuzzy. Her voice made his temples throb.

"That's all you ever do anymore. When are you gonna git a job?"

He shrugged. He was a welder, but things had been lousy in Louisiana since the gas crunch had hit. The state government had started cutting things back and closing everything down.

He hadn't been looking in a while. It was easier to hang out with his friends and pick up a few dollars on odd jobs when he could.

Bess worked in a twenty-four-hour place, and that brought in a little cash too. With their limited expenses they squeaked by. They'd do even better without their dogfood bill.

"Are we gonna live in squalor as long as we're together?" she demanded.

"I don't know," he muttered. He didn't feel up to an argument. All he really wanted to do was go to sleep.

She threw a magazine across the room, hitting him with it. The spine of it was hard and hurt when it made contact. He sat still anyway.

In her present mood, she might be on the verge of leaving, and he didn't like that idea. It would mean he would have to look for somebody else to keep around, and he didn't want to go through that pain in the ass again. It was tough to find somebody he didn't want to strangle every minute she was out of bed.

Bess wasn't as beautiful as she'd been when he'd first met her, but she still functioned all right on her back. That was the important thing, the way Gunter saw it.

He could put up with her mouth for a while if he had to. She'd settle down soon enough.

"To top everything off, Petro is missing," she said.

She had the weirdest damned names for her dogs, and with so many of them, how could she tell one was missing?

"How long's he been gone?"

"A day or two. He hasn't come back for his food like the others."

"He probably just wandered off," Gunter muttered. He still wasn't sure which dog she was talking about.

"Maybe you should go look for him."

38

"Not right now. I'm too tired. I need some rest and some food."

"What if he's hurt? He could be in pain somewhere. Stuck out there in the swamp or something."

"We'll find him. Just let me rest up a bit."

She pouted, lower lip sticking out. "You sure?"

"I promise, baby." He held out his arms, and she came to him, accepting his embrace.

They kissed, and he slid his hands over her slowly. She'd put on a few pounds, but she still had a decent shape. As long as she came across, he could spend some time in the woods hunting her dog. Why not? The mutt had to be out there somewhere.

Chapter 3

The stop by the emergency room to have Jag's hands bandaged took hours because of the crowd. Car wreck victims who'd lost control of their vehicles in the rain were being hauled in and out of treatment rooms on stretchers. A heart attack victim was stuffed into a side room and attached to a monitor, and nurses jogged back and forth to another room where they were trying to keep a shooting victim alive.

Jag's victim had already been admitted.

When they were finally ready to look at Jag, he remained silent. A nurse wrapped gauze around his bruised knuckles. He hadn't noticed how badly they'd been cut. But they were the least of his concerns.

He was still silent when the cops dragged him back to the squad car. He looked out at the dark, wet streets without speaking as the vehicle cruised downtown.

The rain had subsided, and the streetlights gleamed across the surface of the puddles that remained. He kept seeing Caroline's face reflected against the glass. The features were familiar, but he was looking into the eyes of a stranger.

Everything he had felt had been bogus; she was not the person he had believed her to be. He had fallen in love with lies and deceptions, and somehow that made the agony that throbbed inside him more intense.

He could not believe he had lost control. He'd never fought much, not since school really. The instinct for violence was frightening because even in his worst anger he had never been inclined to hit anyone.

He'd let things bother him too much; something had snapped. Pain, pride, infatuation, they all worked together to strip away the checks and balances inside him. When he looked down at his hands, he saw they were trembling.

He bowed his head and rode silently as the car headed toward the parish jail. The city jail was too crowded, so he had to wait for his release in the sheriff's drunk tank. It was the only safe place to house him.

The cops had questioned him at the apartment while ambulance attendants worked on his victim, who turned out to be a jewelry salesman named R. Thomas Baldwin.

Caroline had not hesitated to volunteer information about how Jag had come bursting into the room.

While she talked, he had sat by quietly, not really worrying about the consequences he was facing. Whatever they sentenced him to, he would deal with, and if he lost his job, it wouldn't be the end of the world. He didn't like his work anyway.

The patrol car finally reached the courthouse. Once inside he rode the elevator in silence with the blue-uniformed police officer named Creston.

The fellow had short black hair and a mustache. He was not pleasant. All business, he had kept his eyes on Jag since they'd handcuffed him, his wrists fastened in front because of his injured hands.

When they reached the jail floor, the top floor of the courthouse, the elevator wheezed open, and they were buzzed through the security door and ushered into the lobby area.

The jailers sat in an enclosed glass booth with an array of television monitors behind them. Gray images depicting empty corridors filled the screens.

They put Jag in a chair in front of a small window and began the process of booking him.

He answered questions about his health insurance and with difficulty signed a form stating that he understood his rights. His hands ached, and his head was beginning to throb now as well.

They charged him with assault and battery. He only nodded as they went through the motions, and he didn't argue when they took his belt and other personal belongings and stuffed them into a large yellow envelope.

"You messed up, son," said the burly jailer who sat behind the desk. His nametag read Honeycutt.

Jag nodded.

The jailer gave him an almost fatherly look. "She must have been some kind of lay for you to mess a man up like that." Word travelled fast in the system.

"We weren't sleeping together," Jag said absently.

41

"I'd hate to see what he would do for pussy," one of the other jailers muttered.

When the booking was complete, they let him make a phone call. He dialed the paper, got the front desk and asked them to relay word to the editors.

His parents were living in another town. He didn't want to let them know he'd been arrested, and he didn't really have anyone else he wanted to call. If the editors wanted him at work, they could come and get him.

When he hung up, Honeycutt guided him around the booth and down a yellow hallway. The smell of chemical disinfectants assailed his nostrils.

They walked past a bank of doors, setting off a flurry of racket behind the narrow windows. Inmates began to bang their fists against the metal inside.

"Bring that sissy in here," somebody yelled through one of the windows. "We'll have a good time. We'll turn him out." Another fist slammed against the thick glass.

"What do they mean?" Jag asked.

"By turning you out?" Honeycutt turned around and looked at him. "They mean they want to turn you into a woman."

Jag's expression didn't change.

"You're not going in there," the guard said. "Not right now. Those are the hard cases. If you do go in later, you're big enough to take care of yourself. You just have to let them know you're not going to take any shit. Or they'll do what they say."

With a large metal key, Honeycutt opened another door.

Jag walked slowly into the narrow room. It was barren and dimly lit because metal grates covered the lights. Two wooden benches were bolted to the walls, and there was a metal toilet behind a curtain in the back. The smell of stale urine and alcohol overcame the antiseptics.

A man huddled in one corner, groaning under his breath. Since it was a Tuesday morning, there was not a crowd.

"Your buddy here registered 3.74 on the drunk test when we brought him in a little while ago. That's a local record. Four points is legally dead. He's had a lot of alcohol. Enjoy his company."

Jag sat down on the opposite bench and stared at the dull yellow paint as the door slammed.

He'd felt worse, but really couldn't remember when.

"What are you in for?" The words were badly slurred and seemed to ooze from the man's lips. He had rolled over and discovered Jag sitting there.

He was like a grizzled tree trunk that had been felled across the bench. The smell of perspiration and whatever he had been drinking drifted from his body.

"I beat the shit out of a guy," Jag said, hoping the wino would take a hint.

"You're a pretty big fellow," the wino said. "Looks like the other guy gave your fists quite a workover."

"Messed up my knuckles real bad."

The wino sat up and fumbled into his pocket. He found a badly crushed Pall Mall package, but he didn't have any matches. The cigarette he selected was twisted and damp.

"Light?"

"Sorry."

The old man put the cigarette between his lips anyway, letting it roll against his tongue. "Still raining outside?"

"Quite a bit."

"Ah, nasty weather. This is your first time in jail, ain't it, kid?" He was more coherent than Jag had expected.

Jag leaned his head back against the wall, his eyes looking off into oblivion. "It is," he conceded.

The old man laughed and shook his head. "I been in and out of jails for twenty years. I can't seem to leave the juice alone."

"Well the accommodations are pretty nice."

"Ain't they, though?" His eyes rolled around in his head. "Little tight sometimes," he noted, and the way his breaths labored seemed to indicate he was not joking.

"First time I was ever in one of these it was for a fight in a bar. Remember that old pool hall down on Front Street, by the levee?"

"They tore it down."

"Hell, this was back in the sixties. I was in there with this lady. She had long dark hair and these great big boobs." He held up his hands to illustrate what he was discussing.

"I see," Jag said, not showing any interest.

"Helen Anne Jackson her name was. She was leaning against the table, and some guy tried to make a pass at her. I guess I'd had a few drinks. I broke a pool cue over his head. I should have been home with my wife. I was never with her when she needed me."

"Wish I'd had a pool cue," Jag said. "My fists wouldn't hurt so bad."

"They put me in here with Johnny W.," the old man said.

"No last name?"

"He was a slick one, boy. You know the cops around here ain't too bright, boy. They never could hang anything on Johnny. He ran his share of scams too. He always had the finest clothes, and you should have seen his women."

Jag was thinking about Caroline.

"Not many remember him," the old man muttered. "They got him. Took him away. They took him off, into the swamp."

"What do you mean?" Jag asked.

"Ain't you never heard what happens to prisoners around here that the law can't convict?"

Jag shook his head.

"Sheltered life, eh? I thought everybody knew about the disappearances."

"They disappear?"

"You never know when it's coming. But you get out and you find out nobody's heard from your friend that was released two weeks before you were. 'Fore long you know you're never gonna hear from him again. Shallow graves. That's my theory."

"What?"

"They bury 'em in shallow graves, hide the bodies." His voice cracked.

"You're saying someone kills people, murders them?"

"That's what I'm saying." He gave Jag a quick confirmation nod. "It's real."

Tears began to trickle down the man's cheeks, and his voice began to grow louder.

"They could come for us, boy. You never know when it's gonna happen. It does happen. They take 'em. It stopped for a while. Now it happens again."

His eyes grew wide, as if they might pop out from their sockets. He began to look around the room, frightened suddenly by his own warnings.

"They might be comin' right now," he said. "You cain't tell. You never know."

He drew in a deep breath that rasped through his lips.

Jag slid down the bench, trying to get as far away from the man as possible.

Willis was on his feet now, hands out at his sides as he twisted his head left and right.

"They take you out. They tell you you're gettin' out, but that's not what happens. Mark my words, big fellow, they

44

don't let you go. No, no they don't let you go. They take you."

He began to scream, his voice echoing off the concrete block walls. Jag got to his feet and moved to the end of the room, pressing his back against the door as he watched the man flail about.

Willis was striking out at invisible attackers, shouting insults and spraying spittle in all directions.

"I don't want them to take me. Not me. I don't want to go like Johnny W."

He stopped for a moment, burying his face in his hands. "And not like the fire either. I don't want to burn. So many mistakes. So many mistakes."

He crumpled to the floor, cradling his face in his arms as he wept. His shoulders began to heave, as his cries and moans rose up from his huddled form.

Reluctantly, Jag moved toward him. He was frightened of the man, hesitant, but he finally placed a hand on his shoulder.

"It's all right, old-timer. There's no fire. Nobody's after us. You need to rest and sober up."

The man moaned again.

"Come on," Jag said, "Up here, come on." He took the man's elbow and half pulled him upward.

Obediently the man got onto his knees, then onto his feet, allowing Jag to guide him to one of the benches.

Jag was attempting to help the man onto a bench when the convulsion started. The wino began to heave and clutch at his chest. Tumbling onto the floor, he drew his legs into a fetal position, gasping and coughing as loud growls issued from his throat.

Jumping back from him, Jag stood in stunned silence for a second. Then he spun around and ran back to the door. Pounding on it, he began to shout.

"There's a man sick in here," he called. "Can you hear me out there?"

He slammed his injured hand against the metal, hoping the reverberations would carry through into the hallway.

"Don't let them take me," the old man screamed through saliva and phlegm. Then he moaned again and rolled back to the floor. If it had not been so hideous, it might have been comical.

After a moment the shudders stopped, and the old man was on his knees, then his feet. Standing at the center of the room, he began to flail his arms wildly at imaginary attackers.

"You won't take me, you bastards," he called. "No matter

what, you won't take me alive. Fuckers."

He continued to swing and curse, his eyes rolling about in his head. Jag backed into a corner, positioning himself as far away from the old man as he could get. A second later the door burst open, and Honeycutt rushed into the room, followed by another jailer.

"Get away from me," the old man hissed. "Get away, you bastards."

"Easy now," Honeycutt whispered, trying to sound soothing, "Easy, boy."

The old man moved back to the end of the cell in a futile effort to stay away from the guards.

A third guard entered the room to keep an eye on Jag while the other two confronted Willis.

"We're going to have to put him in the isolation tank," Honeycutt determined, speaking into the microphone attached to the shoulder of his uniform.

"Don't take me to the swamp," the old man pleaded.

"It's going to be okay," Honeycutt soothed. "We're going to get you some help."

"Leave me alone." He pressed his back against the wall, his hands in front of him, ready to strike if anyone moved too close.

The guard on Jag urged him out of the doorway as a couple more uniformed men arrived with clubs.

The man's cries emerged from the cell as Jag stood in the hallway, but there were no sounds of him being struck.

After a few moments the contingent emerged. The old man was in the middle of them, his hands cuffed behind him. He tried to struggle, but they gripped him tightly, forcing him along the corridor.

"Be still," Honeycutt urged. "You're just going to make it worse."

"I know what's happening. I remember. I've seen it. No, no, not me, please."

His cries continued as they dragged him down the hall and forced him through another narrow doorway.

Honeycutt returned in a few moments as Jag's guard was ushering him into the cell once more.

"I'll turn the key," Honeycutt said, taking the ring from the other man. He remained a moment after the guard had gone.

Jag was trembling. He settled down onto a bench and heaved a heavy sigh.

46

"You didn't know your room included a floor show, did you?" Honeycutt asked.

"What was he talking about?"

"He's drunk. No telling what the liquor's done to his mind. Maybe we can get him taken care of."

Jag started to ask something else but then remained silent, only nodding.

Honeycutt stepped through the doorway. "Maybe somebody will be coming for you soon, son." He slammed the door behind him, the sound echoing through the narrow room with an empty thud.

When LaFleur was relieved from the desk, he headed into the locker room to change into his street clothes.

The chief had spoken to him briefly about handling public information, but there had been no formal reprimand. He was glad of that. He wasn't afraid of White, but he knew the chief's ire could be substantial.

While much of the time White was a jovial good ole boy, he could kick ass when he wanted to. He'd been a tough guy on the streets, and that hadn't changed when he'd worked his way to detective and finally been appointed chief.

Now it was good to keep the chief happy. LaFleur had been a cop sixteen years, and he could see the ins and outs of police politics. He didn't choose to play the games, but he knew when to stay out of people's way.

Shrugging off his uniform, he massaged the ache in his shoulder where he had once been shot. The scar where the bullet had entered was like a huge white smear on his skin. The wound always ached when weather got damp, and it always reminded him of the night he'd stopped the liquor store robbery.

He'd never killed a man before that, but after a month and a half of shooting reviews, he had been vindicated. They'd raised hell about it in the newspapers for a few weeks, but nothing stuck. The guy had been committing a crime and had tried to kill a police officer, and LaFleur had been practically put on trial.

On top of everything, he'd had to go through physical therapy to get his arm working right again, and the city's insurance hadn't covered everything the way it was supposed to. He'd wound up paying out of his own pocket. Now he had to carry extra insurance, just in case. He didn't have the money to spend to get well if anything else happened to him.

As he cursed the world under his breath, he changed into a pair of dark-brown slacks and a plaid shirt. When he had tugged on his cowboy boots, he slipped on a shoulder holster and transferred his .38 into that. He took his leather jacket from the locker. After he slipped it on, he checked in the mirror on the inside of the locker door to make sure no bulges showed.

Satisfied, he reached into the locker and took out the small Walther PPK .380, his backup weapon. He'd had it for years. He'd bought it from an FBI agent back in the days when you couldn't get the weapons in America because they were too small for federal import regulations. Now they made them here and it didn't matter, but he was glad he had it anyway. It gave him a feeling of security.

Reaching behind him, he tucked it securely into the waistband of his pants so that it was concealed in the small of his back.

A yawn caught him as he closed the locker door.

He'd pulled a couple of hours extra on his shift to fill in for another officer this morning, and he was tired. After he got some breakfast somewhere, he would probably go home and sleep.

There was no real rush, though. There wasn't anybody waiting for him anymore. That hit him every time he got off work. Sandy had been gone a long time now. She'd grown tired of being married to a cop.

Or at least she had grown tired of being married to LaFleur. He'd never been able to talk to her about his problems at work, and she identified that as "shutting her out."

The divorce papers had said something about mental cruelty. LaFleur had never beaten her, but he did have a way of being gruff and cold. Lawyers could not do a lot with a man's personality.

He hated lawyers. They always snooped around and found loopholes to let guilty bastards go free.

As soon as an arrest was made these days, criminals started screaming about their rights. It was impossible to get anybody convicted.

LaFleur had had his share of trying to get people put behind bars. The lawyers would get the police on the witness stand and play with questions until the facts were screwed up in the

48

jurors' minds.

On the stand, LaFleur always tried to be concise, leaving as little room as possible for confusion. It didn't always do any good.

It hadn't when he was on the stand for Sandy's lawyer either. She'd sat at her table, crying periodically for the judge's benefit, LaFleur suspected.

It had worked. She got their house. He lived in a trailer now. It was all he could afford, and he'd had to scrape to get enough for that, even borrowing against his insurance.

It was a screwed-up world, he decided as he headed for the door. He worked all his life to stop criminals and make something of his life, and the courts let the criminals go and gave everything he owned to his ex-wife.

At least now and then he got a chance to make things right in the world. Somebody had to just to keep things in order.

Chapter 4

Serena Rand's coat kept the wind and rain off her dress, but the bite of the cold air stung her face as she moved through the trees behind her house.

Her father didn't like her out in such bad weather; but her cat had not come back since she had let it out earlier, and she was worried about it.

Besides, she got tired sitting inside watching television all the time, which was about all her father let her do. He feared so much for her safety that being under his care was a bit like being in prison. The food was probably better, but that was the only positive thing she could say.

Since they had moved from Texas several years ago, he had provided a private tutor for her schooling, so she had no friends her own age. The only people she saw were on the small household staff.

He meant well, but she didn't appreciate his smothering attention.

Whenever they went out for their occasional dinners in town or for shopping, he did all but keep her on a leash. She was never allowed to shop alone, and she was not allowed to make her own choices of fashion. She tried to pick out things like those in the magazines or the clothes she saw on television, but her father was not very contemporary in his thinking.

"Your mother would never have worn anything like that," he would say, or "You know your mother wouldn't want you to dress like that."

She wasn't so sure about how her mother might have handled things, but it did no good to argue with her father. He seemed to have an idealized memory of her mother, and it served him well in keeping Serena in the Victorian Age.

She wore her long black hair straight in the style he prescribed, and her dresses were either simple things or so elegant that they seemed too delicate. She could not make him understand she wasn't comfortable wearing elaborate gowns around the house.

They were the clothes many girls dreamed of, but they were more suitable for proms and cotillions than for watching *The Young and the Restless* and reading whatever magazines he let her subscribe to.

She kept having to hold up the hem of the dress she wore this morning, trying to avoid staining it with mud from the forest floor.

Occasionally, she stopped and called for the cat. "Here kitty, kitty. Come on."

She'd had the pet only a short time; but she had learned its habits quickly, and she wanted to keep up with it. She had grown attached to it. Her father at least allowed her pets, and the animals provided comfort in her loneliness.

The cat, stubborn as always it seemed, failed to comply when she called, forcing her to move deeper into the forest.

Her father didn't like that either. He didn't like her going in the forest, or the city, or anywhere.

Since he spent too much time worrying with his sugar cane crops and his other business to talk to her about it, she didn't bother to worry about his displeasure.

He was mysterious about some of his activities, and he was strange to begin with. His family had lived in Texas forever, but he had been educated in the East and Europe and had airs about him that annoyed many people. He did not seem like a Texan at all.

"Here kitty," she repeated. It was futile. She stopped and sighed, her shoulders drooping in disgust.

She was about to turn around when she saw the man standing near the oak tree.

He was like an oak himself, tall and solidly built. Standing well over six feet, he wore dark clothes which gave him an eerie look, a look accented by his face which was stoic in expression and rough, with a scar on one cheek and a weathered texture. He was a textbook bête noire.

A black eye patch covered his left eye, and his curly black hair fell around his face and dangled to his collar in the back. His hands were in the pockets of the heavy black pea coat he wore, and he did not flinch when Serena gasped at the sight of him.

"Scarecrow, you scared the shit out of me," she said when she was back inside her skin.

"Your father doesn't want you wandering too far into the woods," he said in his thick Cajun accent. "There could be wild animals or somethin'."

"I'm perfectly safe," she said. "Besides, you shouldn't lurk around and scare me like that."

"Several people were killed by animals in Bristol Springs last summer."

"That was because of the drought, and we sure don't have one of those now."

"I've been told ta keep an eye on ya." He didn't smile or offer any indication that he intended any humor with his remark.

She pulled her coat tightly about her because the cold stare of his single blue eye seemed to cut into her.

He was a frightening man. She never heard him approach, never knew he was on hand until he made himself known, and there were other things about him she didn't like. He seemed mean, or perhaps heartless was the word. It was as if there was no hint of anything inside him, no feeling, no humanity. She couldn't understand why her father kept him around.

He was a good body guard, but what good was his protection if he made you so uncomfortable, Serena wondered.

He took a step toward her, and she watched for signs of the weapons concealed beneath his clothing. She knew there was a knife there somewhere and a gun. He carried a .44 Magnum, the Dirty Harry gun. She knew that, although she had never seen it. What was even more frightening was she knew what the gun could do.

"Come on," he said, taking her arm gently.

She allowed him to turn her around and lead her toward the house. Looking back over her shoulder, she cast a final, furtive glance around for the cat. It was still nowhere in sight. She hated to think another of her pets had wandered into the woods and disappeared. That happened too often here in Louisiana, far too often.

Nicholas Rand stood at the window of his study, watching Scarecrow lead Serena back toward the house. He shook his head. She was growing more and more defiant as the years rolled along.

She was headstrong the way her mother had been, a quality he found both endearing and troubling. He could not bear the thought of losing her the way he had lost his wife, and he would not allow it to happen. It was just difficult to make Serena understand that her safety was insured only by vigilance.

Turning from the window, he walked over to the silver service beside his reading chair and poured himself a cup of tea. It was hot and clear, and he used only a touch of lemon to enhance its flavor.

He'd picked up the tea habit while working on business deals in London. That seemed a thousand years ago.

The tea seemed a very civilized thing, and he enjoyed it in this sitting room. He'd had the room decorated with the best of furnishings and artworks to make it a gentleman's chamber. Books lined one wall, and the prints of impressionist paintings offered bright colors to offset the earth tones of the paneling and carpet.

Settling into the heavy leather chair, he picked up the framed picture of Serena and her mother which he kept on the table beside him. Everything seemed a thousand years ago.

The picture represented a time of innocence, harmony. Serena was eight. She leaned back into the arms of her mother, who was kneeling behind her, and bright smiles graced both of their faces.

How much she had grown in what seemed just a few years. She was much like her mother, yet her own person as well. She wanted other friendships, wanted to meet boys. The thought of that horrified him. No one could be trusted.

She was past the age most girls started dating, but he couldn't bring himself to even think about that sort of thing.

Too bad, he thought, that the age of arranged betrothals was gone. He could have accepted that, pledging her hand to some worthy young gentleman from a good family.

He had to laugh. The world was not the place he wanted it to be. He looked into the eyes of his wife's picture and remembered.

It was definitely a world he could not control, and he wanted to shield Serena from it as much as he wanted to change it.

53

He wondered if he had the ability to do either.

Willis awoke to the feeling of moisture on his face. He had slept in puddles before, but as he lifted his head, he realized he was not in an alley or on the street.

He was not in the city at all.

As he placed his palms on the ground to push himself upward, he found he was touching leaves.

He sat back, one leg tucked under him, and looked up at the sky. It was masked by the cover of trees, thousands of branches matted together to block out the gray-metal clouds.

He hadn't been in the forest in ages, not since hunting trips he'd taken in another lifetime. How the hell did he get here? He tried to force the memory, but it wouldn't come.

Nervously he licked his lips. His mouth was very dry, and the ache in his head pounded like a jackhammer. His vision was not blurred, but he blinked his eyes several times in an attempt to melt the illusion.

He must be in jail or at least an alley somewhere in Aimsley. He couldn't be in the forest.

The wind swept over him, rustling the damp leaves as if to confirm his location.

A moan rose from deep in his throat, and he rubbed his craggy face with both hands. He let his head roll back then, moaning again at the ache in his back. He had to think about getting up for a while before he actually made the move.

His knees popped, and his muscles sent messages of complaint to his brain. Once he got his feet under him, he leaned one hand against a tree to steady himself.

A drink would have been nice, but getting the hell out of here was going to be the first order of business.

Except, which way did he go to get the hell out of here?

Looking around, all he could see in any direction were woods and more woods. What was that old line from the show he'd watched ages back? "What a revoltin' development."

He made some snorting sounds, then took his hand from the tree and began to wade through the leaves and over the roots that stuck out of the ground.

He'd just walk until he came to something that would give him some direction. Maybe he'd find a house, and maybe if God was looking down on him, there would be somebody there who had something to drink.

He moved from tree to tree, supporting himself and drawing deep breaths for fortification before each new foray.

It was while he was breathing deeply that the first sensation of being watched began to creep over him.

He looked back over his shoulder, expecting to spot a hunter or some other benevolent soul who would lead him to safety, freedom and drink. More woods.

He spat, then coughed and spat again.

The cold was seeping into his bones, making the joints ache. He had to get out of here.

He moved a little more briskly, still aware of a sensation that he was being watched or at least that he was in the presence of someone else.

What time of day was it? It must be morning. Hadn't he been put in jail?

He heard something move, something other than the wind. He staggered around, looking back in the direction he had just travelled.

Nothing.

Empty woods.

Leaves.

He shook his head. Imagination.

He spun again and walked on, stooping slightly to ease his back and shut out the cold.

The cry made him straighten abruptly and turn again.

"Is somebody there?" he called out. "What the hell's going on here?"

The creature just seemed to appear, stepping forward from its camouflaged position. It was covered in leaves and mud, a tall thing, broad through its chest. A hideous smell hung around it.

Even in his special alcohol-enhanced hallucinations Willis had never seen anything like this. It wasn't the type of horror his mind conjured.

So it must be real.

He started to step backward with that thought in mind. This bastard thing was a genuine threat.

He turned and started to lift his feet, jerking his knees upward as he ran. He hadn't run in a long time, and he found it difficult, more difficult than he remembered.

His lungs began to tighten. The muscles in his thighs threatened to knot. Sweat formed on his face in spite of the cold, and his vision began to cloud.

The real pisser was that his ears didn't screw up. Nope, they functioned just fine. As he went bouncing along through the leaves, kicking them up everywhere, he could hear the footfalls of the thing behind him. They crunched down in the damp leaves rapidly, so rapidly that they left little doubt that it was gaining on him.

His heartbeat was pounding hard now, the fear affecting it as much as the exertion. What had that baseball player Satchel Paige said? "Don't look back. Somethin' might be gainin' on you." He wasn't looking back, but it didn't matter.

He didn't just know something was gaining on him; he knew it was going to — *Holy Sweet Jesus* — catch him.

He tried to run faster, but he was too far out of shape, too far gone. The poor conditions he'd lived in for so long — the alcohol, the emotional turmoil — had sapped the strength out of him.

He spilled through some brush and skidded across a blanket of pine straw, grabbed a thin tree and spun to the right, jogged over a log and was starting toward a cluster of oaks when the thing caught the tail of his coat.

Like a cartoon character, he tried to keep moving for several steps before he realized he was suspended.

He looked back over his shoulder, then into the fiery eyes of the creature. He could read the hatred and the bestial fury.

He screamed as it yanked backward on his coat, dragging him to it. He struggled, unable to get a foothold on the slick ground. He tried to close his eyes, but they were frozen open as he drew closer and closer to the monster.

And then he was in its grasp. Claws dug through his clothing into his skin, and he was screaming again.

The scream lasted until the thing's teeth sank into his throat.

Then the forest was silent.

Once he had Serena deposited at the house for her tutoring lesson, Scarecrow went back to his room, a little apartment constructed behind the mansion.

It was a comfortable spot, one of the better homes that he'd had in his life. It was a far cry better than the shack where he'd grown up in Avoyelles Parish.

He'd lived with just his father, his mother having run off to New Orleans when he was very young.

At one time his father had been a sheriff's deputy, but he

had lost his job over a political matter. From the time Scarecrow was eight years old, his old man had made a living hunting or poaching or running crawfish nets.

It contented his father. His people had lived that way forever anyway, and Scarecrow learned well the methods of tracking and other secrets when he accompanied the old man on hunting trips.

The things he had learned had come in handy after he'd left the Merchant Marines. He'd tried a little work off shore, but the long weeks on the water in the cramped rig accommodations drove him crazy. So he'd headed back inland and went to work for a succession of bail bondsmen, utilizing the hunting techniques on human prey — those who jumped bail and tried to run.

Dealing with desperate men had required that he get tough, tougher than the work at sea had already made him. He'd learned to be prepared for anything, and he'd learned to be brutal when he had to be.

He knew the people he was tracking wouldn't hesitate to use force. That was why he only had one eye now.

He'd been in Texas wrapping up a case when he met Rand. That had changed his life. It gave him a chance to settle down, and since Rand was moving to a spot in Louisiana not far from Scarecrow's hometown, he hadn't hesitated to take on the oilman's task.

Shrugging off his jacket, the Cajun stood in front of the mirror, eyeing the Magnum nestled under his arm. It stayed hidden well with the holster he used.

With a swift motion, he practiced his draw and had the weapon in his hand and aimed in a matter of seconds.

He'd trained himself in the use of handguns, and on the occasions he'd had to utilize that training, it had proven effective.

With a grim smile of satisfaction, he slid the gun back into the holster and slipped the knife from one of his alligator boots. He could access either of his weapons with ease. He could make do, whatever the situation.

Slipping the knife back into the boot, he straightened and studied his reflection. People told him he looked sinister with his grim, sullen features.

A less conspicuous eye patch might have been available to cover the damage the kid had done with the switchblade. He couldn't blame the kid in a way. The boy had been about to

57

go down for his third felony, a three-time loser, which meant he'd be doing hard time. That hadn't stopped Scarecrow from beating the little bastard to a pulp, smashing his jaw and rupturing his spleen.

As the kid was carted away to the hospital, no one questioned Scarecrow's use of necessary force. Not when they saw his eye.

Scarecrow wasn't really worried about being handsome, although in a way his features had that quality. Somewhere back in his family there was some Indian blood, and it gave him a lean high-cheekboned face.

He was given to not shaving regularly, however. When he let the beard grow a day or two, the covering of stubble gave him a rugged look. It almost created a gunfighter mystique.

In reality, he was something of a gunfighter, he had decided. Hell, he'd been a bounty hunter; that was right out of the Old West.

Except they hadn't had the martial arts training back then. He was tougher than a gunfighter. He'd worked with a guy on one of the ships who'd studied some kind of Korean karate. It was something Scarecrow couldn't pronounce, but it was effective. He'd learned the moves well, and he'd used them on more than one occasion when he'd been called on to drag big bastards back to justice or whatever slap on the wrist awaited them in the courts.

As a bounty hunter he'd had to walk into some real hell holes after people. You couldn't back up from any of them or let them know you were afraid.

That was behind him now. This job wasn't easy, but it didn't require him to stand toe to toe with whole hoards of the Lucifer's Disciples motorcycle gang either.

He owed Rand a great deal, and he knew it. That kept him loyal, no matter what.

Corey Johnson and his brother Kyle sat in the front seat of their old Impala, waiting for Turk Harper to show up at his house. Kyle bounced about on the seat, nervous and unable to find a comfortable position. Corey handled his concern slightly better. He was the tough one, as the people who knew them always said.

While the rain splattered off their windshield, their eyes darted about. As each car passed, they looked at it to see if

58

Turk was coming home and to make sure it wasn't a prowl car.

They had a trunk and a back seat full of hot merchandise including some televisions and a stereo.

They'd been burglarizing Aimsley's affluent neighborhoods for a month and a half. So far the cops weren't even close, and Turk assured them they wouldn't get close as long as the boys didn't do something stupid.

Turk ran a pawn shop; so he had a perfect outlet for moving what they picked up, and he had some connections with stores in other towns that let him channel recognizable stuff like jewelry fairly easily.

"Where do you think he is?" Kyle asked. He was the younger of the two and the most nervous. Corey had been in trouble before, but the burglaries were Kyle's first experience with illegal behavior.

"He'll be coming," Corey reassured, then looked back up the street for some sign that would make his statement true.

Corey was twenty-two, and Kyle was nineteen. They both had long blond hair and wore tee shirts, blue jeans and leather jackets. They had the look for an MTV Headbangers Ball video.

Neither had a job, although they liked to think of themselves as musicians. They had elaborate electric guitar systems, and they could rattle roofs for blocks with their heavy metal riffs. Unfortunately there wasn't much demand for roof rattling in Aimsley, so they played for their friends and heisted television sets for money and blow.

Both of them felt relieved when Turk's car showed up. There was a thrill in being outlaws, but it was sometimes offset by the tension involved.

The sight of his car meant everything was going to be all right. It meant they could unload their haul.

The white Lincoln cut a slow path through the standing water. It cruised up the street and turned into the driveway, disappearing into a garage opened by remote control.

They waited a few minutes before climbing out of their car and dashing through the rain to Turk's front door.

It took a few minutes for Turk to show up. When he did he only nodded his welcome.

They took it as an invitation and followed him into his living room. It was a match for his personality, because there was something seedy about it. The furniture was all vinyl, and a painting of a conquistador hung over the black couch.

Turk was about forty, with graying hair that had grown thin on top. He was wearing jeans and a gray sweat shirt. On his hands were jewels that looked more gaudy than elegant. A thin gold chain circled his wrist, and more chains dangled around his neck.

As he settled into a chair, a blond girl who couldn't have been more than eighteen walked from the kitchen with a cup of coffee for him. She wore a tight tee shirt and black jeans that hugged the curve of her hips.

She nodded a greeting to Kyle and Corey and then settled onto the arm of Turk's chair in a submissive fashion.

He put his hand on her knee and nodded toward the boys. "This is Diane."

They told her hello, but she only nodded gently in response.

"You can talk in front of her," Turk promised. "What have you guys got for me?"

Corey gave him a quick rundown.

Turk sipped his coffee and nodded. "Sounds good. I'll move it for you, but I got somethin' I need you to do for me."

"What's that?" Corey asked.

"Want you to do a job. It's not outside y'all's usual area. It's on Walters Lane. That big house with the white columns."

Kyle nodded. "I've seen it."

"The old bitch that lives there has some diamonds. Lots of 'em. I got a guy who's already cased the place, and I can sell the shit for top dollar if you guys can lay hands on it."

Corey chewed his lower lip. "What's our cut?"

"You guys get fifty, I get fifty."

"You don't have to give your man a cut?" Corey asked.

"He'd owed me. Now, what do you say? We can set it up for tonight. Sound okay?"

The brothers looked at one another.

Kyle's eyes widened. "I don't know."

"We could use the bread," Corey said with a shrug, then looked back at Turk. "How big a risk are we taking?"

"Hell, you've slipped the cops on every other job you've pulled. This is no different."

"She don't keep these things in a safe or anything?" Corey asked.

"Jewelry box. She thinks she's safe."

Kyle looked at Corey again. "I don't know." His affection

for this business was limited.

Turk laughed. "Come on. It's a piece of cake. It's not anything you haven't handled before. It'll be quick bucks for just what you've been doing anyway."

Corey thought it over a few seconds before he nodded. "Why not? We probably would have hit somewhere tonight anyway."

"Good. I knew I could count on you two," Turk said with a smile. He tossed them the remote control for the garage door. "Unload your stuff and get out of here for a while."

He slapped the girl's knee. "I have some other business to attend to."

Chapter 5

Around one P.M., the door on the holding cell opened again, and Jag looked up from the bench where he was lying back with his head propped on his coat which he had rolled into a pillow. He'd thought about fashioning a noose from it, but that had seemed too difficult. He didn't have the energy to hang himself.

He'd been dreaming about Caroline, something to do with her and her other lovers, and the hurt of the images lingered as he awoke. He found himself staring at Honeycutt again.

"Get up," the guard said.

Jag rolled off the bench, discovering pains in his muscles he had not expected. His shoulder was stiff, his arms ached and his hands were sore. Being up all night, fighting and then sleeping on the hard wood bench had taken their toll.

He rubbed his eyes, then picked up his coat.

"Where are we going?" Jag asked.

"Just follow me."

He trailed Honeycutt into the narrow corridor and stepped along, trying to match the guard's brisk pace.

At the booth, Honeycutt was buzzed through the heavy metal door, and once he was seated in his swivel chair, he motioned Jag around to the window. Through the openings, he shoved the brown envelope with Jag's belongings.

"What's going on?" Jag asked. "Did somebody post bail?"

Honeycutt shook his head. "You're being sprung. Charges dropped."

"Why's that?"

"They just were." He shoved a clipboard through the window opening and nodded for Jag to sign. "That just shows we didn't steal anything," the guard said.

Jag looked into the envelope and shrugged. "Looks like my

62

change is still here," he agreed.

He signed awkwardly with his bandaged hand, then turned to see if the front door would open.

"Just a minute," Honeycutt said.

Jag pulled his coat on and stood outside the booth while the guard walked around into the foyer.

Taking his arm, Honeycutt pulled him a few steps to the side, out of everyone's earshot. His expression was hard. "Between you and me, you got lucky."

"How's that?"

"The guy you beat the crap out of came out from under the drugs they pumped into him long enough to realize what was about to happen to him. He's married, and his old lady already suspects he's been dipping into twenty-year-old poon tang. With a trial, there'd have to be testimony and all that shit. This way he gets off the burner, and we both know your paper is going to hush this."

Jag nodded.

"You could have been in deep for this," the guard continued. His voice grew stern. "You better learn to bridle your temper. I can tell you're a good kid. I don't want to see you back in here. You hear?"

Jag nodded. "I don't want to come back," he said. He rubbed the back of his neck where the ache had nestled. "You guys don't have the best accommodations in the world."

"We're overcrowded. And . . . kid?"

"Yeah."

"Between you and me again?"

Jag nodded.

"You kicked ass on that guy from what I heard. Taught him a lesson. Let him take his chickenshit ass back to his wife's bed where it belongs."

"Yeah," Jag said. "I guess I showed him."

He walked to the door and waited for the buzzer to let him out. He didn't feel like a hero.

The elevator opened, and he climbed on board, digging into the envelope to return his change to his pockets on the way down. He found his belt and put it back on as well, then stuffed his wallet back into his hip pocket.

Wadding the envelope into a ball, he tossed it into a corner of the elevator car.

Again the pressure of tears crept up behind his eyes. He wanted to go somewhere and curl into a fetal position and shut

63

out the world.

Why had Caroline zeroed in on him? If she hadn't wanted him, why had she put him through this?

For a while she had seemed to be a refuge from the terrors of his job. Now his world was in an even more confusing state, and there was no refuge at all.

The elevator doors wheezed open on the ground floor, and he stepped off, moving across the front lobby of the courthouse and out onto the street.

The wind hit him like a cannon blast, and rain was still coming down. He buttoned his coat and turned up his collar.

His car was apparently still parked at Caroline's building. The newspaper offices were several blocks away, but he would have to walk.

Plunging his hands into his pockets, he started along the sidewalk, trying to ignore the rain. It was a harsh assault, worse then Louisiana was supposed to get.

He tried to think about something besides Caroline as he walked, but she kept creeping back from his subconscious to torment him until he reached the *Clarion* building.

Moving through the front glass doors, he paused in the reception area to let the warm air caress him. Charlotte, the receptionist, looked up at him as he was unbuttoning his coat.

"Hi, Jag." Her voice was thick with a Southern accent that did funny things to vowels.

He nodded in greeting and wiped wet hair off his forehead. "Anybody looking for my head?" he asked.

"Mr. Roberts said he wanted to see you if and when you showed up."

The managing editor.

Jag put his hands back into his pockets and followed the hallway around to Roberts' door. It was, as promised, always open.

Roberts was on the phone, but he motioned Jag into the room. Stepping through the doorway, Jag settled into a chair across from the desk.

The editor, who was heavy set in traditional journalistic fashion, sat in his swivel chair like a round beach ball. His hair was gray at the temples and messed up at the moment. It was just one sign that he wasn't having the best of days.

The sleeves on his blue-and-white-striped shirt were rolled up, and his tie was loose. He hung up the phone and looked across the desk with a glare that made his brown eyes intense.

"Don't go the bond," Jag said. "I escaped."

Roberts' expression didn't change as he took a cigarette from his pocket and stuffed it into his lips. "Mr. Carson at our lawyer's office tells me the charges were dropped. He learned that at the D.A.'s office. We were preparing to get you out with the bond being considered a company loan. We don't normally do that sort of thing, but somebody pointed out you're young and stupid." He found some matches and ignited his Kool.

"Thank you." Jag found his voice growing a little hoarse. Since levity hadn't worked, he wasn't sure how to deal with the situation.

It appeared to be growing worse. Roberts got out of his chair. Jag had heard if he paced while he was reaming you a new one, he was really in a foul mood.

"I've talked with the publisher about this matter. You're not doing bad for one of your experience. We trust your work will improve." Roberts sighed. "This present situation is upsetting, however, to say the least. The paper expects its people to behave with some restraint."

He took a long drag on the cigarette and then used it to gesture at Jag. "I know things can get difficult with girls, son. Don't get me wrong." He shook his head. "To let things go to the extreme you carried them is another matter. We can't have our reporters being arrested and thrown in jail. It would be an embarrassment to the Big Man. He's upset about the length of your hair, while I'm thinking about it."

Roberts gave him the stare then, that look everybody always talked about. It was like the evil eye, a death ray and Bela Lugosi's leer all rolled into one. "I'm going to warn you not to let anything like this happen again," the editor said. "You people in that newsroom have to be unimpeachable. You understand that? We have to be without tarnish. We can't get traffic tickets fixed or accept free favors from politicians. We can't do anything wrong because we can't report on other people if we're in and out of jail ourselves."

He inhaled more smoke and let it seep out through his mouth while he talked. "For God's sake, son, straighten yourself up."

Jag's voice was very low now. A "Yessir" was all he could manage. He started to get up.

He'd thought his lecture was complete, but Roberts' diatribe continued, the words freezing Jag in his seat.

"The publisher has a lot of pride in his people. You know when you screw up, son, when you make a little mistake in an obit or when you do something like this, you don't just hurt yourself. You hurt all those people out there who make their living in this place. Good people who work hard to get stories and do their jobs right."

Jag tuned it out. His eyes were drawn to the doorway as the girl walked past. She looked to be in about as bad a condition as he was. Her hair was damp, and her eyes were weary; but that didn't detract from her beauty.

He leaned back in his chair, trying to figure out where she was headed. He couldn't see that far down the hallway, so he turned back to Roberts.

As the lecture finally wound down, the managing editor made his way back to his seat. When he leaned back in his chair, that meant the attack was complete.

That was something else Jag had been told about the process.

"What time does your shift begin?" Roberts asked.

"About now."

"Well, you need to get cleaned up. Check in the newsroom for any assignments, then head home for a little while. And remember, don't let anything like this happen again or I'll fire your ass."

"Yes, sir."

Jag got up and walked from the room, stooping his shoulders slightly as he moved along the hallway in hopes of avoiding contact with anybody.

It worked until he made the newsroom. For a few seconds all was quiet, until Harvey Dotson looked up from his computer terminal and spotted Jag.

"Hey, Jag? How was the food?" he quipped.

Jag ignored him, settling into his desk and calling up the reporters' schedule.

"Jag," Tom Woodrow called. "What kind of bird don't sing?"

Jag was silent, scrolling along the computer tag that held the assignment listings.

"Give up?" Tom asked. "A jail bird." He guffawed.

Jag found his name on the schedule and glanced at his assignment.

— TAKE CARE OF OBITS

—DO BUSINESS REWRITES

—CHECK FILES TO SEE IF ANY UNIDENTIFIED BODIES HAVE BEEN FOUND IN LAST FEW MONTHS.

He was pondering the last entry when he realized someone was looking down at him. He glanced up, recognizing the girl he'd seen in the hallway.

"Are you Mr. Walker?" she asked.

Looking at her closely, he realized she was even more beautiful than he'd thought before. It made him wish he'd at least combed his hair.

Too late now. "Call me Jag," he said. "What can I do for you."

"They told me this morning you'd be in around one-thirty P.M., and that you might know if something had appeared in the paper."

Apparently she'd been shuffled through the newsroom bureaucracy and wound up being sluffed off on him.

When no one knew what to do with visitors to the newsroom, Jag always wound up with them. Usually they were old ladies with garden club news or family members who wanted to turn obituary information in personally to make sure their loved one's death appeared correctly in print. Those were always the ones that got screwed up in the typesetting.

He didn't usually get beautiful women. In fact, he never got beautiful women assigned to him, but in his present mood, he didn't feel particularly uplifted. She wouldn't be interested in him. Caroline lingered on his mind, and he was conscious of looking like a dish rag.

"What can I do for you?" he asked.

"My name is Debra Blane. I'm looking for my brother, and they told me you handle a lot of the incidental stories. You take dictation from correspondents and police news."

"It's called catching," he said. "A lot of calls come in at night."

"I talked to the police reporter, Mr. Walden, and he said there was no record of my brother being found or anything. They said something little might have come in late one night, and that you would know. Your staff librarian is out sick today, so I came back to see you."

"What's his name? Your brother?"

"Mark Turner. He's my half brother."

"Doesn't ring any bells. What kind of story do you think we

67

would have written about him?"

"They said you wouldn't report minor arrests. I don't know. I was just hoping for any thread. He's been missing since the fall." She sat down in the visitor's chair beside his terminal, and a hurt expression furrowed her brow.

"Maybe something like a death notice," she said. "An unidentified body, something like that."

Jag took off his glasses and rubbed his eyes. She was in luck. Some things stuck in his head. "We've had one unidentified body that I know about," he said. "That was north of us, near Bristol Springs."

He bit his lip slightly as he put his glasses back on and looked at her. "It was kind of gruesome. I hope it wasn't your brother. Some guy was sleeping on a railroad track, and a train came along. Last I heard they hadn't identified the body. They were working with dental records."

" 'They' being?"

"The Bristol Springs police department. They've got a new chief up there, and the department is a little disorganized. The old chief got killed last summer in . . . sort of a hunting accident."

"Would they still have the body?"

"Probably sent it to Bossier City. That's where they have the forensic pathology cases handled around here."

"That's near Shreveport?"

"Right."

"Oh, God. That's a long drive, isn't it?"

"From here," Jag confirmed.

"Do you have a copy of the article?"

Jag looked over at his desk. A manila folder stuffed with clippings that had his mistakes circled in red rested next to his Associated Press stylebook.

He picked up up and flipped it open. It would be easier than going to the filing cabinets in the library. He could never find anything under the paper's filing system anyway.

The article on the body was relatively short and clean, and he didn't think twice about showing it to Debra, since he'd given up hope of impressing her anyway.

She took the small piece of paper and studied it carefully. "Can you tell me how to get to Bristol Springs?" she asked.

"I could call the police station for you. Save you some trouble."

"Have you got the time?"

"I got nothing but time," he said. It was true. He really had nothing.

Checking his call list, he dialed the police station number and got a radio officer.

"This is Jag from the *Clarion*," he said. "Have y'all ever gotten an ID on that body you found? The one on the railroad tracks." He looked at Debra and shook his head when he had an answer.

She was leaning forward, her lips trembling. "Ask if they took pictures."

"You guys have photos? I've got a lady here trying to find her brother. She's afraid that might be him." He nodded a few times. "Thanks." He hung up. "They say they've got them," he said slowly, hesitating. "They don't know if you want to see them."

Her expression showed her determination. "There might be something of his I could identify even if the body was messed up. I've got to try."

Jag ran his hands through his hair. It probably looked like Einstein's on a bad day. "Okay, to get to Bristol Springs, you head northeast." He took a map out and showed her the route. "It's kind of nestled up in the corner of the parish," he said.

"Hard to get to?"

"Not too bad. It's isolated, but the road is decent. It'll take a half hour if you cut through Penn's Ferry."

"Not much of a lead but at least it's something. More than I had earlier. The cops in this town are really assholes."

"I'll drink to that," Jag said. "I run the police beat on the weekends."

She got up from her chair. "Well, Jag, I appreciate your help."

"Good luck," he said. "I hope you find your brother."

"Thanks."

He settled back and watched her depart, his gaze following her jeans until she left the newsroom. Then he picked up the early obits and started hammering the keys.

He'd finished a couple of them when Parkinson found him.

Park, the daytime assistant editor, was a big guy with a stern face, but he was half human. When he could, he took time to try and help Jag with his work. "You look like shit," he said.

"Thanks," Jag said.

"You're not going home?"

Jag shrugged. He didn't really want to be alone in his apartment. His thoughts would assault him there. Caroline, cops, Caroline . . .

"Get out of here," Park said. "You've been through a lot in a short time. We can handle everything."

Jag nodded. He needed to go get his car anyway. "You talked me into it," he said.

He headed out the back door after catching only three more jail jokes, mostly about bending over to pick up soap.

It was still raining when he hit the sidewalk. He turned up his collar and started walking toward the bus depot a couple of blocks down from the office. He could make connections and get dropped at the apartment complex in about thirty minutes.

He was bowing his head to avoid the wind when he heard the tires splashing along at his side. He looked over and saw a dark blue Volvo slowing to a snail's pace beside the sidewalk.

When the driver rolled down and window, he realized it was Debra.

"Can I give you a lift?" she asked.

"I'm just going to the bus stop."

"Come on. The weather is lousy, and you were a big help to me."

"I have to pick up my car," he said. "It's kind of on your way to Penn's Ferry."

She put on her brakes. "Then, get in."

It felt good to be out of the cold. The car heater was dialed to "High."

"How'd you hurt your hands?" she asked, setting the car into motion again and twisting the gear shift.

"Long story," he said.

She made a faint sound of acceptance.

"What happened to your brother?"

"Personal tragedy. Girlfriend got killed. He kind of wigged out a little."

"That's what happened to me," Jag said.

"Your hands?"

"Yeah."

"Somebody died?"

"Not exactly. Next right."

She hit the turn signal and followed his directions onto a cross street. "All towns start to look alike after a while," she said.

"This one looks the same every time I look at it," Jag agreed.

70

They cruised on through the rain, talking, even laughing a time or two in spite of the grimness of their moods and the weather.

"How long have you been a reporter?" she asked.

"Forever. Six months."

"I took some journalism courses."

"But you got smart?"

"Didn't like the idea of working under deadlines."

"It gets old. Next left."

She braked, avoiding a skid, and managed the turn with limited difficulty.

"I could have used you a long time ago," she said. "I've made a lot of wrong turns and wound up on a lot of little country roads that go nowhere."

Jag nodded. "Maybe I should ride to Penn's Ferry with you."

"I know you don't have time to do that."

If he went home, he would only try to sleep, probably unsuccessfully. He didn't want to be alone. As long as he was doing something, he wouldn't think about Caroline as much.

"I've got the afternoon free," he said. "I don't mind."

"You're sure?"

"Veer left."

Kyle and Corey cruised along the street, an Anthrax tape booming on the car stereo as they turned their heads toward the house. It sat back off the road, a mansion with thick white columns reminiscent of a plantation home.

A circular driveway curled in front of it, and even in the winter cold the hedges along the front of the house were neatly trimmed. Bright green winter rye grass blanketed the grounds.

It would be easy enough to get behind the place, Corey decided. They'd hit other houses on the street the same way, although it had been a while since they had pulled a job in the neighborhood. They spaced things out to let complacency return to residents.

A day or two after a neighborhood burglary, everybody was on the lookout for suspicious cars or movements in the shadows.

After a week, they were more interested in the latest episode of *L.A. Law*. Another week and you could lift the roof off without stirring suspicion.

"Any sign of the old lady?" Kyle asked. He was behind the

wheel, so he couldn't stare as intently as Corey.

"No movement."

"You think she's even at home? Maybe she's out getting the Mercedes serviced."

Corey shrugged. "We'll let it get late. She'll go to sleep." He pointed toward the house. "With all those windows, we'll be able to watch the lights. I'd bet her bedroom is on the top floor. When everything goes out downstairs, we know it's sleepy-time."

"Turk will be able to give us a little more of a layout, won't he?"

"It would help. If not, we'll play it by ear. That's always worked before."

"If we make good bread on this, maybe we could swing down to New Orleans," Kyle said. "We might be able to gig some, and we could hook up with maybe a good band or something."

It was a dream they discussed often. Corey nodded. He'd learned not to let his hopes rise too high. Doors never opened for them in the world. Kyle, however, never stopped dreaming.

Sometimes Corey let himself believe it could be true also, that they could become real musicians, playing to packed coliseums on tours and shooting videos with gorgeous models hanging on them.

He believed it before each job, actually. Each one was supposed to be the last. Each haul was supposed to net enough to let them get their feet on the ground and plot some career moves.

It just never seemed to happen that way. They wound up with some televisions and other shit that didn't sell for that much, and that meant looking to a new job for their rent money and food bills.

As they eased past the house, he let himself hope just a little bit, let just a touch of brightness touch his spirit. They would be going after jewels tonight. With jewels, the potential for some big money existed.

If he pressed Turk, a fair price might come their way. A fair price might make the trip to New Orleans viable. And from New Orleans, who knew where they might be able to move on to?

They might even be able to get out to L.A. That's where they really wanted to be; that's where they could establish themselves.

He cracked his knuckles. "Let's go get some food," he said. "I don't want to do this on an empty stomach."

As Kyle prepared to turn the car at the end of the street, a Mercedes swished past them, splashing water.

A woman with faded blond hair was at the wheel.

"Think it could be her?" Kyle asked.

"Guess she really does have a Mercedes. Could be."

Swinging the car around, Kyle paced the Mercedes until it turned into the driveway.

"That's her," Corey said. "Pass slow so we can get a look at her."

The woman was climbing out of the car when they reached the front of the house. She was trim, dressed in a dark wool skirt and jacket.

From the road it was hard to judge her age, but Corey realized she had been beautiful once.

"Least we know who we're robbing," Kyle said.

"Hope she doesn't stay up late."

"Nah. She's on the go. Needs her rest."

"I hope so," Corey said. "I want to get this over with."

For some reason he had a bad feeling about this job, a really bad feeling.

Chapter 6

The rain had subsided a little when Debra and Jag reached Bristol Springs. They followed the main drag past the fast food restaurants, and Deb turned at Jag's directions on the street which led back to the police station.

She was glad he was with her. Sometimes a stranger could be a friend, and she needed a friend right now. Occasionally he would make a joke or say something that eased her tension a little, and she needed that.

He had finally told her his story, admitting he had been rash and stupid. He was ashamed of what had happened, and telling her about it seemed to be a confession.

Debra could tell violence was not his true nature; she granted absolution with small words of understanding. She'd known of men who had done much worse.

He returned that understanding as they pulled up to the police station; he tried to console her. She knew she might be walking into a place to find out her brother was dead.

The fear of that shuddered somewhere inside her. The strain of travel had caught up with her, and the anguish that came with not knowing her brother's fate gripped her heart.

She realized she was trembling as she parked the car against the curb.

The police station was a cramped little place that looked like a storefront with a large plate glass window lined with dust around the edges. A shiny decal of a badge graced the front of the glass door, but its surface had begun to peel.

When they stepped inside, Deb discovered the front room resembled the set for a television show about small-town police.

A fat woman with a round face and curly black hair sat at a desk, working on a crochet pattern with yellow yarn.

"Is the chief around?" Jag asked.

"In his office. Who's calling?"

"I'm Jag Walker from the *Clarion*. I think we've talked on the phone."

She looked back over her shoulder and yelled in a shrill voice. "Chief?"

The door to the inner office opened, and a man who resembled a gorilla walked through it. He was about five feet seven inches, and his body was broad, his stomach stretching against the seams of his blue uniform and his gunbelt like an overstuffed sofa.

He rested a hand on the pistol that dangled at his side as he walked forward. A huge blue tattoo snaked around his forearm, and he had a face to make J. Edgar Hoover look like Bert Convey.

"Can I hep you?" He had a north Louisiana speech pattern.

Jag identified himself again.

"You the one that called me a Nazi?"

"Must have been somebody from the television station," Jag suggested.

"Seems like it was from the *Clarion*."

"Wasn't me," Jag said.

He introduced Deb, and the cop's features softened a little. He extended his hand in a polite greeting.

"How are you doing, Ma'am? I'm Ronnie Malone. The acting chief. What brings y'all up here?"

She stammered, searching for the right words. "I'm trying to find my brother." Her voice was quivering. The fatigue was beginning to exercise its hold on her. She fought it, angry with herself, frustrated that she could not keep control.

Jag took her arm and helped her to a chair. She struggled with the tears, but they could not be stopped. They tumbled out followed by sobs.

The receptionist got up and came over to her, touching her shoulders. "Now, now, dear," she whispered.

"A little water," Malone instructed, sending the woman off toward a cooler that stood in a corner of the room.

Jag knelt at Deb's side, touching her arm. "It's okay," he said. "Really."

She nodded. "I'm sorry. I'm just so tired. I'm not really this emotional." She felt her face flush with embarrassment and willed herself under control.

The water arrived, and she drank it; then the woman produced some tissue to let her wipe her eyes and nose.

"Let me run this past you, Chief," Jag said. "Her brother is missing. He was a drifter, and he was on his way to Aimsley when she last had track of him.

"We were checking to see about that unidentified body you guys found up here."

Malone nodded. "We still haven't found any match up on dental records on that fellow. He'd never been in the armed services."

"Mark never served," Deb said.

Malone looked down at her. "The body is up in Shreveport," he said. "I have pictures, but they're rough to look at."

She swallowed, closing her eyes for a second to collect herself. "I have to see them. Whatever the remains look like, I might be able to find a clue that would let me know if it was Mark."

Malone looked to Jag. He raised his eyebrows in question. Jag returned the look with an expression that it was her decision.

Deb noticed it, a man to man thing, but she did not let herself feel resentment for Jag. He was only playing the chief's game.

"Okay," Malone said. "Brace yourself."

He walked back through the door of his office where he opened a file cabinet and pulled out a folder.

Paper flapped around the edges of it as he carried it back into the front room. He flipped it open and pulled the eight-by-ten pictures out in a stack.

"You sure you're going to be all right, Miss Blane?"

"I'll handle it," she said.

He passed the stack to her. She placed them facedown on her lap at first.

Jag stood at her shoulder, waiting as she wiped her eyes and drew a quick breath.

Then in a slow, determined movement she turned the folder over.

The first photo was bad. It showed the mangled limbs and shredded flesh where the wheels and the weight of the train had ground down.

The severed legs were angled off at one side of the frame, and one hand was visible beside a portion of the torso. The flesh had been ripped away from the cracked ribs, and the mashed jelly that had once been internal organs oozed through the open chest cavity.

She felt bile in her throat. She had nothing in her stomach to throw up, but the muscles that would have set the process into motion stirred.

She wondered if it would have been worse if the shots had been in color. Somehow the black and white made the sight seem more hideous. The photo had been snapped without thought of composition, and that seemed to make it more stark and horrifying.

She was conscious of Jag stirring beside her. He was as upset as she was.

With fingers that could barely grip the paper, she turned the first photo and looked down at the second.

A portion of the face was visible. It had been raked along the railroad track, cut from one ear along the cheek and across the chin. The nose was flat and torn, and blood and dirt covered the flesh.

She let the photos slide from her hands. They fluttered off her lap onto the floor.

"It's him," she whispered as she leaned against Jag. He knelt quickly, and she placed her hands on his shoulders.

She thought she was going to cry immediately, but instead a wave of shock swept over her. Her skin felt hot, and the muscles of her jaw began to quiver. She clutched at Jag's coat, grabbing handfuls of the fabric.

He embraced her, trying to lend support. She could tell he was startled and unsure of what to do, but she had to cling to something.

A whimper formed in her throat, followed by a groan that finally became a sob. When the tears broke, she felt like collapsing. She placed her head against Jag's shoulder.

"I know it's rough," he said.

"We can let her lie down in the cell," Malone said. "We haven't had to use it in a while. The linen is clean in there."

She didn't resist as Jag helped her from the chair. Leaning against him, she closed her eyes as they moved through a doorway at the back of the station.

The cell door rattled as Malone pulled it open. Jag whispered something softly and guided her through the door.

She opened her eyes long enough to look at the narrow bed fastened to the cell wall, then closed them again as Jag helped her sit down on it.

As she eased her head back on the pillow, her thoughts were

a twisted swirl of memories. She could see Mark as a child, playing with their dog Alamo, building forts in the backyard and teasing her about her Barbies.

She remembered him trying to repair the old yellow Cutlass convertible he'd bought with the money he earned at his first real job the summer of his sophomore year.

She remembered him in his tux for the senior prom, remembered him at graduation, remembered him entering med school. It all rushed through her thoughts as she faded back into the semi-bliss of unconsciousness.

Gunter had been able to delay the dog hunt most of the day, using the rain as an excuse. When darkness fell without the dog's return, however, no excuse was good enough.

Bess was convinced the animal was hurt somewhere, suffering in the cold. She would not consider the possibility that the animal, a stray to begin with, had just wandered off somewhere for a better handout.

So with the sky dark and the temperature dipping while the rain continued in sporadic drizzle, Gunter found himself shrouded in his hooded green raincoat and armed with a flashlight to trek through the woods. He had no idea of where to begin a search for a lost dog.

Bess was confident he would hear the cries when he got near it.

He dreaded the scene that would face him when he returned home empty-handed. Maybe it was time to start thinking about moving on. With a little luck he could hook up with somebody else quickly, somebody who didn't have Bess's concern for the downtrodden.

Then he would be able to avoid treks through the woods in search of lost mutts.

He trained the flashlight beam ahead of him, swinging it from side to side to let the light flow over the shadows. He thought it might bounce off the dog's eyes if it really was out there somewhere.

He thought about whistling, but the animal had never responded to that summons before. It seemed senseless to expect that now. He slogged on through the trees, pushing branches out of his way and ducking the wet strands of Spanish moss that dangled down across his path like locks of curly gray hair.

He was closer to the bayou than he'd thought. Once again

he considered the possibility that the dog had fallen in and, chilled by the cold, had been unable to struggle out of the rushing water.

That would mean the carcass had probably been carried away, into the network of tributaries of the swamp. He wondered if he could convince Bess of that without having to drag for the body.

It was getting colder now. He wasn't going to be able to stand much exposure in this weather before he had to go back to the trailer, scene or no scene. A little argument and the cold shoulder from Bess for a while would be preferable to pneumonia. Pneumonia would last a lot longer than one of her bad moods.

He broke through the trees near the edge of the bayou and began to walk along the bank. The ground was slippery, but he placed his steps carefully, shining his flashlight on the ground just in front of him to make sure there were no roots waiting to trip him and spill him down into the water.

He'd travelled about a hundred yards when the beam fell across the tattered fur.

The sight made him stop walking. The remains of the dog were broken and twisted. Streaks of blood stained the fur, and portions of the innards streamed out of the abdomen like snakes crawling to freedom.

Some kind of animal had found it. He hadn't thought about any of the animals in this area being dangerous.

He walked toward the mess slowly, preparing to kick it into the bayou. It wouldn't do to have Bess see this.

He would break the news to her gently and convince her that he had buried the remains. She would believe him. She always believed him when he told the truth. It would just be a burial at sea.

Revolted by the sight, he turned his face slightly as he prepared to lift his foot and shove the body away.

Out of the corner of his eye, he caught the sign of movement in the shadows. He turned the flashlight toward the trees, but he saw nothing but the sway of the wind.

Puzzled, he took a step forward, unsure of why he had a funny feeling. He was not afraid of wild animals. One would be too frightened of a man to attack, he reasoned.

He realized he was fooling with something's dinner on the other hand, and an animal might be protective of that. He took a step back from the dog's body, keeping the light on the trees.

He could still detect no sign of movement other than the wind. Maybe it would be better to leave the carcass alone anyway. Whatever had killed the dog could come back and finish it. Bess certainly wasn't going to be coming out this far.

Backing up a few more steps, he prepared to turn around and move back in the direction he had come. He would enter the trees at the same point he had exited and hurry back to the trailer.

The cry made him stop. It rode on the wind, a shrill, harsh sound that added a new angle to his discomfort.

He breathed deeply to try and control himself. He had nothing to be afraid of. He knew that. All he had to do was walk back to the trailer. He'd been out in these woods dozens of times.

He shone the light toward the trees again, and this time through the rain he caught the reflection of something. Possibly eyes.

They didn't glow green the way an animal's eyes would have though, not quite. Yet they didn't look quite human either.

"Who's there?" he asked.

He got only the wind's answer.

Okay, his mind was playing tricks. The weather was getting to him. He'd been exposed to the cold for too long, and his brain was getting numb.

He would go back to the trailer now.

The branches parted.

At first he thought it was a man.

That impression lasted until the flashlight beam played over the figure standing before him.

He could see an eye. It glared through a tangle of—what was it? Hair? Something covered the creature from head to toe, a nasty, messy-looking pelt matted with leaves, mud and moss, and the one eye peered out through the tangles that covered the face and head.

It was a wild eye, and before Gunter could think, the thing's mouth dropped open and a scream issued forth. It was deep and guttural, a beast sound.

As it echoed through the forest, the trees began to rattle and bushes began to shake. In a moment it was joined by two others like it.

They huddled, about two hundred feet apart at the edge of the trees. One crouched, and the other, which seemed slightly

80

heavier, stood upright.

As fear gripped him, Gunter raised one hand to his face, wiping his eyes, hoping that he would discover it all to be an illusion.

They were still there when he looked again. All of them stared, all eyes glazed with a wild look of hunger.

Turning now, he tried to run. His feet slipped immediately on the ground, and he went sprawling.

He landed facedown in the dirt, the flashlight bouncing out of his hand. He saw the beam flopping from side to side as it rolled into the bayou.

He tried to get up, but before he could move, the first creature was on his back, straddling him. He felt claws digging into his shoulders, bending him backward.

He screamed as the pain shot through his muscles, and the creature abruptly shoved forward, slamming Gunter's face into the ground.

The creature lifted him upward again, and a moment later he heard the others moving toward him. They crouched near him, grabbing at his limbs. They seemed to want to pull him apart.

With a strength he did not know he possessed, he pushed upward, forcing the one off his back and swinging wildly at the other two. He hit one of them a glancing blow then started to run, being more careful with his steps this time.

He was able to take two before they grabbed him again. Holding his ankles, the heavy one yanked his feet out from under him, and he tumbled over the edge of the bank.

Plunging into the water, the chill paralyzed him, and he felt water rushing into his lungs.

The current pitched him about, but he found some inner strength and flailed his arms enough to get his head above water. He coughed and sputtered, and before he could begin to struggle, they had him again.

Their claws closed on him, pulling him up out of the icy water. Mercilessly they slammed him down onto the shore, and all of them moved on top of him now, forcing their weight on him to hold him down.

He had no more time to resist as their teeth tore into his numb flesh.

Chapter 7

After Debra had rested for a while at the police station, Jag drove her back to his apartment. The Volvo had the aerodynamics of a brick, but he got the feel of it without much difficulty and made fair time getting back to Aimsley.

She was silent for most of the trip, staring out the window at the rain as they travelled. He could tell she was pulling herself together, or trying to.

Jag didn't make any effort to engage her in conversation. He didn't know what to tell her, and he'd run out of things to talk about.

He had talked briefly with Malone while Deb rested. It puzzled him that there had been no personal effects on the body. It didn't seem realistic to believe the train had destroyed everything. There was no wallet, no jewelry, nothing for Debra to claim.

He felt bad for her. When she claimed her brother's body for funeral purposes, she would still have nothing. A closed casket would be required, so she would be left with no final remembrance of him.

Jag lived in a garage apartment in a residential district just a few blocks from downtown Aimsley. The houses were mostly white frame buildings, and old oak trees grew in most of the yards, giving the neighborhood a quality of forgotten years. In many ways the district resembled the 1950's.

His apartment sat behind a small residence on a side street. The house was occupied by an old woman named Myerson who rarely left her dwelling and said little to Jag. He tried not to speculate on the nature of her psychosis. He'd read enough Faulkner to make the possible scenarios unpleasant.

He pulled the Volvo up the driveway, past the house and into the garage. Then he got Deb's suitcase from the trunk and led her up the wooden steps to the porch. It was screened and stretched the length of the building.

The boards creaked under their weight as he unlocked the front door and led her into the small living room.

It was cluttered with newspapers, and the coffee table was piled with dishes, pizza take-out boxes and a manual typewriter.

His couch was a bit lumpy, but he let her sit there while he placed her luggage in a corner and hung her coat on the edge of a bookcase filled with rumpled paperbacks. He tossed his own coat over a chair before moving into the kitchen to fix coffee.

"I can't believe I'm imposing on you like this," she said when he had the cups ready.

"It's okay. I need the company. It's cool as long as my mother doesn't find out. She'd never believe there wasn't something going on."

She drank a couple of swallows. "It doesn't seem real," she said. "That he's dead I mean. I can't believe it."

"Things happen, and you don't think they can be happening to you," Jag said, considering his own experiences. He looked toward the window where the rain was spattering against the glass.

"Why would he be there, on that track that way?" Deb asked. Her voice was coarse and weak, tainted with confusion.

"It doesn't make a lot of sense," Jag agreed.

"Unless he was drunk."

"I guess he could have been riding trains," Jag suggested. "Otherwise it's odd. The tracks in Bristol Springs are mostly in the woods. Not the kind of place you'd stumble to."

"And where's his stuff? He had to have had some kind of personal effects besides just his clothes."

Jag nodded. The death seemed odd to him too, but strange things happened. He suspected Deb's reaction was natural. She was clutching, hoping to find some kind of meaning or reason for her brother's death.

In his short time on the job, he'd come to realize people died every day, and there were no reasons. They just died. They dropped dead or got hit by cars or shot by nameless criminals.

"You're sure it's all right if I stay here?" Deb asked. "I could get a motel."

"No need. You don't need to be alone."

83

"You're very sweet."

Caroline had always told him that. "Maybe I am," he said.

"Some people would say I was crazy. I mean, we just met."

"I have friends who can certify I'm not an ax murderer in spite of what I did."

A hint of a smile came. "I know. I can tell. There's something about you. I don't know what it is."

"I'm just me."

She set her coffee cup on the table. "I think I need a shower. I feel like I'm covered in grease and sweat."

"I'll fix something to eat," Jag said. "Something good."

He showed her to the bathroom and returned to the kitchen. He had steaks in the freezer. He'd been saving them for a special dinner with Caroline. Now seemed like a good time to use them.

He plopped them in the microwave to thaw before placing them on a broiling pan, seasoning them the way his father had taught him, then slipping the pan into the oven.

He had already turned them over when Deb returned. She was wearing a bath robe, yellow terry cloth, with a towel wrapped around her hair like a turban. Her eyes were still weary, but her face seemed vibrant and beautiful. Scrubbed free of makeup and grime, she looked fresh and natural, a princess out of a fantasy.

"You didn't have to go to all this trouble," she said.

"My pleasure." He was silent a moment. "It's good to do something nice for somebody without thinking about a reward. You have to do that now and then, just for the sake of the world."

The oven timer buzzed, ending the conversation for a moment as Jag removed the tray and plopped the steaks onto plates.

"Medium rare all right?"

"Fine," she said.

He pulled baked potatoes out of the microwave, and they sat down together at the table.

He was pleased with the way the food turned out. He was no gourmet, but the meal was good.

"When we were kids, and we had steaks, I used to cut Mark's for him. He was younger, and it took him a while to get the knack of it. For a while we were with a foster mother named Mrs. Nicholson. She was nasty. She wouldn't tie his shoes for him or anything."

Jag laughed. "Sounds like some of my school teachers."

"Sometimes living with foster parents was like that. Just imagine having to spend day in and day out with your teacher. We had some good ones too, though, and we were lucky. We got to stay together."

A new sadness touched her features, and Jag fell silent as she dealt with it.

After dinner, Jag piled the plates in the sink.

There wasn't much on television, so he put on a Tangerine Dream tape called *Green Desert*. It was kind of different, a gift from a college friend one Christmas. The tones seemed to be appropriate.

"I can't see how he got back so far in the woods," Deb said. "He would have been hitchhiking along the highways. You can hardly get to Bristol Springs, and when you get there, you don't really have anywhere to go. He'd been going from city to city, but the road to Bristol Springs doesn't lead anywhere else. Bristol Springs isn't on the way to anywhere."

"That's true. You really have to want to go there, and not many people do," Jag said.

"If he was riding a train, he wouldn't have fallen off it into the middle of a track," she added.

Jag had to agree with that too. He'd heard of hobos slipping off box cars and getting snagged by the wheels which severed legs. He supposed it would be possible to be dragged completely under a train, but that would have been difficult.

"The cops had no record of him?" he asked.

"No."

"Did you check the parish jail?"

"I didn't know about it. Why?"

"Just curious."

"Maybe I can do that tomorrow."

"Good idea. Maybe I could go with you."

He changed the stereo to an old Gordon Lightfoot tape and settled back into his chair.

They talked until drowsiness made them incoherent. Jag gave Deb the bedroom and crashed on the couch while he listened to Gordo singing about sailing to a place called Christian Island.

Later he would wonder what different course his life might have followed if he had made some other decision besides getting into her car on that rainy winter afternoon.

The Impala pulled to a stop near the curb about a half a block from the driveway. The rain had become only a light drizzle in the darkness. Corey killed the lights and looked out his window toward the house.

Kyle pinched out the joint he had been smoking and put it into the pocket of his leather jacket. He always smoked before a job. It calmed his nerves. Kyle was not really cut out for crime.

After a few seconds, Corey climbed quietly out of the car and opened the trunk. He took out a small athletic bag and looked in each direction before easing the trunk lid closed.

"You ready?" he asked, his voice little more than a whisper.

Kyle climbed out of the car to join him, and together they walked across the street. On the sidewalk, they paused for a moment to look around for unexpected witnesses, then sprinted across the broad lawn. They covered the distance better than track stars, the adrenaline impelling them as it tingled in their systems.

Near the house they crouched in the shadow of an oak tree. While their breathing slowed back to normal, they watched the windows for signs of movement. The house's lights were out, but it never hurt to take precautions.

"Back door," Corey said after a few moments, and they moved around a rear corner of the building.

Corey checked his watch as they stood with their backs pressed against the wall. He could see by the glowing dial it was getting close to midnight.

The wind roared as they moved across the patio to the French doors. Kneeling beside the latch, Corey pulled a pair of picks from the bag.

The tumblers on the doors offered little resistance, and after one more quick look around, he pushed them inward.

The house was warm when they stepped in out of the wind. Corey closed the door and handed the bag to his brother.

Kyle raised his eyebrows. "What should we do?"

"Let's hit it like we'd do any of them."

"You sure?"

"There's bound to be silverware. We might as well snag that and the jewelry and the VCR if it's handy."

They stood in silence for a few moments, listening for any sounds or movement that might indicate someone was stirring.

When they were content with the silence, they began to move, placing their steps delicately.

Systematically they worked their way in and out of rooms, stuffing things that looked valuable into a pillowcase Corey pulled from the bag. Within a short time it had become bulky with candlesticks and ornaments that tended to rattle.

Corey pulled out another pillowcase and passed it to Kyle before lowering the first case to the floor of the dimly lit hallway where it could be picked up on the way out.

"Let's find the jewelry box now," he said.

They crept along the hallway, each holding his breath. The double doorway at the end of the corridor was slightly ajar.

Beside him, Corey could feel Kyle's fear. It seemed to flow out from his brother in little waves. Reaching over to the golden handle, Corey pushed the door gently inward, moving it slowly in case there was a creak. The hinge was silent.

He looked at Kyle, locking on his brother's eyes for reassurance. Then he led the way into the shadows, his eyes adjusting slowly to the darkness. He was still holding his breath as he looked first toward the bed.

He expected to see rumpled blankets and the outline of a person. His heart jumped when he realized the lace pillows were in place and the bedspread lay undisturbed.

The woman wasn't asleep. Where was she? They could be caught if she was roaming around the house somewhere or nestled in some forgotten corner reading by a dim night light or one of those damned book lights.

He started to turn toward Kyle, but his eyes were frozen on the outline beside the bed.

She lay huddled on the floor, her knees drawn up toward her chest beneath her nightgown.

As his eyes adjusted further, he could see her head with tousled silver hair was twisted to one side. Her left arm stretched out over her body, the fist twisted into a tight knot.

Corey swore quickly under his breath.

"We've got to get out of here," Kyle said.

They bolted, scurrying down the hallway, past their pillowcase and to the stairs.

Using the hand rails, they vaulted down the steps several at a time and rushed across the floor to the doorway. Kyle yanked it open and they were through in a second and on their way across the patio.

The rain had started again, and it showered down on them,

splashing into their eyes as they set a new speed record on the trip back across the lawn.

They were soaking and half-frozen by the time they made it to the car. Corey dropped the keys before he could get them into the ignition. He fumbled around for the ring on the floorboard, then finally found it and picked out the ignition key.

The engine sputtered.

"We gotta get out of here," Kyle demanded.

"I'm working on it," Corey said.

The engine roared at last, and he shoved the car into gear. It sloshed through the water against the curb, and the tires spun for a moment until they found traction.

Corey fought the wheel to keep it steady and guided the car up the street until he saw a place to turn. He pulled the wheel hard and followed the twisting street that branched off to the right. He was heading for another thoroughfare that would speed them away from the death.

He had just turned onto Melton Street which would connect with Nicholas and take them down through the railroad yards when the blue lights appeared in the rearview mirror.

"Shit!" he shouted. "Shit, shit, shit!"

The lights did not go away.

He pulled the car over and watched the rearview as the door of the police cruiser opened.

Silhouetted in the blue light, the policeman emerged in a bright yellow rain slicker. Resting his hand on the pistol at his hip, he stood at the rear fender of the Impala.

"Would you gentlemen step out please."

He was alone in the car, but he had probably already called for backup. There was no way to run.

Jag woke up around one A.M. and sat up on the couch to look at the rain spattering against the windowpanes. He was staring at the drops that caught the light from the dusk-to-dawn lamp outside when he heard the creak of one of the hardwood panels of the floor.

He turned to see her moving into the room.

"I couldn't sleep," she said.

"Me either," he admitted. He had been thinking about Caroline, or perhaps more about himself. He'd been an idiot, crazed. He couldn't believe what he had let himself do.

"You going to Shreveport to claim the body?" he asked.

88

"Not right away. I need to pull myself together." She joined him on the couch. "I'm trying to get the images from those pictures out of my mind."

"Can you think about the good times?"

"Some. It's not easy. I can't accept that he's dead."

He looked over and saw the tears glistening in her eyes.

He'd never had a brother, and the only relatives of his who had died had been elderly. He could only imagine her pain. He tried to tell himself she was the one who really had something to be hurt about. It didn't lessen his own feelings, but perhaps it slightly altered his thoughts about them.

"I wish there was something I could do," he said.

She tried to smile. "You've done so much. I mean, I don't even know you."

"I'm a nice guy for an imperfect stranger."

She slipped off the couch and walked over to the window. The shadows of the raindrops fell across her face.

"He shouldn't have been on those tracks," she said. "I don't know what the reason is. I can't understand it. I've got to find out. Somebody must have some answers. Somebody must have seen something or know something. Here or in Bristol Springs or somewhere. I have to know, Jag. I have to find out."

He studied the shape of her body in the silhouette at the window. Her form was rounded but her waist thin, and in the sweat shirt the outline of her breasts was full. Her legs appeared smooth and firm, the calves displaying a hint of muscle, but not so much that the feminine elegance was lost.

She turned back, and he averted his gaze, embarrassed that she might have noticed him staring.

The stirrings of attraction frightened him. He didn't trust himself at the moment. His emotions were tainted, and he was afraid of more hurt.

Even though they had just met, eye contact might call for some kind of action. He wasn't sure if he needed anything more right now even if he wanted it.

"Where do you start?" he asked.

"Maybe the parish jail."

"Nice place," Jag said. "I've been there."

The interrogation room had a mirror that dominated one wall. Corey imagined someone on the other side of it, observing them while swilling coffee and chewing cigarettes. He and his brother remained silent as they sat in the stark white room watching the walls.

They seemed to be closing in.

Kyle jumped when the door opened, and a tall, rough-looking cop walked in. His nametag read LaFleur.

His expression was nasty, and he leaned across the table to stare at Kyle. He'd probably been observing through the mirror and figured out which was the weaker of the two.

"You guys were in that house, weren't you?"

"What house?" Kyle asked.

"What house? What business did you guys have in that neighborhood at one in the morning. A motion detector was triggered in the home about five minutes before Officer Watkins spotted your car."

"We were riding around," Corey answered. "We do that sometimes. This is a real boring town."

"You two don't do well enough with the girls? That's who you ought to be riding around with."

Corey remained silent, and Kyle bowed his head.

"If somebody dies in the commission of a felony, it's murder," LaFleur said. "That old woman had a heart attack because she heard you bastards rummaging around in her house. You know that. We know that. Your car has been seen in the vicinity of a lot of burglaries."

"We weren't in her house," Corey said. "And there are lots of Impalas on the road." He was beginning to feel a little better. He'd been shaking inside for the hour they'd let them stew, but if the cop was pushing this hard, it meant they didn't have anything solid.

"Have you found a lawyer for us yet?" he asked. Aimsley wasn't big enough to have a public defender's office. Appointed lawyers had to be rummaged up.

"We're making some calls," LaFleur said. His glare was harsh. He looked like he wanted to hit someone.

"We'll wait."

With something like a growl, LaFleur turned and walked out of the room.

Corey only looked at Kyle for a moment to let him know with his stare that they had to bide their time. The hours would drag, but he was confident that as long as they kept cool they were going to be all right. If the cops thought they could hold them, they would have been booked by now.

They had been rousted by cops before, never for anything

90

this serious, but at least he had some experience.

The boys' parents were divorced. During their junior high and high school years, their folks had been more concerned about their own problems than watching Corey and Kyle.

The two had spent a lot of time cruising and drinking and dealing some marijuana. They had grown it in a field outside Penn's Ferry with a guy named Deke Taylor who had dropped out of school. He played in the band with them, had been damned good on bass guitar and anything else he took a mind to play.

He'd conceded to make one visit to school for a talent show. The rest of the crap in the show had been meaningless, but when their band, The Cynosure, had performed *Free Bird,* it brought the house down.

The gym where they held the event, filled with discontented students sitting in uncomfortable metal chairs, had rattled with the roar of applause and cheers.

Corey could still remember the thrill that had filled him that afternoon. Back then it had seemed like they were really going places.

That was before Deke got arrested, before graduation and unemployment, before meeting Turk.

They were supposed to be sitting in the dressing room after one of their concerts now instead of in a police station. The world didn't turn out the way it was supposed to.

Chapter 8

Jag's car was where he had left it, unchanged except for the decoration of raindrops beaded across its surface. He climbed out of Deb's car and walked over to it.

The rain had stopped, but the day was gray and cold.

He paused just a moment to stare back across the parking lot but saw no sign of life in Caroline's apartment. The drapes were drawn, and the door had already been replaced. Evidence of his temporary insanity had been removed.

Slowly he got behind the wheel and fired the engine to life. It came alive slowly because of the dampness and the time it had been left sitting, but when he coaxed it, the machine roared.

Debra followed him in the Volvo back into town, and they finally found parking places outside the courthouse.

It was a little strange for Jag being back there. He stood on the sidewalk while he waited for Debra to get out of her car and walk up the street from her parking place.

She was wearing a brightly colored, oversized sweater this morning with her jeans, and with her hair brushed loosely to her shoulders, she looked even prettier than before.

"You ready?" he asked.

"These cops can't be any worse than any of the others," she said.

He led her inside to the elevators, and they rode up to the sheriff's department. She'd refused his offer of help at first, but he had persisted. He had several hours before he was due at work, too many hours to fill on his own.

They talked with a young desk sergeant who surprised them with his pleasantness and made the call to the jail which would allow them entry.

On the jail floor, when they were buzzed into the front

room, one of the guards whooped at the sight of Jag.

"He's back," another one called. "Is she the culprit?"

Ignoring them, Jag led Deb over to the window where Honeycutt sat.

"What happened?" the big jailer asked. "You like it so much you came back?"

"I'm here to check something about my brother," Deb said. "I need to know if he was ever held here."

"This is Debra Blane," Jag said. "I thought you might be able to help her."

"That stuff's public record. If you're good. What's his name?" Honeycutt asked.

Jag was beginning to get the idea he might be a decent human being.

"Mark Turner," Deb said, leaning down to speak through the mouthpiece in the glass.

Honeycutt raised his eyebrows. "That sounds familiar."

He turned his chair around to the computer terminal at his side and typed in the name. The green letters crawled across the top corner of the screen.

A few moments passed as the memory search was processed.

"He's not in the computer," Honeycutt said. He reached beneath his desk and pulled out a huge book which held bound copies of computer printouts.

For several minutes he scanned the pages. Leaning over it, he pressed one finger against his temple without realizing he was doing it. He gaze moved along the lines of print carefully.

Finally he shook his head. "We don't show him, but I know I know that name. Dammit. It goes back a while. A year or two."

"No," Deb said. "It wouldn't have been that long. It would have to have been in the last few months."

"I must be mistaken then," Honeycutt said. "We serve a lot of customers here. Sorry we couldn't help you. What's going on? You got a man missing?"

"He's dead," she said. "I'm trying to retrace his steps."

Honeycutt shook his head. "I'm sorry to hear that. Wish there was something I could do. Did he have a criminal record?"

"Just vagrancy."

He nodded again.

Jag leaned against the window. "The old man, he all right?"

"I guess. We put him in an isolation cell, and that's where he was when my shift ended. When I came back to work today he was gone, so I guess he's been released."

"Is he safe?"

"Ah, he's harmless," Honeycutt said. "We'll probably be accommodating him again in a day or two."

Jag leaned back from the window with a raise of his hands and a mock air of pleasantness. "Well, we thank you," he said. He took Deb's arm, and they walked back to the door together to be buzzed out.

"Who were you talking about?" Deb asked when they got back into the elevator.

"Guy I met when I was in jail yesterday. A local wino. He went a little crazy, got scared the cops were going to hurt him. They said he was so drunk he set the record for blood-alcohol levels."

"Nice people you meet in jail."

"Yeah. I don't plan to wind up there anymore. I've learned my lesson."

"Stay away from women?"

"Keep control of your own head," he answered. "Don't turn it over to the beast within."

Bess had dropped off to sleep reading a book by Louis L' Amour that Gunter had left lying around. She didn't like westerns, but she'd needed something to pass time while she waited on him to return the night before.

Sliding off the couch, she checked the bedroom to see if he'd slipped in past her. The bed was undisturbed. She threw the book down on the pillows. She'd been worried about him, thinking he was out searching late, when obviously he'd slipped off with some of his friends again.

She didn't have her dog back, and she didn't have Gunter to chew out. He was probably with some other woman. She'd seen the girls who hung around with his friends. They weren't the types that care if they took somebody else's man.

She lifted her hair and let it slide through her fingers. She wasn't sure if losing Gunter would be a big problem. She did all the work, and he just showed up to eat and sleep and use her if he was in the mood.

He had seemed nice when she'd met him. There had been

no way to predict that he was shiftless that first night. He'd told her he was looking for work. At the time that had seemed noble, a blue collar man coping with his times.

The nobility of it had worn off quickly. She wasn't a computer programmer herself, but she hustled to keep her job. Lately she was asking herself why she broke her back for him.

Pulling the front curtain aside, she saw his truck was still in the driveway. She couldn't remember hearing any cars pull up during the evening, but evidently someone had come along and picked him up. That was the only explanation that fit.

She knew Gunter wouldn't spend the whole night out beating the bushes for Petro.

When she saw him again there would be some discussion. If she couldn't reform him, she was going to abandon him.

She walked into the small bathroom which connected with the bedroom, what there was of it. She'd never expected to live in a mobile home.

The mirror was small, and the fluorescent light over it was dim. She stared at her reflection with mild apprehension. She was not as young as she had once been. The developing signs of wrinkles didn't concern her as much as the limp look of her hair.

She reached in and flipped on the shower. She had to be at work soon.

A half hour later she bolted from the door of the trailer for her car. She didn't bother to lock the door because no one ever came out to this godforsaken cranny of the world, and she wasn't sure if Gunter had taken his keys. He'd be pissed if she locked him out, and she wanted to have the edge of being the angry one when she confronted him.

As she twisted the car around to leave the driveway, she didn't look toward the forest. She had no reason to. Not that she knew of.

Kyle and Corey were bleary eyed when the cops finally let them go.

There had been, as Corey suspected, insufficient evidence to hold them. They drove over to a restaurant for breakfast and selected a corner booth that isolated them from the businessmen and other patrons.

"Do you think we did cause it?" Kyle asked when they had

95

placed their order.

Corey shook his head. "She'd been there awhile. She caught it on her way to bed." He was sure of that, and he was forcing himself to believe it.

He understood his brother's feelings. The thought of taking a human life was sickening to him, but he was certain they had not been responsible.

"What if she did hear us and get scared? What if it was our fault?"

"We didn't hurt the old lady," Corey said, staring hard across the table at him. "We were there to steal some stuff, that's all."

Kyle looked around uncomfortably. "We never hurt anybody before, Corey. We've stolen, sure, but the stuff we take is from people who can afford to buy more."

"Just settle down. We didn't do it."

"You don't know that, man. You know how close we came to a murder charge? They would have thrown us in jail with the tough bastards, and you know what they'd do to two skinny boys with long hair."

"Settle down. There's no way to tie us in. The satchel didn't have our prints on it, and there was nothing in it that could be traced. That's the only way that they could get us. The best thing we can do is lay low for a while. We'll stay away from Turk, and we'll just play it easy. The heat will get down as soon as they get something else to worry about."

Kyle looked out the window, and his shoulders sagged slightly. "We're supposed to be singers, man. That's all. I never thought of this business as being dangerous to anybody."

"It's risky. That's part of it. Just don't worry. I'm telling you it wasn't our fault."

Their plates arrived, and Corey picked up the syrup to douse his pancakes. "Just relax," he said. "This is all going to blow over."

After Jag went to work, Debra cruised the streets alone, wondering what she should do next. How could she find people who had seen Mark or might know something about him?

That seemed like a waste of time in many ways, futile, yet she wanted to know what he'd been doing in Bristol Springs.

His patterns did not seem to lead him to small towns. The

96

path she had traced had been an urban one. He'd trekked through places where he could be left alone for the most part, where he would have anonymity.

She suspected he had avoided trouble staying out of places like Bristol Springs, considering his long hair and faded clothes.

That's why it didn't make sense. There was no reason for him to head up to Bristol Springs. It deviated from his style. The feeling that something was wrong kept creeping up through the coils of pain that gripped her heart.

Mark should not be dead. He had been going through a bad time, but he was not a bad person. He would have been able to get over his grief. He would have made a fine doctor if something had not intervened.

As much as the personal loss, she lamented the destruction of his dreams. She had heard from him, had shared them. Now all of the things that he had ever wanted to be would go unfulfilled.

Life seemed so meaningless. Things ended before people had a chance to find their way. Doors closed. Colors faded, and nothingness took over.

There were the lies, that you could be anything or do anything, but they didn't take everything into account. They didn't factor in emotional pain or outside forces that shaped the direction of peoples' lives.

She turned a corner, and her gaze fell on the church. It was a huge old building with a large vaulted doorway and a towering steeple and bell tower. It reminded her of the church she had attended while growing up. It looked like it might offer comfort. Pulling to the curb, she got out and walked through the wind to the front door.

She found it was open.

Inside, the pews were empty, so she strolled silently through the sanctuary. The room was dark, and the light that filtered through the stained-glass windows was dim because of the clouds outside.

Everything was tinted violet.

At the edge of a pew she knelt and genuflected before walking on toward the front of the sanctuary where a rose window cast a spiral of colors that spilled rosy shadows down on her. Moving along in front of the altar, she found a stand displaying candles in small red holders. A few flames already flickered.

97

Selecting a lighter, she set a new wick ablaze, praying for Mark as she watched it flicker.

She thought she would cry, but she felt only a tightness in her throat. Turning from the candles, she walked back to one of the pews and sat down to stare up at the figure of Christ on the cross that hung above the altar.

She didn't notice the priest until he had walked along the outside aisle of the other set of pews and begun moving across the front row toward her.

"You're a bit early for the noon mass," he said.

"I won't be staying," she said. "I just needed somewhere quiet to sit for a while."

He was tall with blond hair that was long in the back, and he wore a thick mustache a shade darker than his hair.

He leaned back against the edge of a pew. "Is it something you'd like to talk about?"

She knew he could read her pain.

"My name is Father John Larson," he said, offering his hand. She could detect a Cajun flavor in his voice.

She looked up at him. He was young, probably not long out of seminary, yet he had an air of confidence. She sensed a warmth in his pale blue eyes.

"My brother passed away," she said as she accepted his hand.

"I'm sorry." He sat down beside her. "Was it an accident, an illness?"

"I'm not sure what you'd say it was."

"At times it is difficult to accept the Lord's will."

"Yes it is, Father."

He rested one arm on the back of the pew, remaining very casual. "He has a purpose for whatever He does, even if that purpose is beyond our understanding."

His voice was soft and firm, and she could tell he believed what he was saying.

She wished his sincerity was enough. "Why Mark? He was so young." Tears came now. She'd thought they were all conquered, but the emotion was too raw.

The priest took her hand. "I can't answer that for you . . ."

"Debra."

"In time, perhaps He will let you know. Or He will let you come to accept it. God has provided us with the process of grief."

She took a tissue from her purse and wiped the tears.

"Would you like me to pray for you?" he asked.

She had planned on praying, but alone. Right now she did not want to sit here and try to contemplate the scope of her grief and its divine purpose. "Keep me in your thoughts," she said. She got up. "Pray that I'll find a reason."

He smiled. "I hope that you will. You are from out of town?"

"Yes."

"Drop in if you need someone to talk to."

"I'll keep that in mind, Father. Maybe I'll be back."

LaFleur parked his pickup truck on the small parking apron in front of Nicholas Rand's house and climbed out, picking his cowboy hat up from the front seat and squaring it on his head before walking toward the front door.

He knocked and was greeted a few moments later by a dark-haired maid. He tipped the hat brim politely and asked her to announce his presence.

She showed him into the small entranceway which was illuminated by a golden glow from an overhead light, and leaving him there, she disappeared for a few moments down a darkened hallway.

He never got over the elegance of this house. Rand had spared no expense in creating the luxury. It was the kind of place LaFleur would have loved if he'd had any way to scrape that kind of money together. He might have decorated a little differently, but. . . .

It would never happen, but he could dream.

Returning, the maid summoned the policeman back through the hallway.

At the end of the passage, they entered a large paneled den which was lined with glass cases displaying all sorts of rifles, shotguns, pistols and military paraphernalia. One shelf contained an assortment of .45s including an old Singer model from World War II.

LaFleur always felt himself drawn to the cases. He admired weapons and wished he had the money to pursue the hobby the way Rand did.

It all seemed to boil down to money. If he'd had money, his wife probably would have stayed with him, too.

Still he admired the guns. He knew the businessman's collection had been put together quickly thanks to the pocket money he had available. The pieces had come from legal and illegal sources.

Rand stood at a corner of the room now with Scarecrow at his side, the tall man looking more like a nightmare than ever. He seldom spoke when LaFleur was around, and the gaze from that one eye always sent shivers through the cop.

"Good morning, Sergeant," Rand said. "It's been some time. We had one bit of trouble we took care of."

"I heard. I have some other news. Maybe something that would be of interest to you."

"Ah?"

LaFleur took his hat off and turned it about in his hands in an unconscious motion. "Couple of guys who started out as burglars. Last night they pushed it a little farther. Caused the death of a little old lady, but we couldn't prove it. They're back on the street."

"This death," Rand asked. "How did they bring it about?"

"They broke into her house, and it scared her to death."

"No evidence?"

"Nothing firm. They left some stuff in the house that couldn't be traced. The detectives threw it out. They spend enough time in court on stuff we have a chance of winning."

"Have a seat," Rand said. They walked over to the other side of the room where a couch and some chairs were arranged.

"Would you like coffee or anything?" Rand asked.

"Nothing," LaFleur said. He watched Scarecrow settle into an armchair. The guy always sat down slowly because he was so heavily armed.

The cop took comfort in the slight bulge in the small of his back. The Walther was all the security he needed.

"Now, these people you are referring to," Rand said. "You know their whereabouts?"

"Right. They're brothers. No other family. I ran a check. This time I'm sure."

"Mr. Turner's sister? Is she taken care of?"

"She has no idea he was ever with us."

"Then perhaps it is time we took another step or two. Can you gather the council this evening?"

"As long as we make it quick. I'm off duty tonight, but a couple of the fellows might have to slip off to be with us."

"If you have your answers ready, it should not take long," Rand said.

"I'm ready. These guys are scum. Long hair, the works.

We've had an eye on them for a month and haven't been able to nail them. Now they've cost somebody's life."

"That puts them into our realm," Rand agreed, his voice still cool and elegant. He never dropped his practiced demeanor. He was always calm.

The ice water in the man's veins never stopped amazing LaFleur. The cop considered himself made of stone, but Rand topped anybody.

At first LaFleur had believed him to be another millionaire looking for kicks, but there was something more to the man than that, something complex.

Whatever it was didn't really matter, though. As long as Rand's agenda matched LaFleur's it was good enough.

With his fingers pressed together, Rand smiled. A glow always came to his eyes when he was planning things.

"I feel the excitement building already," he said.

He looked a little like Satan with his black beard.

Chapter 9

Jag left the obits on his desk and told Breech he had something he was checking out.

Breech was skeptical, but Jag persisted, stressing that he might have something that could turn into a story.

"I just have to check on it," he said. "Give me a little time. The obits aren't going anywhere."

Breech thought that over a minute before nodding. "What is it you're wanting to nose into?"

"Let me check a few things. It may be nothing, or it may be a story. Come on, Breech, you keep me in the building all the time. I'm stagnating."

"We keep you in the building because that's where you do the least damage."

"I could spill coffee into my computer here. There are no guarantees."

Breech raised one eyebrow. "Is that a threat?"

"I don't even drink that much coffee."

"All right. Go play awhile. Be back by around four so that you can answer the phone while people are going to supper."

"You got it, Chief."

Breech hated to be called chief. It reminded him of the style of editor William Conrad played in *-30-*, the old Jack Webb film. Breech preferred to think of himself as one of the new breed of newspapermen, hip and sophisticated.

Jag got his overcoat and made tracks out of the newsroom before Breech had time to change his mind. On the street, he turned up his collar and walked at a brisk pace, following the street behind the building down toward the decaying corner of Aimsley's bleaker downtown section. A couple of blocks from the *Clarion* things got nasty.

102

It was the place the drug deals were made, and the dives were open most of the time.

The three-block walk left him shivering as he found the doorway of a place called Nebo's. It was dark, little more than a hole in the wall with pool tables crammed into it. Smoke hung in the air the way it was expected to in this kind of place.

The bar was parallel to the back wall, and except for a few men clustered at one end, the place was vacant.

A woman who could have been anywhere from forty to seventy was behind the counter. Her frosted blond hair swirled in a bouffant mass around her wrinkled face. Her glasses were old-fashioned, the frames oddly shaped, giving her face a catlike appearance.

"Can I help you?" she asked. Her voice had the hoarse quality developed from too many cigarettes.

"I'm looking for somebody," Jag said, adjusting his glasses.

"Who would that be?"

Eyes were on him now.

"He's probably one of your regulars," Jag said nervously. "Willis. Big fellow."

"I know him. He ain't been in in a few days."

"What the hell are you? A lawyer. You got a Porsche parked outside?" The voice was abrasive and came from the end of the bar.

Jag looked through the shadows at a man with a stubbled face and a baseball cap tilted back from his forehead. He wore a dark-blue work shirt with sleeves rolled up over his biceps in spite of the cold outside.

"I'm a reporter," Jag said. "I just want to talk to him." He walked toward the man, who looked down into his beer as Jag approached. Conversation didn't seem to appeal to him. "Do you know him?" Jag asked.

"Seen him around," the guy said, his hostility defused a little.

"Have you seen him lately?" Jag asked. He was feeling a little intimidated, but he tried to keep that hidden.

"No, he ain't around," the guy said. His shirt had the name Mike stenciled over the pocket.

"Anywhere else he hangs out?"

"There's a place called The Outbreak. Couple of blocks over. You got any spare change?"

"I left it in my Porsche," Jag said.

The Outbreak was like a clone of Nebo's. For a moment Jag thought it looked like the same four extras clustered around the end of the bar. They looked like a casting director had just put different coats and hats on them.

The bartender here was a big guy with red hair. If he'd had the right Irish accent, he would be been a perfect cliche.

Jag described Willis again.

"He comes in," the guy said. "Haven't seen him in a day or two."

"He got arrested," someone at the end of the bar said.

It was a heavy man with gray hair. He wore a thick coat and a hat with a badly compromised brim.

"I heard he got out of jail."

"Hasn't been around since we heard he was picked up," another of the men said.

"What are you, his grandson or something?"

"Yeah, the family wants him to come home. That's why I'm trying to find him," Jag lied.

"You ain't really his grandson." It was another of the extras. Somebody had written dialogue for all of them, Jag noticed. This guy was thin with a drawn-up face and a balding head. He was so thin he looked like a skeleton somebody had wrapped in wax paper.

"We were cellmates," Jag said. He had his hands in his pockets, and he clenched his fists tightly. He was still quivering inside. He wasn't cut out for this. "Nobody here has any idea where I can find him?" Jag asked.

"Nil," the gray-haired guy said.

"You might try Ernie's," one of the others suggested.

By the time he left Ernie's, Jag was developing a sense of déjà vu.

No one had seen Willis there either. Bowing his head against the wind, Jag meandered through the maze of streets that stretched out behind the bars.

He was travelling on impulse now. He'd never done anything quite like this. In college he'd done his share of reporting that had rattled the administration, but at the *Clarion* he'd become lost somehow.

Outside the academic setting, he lacked something. He wasn't a fighter. He wasn't a tough guy when it came down to the wire. He was beginning to wonder if his newspaper career was a mistake. This little hunch he was playing was taxing his nerves to the maximum.

The guys in these bars had put him on edge, and now, squirling through Aimsley's answer to skid row, he was starting to feel like a teenager who'd never seen the world.

He stumbled over a guy in a box at one corner, and bumped into a man wrapped in newspapers at another.

Neither of them had seen Willis.

"This is where he usually hangs out," said the man with the newspapers.

"Tell me something," Jag asked. "You ever hear of the swamp or anything?"

"Spare change?"

The guy was old and grizzled. Jag gave him a couple of bucks.

"Been mentioned," the old man said, running his tongue over his false teeth.

"Who would know something about it?"

"Not winos."

"Who?"

"You'd have to check with some of the dealers. They might be able to help you."

"Thanks," Jag said.

Now all he had to do was pretend he was trying to score some crack and risk getting his throat slit trying to find an old man who probably had nothing to do with the disappearance of Debra's brother and would not lead him to a story that would deliver him from the obit desk.

It was better than sitting in the office.

Kyle and Corey decided to lay low at Ruth Sanders' house. Her mother was at work, so they picked up a six pack and piled into her rec room where they turned on *Club MTV* on the stereo television set. The whole house was a study in domestic tranquility, and the rec room with its pool table, Nintendo games and pinball machine right out of *The Sharper Image* catalog was unparalleled in middle-class luxury.

Ruth was a dark-haired girl with a slender build that made her look younger than her nineteen years. She had the look of a princess, and her mother expressed frequent dissatisfaction that she spent time with Corey and Kyle. She feared Ruth didn't devote enough attention to her classes at Pine College in Penn's Ferry.

That was why Corey and Kyle tried to visit mostly while her mother was out.

She was one of the few bright spots in Kyle's life, and Corey hated to see him suffer. Besides, she was crazy about Kyle too.

Once Kyle was seated, she settled into his lap and curled her arms around his neck, nibbling on his ear while Corey stared at the television set as the dancers bounced about to a new song by Samantha Fox.

It wasn't Guns and Roses, but it would do. Corey had to have something to do while the couple necked.

He guzzled a couple of beers, hoping for a buzz to take his mind off of the mess his life had become.

As a new song was announced, he tried to shut out the groping sounds behind him. He hadn't had a girlfriend in a while, and he didn't want to think about that emptiness on top of everything else.

Pulling another beer from the plastic ring, he left the rec room and moved into the front of the house. Everything was in place in the living room, the furniture perfect, everything dusted, magazines neatly stacked on an end table — *Redbook* and *Good Housekeeping*.

It was the kind of place he and Kyle had never known. The house they'd lived in growing up had been nice enough, just never particularly well kept. Neatness had never been a priority.

Nothing had been a priority. Seeing the living room, the symbol of the American dream, made him aware of the emptiness his own home had represented with newspapers strewn about and dishes piled up on the coffee table where his old man put them while he watched television.

If he wanted to, Corey could make a pretty good case for turning out bad.

He just didn't want to. It was time to turn things around. He knew they weren't the cause of the old woman's death, but they easily could have been.

106

Next time they might not be so lucky about avoiding police problems, and Corey didn't have just himself to think about. He had to consider Kyle too.

Kyle didn't like being a criminal anyway, and while he wasn't focused enough to make any decisions on his own, Corey didn't want him to wind up in jail.

Maybe they should just head for California now and hope they could hook up with some bands out there. They had the skill. There was no question about that, and it was probably a good idea to get out of Aimsley.

The cops would be on their tails now. They had known the Impala last night. That meant they were pretty close to snagging them.

Kyle wasn't going to want to leave Ruth, but if they hit it big, they could bring her out to L.A. If they didn't, there'd be ladies out there to take his mind off her.

Too many thoughts raced through Corey's head as he paced the floor of the living room. There was much to decide in a short period of time. He was no good at decisions.

They could scrape together a little cash, enough to cover gas. Would there be enough gigs along the way to pay for the food?

He chugged down some of his beer and let the warmth soothe him a little. He could see the gray light of the afternoon through the front window. Moving over to it, he stared up at the gray clouds.

He didn't pay much attention to the car that sat across the street. It was a dark Chevy, and there was someone in the driver's seat. It didn't look out of place on the street. A lot of the families' second cars were Chevies or Olds.

Jag found Rudy Jackson in a building that had been a quick-stop grocery at one time. Now the front of it was boarded up, and dingy grime seemed to cling to the structure on Nora Street, Aimsley's Drug Corridor as the cops called it. Nora had been the wife of one of the mayors, but that had been long ago.

The entrance was now on the side of the building. Jag knocked and was greeted by a skinny blond-haired kid whose clothes were too thin for the weather. He wore a tee shirt and a leather vest. Chains were draped around him as part of his

107

outfit, and on his hands were gloves with the fingers clipped out.

"You look like a fuckin' narc," the kid said.

"If I were a narc, I'd be dressed like you," Jag suggested. He managed to keep his voice steady.

"Yeah, we've been expecting you." The guy puffed on his cigarette and motioned Jag into the darkened interior.

The smell of perspiration permeated the room, and drab blankets and old mattresses lay piled about. A portable radio the size of a radiator sat against one wall, booming music from a group Jag had never heard.

Jackon sat beside it on a chair that resembled a throne. He was fat. Seriously fat, a poster child for cholesterol and diet pills. His head was as large as a bowling ball and almost as round, and his stomach stretched against the seams of the dark pants he wore. His dark-blue overcoat was the size of a tent. A carnival barker trying to guess his age or his weight would have been a loser.

His left eye angled wildly to one side, looking out of place in its socket. A sick, milky yellow haze clouded the pupil, giving it a purple look.

His black skin was so dark he seemed to blend with the shadows. He smiled casually when he saw the expression in Jag's eyes.

"Scared?"

"A little," Jag said. He kept his hands in his pockets.

"You're not my idea of a tough investigative reporter. You don't look like Joe Rossie," Jackson said.

"You just can't rely on stereotypes," Jag said.

"Guess not. Listen at how smart I talk, and they say blue niggers is all dumb asses."

"Blue?"

"Blue gum." He grinned. "I forgot white boys don't know all the terminology brothers use. A light-skinned brother is bright. A dark boy like me is blue. A lot of mammas pray their babies won't come out blue. They teach you that in the sociology classes you took at your white ass college?"

Jag swallowed. His intestines were tense, his knees threatening to knock. "Never came up."

"Well, that was your free fuckin' lesson. What else did you want? I figure you rich boys have better outlets for your blow than this. Go sit in somebody's livin' room in Wilmington

108

District. I hear they invite you in over there to do the deals."

He put a cigarette between his lips and touched a match to it.

The room was cold, but he seemed oblivious to it. "I don't like it here much myself, but it's where I do biness. You know?

"What you want to know, white boy? You trying to do an exposé on my supplier?"

"Somebody said you might know about a rumor I heard."

"What's that? I hear a lot of rumors."

"The swamp."

"That's bull *shit*, Ain't no swamp."

"What's the story on it?"

"Just something pussies tell when they're sittin' in the jail cells waitin' on they lawyers."

"You've heard of it?"

"I've heard the story. That's all it is. A fuckin' story. Ain't nobody ever confirmed it."

"Well, fill me in on the story," Jag said, summoning what courage he could muster to pursue the questioning.

"It's just talk."

"I've never heard of it."

"You ain't been around that long. Lots you ain't heard of. Some things ain't discussed in po-lite society."

"Then, tell me, Rudy."

The blond-haired guy was hovering at Jag's shoulder. Jag tried to keep an eye on him with his peripheral vision while also trying to focus his attention on Rudy.

"What good would it do me to tell you something that's bullshit anyway?"

"If there's something wrong, maybe I can do an exposé on that."

"That's not an immediate benefit," Rudy said. His head jerked suddenly, and the blond guy was on Jag.

Grabbing one arm, he twisted it behind the reporter and shoved him against the wall.

Jag's face was pressed against the jagged wood, and he felt the guy's hands probing his pockets.

He tried to pull free, but the grip was too tight, and at the angle he was held, struggling sent sharp pains through his shoulder.

He felt his wallet slide from his hip before he could protest.

"Not dick here," the blond guy said. "Fifteen lousy bucks."

"Take six," Rudy said.

Letting go of Jag, the guy pulled six ones.

Jag took the wallet back when he was through with it.

Adjusting his coat as a way of regaining his composure, he stood in front of Rudy again. "Have we proven something?"

"Rudy don't give anything away," the blond guy said. "Money talks. Bullshit walks."

"So tell me. What's the swamp?"

Rudy grinned broadly, and the smile faded into a chuckle. "You don't give up. The swamp. That's where they keep the pond scum."

"And?"

He chuckled. "It's talk. When you in jail on those cots with nothing to look at but the ceiling, you come up with shit."

"What kind of shit?"

Rudy stopped laughing. He closed his mouth and narrowed his eyes a moment. "Talk. 'Bout what happens to people in jail. Some of us don't do a lot of time. Some of us are slick. Ever once in a while somebody goes to jail, then they get out and disappear. Not odd. Sometimes a guy sees he ain't got an out so he skips town."

"And nobody ever hears from him again?"

"People involved in businesses not sanctioned by establishment sometimes have to alter their identities, and it don't pay to be in contact with old friends that'd probably slit your throat for six fuckin' dollars. Know what I mean? Know what ball park you're playing in here, dickless?"

"When somebody disappears, it's called going to the swamp?"

"Some people have imaginations like I told you, home boy. They think somethin' happens besides just them skippin' town."

"What's the rumor?"

"Why you so interested in this?"

"I've got six bucks invested." It was a good line, but he didn't deliver it well. He didn't sound tough at all.

"I have a friend," Jag went on. "Her brother disappeared. He had a history of getting himself put into jail. He was supposed to be somewhere in Aimsley, but he was nowhere to be found. I heard about the swamp from this old man, I also can't find. It's a hunch. Coincidence or whatever. Some people directed me to you."

"The rumor is that the guys that disappear are bumped off. Not by other criminals."

"What do you mean?" Jag asked. "Cops?"

Rudy lifted his finger to his lips. "Shh. We don't want to actually say that. It could be troublesome. Some things it's better not to know."

"That's what people believe?"

"Shit. Some people. I didn't say I did. It's just what I told you. Nobody could prove shit, and who'd want to? The world can do without the people that disappear. You think I don't know how the people who sit in their living rooms in Wilmington District feel about people like me? They git their money nice ways. Fuck 'em. Fuck you, home boy. Don't come down here and stir up a bunch of stuff that's gonna make life hard on all of us. Them fuckin' ministers over there that all think they're Martin Luther King make it bad enough down here. Want to mess with my livelihood. Say they gonna take their neighborhood back. Shit. This is my neighborhood. Been here all my life, workin' anyway. My house is somewhere else. Anyway, you rock the boat, you get hurt and get a lot of other people hurt too. That's bad for business."

"You could be one of the victims some day."

"If it was true" — a frown crossed Rudy's brow — "I'd be a prime candidate. What ain't true don't hurt me."

"If people are dying by vigilante justice, something has to be done. My God, that's the same thing as lynching."

"Got your fuckin' liberal blood boilin'? If you stir something up, I won't help you. If you get into trouble, you're on your own."

Jag studied the dealer's features. "You do believe it, don't you?"

"I believe if I don't wipe my fat ass it'll itch," Rudy said.

"What else do you know?"

"Nothing. Not a damned thing. Show Mr. Walker out."

The hands closed on Jag's shoulders, and in a matter of seconds he was back on the street, feeling frightened and confused.

He'd been trying to play a hunch, and he seemed to have scratched the paint off something much deeper than he'd expected.

111

In the parlance of the old detective novels he'd read, he'd stumbled onto something big.

Even with that in mind, he didn't know what he was letting himself in for.

Chapter 10

Bess's feet were aching when she got off work.

Standing behind a check-out counter for nine hours would do that. She was becoming used to the sharp pain that nestled almost constantly in the small of her back, but the ache in her feet seemed to have become a new problem. The feet were the latest thing to go.

Today the rain had most of the customers disgruntled, compounding the frustration of the job.

She'd managed to maintain her politeness, even while she felt her nerves fraying. She found herself thinking about Gunter more and more, frustrated with his whole attitude toward life.

Finally the agony of work ended, giving way for the true source of pain in her life.

What an evening she had to look forward to, sitting around the trailer watching the bland gray television programs on the old black and white TV while Gunter drank, if he came home at all.

She needed to get out of this situation before the hole got too deep.

She didn't drive fast, but eventually she made it home anyway, her car splashing through the potholes of the driveway.

She climbed out of the front seat, slung her purse over her shoulder and stalked up the front steps. Gunter's truck was in place, but that was no sign he was home. He might still be out with whoever had picked him up last night.

Grasping the front knob, she yanked the door open and stomped into the front room. It was just like she had left it. She turned on a lamp and glanced around. Gunter wasn't hiding in the shadows, but there were clumps of dried mud on the carpet. He'd apparently staggered into the bedroom. The door was closed now.

If he was sleeping off a hangover, she saw no reason to bother him. He needed to be sober for their confrontation, just so he'd remember it. She turned instead to the kitchen.

There were a few beers in the refrigerator, but she decided against one, choosing a Tab instead. She wanted caffeine more than relaxation. She'd never liked the taste of beer anyway.

Tossing her purse onto the counter, she popped the can open and yanked a Swanson frozen turkey dinner from the freezer.

Plopping it onto the oven rack, she closed the door with a whack before dialing the heat setting. Maybe the racket would bring Gunter out of his stupor and summon him to battle.

Moving back into the living room, she flipped on the stereo. It was dialed to an oldies station that was playing The Big Bopper's *Crazy Blues*. If that didn't stir Gunter, nothing would. She grabbed the volume knob and twisted it to a louder level.

She dropped onto the couch, propping her feet on the coffee table atop the confession magazines Maxine had loaned her. She'd read them and hadn't returned them yet.

She heard movement in the bedroom now. Maybe Gunter's drunkenness was fading. Picking up one of the magazines, she began to scan the ads and the headlines again, wondering how her own true confessions headline would read. "I Moved in With a Slob and I Can't Seem to Shake Him."

Footsteps vibrated the floor, and the bedroom doorknob began to twist slightly.

He was up all right. She flipped a page hard then another, the sound making a whishing sound as it cut through the air. He sounded groggy.

"You up, Gunter?" she asked.

There was no reply, just the sound of movement. He wasn't doing much good with the door, an indication of his condition, she suspected. Fine. She would have it out with him, and it would be up to him to remember it.

She threw the magazine down and waited, the thought of his staggering form firing her anger.

Finally the latch on the door turned, and it began to swing open.

"I guess you located Petro," she said. "You were out long enough looking for him."

She watched the edge of the door slide from the frame, and a coarse rattle of breath escaped.

A smell touched her nostrils. It was awful. God, where had he been? If she stayed here tonight, she'd have to change the sheets and force him to have a shower. Getting him to sleep on the couch would be even better.

Feet scuffled on the floor, and the door swung outward, thumping against the wall.

"Gunter, what the hell's wrong with you?"

She wasn't looking at Gunter. She wasn't looking at anything that looked human.

It was a biped—she'd been taught the word for two-legged animals in high school biology—but that was where the similarities ended.

The form filled the narrow bedroom doorway. A mass of leaves and moss covered its body and head so that she could not be sure of what was beneath. There was no sign of fur, but that didn't make it any less frightening. It was holding a blanket in one hand, the cloth trailing down its side.

The creature's yellowed broken teeth were bared, and saliva dropped off the pulp that surrounded the lips. The eyes which glared through the mess on its face were wide and full of madness.

She was frozen only a second, gawking, before she started scrambling to get off the couch and head for the door.

The sunken seat seemed to hold on to her, slowing her progress. She had to force herself forward, getting her feet under her as the creature let out a loud roar.

The Tab spilled off the table, sending a spray of foam across the carpet. She didn't look back. She rushed across the narrow floor to the kitchen counter where she grabbed her purse. She'd have to have her car keys if she was going to escape. . . .

Her feet slid on the tiled floor, but she kept them under her, grabbing for the front door.

The creature was scrambling through the living room after her. It stepped up on the coffee table and walked its length, grunting as it lunged for her, the blanket flagging behind it.

She escaped the hand that was extended for her and shoved the front door open. Her breath was gone. She could not find air for her lungs, and her heart was hammering in her ears.

She was about to race down the front steps when she saw the other creature, standing on the second step.

Its hands reached out for her as well.

Ducking, she slipped backward, moving between the two creatures and scurrying once more into the kitchen. They began to scramble after her.

She retreated to a corner beside a cabinet. The window over

115

the sink was too small for her to wriggle through. There was no escape in that direction.

Frantically she tore open a drawer and raked through its contents. No butcher knives, nothing formidable. She selected the best weapon she could find, a slicing knife she'd picked up at the supermarket.

Grasping it, she whirled around to face the creatures. Her mind did not have time to process her fear and confusion.

They were moving toward her cautiously, their shoulders hunched a bit, grunts still uttering from their mouths.

Her stomach threatened to heave as the smell of them reached her once more. They stank like sewage and filth.

Brandishing the knife, she pressed her back against the cabinet. With the handle between both hands, the blade was visible, but the creatures did not seem frightened of it. The one with the blanket moved slightly forward, flagging the cloth in front of itself.

She slashed at it and missed.

The motion elicited a loud growl from the monster.

Bess began to cry. Tears flooded from her eyes, and her mind felt as if it were throbbing. Reality had been wrenched from her without warning. One moment things had been normal, shitty but normal; now she was center stage in a horror movie.

The first creatures made another move for her, avoiding the blade and flapping the blanket toward her.

She realized, too late, what was happening. The cloth lapped over her face, and the creature closed on her. She could not see what was happening. The musty smell of the fabric filled her nostrils as she felt hands or claws raking over her.

Screaming, she found her voice was muffled by the cloth, and the creature dragged her across the floor.

Her arms were pinned, so she kicked with her feet until one of them grabbed her ankles. She screamed again, terrified by what her imagination was conjuring, a fate more horrible than could be created in a thousand years of nightmares.

They crouched over her in the living room. Weight pressed down against the blanket, holding her as she twisted and tried to pitch her body upward to wrench free.

Then she was turned over, onto her face. The weight fell on her shoulders, and her nose was pressed down against the floor.

The blanket filled her nostrils, smothering her.

Screaming was impossible now. She closed her eyes, praying as she felt their touch. Nails dug through her clothing into her flesh.

The pain was sharp. It shot through her brain, clouding her head. She was on the verge of fainting, but the pain cancelled out the shock to prevent unconsciousness.

They weren't ripping with their claws. It was their teeth. They were biting at her. Devouring her.

She felt their bites, felt her flesh ripping free from her back, and still she could not lose consciousness.

She was going to have to endure her death in full awareness, feeling her life torn away bite by bite.

When Jag got back to the office, Breech gave him a stack of obits and assigned him a weather story.

Weather stories were unanimously hated by staff but had become a staple of the *Clarion*'s reporting.

It was between calls to the National Weather Service and mayors from the various municipalities of Riverland Parish that Jag lifted the key to the paper's morgue.

The mayors offered various comments about the bad weather, including Walter Perkins of Penn's Ferry, who expressed concern that an ice storm might hit.

Jag tied them together in an essentially meaningless story and hammered the obits into the system, then slipped away from his desk and ducked back down the hall to the narrow closet of file cabinets.

In the dark, the room looked like a real morgue, filled with shadows. The drawers might have pulled open to reveal bodies instead of folders full of clippings.

He flipped on the lights and walked across the tiled floor, his shoes tapping as he moved over to the small computer terminal. Slipping the stool back, he flipped on a switch and watched the orange-on-black, letters slowly come to life.

Accessing it with his password, he began to search for listing about prisoners.

He found no files listed as *Inmates* or *Prisoners*. He had to sift through every possible title in his head before he came up with *Jail*.

Jail seemed the least likely heading for a file. He should have checked that first. He'd heard horror stories about the *Clarion*'s filing system.

He memorized the call code and shut the computer down

before walking back through the file cabinets to pull out the folders he wanted. They were thick, stretching back five years. Before that things were on microfilm.

He wasn't sure what he was looking for, so he sat down at the librarian's desk and began to scan headlines. He saw articles about leaking roofs, a mention of a fire and other notices about needs for improvements and overcrowding stress — nothing out of the ordinary in considering typical prison problems in thirty-year-old buildings. The reports on the Aimsley jail and the parish jail were virtually interchangeable.

He was about to refile the folder and head back into the newsroom when he spotted the escape headline.

It was about a year and a half old, an account of three prisoners escaping from the parish. They'd used cigarette lighters to melt through a plexiglass window in a rec room.

One of them, twenty-five-year-old named Melo Templeton, had never been caught, according to subsequent articles.

Jag shuffled the clippings several times to find a report of Melo being recaptured, but nothing turned up. He finally resorted to consulting the typed sheet at the beginning of the folder which listed the stories by dates.

The follow-ups trickled off as more pressing news took over, and no indication that anyone knew where Melo had gone was in print.

Since it was the closest thing to a disappearance that he could find, Jag took the clips over to the photocopier in the corner of the morgue and flashed off copies of the coverage of the escape.

Returning the folder to the cabinet, he folded the copies and stuffed them into his pocket.

As soon as he returned to the newsroom, Breech ambushed him.

"Can I ask a question?" Jag asked when the interrogation was complete.

"Sure," Breech said, not looking up from his work.

"Whatever happened to Melo Templeton?"

Breech cocked an eyebrow. "Why are you interested in Melo Templeton?"

"Curious."

"We haven't done a 'Melo is still at large' story in a while."

"So he still hasn't been caught?"

Breech looked up and grinned. "You going to find him where all the law enforcement agencies have failed and win a

118

Pulitzer, Mr. Stanley? Could he be in the darkest Africa?"

"It just seems odd that he could elude capture with all the things cops have going for them."

"He disappeared somewhere. He's probably under a rock," Breech said, looking back to his screen.

Jag sat down in a nearby chair. "What did he do?"

"Killed a girl and beat up her boyfriend."

"Why?"

"He didn't like the television program they had on."

"Really?"

"Oh, something like that. It was arbitrary. He just wanted to kill somebody, and they were handy."

"Then he got arrested and escaped and never got caught?"

"You've summed it up. Mr. Walden, our esteemed police reporter, contends that they haven't tried that hard to find him because he couldn't have been convicted."

"Why?"

"I don't remember exactly. Remember, this goes back a while. Ancient history in a business of immediacy. They screwed up evidence or something. I think the D.A.'s office was pretty much ready to throw up their hands on the matter when the escape came."

"That's interesting."

"So's your spelling of Gremillion." Jag tried to protest, but Breech dismissed him. "I know, I know. That's the way they told you over the phone."

"Right."

Jag got up from the chair and headed for higher ground before Breech had time to find something else wrong.

The lights from Jag's car washed through the living room around ten. Debra watched them chase the shadows and got up to meet him at the door. She was wearing gray sweat pants and socks under a fluffy oversized shirt that had seen better days.

Her reading glasses rested on her nose, and she had pulled her hair back into a pony tail. She hadn't given much thought to how she looked while she was getting comfortable, but she considered it as she heard Jag climbing the stairs. She surprised herself in caring that much. It was too late to do anything about it.

He looked tired too when he entered, but a spring was visible in his step. He shrugged off his overcoat and motioned her over to the coffee table. He was unconsciously rubbing his bruised knuckles.

She'd been watching the news, but she switched it off as he started tugging papers from his pockets.

"I had a busy day, and I may have found a lead. It's a long shot, kind of weird, but you can never tell."

"What's that?"

He put the papers on the coffee table. "Other prisoners have disappeared from the local prison system, and the local criminals have sort of a legend about it."

"Mark never made it into the local prison system."

"Maybe not. Or maybe, just maybe, he did."

"What are you saying?"

He sat down on the couch and looked up at her, excitement visible in his eyes. He explained his search for the old man and what he had learned about the prison rumors. Then he unfolded the clippings about the jail break.

"This guy was never found," Jag said. "People do elude capture, but it's hard. You realize how unlikely it is that somebody would break out of jail and get completely away with all the computer stuff the police have today?"

"It's been done. Often I would think."

"But this guy was not a criminal genius, and I found out something was screwed up with his arrest. They didn't read him his rights properly or something, which means he could have walked away if he hadn't escaped."

"So what does that mean?"

"Two things. One, he had no reason to escape, and two, I was told that usually the people who disappeared to the swamp were people who weren't going to be convicted. They were going to get away with their crimes. Then they just disappeared."

An edge was evident in his voice, an animation. He was enthralled with what he had discovered or thought he had discovered.

Debra could not conceal skepticism.

"Jag, that's so bizarre. How could they get away with that?"

"Cops cover things up all the time around here. They violate the public records law with impunity. There's not really a check on them."

"I can't believe this, and even if it's true, what could it have to do with Mark?"

"Suppose he did get picked up when he came into town?"

Suppose he was in jail for a while, and then the cops did whatever they do to people. That could explain how he wound up on the railroad tracks."

"I thought the others disappeared completely."

"Maybe some did. Maybe some bodies turned up the same way his did in other areas, badly mangled or decomposed so that they didn't reveal the true cause of death."

"All right, but the fellow in this article is a murderer who was going to get off. If they were punishing people to bring justice or something, why should they pick on Mark? I know he wouldn't have hurt anybody, and the worst crime he probably would have committed was vagrancy or maybe possession of drugs. Victimless crimes. Mark hurt himself, not other people."

Jag threw up his hands. "I can't answer everything. This could be a lead, like I said. It's something I've found totally by coincidence. You can't expect it all to fall into place right away. There are other answers that we'll have to look for."

"Jag, I know you're a journalist, but this seems so farfetched. You're drawing a conclusion from a few things you've found out."

"It's just a start. With a little checking, we can figure out whether we're barking up the wrong tree. We try to find out if there really are others who have disappeared. It's scary; but it could be true, and it could be an explanation for what happened to your brother."

"But to think the police are involved."

"Maybe it's not all of them. I know it couldn't be, but they did give you a runaround when you tried to check on him."

"That could be just their typical bureaucracy."

"Or it could be a cover-up. We need to check it out."

Her eyes widened. "Jag, if it is cops, then you're talking about something dangerous."

"I know that."

"Have you talked to the newspaper about this?"

"Not exactly. I don't know what to tell them. They're not going to believe me. I'm just the green kid. *You* don't even believe me."

"It's just that everything has happened so fast. I just found out my brother is dead, and you come home and tell me it may have been the cops on some crazy vigilante binge. It's hard to believe something like that could happen. The police are supposed to protect people."

"You have to **remem**ber a lot of policemen aren't nice people. They deal with criminals all the time. They get hard. Some of them are good people, hard working, but others are mean, as mean as criminals. I've seen some of them. They're vicious. If they think some guy is slipping through the loopholes, they resent it."

"All right, Jag. I want to find out what happened to my brother. How do we go about checking it?"

He was silent a moment, thinking. "I'll have to do as much checking as I can about disappearances. If there's really something here, there's bound to be some kind of pattern."

"What happens if we get into trouble?"

"We'll just have to be careful."

She looked at him for a long time, studying his face. "What do you get out of this?"

"If it turns out to be true, I'll have a story. Maybe that'll be enough to get Norman Breech to let me off the obit desk."

She thought she caught a sparkle in his eye, more than just excitement over his investigation. It made her feel a twinge of apprehension, but absently she reached up and smoothed her hair.

Deep in the forest, the creatures crouched around the remains of Bess's body where they had dragged it, finishing their meal in the safety of the thick trees.

Little sign of communication passed between them, except when they swatted at each other, fighting over bits of skin and chunks of other tissue.

When they could they grabbed the morsels and stuffed them quickly into their mouths, snatching from each other the choicest pieces that remained to chew and swallow with bestial grunts.

Finally, the taller one picked up the remains of the girl's right arm and threw the blanket around its shoulders before moving off through the trees. After snatching a few more bites, the others followed, leaving the ruined corpse unattended.

It was more skeleton than flesh now, except for a few scraps of skin and the internal organs which, though exposed, were still stuffed inside the chest cavity.

Chapter 11

The night seemed to have a fate all its own.

Corey and Kyle parked their Impala at the edge of Aimsley's park and drank beer for two hours while they listened to the jam box in the back seat.

They'd left Ruth's house shortly before her mother was due to get off work, and they'd cruised until they'd burned enough gas.

Going home didn't strike their fancy, so they finally settled on the park. In the cold, the cops didn't patrol it that heavily.

From their perch, they watched a couple of crack deals go down, and saw some guy walking a pointy-eared boxer that looked like the devil, and a couple of people jogging in spite of the cold.

It was not the most entertaining scenery in the world, but it sufficed as a backdrop for their contemplations.

"We need to get out of here," Corey said.

"Ride around some more?"

He shook his head, the long locks of his hair bouncing about. "Not that. I mean we need to blow Aimsley, head on out to the coast. "We're not getting anywhere here. It's shitty."

"We don't have that much bread," Kyle said. "Shit, Corey, the cops almost put us under the jail. We can't pull another job. Besides, I don't want to. I keep thinkin' about that poor old lady."

"I know. We'll hock some stuff. We don't need all the sound equipment we've got. We could part with some of that, just keep our basic stuff. We could let the jam box go. It's still in good condition, so what the hell? If we get work in L.A., we can get new shit."

Kyle sat up in his seat. He tilted his head back and poured beer down his throat before crushing the can. His eyes had widened. Corey's proposition was beginning to sound more viable. "You really think that would work?"

"We're never goin' to get there if we just keep sitting around talking about it," Corey said.

Kyle nodded. "You're right. We could get our shit together tonight, you know it? We could sell what we want to get rid of to Turk and just haul ass. Why not, man?"

"We could do it tonight," Corey agreed. "It wouldn't hurt. We could be on the road in a few hours. By daylight we could be halfway across Texas."

"We can sleep in the car," Kyle added. His voice was rising as the possibilities jangled through his mind.

Corey dropped his hand to the ignition. "Let's roll, man." He coaxed the car engine to life. It was reluctant because of the cold, but it finally coughed and sputtered to a constant roar.

"We'll find a phone and yell at Turk, then we'll pick up our stuff." There was excitement in Corey's voice as well. The dream had been there so long, seeming so far way. Now it was looking like reality. He couldn't imagine why they hadn't just done this before. It made sense.

He eased the car onto the narrow street which curled through the park. The buzz from the beer complemented the complacent feeling that was oozing through him. Things were going to get better, he decided. Once they got to California, things were going to be hot and wild.

Just pick up and go, that's all they needed to do, get a little cash together and kick off.

Everything was going to be cool from now on. They'd be out of Aimsley in a few hours and on the road to somewhere better.

He didn't notice the black pickup truck behind him. It was parked behind a stand of pine trees, and it remained silent and dark for several seconds after the Impala drove past.

Once the Impala had rounded the first curve on the street, however, the white eyes of the truck's headlights blazed to life. Almost silently it eased onto the street as well and began to trace the Impala's path.

A stop at a pay phone outside a quick-stop grocery store confirmed that Turk was at home. He agreed to look at what they had to sell, so Corey jumped back into the driver's seat and wheeled the Impala onto the street toward their house.

"How much you think he'll cough up?" Kyle asked.

"Not enough. We'll have to push him a little, get as much as we can."

"If we give him the jam box, the speakers, the TV?"

"Whatever's not tied down," said Corey. "We're not goin' to need it."

He pushed the gas, not wanting to waste any time. Since the street was slick, he concentrated more on the road in front of him than the rearview mirror.

Skidding through a few red lights, he reached the house in record time. It was a sagging, old frame house with peeling white paint, and the boards on the front porch were decaying near their ends. The rent was paid through the end of the month, and the businessman who owned the place would find out soon enough that they'd vacated it.

Slamming the doors, they climbed onto the porch and headed for the front door. As the door closed behind them, the black truck pulled to a slow stop against the curb across the street. The lights went off abruptly, and the machine sat silently except for the pops of the engine cooling. The windows were tinted, almost so dark as to be illegal. Even in daylight it would have been impossible to see into the cab.

For several seconds there was no sign of movement, but then slowly the driver's door opened.

LaFleur slid from behind the steering wheel, his boots touching the street silently as he eased the door closed. He was wearing a black leather jacket and dark jeans that allowed him to melt into the shadows. He crossed the street quickly and slipped into the darkness at the base of some oak trees that stood in the front yard.

Seconds later he was joined by another man dressed in black. His name was Idal Taylor, and he was a bulldog with jowls that sagged out from his cheeks. A beard might have helped, but departmental policy didn't allow it. Stiff black hair swirled around his head in wiry waves.

He weighed well over two hundred pounds and carried it on a six-three frame.

"You see them?" he whispered to LaFleur.

"They're in there. That's all that matters." He reached beneath his jacket and pulled the Walther from its holster, using it to motion Taylor forward.

Kyle and Corey began to sweep through their own house the way they might have hit one they planned to burglarize. While Kyle disconnected the television set, Corey hauled their sound equipment from closets and rifled the other rooms for things of value.

"It's going to be beautiful," Kyle said as he set the television down in the center of the living room. "We're going to hook up with some great bands out there, man." He raised his voice as he walked down the hallway into his bedroom to begin pulling his clothes from a drawer. "We're going to be in the big time," he said. "Just like we've always wanted."

In the living room, Corey smiled as he listened to Kyle's fantasies. Corey couldn't be quite that optimistic. He knew things were going to be tough for a while. They'd have to get jobs, but that should be easier out there than it had been here. The economy was better in L.A. than in Louisiana.

"There are gonna be a lot of chicks out there, too," Kyle continued. "Lots of them, man. Models and all that." His voice stopped abruptly, and he appeared in the doorway a moment later.

"Shit, I forgot about Ruth. What am I gonna tell Ruth?"

"Take it easy," Corey said. "You can call her from the road, and we'll send for her when we get the cash. It'll give her old lady time to settle down."

"I guess you're right. I wish we could take her now."

"Her mom's never goin' to stand for that. Later is better."

"You sure, man? I'm gonna miss her."

The last thing Corey wanted to deal with was dragging Ruth along. Her mother would have cops after them in no time.

"Sending for her is best," he said, knowing Kyle would fall in love again soon enough. The kid was a romantic. "Don't think about her right now. We've got stuff to do. Give me a hand with the amplifier."

Together the cops moved across the lawn like combat soldiers approaching an enemy camp. Their booted feet slid across the dry winter grass silently and up the front steps, creeping across the porch so that they would not rattle the boards. The old planks creaked under their weight, but the sound was faint.

LaFleur paused at the door, listening for only a moment before he lifted his foot and slammed it against the latch. The old wood crushed inward without much resistance, and LaFleur charged forward, leading with the gun.

The kids were standing in the middle of the living room, holding a large amplifier between them. They froze as they saw LaFleur, and as the big man entered behind him, their eyes bulged.

"Put that down slowly," LaFleur demanded, leveling the pistol at Corey.

"What's goin' on?" Corey asked.

"Just put it down and shut up," LaFleur said.

They eased the speaker to the floor as directed.

"Now raise your hands," LaFleur ordered.

Idal reached behind his back and pulled out a pair of handcuffs. Keeping his pistol ready, he moved over and slapped a bracelet on Corey's wrist, then turned him around and clipped the other shackle into place.

"Are we under arrest again?" Corey asked stoically, almost as if he were bored.

"Just shut up," Idal said, "before I crack your skull open with this pistol." He reached back, and LaFleur placed another set of cuffs into his palm which he used on Kyle.

"Now check the front way," LaFleur suggested.

Idal looked out through the front door, his eyes quickly surveying the surroundings.

"Looks clear," he said. "They were nice enough to rent a

house at the end of the street. It's secluded."

LaFleur grinned. "Good." He nodded toward the materials on the floor. "Were you boys going somewhere?"

"Leaving town," said Corey. "We were heading west to be out of your hair."

"You steal this stuff?"

"It's ours," Corey said. "We were going to sell it to get travelling money. That's all."

"So you were about to go see your fence? He know you were coming?" LaFleur asked.

"You've got nothing on us," Corey said.

LeFleur lifted the hand with which he was holding the Walther and brought it back across Corey's cheek with a backhanded blow that rattled the kid's teeth.

He dropped sideways and bounced on the floor, unable to break his fall since his hands were bound.

LaFleur put the sole of his boot against Corey's shoulder. "You're right. I can't prove anything; but I know what you did, and there's something I can do about it. You've made it real easy. Everybody's going to think you're leaving town. Your fence will tell that. Nobody will miss you. You're the kind of scum nobody misses."

Kyle stood helplessly, watching the cop apply pressure to Corey's side. "Leave him alone, man."

"You want some of this?" LaFleur asked. "You little piece of shit. I can grind either one of you into the ground."

"What about our rights?"

Leaving Corey on the floor, LaFleur walked toward Kyle. A grim smile spread across his lips. Carefully he inserted the barrel of the gun into the kid's left nostril.

"You don't have any rights anymore. There are no judges to protect you now." He chuckled. "You know what a bullet does when it goes up your nostril? There's a lot of blood, and you watch it pour out of your face in the split second before the bullet bores into your brain."

Kyle began to tremble, and beneath his gasps for breath a slight moan was audible in his throat.

LaFleur moved the gun and looked down at the crotch of the boy's pants where the fabric was darkening in a slowly spreading circle.

Laughing, LaFleur looked back at Idal. "Five bucks," he

said. "I told you I could make one of them piss himself."

"Ten bucks says you can't make the other one," Idal said.

"No time," LaFleur said. "Let's get them to the truck."

Stooping, he grabbed Corey's collar to lift him to his feet and shove him toward the door.

Scarecrow was waiting at the front driveway when the truck arrived. He had the collar of his pea coat turned up around his neck to try and combat the cold, and his hands were plunged deeply into his pockets. A cigarette dangled from one corner of his mouth. He plucked it out as he lifted his hand to wave.

LaFleur rolled down the window and leaned out.

Scarecrow questioned him with a twitch of his head.

"In the back," the cop said.

Scarecrow walked to the side window of the camper cover of the truck bed and peered through it. Two long-haired kids lay facedown. Their hands were cuffed behind them, and Idal sat over them with a revolver.

"Let's put them in the holding tank," LaFleur said.

Taking his time, Scarecrow walked silently around the truck to climb in on the passenger side.

LaFleur eased the truck on past the driveway and turned onto a narrow road a few hundred feet beyond. It wound back through the trees, a soggy trail of mud and tire ruts.

The wheels on the truck were just broad enough to keep it going without bogging down, and the cops guided it with ease, taking the familiar curves and twists without much trouble as the headlight beams bounced up and down.

"Cold enough for you?" LaFleur asked.

Scarecrow reached into his pocket for a new cigarette without speaking.

The truck continued on through the trees another hundred yards before the headlight beams fell upon the dilapidated shack. Its gray planks were rotted and cracked, and the entire building seemed to sag at the center of its frame.

LaFleur took the truck out of gear and climbed out.

Scarecrow met him at the tailgate, slipping the Magnum from beneath his arm as LaFleur reached for the camper handle.

Flipping the back of the camper open, the cop slowly eased the tailgate down.

"Come on, boys," he said, grabbing Corey's feet and yanking him along the length of the truck bed and across the gate.

Unable once again to break his fall, he landed on his shoulder in the soggy pinestraw and rotted leaves that were matted across the ground.

"What are you doing?" Kyle demanded. He had managed to scramble to his knees, and he looked from the back of the truck at his brother.

Behind him, Idal lifted one foot and placed it against the kid's shoulder blades. With a shove he sent Kyle plunging off the tailgate.

He landed on his face, the fall flattening his nose and stuffing dirt into his mouth. He rolled over spitting, and blood bubbled out of each nostril.

"What the fuck are you guys doing?" he demanded.

LaFleur reached down and took hold of the boy's shirt. "You don't ask the questions here unless you want the shit beat out of you. Now get up."

Together the brothers struggled to their feet, standing side by side.

"Let's get in the house," Idal said.

Together they moved along beside the truck and toward the narrow front door of the shack.

LaFleur walked ahead of them and took out a ring of keys to undo a heavy Yale lock. The house was not as dilapidated as it looked, and the door was apparently solid.

"What are you going to do with us?" Kyle asked. He was fighting not to cry.

"What the law won't," LaFleur said.

He pushed the door open, and Idal urged the two through the frame into a dark, narrow front room.

"You're not going to leave us in here?" Kyle said.

"Not in here," Idal said. "Under here."

He pulled open a closet and took out his Zippo lighter. Flicking it on, he held it up so that some of the glow

130

spilled down to the floor of the narrow chamber.

Squatting, he gripped a metal ring and pulled upward. It looked at first as if he was ripping up the floor.

The flickering flame quickly revealed an opening, a hole that led down into darkness. A narrow ladder stretched into the nothingness.

"Come on, guys," Corey said.

"Climb down or get pushed down," Idal said.

"What are we going to do?" Kyle asked, looking at Corey.

LaFleur gave him the answer instead. Grabbing a handful of the back of Kyle's hair, he pulled the boy's head backward. The other hand went under Kyle's chin, gripping tightly.

"You're goin' to do what you're told," LaFleur said.

He squeezed the muscles of Kyle's jaw for a moment to bring pain, then gave him a push that sent him stumbling toward the edge of the trapdoor.

"Down you go," LaFleur said. He lifted the Walther and leveled it at Kyle. "Down the ladder."

Kyle looked over the edge of the hatch. "I can't even see down there. You expect me to climb into that with my hands cuffed?"

"If I shoot you, you'll fall in the hole."

Kyle swallowed, looked at the gun in the flickers of moonlight and the glow from the lighter, then glanced back at the hole.

"Go ahead," Corey said.

Kyle's eyes displayed his confusion.

"We don't have any choice," Corey said.

Sniffling, fighting tears, Kyle eased his feet over the edge of the hole, lowering his shoes onto the top rung of the ladder.

He had trouble balancing himself. He sat at the edge of the hole, trying to position himself so that he could move down the ladder without his hands. Awkwardly, he tried to move his left foot down a rung. He managed it and got his hands onto the top rung.

His descent into the darkness was slow; but finally he disappeared into the hole, and LaFleur urged Corey over to do the same. Corey moved with the same awkwardness, but he managed also.

With a laugh, Idal slipped the door back into place.

"They should be pretty wild by the time we're ready for them," LaFleur said.

"Yeah," Idal agreed. "It'll be a good hunt. This time we'll get to them first."

LaFleur laughed. "Maybe. It doesn't matter. The end's all the same."

Idal lifted his gun and sighted down the barrel. "Yeah, but I haven't picked off a criminal in a long time."

"It's just like seducing a virgin," LaFleur said. "You don't forget how."

Chapter 12

Jag was up around six the next morning, eager to get to work on his investigation.

He was dressed and stirring around in the living room when Deb strolled out rubbing her eyes. The hardwood floor creaked under her footsteps, prompting him to turn and see her in the gray light that streamed in through the side window.

She was wearing one of his shirts, so the tail fell to about mid-thigh; and her hair was uncombed and loose about her face, the unkemptness somehow making her seem more sexy, more attractive. He paused for a moment, taking her in before averting his gaze.

She was yawning. Apparently she had not slept well.

"What are you up to?" she asked, dropping into a chair and tucking her legs under her Indian-style. The shirt tail rode up ever farther.

Jag adjusted his glasses a bit nervously, trying not to let his gaze linger on her thighs. "I figured I'd have some time to dig around," he said. "I'm not sure what I need to do next."

She rubbed her eyes. "I kept thinking about the things you said while I was trying to go to sleep. It seemed wild. It still does."

She clenched her teeth, a ripple pulsing in the muscle of her jaw. "It makes me angry if it's true. If that's what it was, I want to get them, Jag. Whatever Mark did, he didn't deserve to be murdered."

"I know," Jag said.

"Are there any cops you can trust?" she asked. "Any that might not be involved in this?"

He shrugged. "It'd be dangerous. Who knows which ones might be involved?"

She thought for a moment. "What about that guy at the jail? Honeycutt? Wasn't he pretty nice to you?"

"He seemed decent enough," Jag said. "But if they were carting people out of the jail, he'd have to know about it."

"We don't know that they took them out of the jail. If this is real, they'd have to take extreme steps to keep people from finding out. They'd have to be very cautious. The more people that know about something makes it harder to keep things secret."

"I suppose you're right," Jag said.

"Maybe we can talk to him," Deb said. Her tension and anger were still apparent in her voice and her expression. "Who else can we ask?"

"It's hard to know who to trust. If he's in on it, we'd be taking a dangerous step. They can't afford to let us find out what's going on." He felt some of the enthusiasm sinking out of him. The prospect of treading into a situation that could actually be life-threatening took the thrill out of it.

"We've got to find a way to approach him," Deb said. "Maybe we could talk to him away from the jail."

"It's still a risk," Jag said, "but that may be the only way we learn anything."

"We can ask the questions like we've just heard rumors," Debra said. "We don't have to tell him what you found out about the old man." A partial smile wrinkled across her lips. "We're sounding like the Hardy Boys here, aren't we?"

Jag sat down on the couch. "That would make sense, though. Approaching it that way, I mean. The rumors go around. Anyone could hear them, so Honeycutt wouldn't have to know we hadn't just picked them up on the street." Jag threw up his hands. "It still doesn't keep us safe if he's in on it. If they've killed people, they won't hesitate to do it again."

"Except that they've been killing criminals, people that won't be missed. You're a journalist."

"Not a very good one."

"Doesn't matter. If something happened to you, think of the attention it would draw. Any time a reporter gets put in jail for refusing to reveal a source, it makes headlines. When one gets killed, even more heads turn."

"You're right. If they do find out we're asking, they might just try to lay low and hope we shut up. Maybe the fact that I'm a lousy reporter will work to my advantage. They'll figure I'm not a threat."

"Don't put yourself down," Deb said. "You've helped me a lot by just being here. You've done more than I could ever expect anyone to do, especially anyone I just happened to meet. I feel like I can trust you," she said. She slid out of the chair. "Let me get a shower, and then we'll see if we can find Honeycutt."

"I'll be here," Jag said.

She touched his face gently with her palm as she walked past.

He let the sway of her body as she moved from the room take his thoughts off his anxieties. Her beauty was intimidating, yet her manner with him put his fears at ease, even the ones about death.

The air in the pit where Kyle and Corey were confined was heavy and damp, making it hard to breathe. Only a few cracks let in any air at all.

The stench from the corner they had been using to relieve themselves filled their nostrils, and the cold bit through their clothes. The floor of the pit was soggy with ground water that soaked up through it, and the walls were slick with slime. Stumbling around in the darkness, they had tangled in spider webs. Kyle had been afraid there might be black widows.

So far nothing had bitten them.

That was the only bad thing that hadn't happened, Corey thought.

They leaned against the wall near the ladder, looking upward without seeing anything. It was too dark. Not even a sliver of light made its way into the room.

"I think this is probably what hell is like," Corey said. "No fire, just cold and dark. Like a dungeon."

"We're gonna die down here," Kyle said. "They're just going to leave us here and let us rot."

They had already taken turns climbing awkwardly up

135

the ladder, each trying to budge the trapdoor by pressing against it with his shoulders.

Despite repeated efforts which had left them sore and frustrated, the door did not budge. It was old but solid enough to keep them confined.

"Try to relax," Corey said. He didn't know what good it would do, but it felt like they were kids again. He'd always had to calm Kyle down after vampire movies on television or bumps in the night that frightened him.

He felt like a big brother again, protective and responsible. Kyle had never seemed quite as strong, so Corey had always stood up for him, facing schoolyard bullies and anybody else who bothered him.

Perhaps he had done too much for Kyle over the years, letting him grow to expect protection. Kyle had to have someone to take care of him, and that was bad. Corey worried that Kyle would never be totally independent.

This was not a time to think about that. They were in deep shit, almost literally considering the slimy dirt floor beneath them.

It was like the Black Hole of Calcutta. Apparently this place had been dug just to stuff people into for whatever game these cops were playing.

Corey didn't like it all. It wasn't the kind of thing they let you walk away from.

Beside him, Kyle was shuddering, and his shoulders were heaving up and down with his sobs. He had contained his emotions as long as possible.

"My feet are like blocks of ice," he said. "I'm freezing down here. We're gonna die down here, Corey. If we don't freeze to death, they'll starve us. Why are they doing this to us?"

Corey wished he could put an arm around his brother to comfort him. He had to settle for speaking a few quiet words of reassurance instead.

Kyle didn't stop crying.

"We'll figure something out," Corey said. "Give it some time. All we can do is ride it out. They'll come back for us, and we'll watch for an opening."

Kyle's sobs made his body quiver. "That's never gonna work."

"We're still alive. We've got a chance." He wanted to tell

136

Kyle to shut up, but he knew he couldn't do that. The kid was upset enough without having his brother turn against him.

"Why are they doing this?" Kyle asked again. "We've never hurt anybody."

"The old lady. They think we caused it."

"It wasn't our fault. She was dead when we went in."

"They don't believe that" was all that Corey could say. It didn't have much meaning.

He let his head roll back against the wall. He stared upward, but his eyes saw nothing in the darkness.

He couldn't really disagree with Kyle. When the cops came back, they would have guns. There would be no opportunity to run, no real hope of any chance of escape.

He hated to think of what lay in store. They had to be crazy to be doing this kind of thing. The vigilantes would probably take them farther into the woods and kill them execution style, then stuff their bodies into the ground somewhere.

They'd never be found, and they would never be remembered. Not even on headstones. No one would ever record their music, and they would never play to large auditoriums the way they had dreamed.

A sadness crept over Corey as he looked back over his life. What had he ever done that was worth a shit? He'd taken care of Kyle for the most part, but he'd never done Kyle any good really. Poor Kyle. Poor good-hearted Kyle.

What a mess. Of all the shitty things that had rolled along in their lives, this was the worst.

This was how it ended.

At least it would be over soon.

He realized he was giving in to hopelessness, but in spite of what he'd told Kyle, things were pretty bad. He couldn't come up with any scenario in his mind that would lead them to freedom. All possibilities ended with them floating in the swamp.

What came, however, was not what he expected.

It began with the sound of scratching, of nails against the wood over their heads. The sound crept down to them through the darkness, and something began to tear at the door from the outside. Something wanted to get in.

With a phone call to the jail, Jag confirmed that Honeycutt was off duty. He couldn't get a home phone number out of the man who answered, so he and Deb had to go by the public library and check the city directory to get a home address.

The jailer lived on the outskirts of Aimsley, along a stretch of road that was not quite a suburb, yet it was beginning to lose its rural edge. The gradual sprawl would overtake it soon.

A Ford Bronco was parked in the driveway, and the number over the door matched the address from the directory.

Jag pulled up behind the Ford, and he and Deb approached the screen front door where a small white button was set into the door facing. Jag hit it with his thumb.

A chilly wind hit them as they waited, but the day had turned out to be a little warmer. The sky was still overcast with a slate-gray sheet of clouds.

Jag allowed his gaze to wander over to Deb. She was wearing a loose white sweater that fell long on her, and her stone-washed jeans hugged the shape of her legs.

He kept feeling drawn to her. Part of it was the rebound from Caroline, and part of it was physical. He knew that. It didn't change the fact that he had a growing admiration for her.

She had a toughness, no doubt born of her struggles as a young person, and a determination. He would never have been able to have plunged this far into something so dangerous without her support. Somehow, in a way he didn't understand, she had tapped something inside of him, or helped him tap it.

When the door finally opened, a woman in a pale floral house dress stood on the far side of the screen, her hands gripped tightly around the handles of an aluminum walker.

She was not old, but something had taken the youth out of her. Her face was drawn and pale, her hair a mass of blue tangles.

"Can I help you?" she asked.

"We're looking for Mr. Honeycutt," Debra said. "Is he

at home?"

"He's here." Her voice was weak, and she had to struggle for her words. "Out back. Does he know you?"

"We've spoken to him," Debra said. "It's about a matter at the jail."

The woman swallowed. "He's out in the back with his dogs. He likes to work with them when he's off his job." She seemed to accept what they had told her. "You can come through," she said. "You'll have to find him out the back door."

Awkwardly, she moved backward to give them entrance.

The house was a typical suburban job with thick pile carpet, discount furniture and an unmemorable landscape visible through the sliding glass door beyond the couch.

They moved quickly through the hallway to the kitchen where a door opened out onto the patio.

The backyard was beyond and stretched farther than Jag had expected. The grass, browned by the winter, crawled back across a half acre, then the ground sloped downward toward a cluster of pine trees.

They traversed the yard quickly, toward the edge of the trees where they could hear an occasional whistle and the gentle thump of dogs' paws against the ground.

A pair of black Labrador retrievers came bounding out of the woods, one slightly ahead of the other, carrying a sock between its teeth.

Honeycutt came jogging along behind them shortly, a baseball cap tilted back over his hair and a red plaid hunting jacket flapping around him.

He was smiling; but when he saw Jag and Debra, he stopped in his tracks, and his expression melted.

"What the hell are you two doing here?"

Jag had his hands in the pockets of his coat. He removed them and held them out at his sides, palms upward. "Just came to talk," he said. He'd noticed the jailer's arm creeping beneath the plaid coat where there might be a weapon concealed.

"What do you want to talk about? The good old days of being locked up?"

"We're still looking for information about my brother," Debra said. "We didn't have anybody to turn to, so we thought we'd come to you."

139

"I don't know what I could do to help you," the big man said. "I told you we didn't have him in our lockup."

"His name sounded familiar to you."

"Hell, sweetheart. You know how many names I have to deal with on a Saturday night alone? They all start to run together." He walked toward them a few more steps, his manner becoming a little more comfortable.

The dogs trotted back to him and began to wag their tails and jump up on him. The one with the sock dropped it at his feet as if proud there were no teeth marks. It had been stuffed with rags to simulate the shape of a duck in order to teach the dog not to tear up game when retrieving it.

"Good boy, Digger," Honeycutt said, rubbing the dog behind the ears. The other, jealous, forced its nose between Digger and its master.

Laughing, the jailer petted the second dog too. "Easy, Honey. I haven't forgotten you."

"They're nice dogs," Jag said.

Honeycutt looked up and smiled. "I spend as much time with them as I can. Have a look at this."

He picked up the sock and carried it over to the fork of a thick magnolia tree at a corner of the yard. The tree did not grow straight, so one side of it curved at an angle.

Wedging the sock into place, he stepped back.

"Seek."

Digger's claws kicked up tufts of ground as he hurried across the lawn and bolted up the slope of the tree in a quick motion which allowed him to propel himself upward.

His jaws closed around the sock and tugged it free with ease before he jumped onto the ground.

"Good job," Honeycutt said. "You ought to see the other things."

"It seems kind of a shame to go through all this for hunting," Debra said. "It always seems so brutal to me."

Honeycutt did not seemed offended by her remark. "Hunting's a part of life," he said as he continued petting the dog and drew Honey's jealousy once again.

"As long as you keep it in moderation, you're all right. I don't hold to killing in excess. If I hunt, we eat what I

140

kill."

"It just seems that it's primitive, I guess. It goes back to the old ways. I mean, we can buy food in a supermarket."

Honeycutt chuckled. "I suppose you're right. It's one more reminder that we're not that far removed from the savages."

"We didn't really come by to talk about sociology," Jag said, trying to steer things back on course.

"You're still looking for something about her brother; well I wish I could help you. I sympathize. I know it's tough when people you love suffer."

He paused a moment, and it was apparent he was referring to the woman in the house. Jag wasn't sure what her problem was, but it had obviously taken its toll on the big jailer.

"There's no understanding some things," Honeycutt said.

"I think there's an answer to why my brother's body was on that railroad track," she said. "I've just got to find it."

"We came to you because we thought we might be able to trust you," said Jag. "We've heard some things, things we have to check out with somebody."

"Is this for publication?"

"No," Jag said. "I'm not interviewing you. I'm just trying to get at the truth."

Honeycutt straightened up from the crouch he had assumed to pet the dogs. "What are you after, son?" His voice was firm.

"We need to know about the swamp," Debra said. "It's a rumor that goes around. Is it true?"

The blood drained out of the jailer's face.

"I don't know what you're talking about."

"It's just a rumor," Jag said. "We had to check with someone and see if there was any truth to it."

"I've never heard anything about it," said Honeycutt.

He knelt back to his dogs, pretending to be more enthralled with their presence than he really was.

"Let me show you something else," he said, taking the sock and pitching it across the lawn. "Get it," he shouted, and the two dogs set off at a dead run, each struggling to reach the sock first.

Honey outran Digger this time and snatched up the

cloth triumphantly, trotting around a half circle before heading back toward Honeycutt.

"It's something all the criminals seem to talk about," Debra said.

"It gets boring in jail," Honeycutt said. "They sit around the bull pen and make up stuff to scare each other. Some of it they do to intimidate the younger prisoners." He looked at Jag. "You weren't in there that long. You'd have found out. They tell all kinds of legends about the jail."

"What do you think happened to Melo Templeton?" Jag asked.

"He escaped. That's all. You might as well just forget about rumors. They're not going to help you find what you're looking for. You'll be better off leaving things alone, son."

Jag thought he could hear a quiver in the big man's voice.

"You never know who you'll make mad prying into things. You start talking a lot, you'll just spread the rumor farther and make a bunch of people look bad. You know yourself cops don't like to look bad."

Looking at Honeycutt's face was like looking at a ghost. His skin seemed to grow more pale each second.

"What if it were true?" Debra asked. "What if people were dying? You seem like a good man, Mr. Honeycutt. Wouldn't you try to stop it?"

"My wife needs me to take care of her. She's very sick. Crusades are for younger men, men who aren't just a few years from retirement and pension. You understand that?"

He knelt back down to pet his dogs. Jag and Debra cast each other quick glances which offered mutual acknowledgement of the futility of the situation.

"I guess we'll be going," Jag said. "We shouldn't have bothered you."

"Well, I hope you get some satisfaction about your brother, miss," the jailer said. "You might find something, but you don't need to chase rabbits. You're looking at what they'd call a red herring in the mystery books. Y'all take care of yourselves."

He waved good-bye as they walked back across the yard and looped around the house to get back to the driveway.

142

"What do you think?" Debra asked as they settled into the car and got the heater going.

Jag held his hands in front of the vent, letting the warming air bring feeling back to his fingers.

"I think we've seen confirmation that it's more than a rumor."

"You think he's in on it?"

Jag frowned. "No. I think he knows something, though. Maybe everybody knows something, and it's something they overlook. Maybe they have to."

"It's getting scary," said Debra. "We may have put ourselves in danger after all."

"So we start watching our backs," Jag said.

"What do we do next."

"Something kind of difficult. We look up Melo's family and see if they really think he's hiding out somewhere. If he's alive, he's bound to have tried to contact them."

"Do you think they'll talk to us?"

"Not if they've heard from him. If they haven't, they may be ready to spill their guts."

Honeycutt entered the house and went to the front window where he watched the car pull away.

Then, turning, he paced the floor. His wife was resting on the couch. With difficulty she lifted her head a bit. "What's the matter?"

"Those kids. It's nothing really. Don't let it worry you."

"It worries you . . . I can tell."

"They've heard about something. Something I thought was over. They both seem like nice kids but . . ." his voice trailed off.

"But what?" the woman's coarse voice croaked.

"If they keep going like they're going, I bet something bad happens," Honeycutt said.

Chapter 13

Serena's gaze and thoughts kept drifting toward the window as her tutor droned on about some esoteric geometric concept.

The gray sky did nothing to eliminate the imaginative possibilities of the world beyond the walls where she was confined.

She wanted to go walking. The cold would not be that bad, and she could explore the forest. It wasn't the same as having friends and doing things with other people, but it would offer something different from the routine in which she had been trapped for so long.

Sometimes depression seized her because no change was in sight. Her father offered no chance for any variation.

She could remember when things had been different, back when her mother was still alive. Her father had been different then. He'd been preoccupied with his business, failing to notice things and often being distant, but at least not obsessed.

He had not seen evil in every shadow and had not shackled her with restrictions deemed for her own safety.

How time changed things. How much she missed her mother.

She had been a beautiful woman, a wonderful woman with wisdom and knowledge. She'd been a good mother, too. Being Nicholas Rand's wife had made demands on her, social commitments and civic duties, but she had still found time to devote to her daughter.

Serena remembered the moments they'd had, special times mingled in between the usual spats and disagreements.

Once upon a time Dayana Rand had studied ballet, and

although she had never pursued a career, it had remained a favorite pastime. In their home in Texas there had been a small studio which Nicholas had installed. Sometimes Dayana had taken Serena there, teaching her moves and steps. Serena had loved the exercises, but she had never been able to match her mother's grace.

She recalled Dayana's twirling form, the long black hair spinning around her head as she glided across the floor.

Her mother's exotic looks, remnants of what she claimed to be Aztec blood, had been handed down to Serena, but Serena had always considered her mother to be the most beautiful.

In this new home, Nicholas had paid for renovations to give Serena a studio. He'd offered to have someone come in for instruction, but she couldn't bring herself to dance anymore. It was too painful without Dayana. The memories of the dance were pleasant, but other memories had a tendency to launch assaults if she wasn't careful.

The monotonous voice of Miss Rainey continued, making Serena long even more for escape.

Walks in the woods were pleasant as long as she could avoid Scarecrow. They weren't substitutes for Mother or for friendship, but they were something besides the emptiness.

Raising a hand to her forehead, she closed her eyes. "Miss Rainey, I've had about all I can take for today," Serena said.

"Are you ill, dear?"

Miss Rainey was a silver-haired retired school teacher who had never married but had spent ages caring for nieces. Her maternal instincts for Serena were always quick to click into gear.

Serena seldom responded, however. Miss Rainey was one of her captors, an emissary of her father. She chose not to get close to them.

"I think I just need some fresh air," she said. "I guess I'll be all right for tomorrow."

"Can I get anything for you?"

"Nothing. Thank you."

She watched Miss Rainey gather her things. The old woman moved slowly, and it seemed to take her forever. Serena tried to appear patient, but she was relieved when the woman finally departed.

She sat for a while longer, giving Miss Rainey time to get to her car, and then she listened, making sure all was quiet in the house.

When she was satisfied that Scarecrow was not lurking around somewhere, she went into her bedroom and pulled on a dark suede coat over her slacks and sweater. The chill would bite through the clothes, but it would not bother her much. The leather coat was warm, an essential for her walks.

She pulled the tie tightly around her waist and moved out into the upper hallway, stepping softly until she reached the stairs. She went down them quickly, wasting no time getting across the living room and through the kitchen. The kitchen exit was to the side of the house, only a short distance to the woods.

The cold wind hit her as she rushed across the lawn, but the trees broke some of it when she reached the forest.

She wondered where her cat had gone. She had not seen it in days and reminded herself to watch for it.

The oaks were bare, their leaves long since fallen, but the pines that dominated the forest were as lush as ever, their needles green and thick, covering the sky and building walls of shadow.

She wound among the trees, imagining freedom, imagining that she could keep walking and find friends and diversion.

She wouldn't know what to do with friends now, however. It had been so long she probably wouldn't fit in with people anymore.

They would probably find her weird since she hadn't had contact in so long except with tutors and body guards.

She'd heard people tell her father she should have had counseling after her mother's death, but he had refused to hear of it. He came from the school of pulling yourself up by your own boot straps.

She'd learned to do that out of necessity. For a while she had battled nightmares which made her relive things, recreating scenes she had not witnessed and enhancing them with imaginations that might rival the deft hand of a screenwriter.

They still came from time to time, those little mind movies, but she had learned to deal with the fear; if she had not, it would have consumed her.

She let her thoughts drift past the bad things as she walked. The wind numbed her cheeks and toyed with her hair as she strolled across the damp ground. Thunder threatened somewhere, but it was far away.

If the rain started, she was still close enough to the house to return quickly. She followed a path that twisted around trees and occasional logs which lay rotting on the ground.

She would walk along the edge of the bayou, she decided, letting her thoughts drift along with the gentle flow of the brown water.

Pulling the tie of her coat again so that it would not slide open, she walked down a slope and moved around a thick-trunked oak tree in her path.

A pine had fallen just beyond it, perhaps a long time before. The bark was decaying, and white parasitic growths blossomed across its surface.

She moved to it, lifting her foot to step upward. It was a large tree, so traversing it presented a little difficulty. Climbing onto the log, she prepared to hop down.

The arm lay there as if it might be ready to reach up for her. It was hideous, ripped away from its body at the elbow. Torn muscle and tendon trailed out at the tear, and the hand was partially stripped of flesh revealing skeletal fingers.

The body was about three feet away, a mangled mass of meat. The part still covered by flesh was smeared with blood and the rest was mutilated beyond recognition.

She stood on the tree, eyes frozen on the scene. She felt her heart leap, and she slipped backward, landing with a thud onto her buttocks. She had just touched ground when she began scrambling backward, kicking with her feet and finally rolling onto hands and knees. She continued that way a short distance before getting to her feet and beginning to run.

The scene of carnage assaulted her thoughts. She remembered her mother, remembered walking into the solarium of their old house and seeing her on the floor there, naked and bleeding, her flesh covered with purple bruises that looked like makeup smeared across her thighs, breasts and stomach.

The whimper from her mother's lips returned, that whimper that had haunted endless dreams. It had been so futile and so pitiful, a weak sighing sound of the life leaving her. It was the sound of her giving up, a sound that said she had endured too much to go on.

Serena had never dreamed she would see something that could equal that nightmare.

Her feet skidded across the slick pine straw, and her arms flailed at her sides as she ran.

Blood, crimson, filled her thoughts. The blood on the

147

woman's body was her mother's blood. It was happening again.

There was no safety anywhere. Her father was right.

She didn't realize it, but she was screaming as she moved, not words, just incoherent shrieks.

She retraced the path she had followed, maintaining balance only with difficulty. She broke through the branches and screamed again, conscious of her cry this time as she charged headlong at Scarecrow.

He sidestepped slightly and caught her with one arm, sliding the Magnum from its holster with the other hand in a quick, fluid movement.

"What's wrong," he whispered, the gun ready as he scanned the country in front of them.

Serena had to catch her breath and force her words through trembling lips. "A body. There's a body up there. Torn up."

"Okay," Scarecrow said. "It's all right."

With his arm around her shoulders, he turned her, guiding her back toward the house while his eye kept busy, watching the trees all around them for signs of movement.

"Who is she?" Nicholas Rand asked as Scarecrow pulled a blanket over the remains.

"Must have lived around here," Scarecrow said. "Probably out for a walk."

Rand ran a black-gloved hand across his face. Anxiety was visible in his eyes.

"That wasn't supposed to happen," he said.

"They're dangerous."

"So you think it is them?" He plunged his hands into the pockets of his overcoat and looked away from the body.

Scarecrow straightened. "What else do you think could have done this?"

Rand turned away and stepped back over the log. "They've never ventured this far out of the swamps before."

Scarecrow crossed the log to join him. "The corpse has been chewed. They were after food. They've developed a taste for human flesh."

Rand lowered his head. "Innocent people weren't supposed to be hurt."

"It was an accident. The thing we have to do now is get rid

of the body."

"Bury this one. LaFleur said the one on the railroad tracks is causing more trouble than a total disappearance."

"It had to be done. Mistakes were made. We thought it was best if there was some kind of answer if somebody came looking for him."

"LaFleur said his sister and the journalist are asking more questions. She doesn't believe it was an accident. The simple answer didn't work."

"Everything's going to be fine."

Rand watched the trees and then gazed toward the depths of the forest, as if he could see into the swamp beyond. He didn't see any movement, no matter how hard he searched.

But then he knew the mormo. No one saw them, not until it was too late.

The door above them splintered, forcing Kyle and Corey to slosh back through the water that covered the floor and press themselves against the far wall to avoid the falling wood.

The rats that shared the hole scattered also, some of them swimming past Kyle's legs, causing his bladder to open. The warm urine spread through the fabric of his jeans, which absorbed the liquid like the paper towels in the television commercial. Twice he'd lost control. He felt embarrassment rush in with the fear.

It didn't really matter that the rats had that effect. If he hadn't pissed his pants for them, he would have pissed them when the feet appeared through the trapdoor, large, dirty feet smeared with mud and leaves.

"Wild men!" Corey shouted, confused.

The creatures descended the steps, and he realized he'd been mistaken. They could not be men. They walked upright, but they were bestial, wild.

Three of them approached, low, guttural growls issuing from their throats as their mouths peeled open to reveal yellowed teeth that gleamed in the light that spilled from the open trap.

Kyle slunk back into a corner, shuddering as they crept forward. Protective as always, Corey moved also, trying to block them from his brother with his body.

The two front creatures grabbed his arms, pulling outward. The pain made him shout as they tugged. The arms separated from his torso in a swift movement, tendon and cartilage ripping free. They dropped to the floor, still shackled at the wrists.

Blood began to spray outward from the shoulder sockets in a crimson fountain. Corey watched his dismemberment with disbelief. Color went out of his face as the shock set in, and he swayed back and forth before toppling to the ground with a splash.

The creatures knelt around him, ripping his shirt opened so that their claws could rake across his exposed chest, tearing strips of flesh away.

They crammed the globs into their mouths in a greedy feeding frenzy which gained momentum with each bite. Soon they were peeling at his face and neck, sinking their teeth into his thighs and licking blood off his stomach.

He died somewhere in the midst of it all, spared most of the experience which Kyle had to witness.

Kyle could not take his eyes from the nightmare. He could not move. He crouched against the wall, sopping in his own fluids.

Tears involuntarily dripped out the corners of his eyes, but there were no sobs because his chest was frozen, breaths shallow and almost nonexistent. He was not catatonic, because he was aware of what was happening, but he was removed from reality. At least a part of him was trapped somewhere within his subconscious.

When the creatures had finished with Corey, they turned away and began to move across the narrow room.

Soon they surrounded Kyle, looking down at him with their maddened eyes. He waited for them to attack him, but they did not.

For a long time they just looked at him, and then two of them stooped and took his arms, pulling him to his feet and tugging him along.

His feet dragged across the ground until they reached the ladder. They started up it together, pulling him after them, taking him with them.

He didn't know where.

Chapter 14

Jag and Deb parted company shortly before noon, he to get to work, she to look up Melo Templeton's relatives. A call to the newspaper morgue and a favor from the file clerk had provided the names of Templeton's closest kin — his mother and grandmother. Deb had written down their address. They had agreed it might be better for her to approach them. While he was a newspaper reporter and might seem like an intruder, she was nonthreatening.

She climbed back into the Volvo with an area map Jag had picked up for her at the Chamber of Commerce. She found herself a little apprehensive about the visit, but she knew it could be no worse than anything she'd encountered thus far.

Penn's Ferry was across the river, about ten miles from Aimsley. It seemed farther because there was little along the road besides a few houses and some grocery quick stops to break the monotony. Pine forests covered most of the territory.

The town had started to expand in the last few years with new subdivisions and businesses that let it thrive in spite of the economic conditions in Louisiana, but it still had some distance to cover before it equaled Aimsley.

Deb made the trip quickly, her foot heavy on the gas pedal in spite of the possibility of state troopers hiding along the way. She was impatient for answers.

She found the side street where Mrs. Templeton lived without much of a problem once she'd hit town. Even with its recent growth, there wasn't much of Penn's Ferry to get

151

lost in since it was built mostly around an old mental institution and the small, private Pine College. Except for a few stores and shopping centers, everything else was residential.

A block off Main Street, Debra found herself in a different world.

Chapel Drive was a narrow paved street riddled with cracks. It curled around behind a cemetery and ran along in front of some row houses that were gray and sagging with age.

Rusty, bowed screens enclosed the front porches, and broken toys and ruined appliances littered the front yards where brown grass withered in clumps which had gone undisturbed for several summers.

She drove past the houses, looking at the numbers on the mailboxes or posted over the porches.

She was looking for 505. She found it at the end of the street, a corner lot with a two-story house that could have been Norman Bates' summer home. It was no wonder the guy who'd grown up here had gone on to become a killer. Deb reluctantly pulled into the driveway and killed the Volvo's engine.

There was no sign of life. She expected to see a child with a dirty face peering from one of the windows, but that didn't happen.

She walked across the soggy front lawn and up the porch steps. The screen door was open, so she moved through it to knock on the front door.

A thin woman with dark-gray hair answered, her wool dress faded and limp around her withered frame. Her face was wrinkled like leather, and her chin and nose stuck out as if they were making an effort to meet each other. A cigarette smoldered in one corner of her mouth.

"What do you want?" she asked.

Deb introduced herself. "I'm looking for Mrs. Templeton," she said.

"You sellin' insurance?" the old woman asked.

"No ma'am," Deb said. "I was hoping I could talk to her about her son."

"Not another reporter?"

"No. It's a personal thing. It involves my brother."

"We already got a church. We don't want no *Watchtowers*."

"That's okay. I'm not from a church," Deb said.

The old woman stared at her skeptically for a moment, a look of hostility in her eyes. Finally she let the door open wider and motioned Deb into the front room.

The smell in the air was sour, made worse by the stuffiness created by the heater. Deb wondered if they had mummified bodies hidden in the back room.

The old woman left Deb standing in the center of the living room. The furniture had a worn look, and the lamps that illuminated it somehow seemed to have a brown tone.

After a few moments, a woman with wiry blond hair appeared. She was wearing white spandex slacks and a loose-fitting blouse of a shiny fabric with zebras on it.

"I'm Emily Templeton," she said.

Deb introduced herself. "I'm not a reporter or anything," she assured. "I'm trying to find some information about my brother. He was found dead in the north part of the parish."

Mrs. Templeton only folded her arms and stared. "What has that got to do with us?" The woman had had a hard life which showed in her face and manner. She offered little sign of compassion or compromise.

Deb stammered a bit because she had so much information to convey and Emily was not making it easy.

"My brother may have been murdered, and it may have something to do with the jail."

"What has that got to do with my son?"

"No one's seen or heard from him since he supposedly escaped," Deb said. "Unless you've got some indication that's different."

"How do I know you're not from the police?" Mrs. Templeton asked. "You could just be trying to pump me for information."

"I don't have any great love for the police in this place," Deb said. "They've done nothing but stonewall me."

Perhaps it was the tone in her voice or the look in her eyes that convinced Mrs. Templeton of Deb's sincerity, or maybe she just needed somebody to talk to about her son's disappearance.

"They haven't been much help to me either," Emily said. "We haven't heard from my son since the escape. We really haven't."

"Why do you think he hasn't tried to contact you?" Deb asked.

She shook her head. "I don't know. They say when people escape from jail they try to go home. He never did. He never called or anything. Even on the run, I can't imagine why he'd do that. I know he'd want to protect us, but I can't understand why he wouldn't try to get us a message or something to let us know he's all right. He did what he did, but we're still family."

She motioned toward a couch and settled down beside Deb.

"Have the police given you much trouble?" Deb asked.

"They came around a time or two asking questions. Not much else."

"No stakeouts or anything?"

"Not that I've ever noticed. What happened to your brother?"

"They found him dead on a railroad track."

"An accident?"

"Maybe. Or maybe somebody put him there."

"How is this tied to my boy?"

"I don't know." Deb didn't want to come out and tell her about the suspicion that her son could be dead. "I don't know what could be going on here."

"You think somebody could have done something to Melo?"

"Maybe the same thing that was done to my brother. I don't know why. Did they have a very good case against your son, Mrs. Templeton?"

The woman's eyes narrowed, and for a moment her lips grew taut. She studied Deb, trying to decide if she could trust her. "This is nothing that could be used in court if you're wired. I know something about rights."

"I'm not bugged, Mrs. Templeton."

"I think it's pretty clear he did it," the older woman said. "You know that if you know enough about the case to come lookin' for me."

Deb nodded, a silent confession.

Mrs. Templeton swallowed, half choking on her words. "I lay awake at night and wonder what it is in our blood that could have made him that way," she said. "I don't find any answers."

The harshness in her voice faded, and she wiped a tear from the corner of one eye. "The thing is, though, his defense attorney said things could be worked out. They thought they could get him off, but they couldn't give a guarantee. He might have been found guilty, but he wouldn't have faced the death penalty, they said. He may have done jail time, a long time, but he wouldn't have been killed."

She began to cry. It was not something she did often, and it showed. She bowed her head, embarrassed to be showing emotion in front of a stranger.

"I don't know what I've ever done to have so much go wrong," Emily said. "I carried him in my body, held him in my arms, and he grew up to kill that poor girl. What made him a killer?"

"I don't know," Debra said again. It was becoming a standard answer.

"What do you think happened to him?" Emily asked. "You think something, or you wouldn't have come here." She looked at Debra, her eyes gleaming with tears. It took all of Deb's effort not to cry as well.

"I think maybe he was murdered too," Debra said. "Maybe some kind of vigilantes."

"You really think so?"

Deb looked at her and nodded slowly. "I can't prove anything yet, but I will. I told you I'm not a reporter, and that's true, but I do have a reporter working with me, kind of helping."

"If you find something out, it'll be in the paper?"

"If we find something we can prove. It's a tough road, but yesterday we didn't even have an idea of what was going on. We've had some luck so far. Some things are starting to come to light."

"You have to be careful," Emily said.

"Right now I don't think we're much of a threat to anyone," Deb said. "We just have an idea of what's been going on. We're not close to anything. I don't think there's a problem."

"Well, watch out. And if you find anything about my little boy, let me know."

"We will," Debra said. "We will."

She showed herself out and climbed back into the Volvo. It was true, there was no proof, but more and more she was becoming convinced the things Jag had turned up were true. It seemed like a wild, fanciful tale, but facts kept floating to the surface.

If Templeton were all right, he would have contacted his mother. It might have been a long-distance call or a disguised note, but he would have found a way.

Unless he was dead.

She cranked the Volvo to life and backed out of the driveway, heading up the street the way she had come.

At the end of the street, an unmarked white police cruiser pulled out of a narrow driveway and followed her, moving slowly to avoid detection.

In the *Clarion* office, Jag sat at his terminal, typing rewrites of press releases. The newsroom was almost empty, and he'd spent as much time as he could reading other stories for tomorrow's paper that were sitting in the computer. He'd spotted one news brief in the system about the identification of Mark Turner's body. The Bristol Springs chief had finally decided it was official and made a press release to police reporter, Phil Walden.

Jag realized he should have done the story as soon as he'd learned about the body. Maybe Breech was right; Jag was a screw-up. He was so caught up in playing investigative reporter he'd failed to notice the little things along the way.

Big help he was being to Debra too. How could they get anywhere? Everything seemed hopeless sitting there at the VDT listening to the quiet hum of the machine.

He had begun to type again when the phone rang at Walden's desk. The silver-haired reporter was nowhere in sight, so Jag picked up the call on his own line.

"Newsroom."

The caller asked for Walden.

"He's not in," Jag said. "Can I take a message?"

"This is Max Putnam at the sheriff's office." Max was the public information officer. "I had a little release for him."

"I can take it," Jag said. It would probably be no more than a burglary arrest, but at least it would break the monotony. Breech would hack it to pieces, but he'd be showing initiative.

"It's a missing person report," Putnam said. "Actually two people. Some friends reported them missing. We thought maybe putting it in the paper might help flush things out."

Jag called up a fresh computer page. "Okay," he said. "Go ahead, Max."

"Riverland Parish Sheriff's Deputies are searching for a man and woman who have been reported missing from their home south of Aimsley," Max read.

Jag hammered it out, not worrying about typos. He could clean them up later. The story went on giving the names, Tim Gunter and Bess Jackson, and explaining that deputies were trying to locate them because friends were concerned.

As always when policemen wrote news stories, the lead was buried at the bottom. Max explained how the house trailer the couple had shared was found in a state of disarray when police arrived.

He didn't have much information about what sort of disarray, but he did note that foul play had not been ruled out.

"Now, this trailer is in a kind of isolated area," Max said. "Back out near the swamp around Bayou Fannin."

"I see," Jag said.

"We've had a couple of cars out in the area, but so far we haven't turned anything up. Oh, both people's cars were parked in their driveway."

"Sounds like something did happen to them," Jag said.

"Yep, it does," Max agreed. "Course they could turn up in a motel somewhere too. You never can tell about these things. Friends called, though, so we gotta check 'em out."

Jag thanked him and took just a few minutes to read over the copy before walking over to Breech. "I just put a brief about some missing persons in the system," Jag said.

"Teenagers?"

"Adults. They lived out near the Bayou Fannin swamp."

"Oh, the dark and bloody ground?"

"What's that?"

Breech smiled and shook his head. "Just kidding. That's from the old *Daniel Boone* series, remember? That's what the word Kentucky meant to the Indians. The Cajuns and the Indians have legends about that swamp out there."

"I've never played Cajuns and Indians," Jag said. "What's the story?"

"Boogeyman type stuff," Breech said.

"Bayou boogeymen?"

157

"The Attakapas Indians and the Cajun trappers used to believe the woods out there were a place of evil."

Jag slipped his hands into his pockets. "You're always bubbling over with trivial information, Norman."

"I'm a journalist. Anyway, the story goes that the Indians and the Cajuns were afraid of these men that lived out there. They called them momo, mormo, something like that."

"What were they supposed to do?"

"When I was a kid, they supposedly sighted one. Kind of like Bigfoot. Some of the kids I was in school with were talking about it. They said they saw him wearing tattered human clothes, and he smelled like decaying flesh."

Jag almost laughed. "You're bullshitting me."

"Ah, the legend's pretty obscure, but the kids I was in school with grew up hearing this shit from their grandparents. Aimsley is the city, but not too far from here civilization gets a little backward."

"People were afraid of these things?"

"Of course. They were the unknown, and why do you think momo smelled like decaying flesh?"

"Why?"

"They eat people, Jag." Breech raised his eyebrows. "We consider Cajuns and Indians ethnic groups. Momo consider them food groups."

Back at the apartment, Deb found it difficult to begin making the arrangements for Mark's body. Placing the phone calls made his death seem more real, more final. It was a reminder that his life was over and that she would never see him again.

She called a local funeral home from the Yellow Pages, and someone there agreed to contact a Shreveport funeral home to fetch the body from the forensics lab.

No stretch of the imagination would allow an open casket, but she knew she wanted Mark buried beside her parents. It was important that in death if not in life the family could be together.

In the meantime the funeral homes would be passing him around in a morbid game of musical chairs, doing what they could to keep him on ice. She pictured him dead and cold, on a slab somewhere, and she remembered at the same time a moment when he had been most alive.

One summer not long before, they had driven down the Georgia coast, spent some time in Savannah and then moved on to a place called Cumberland Island. They'd had to take a ferry across the intercoastal.

The island had been rustic, and they'd camped there, lugging their gear back into the woods where wild raccoons cackled at them and tried to raid their campsite. On the beach, they'd seen wild horses and had walked endlessly looking for sand dollars.

It had been a wild trip, allowing them youth they'd never been able to enjoy before. They had huddled in their small tent, laughing in spite of the mosquitoes that tried to carry them off. It was perhaps the closest they had ever been.

Sitting on Jag's couch, remembering, she wept for her brother all over again.

They dragged Kyle through the forest, clutching at his clothes with their filthy hands and forcing him to keep moving even as his breath rasped in his throat. In spite of the cold, his face was flushed red, and he was covered in sweat that quickly congealed in the chill air. The spot of urine on his jeans was like a patch of ice, and his nose was running. With his hands still cuffed behind him, the phlegm ran from his nostrils.

He wanted to stop and sit, but every time he tried to slow down, they pulled harder on him, forcing him to keep going.

They bounded across the rugged ground, the movement sending throbbing pains through his muscles. The pain was not enough to reduce his fear, however. His mind was filled with a near madness watching these wild man-things scurry along. Beneath the matted pelts, he could discern lean muscles, and they seemed tireless in their movements.

He had never seen or heard about anything like them, yet they were real. They had devoured his brother before his eyes, and now they were taking him somewhere, perhaps for the same fate.

Corey had always been on hand to protect him. With that stripped away, he was lost. He had no way to escape these captors, and with his terror he could not even weep for the loss.

He just let them drag him along, stumbling occasionally until they reached the edge of the bayou. For a moment he wondered how they planned to cross it. Then it became apparent.

At the bank, they plunged in, holding him tightly as they kicked against the current, oblivious to the cold which bit into his very bones.

He felt as if he were going to go into shock. His brain felt numb, and his limbs were so chilled that the feeling began to leave them as well.

He was dragged through the current, and on the opposite bank, the creatures climbed out, pulling him to shore.

His clothes clung to him, made an icy paste in the winter wind. He felt as if there were no warmth left in his body. He was going to die of exhaustion and hypothermia.

It would be a blessing. He would not have to live through them devouring his flesh.

He staggered along, trying not to pay attention to what was happening, just waiting for everything to fade. If he could pass out, he wouldn't have to run anymore. If they wanted him somewhere after that, they'd have to carry him.

Without Corey, he had little will to fight. He didn't care about trying to survive. He wouldn't see Ruth again, and that disturbed him a bit; but it was futile and he knew that.

He was resigned to his fate. There was no choice, and he could accept that. He let them pull him back through the trees, deeper and deeper into the uncharted swampland.

The creatures came upon a thicket and began to pick their way through it, following a narrow trail that was invisible at first.

The passage in the twisted mass of brush, vines and branches offered resistance, but the creatures seemed to know their way. They wound farther and farther back through the almost impassable underbrush, lifting Kyle over dead trees and pulling him under other entanglements.

His face was cut open by branches and briars. The blood ran down his cheeks and dripped off his chin. He couldn't wipe it away.

He wondered if anyone besides these creatures had passed this way in a thousand years. Perhaps they were prehistoric, ancestors of man, some forgotten missing link.

He began to cry, helplessly. He didn't want to die here. He wanted to go back and find Corey alive and rekindle their dreams of going to California.

In the blink of an eye everything had fallen apart.

He stumbled again in the brush, but the creatures did not let go. They pulled him onward until some of the branches parted. There they moved into a partial clearing. He prayed they were about to stop. He was breathing heavily and about to freeze as well.

He wanted desperately to get warm, or die. Either would do fine.

The creatures parted some branches and shoved him forward instead. He stumbled and dropped to his knees. At first he thought the monsters had already moved in front of him. Then he realized he was looking at a new group of creatures just like the three at his back.

They peered at him with wild eyes, noses twitching as they uttered grunts of excitement.

Honeycutt slipped away from the jail a few minutes after shift change and took the stairs down to the sheriff's office.

He knew Cormick Holt was the detective on duty that night, and Holt was a guy who could be trusted.

Things were going slowly, so he found Holt in the coffee room thumbing a copy of *Cheri*.

A toothpick dangled out the corner of his mouth, and he had his alligator-skin boots propped up on the table. He looked up and grinned when he saw the jailer. "What you doin' out of the pens?" he asked.

"I was hoping I'd run into you," Honeycutt said.

Holt swept his feet to the floor and tossed the magazine on the table. "If I ever have a daughter, I hope she don't wind up in one of these," said Holt.

He was about thirty-five but looked younger with neatly trimmed brown hair parted on the side. If he hadn't worn a western shirt and dark-brown slacks, he might have looked like a yuppie with his boyish good looks.

He shifted the toothpick to the opposite corner of his mouth and rested one hand on the revolver strapped to his belt.

161

"You look forlorn, old buddy." Holt seemed too happy to be a cop.

"You ever hear of a guy named Mark Turner?" Honeycutt asked.

"Can't say as I have. Common name. Could be anybody." Honeycutt leaned against the door frame and massaged his forehead.

"What's worryin' you?" Holt asked.

"Nothing."

"You'd have your fat ass in a chair up there at the jail aiming your closed circuit monitor at the lady's shower if nothin' was wrong," Holt said.

"It's probably nothing," Honeycutt amended. "Just the old rumor."

"What old rumor?"

"The one about the Circle or whatever. The justice squad."

"There's been talk of that ever since I been on the force. Fifteen years, buddy. Has to be bullshit."

"Does it?"

"Why wouldn't we know about it otherwise? That's not something that could be kept a secret. Not from other cops."

"Word has always been that members of the squad are sworn to secrecy. Besides, Cormick, who would know how to cover a crime better than a cop? People screw up when they do things and try to hide them, because they don't know the signs that stand out, like a cop does.

"Somebody burns their house down for the insurance; they take all the pictures out. They don't want to lose their memories. They don't know an investigator is going to walk in and notice the frames aren't in the ashes. They try to fake break-ins and shatter the glass from the inside, they—"

"I'm familiar with how a police investigation is conducted," Holt said.

"You get my point."

"So there's potential that something could be covered up. That's always been true. What makes you think now that this is real?"

"Just wondering. This fellow Turner was found dead on a railroad track. Why would a man lie down on a railroad track?"

"Could'a been stoned."

"Or it could be he was put there to cover something up, make his death look like an accident."

"Can you prove anything?"

"Not a damned thing. That's why I thought I'd bring it up to you."

"Like I don't have enough to do?"

Honeycutt looked at the cover of the magazine.

"Tex left that around," Holt explained.

"I don't know what to tell you, but the rumor's there. You know the old story. Men from the various departments in town, sworn to secrecy and to carry out the executions of those who escape the law."

Holt sat back in his chair. Honeycutt had set the wheels in motion in his head. He bit down hard on the toothpick. The look on his face confirmed that he'd had the reaction the big jailer had anticipated.

"I've got to get back to the jail," Honeycutt said.

"Right. Get me all hot and bothered and leave."

Holt propped his feet up again, but he left the magazine closed. It wasn't easy, but Honeycutt had turned his thoughts, causing him to lose interest in the nubile bodies of the *Cheri* "tarts."

He had the sinking feeling the jailer was right, and if the suppositions were facts, Holt knew his conscience wouldn't let him rest until he did something about it.

163

Chapter 15

Holt slipped a fresh cigar between his lips as he walked into the dispatcher's station.

Tex Olsen was on the desk.

"You look tired," Holt said.

Tex, a big blond guy who'd been with the sheriff's office ten years, rubbed a hand across his features. "Nights go on forever," he said.

Most of the men hated to take their turn at the dispatcher's desk. It was an endless stretch which alternated between boredom and aggravation. The weird calls came in between midnight and dawn, the paranoid reports and the bullshit that was enough to run you crazy. If they could get to a phone, the inmates over in the mental institution would come up with some really strange complaints like being possessed by demons and seeing dead men walk.

"Get you some coffee," Holt said. "I'll answer the phones for a while."

"You don't have any crimes to solve?"

"Not unless one of the line units requests me, and that don't look likely. Fights between good ole boys don't call for Sam Spades like me."

Stretching his arms out, Tex yawned, his large mouth opening like a canyon. "Maybe we ought to hook up the VCR and check out some of those videos in the evidence room, the ones they got in the raid," he suggested.

"I went over them with the D.A. already," Holt said.

"Any good?"

"Some of it's hot."

In Riverland Parish, hard-core videos could not be sold or rented. When a store owner was caught providing

164

them under the counter, the cases made the papers, so the sheriff always had his eye out for such opportunities.

The men usually scanned the confiscated tapes when they rolled around.

"Go have a look," Holt said. "Take your time; hell, there's nothin' happenin'."

Tex climbed out of his swivel chair and yawned again. "Yell if you need help."

Holt replaced him in the chair. "Hey, Tex."

"Yeah."

"Stay away from the one marked 5-A. Make you sick."

"What is it?"

"Acrobatic guy, you know. His own. . . ." Holt opened his mouth and stabbed a thumb at it.

"Thanks for the warning."

"On 5-E there's a redhead you won't believe."

He watched the dispatcher disappear down the hall. A moment later a line buzzed. He had to send a unit over to check out a report from a little old lady who'd seen a suspicious looking black man outside her window.

When he had that taken care of, Holt spun the chair around and used his heels to pull himself across to the computer terminal. With it he could access a nationwide computer database that contained almost limitless information about criminals and their activities.

He looked down the hall to make sure Tex was still busy and then ran his fingers quickly across the keyboard.

The flashing cursor obeyed his request, and a moment later he had paper spitting through the printer.

He frowned as he looked over the information before him. Something was wrong.

He sat down again and made his request of information once more, his forehead still wrinkled with a frown.

Jag found Deb waiting up for him when he got off work. Her eyes showed the signs of her tears, but she looked no less determined.

"You talked to Mrs. Templeton?" he asked.

She nodded. "No word from her son. Even a killer on the run would call his mother, wouldn't he?"

"I think so," Jag said. "It must be an indication that

165

something happened to him, just like with your brother."

"It's very confusing," Deb said. "Honeycutt was no help. There's nobody else to go to. I can't just let that go. I can't."

Jag took her hand and squeezed it gently. His eyes showed he was nervous about what they were facing, but he tried to seem reassuring.

"We'll stay after it," he said. "People know things. It's just a matter of finding the pieces from each one and putting them into place."

She put her arms around his shoulders and rested her head against him. "Can it be done?"

His uncertainty gripped him. He didn't feel confident, but he didn't want to convey a feeling of hopelessness. There had to be a way to find the answers, and he told her that.

"I'm no super investigative reporter," he said. "but we'll keep looking. Something is very wrong, and somehow we'll get to the bottom of it."

She eased back from him slightly, and they looked into each other's eyes. He bent forward, touching her lips with his.

The kiss was hesitant, unexpected and a bit awkward. He was nervous because they had remained businesslike until now, feelings flickering somewhere beneath the surface of their protective facades.

She seemed surprised, yet she did not resist. Her lips parted slightly, and he slipped his arms around her waist, drawing her closer.

He ran his fingers through her hair and then touched her face. He brushed her cheeks with his palms, and her lips parted even farther, admitting him.

When the kiss ended, she bowed her head, resting her forehead against his chest.

"I didn't expect that to happen," she said.

He put his cheek against the top of her head. "I didn't either."

"This isn't why you agreed to let me stay here?"

"No." The accusation shocked him and made him feel strange. "I didn't have an agenda," he said.

"I didn't think so. You just can't tell with men."

"I guess I'm a little . . . naive," he said. "I mean I've

166

been attracted to you from the beginning. I just. . . ."

She tilted her head back again, looking into his eyes once more. "You don't have to say anything," she said. "Just hold me."

They moved over to the couch, sitting down to face each other. She took his glasses and slipped them off his face, then curled her arms around his neck once more and found his lips with hers.

Kyle's evening was far less comfortable. He was pitched onto a bed of damp pine straw and leaves, and his grunting captors covered him with nasty makeshift blankets made from animal pelts only partially or improperly cured.

He lay beneath them, shivering as he watched the monsters shamble back and forth. Their movements were not like those of primates he'd seen on television, yet he could not believe these things were human in any way.

They were too brutal and bestial, eliminating any possibility that he'd been discovered by members of one of those lost tribes like he'd read about in old *National Geographics*.

Each time one of them glanced in his direction or staggered toward him, he shuddered, fearing they were going to tear him apart the way they had Corey, but for the most part they were ignoring him.

He didn't know what they wanted, and that added to his terror. He counted a dozen of them in varying sizes, all seeming to have excessive strength.

From the way they milled about, they did not seem to have any real organization.

Some of them slept on the ground, others in nests carved back in the thicket. They had no houses, no other signs of anything akin to civilization. They were wild.

Most frightening of all was the litter that covered the floor of this mini-clearing, the litter of human bones. They were everywhere, skulls and femurs and ribs, not bleached white but covered with grime and bits of decaying flesh.

Kyle feared the moment his bones would join those, yet in a way he looked forward to it as well. He wanted his torment to cease.

It was actually just beginning.

In Rand's study they gathered. The bar was stocked, but they didn't drink anything. Their expressions were too solemn.

LaFleur leaned against one of the gun cabinets, his rugged features displaying signs of ashen discontent.

"Why are they out of control?" he asked.

"They've never been *in* control," Scarecrow said.

Rand rubbed his beard. "They've gotten bolder. They used to stay back in the woods and not venture far from their hiding places."

"On the last three hunts they've reached the prey before we have," said LaFleur. "I guess that should have been a sign. Before, there was always a chance we'd finish the hunt first."

"It will be all right," Rand said. "What we're doing is too important to let anything stop us."

"We can keep up the hunts," said LaFleur. "But maybe we should go in and kill these things off before they get too dangerous."

"No. They stay," Rand insisted.

"I could get some other fellows in. There's a trooper from up in Monroe who's been wanting to get in on some of this. A guy from Baton Rouge wants to help out too. It wouldn't be the same as hunting criminals, but it would be close."

"They stay alive," Rand reiterated in a louder voice. "If they're killed, everything is ruined. Everything this is about is negated. I want those bastards out there."

LaFleur held up his hands. "Okay. Okay."

"We just have to be careful." He looked at Scarecrow. "We have to make sure Serena doesn't go out there again."

"Done," Scarecrow said. "She sees the danger now. She won't try to slip away anymore."

"And we just won't use that holding spot anymore," Rand said. Earlier they had discovered what was left of Corey's body. "They've learned what's going on."

"Why did they just kill one of them?" LaFleur asked.

"We've just found one set of remains," Scarecrow said.

"The other one's out there probably."

"If it's not, why did they take him?"

Scarecrow shook his head. "I don't know. We don't know what they do. Nobody believes in momo; so nobody's ever done a scientific study."

"I thought you were the expert."

"Being an expert on something nobody knows anything about doesn't take much," the Cajun said.

"They could rip any of us apart," LaFleur said. "You don't have any way of doing something?"

"They're wild. You're talking about things that the Indians didn't understand and the Cajuns didn't like to talk about. Silly as it sounds, let me tell you it's magic, bottom line bad magic."

"Don't give me the hoo doo shit. We know what they are."

"No we don't," Scarecrow said. "Nobody knows what they are but them. That was told to you a long time ago when you decided to play the game and help us bring the bad ones to justice."

"It's starting to get out of hand," LaFleur said.

"You didn't have any trouble when you and your friends were getting to shoot criminals that'd go free otherwise."

"More than criminals are getting killed, dammit."

"That's a price we have to pay," Rand said. "You're in this because you want to clean up the streets a little. I'm in it because of what happened to my wife, and because I want a better world for my daughter. I want a world where the scum have to cower and not the decent people.

"I want them to whisper their rumors when members of their ranks disappear. I want them to shit their pants when they hear they might get off on a technicality. I want them to think twice before they hurt good people. There has to be a penalty. Death isn't enough. They have to know the fear their victims feel. Punishment isn't enough. They have to become victims; they have to become the animals they are, slithering through the woods to get away from us and falling prey to subhuman monsters just like themselves."

He left the room before his anger exploded. Stomping down the hallway, he found Serena at the end of the corri-

169

dor. She was standing with her arms folded, and her eyes were swollen from tears.

"What's going on, Daddy? What happened out there?"

"An animal," he said. "We're in the wilds, honey. You see why I've always warned you. You see why I've stressed to you the importance of caution."

Her jaw seemed set into stone. "I thought we were supposed to be better off here. I'm like a prisoner. What happened to Mama was terrible, but what happened out there, my God, it's unbelievable. What kind of animal did that?"

"All animals are dangerous," Rand said.

He tried to hug her, but she pulled away from him, folding her arms more tightly around herself to keep him away.

"I want to go away from here," she said. "I want to be somewhere there are other people, somebody besides old tutors and body guards."

"That's not wise," Rand said. "There's so much evil. It's going to get better. Then it will be safe for you. Just be patient."

She frowned. "What do you mean it's going to get better?"

"It just will. The world can't go on like it's going. The scum can't continue to rule."

"Daddy, there are always going to be bad people. We can't shut ourselves away and cower. Mama wouldn't want us to do that. She'd want us to go on."

"We're not cowering. Not at all."

"What are we doing, then?"

"You'll see one day. You'll thank me."

"Thank you for what? Making me a spinster? Hiding me away from everything? You treat me like I'm your fucking property."

His hand swept across her cheek before either of them realized what was happening.

She stood frozen for a second, her skin reddening. Then she turned, hiding her tears as she hurried down the hallway.

Rand rushed after her, trying to apologize, but she outran him, entering her bedroom and slamming the door before he could reach her.

"I'm sorry," he shouted, banging his fist against the wood.

She did not respond, and when he tried the knob, he found it locked. He turned, putting his back against the wall and raising a clenched fist to his forehead.

Nothing was quite working like he wanted. He was supposed to be in control. Someone had to take hold of the chaos and try to make order.

It was his responsibility, his duty. Why did so many people want to oppose him? Why couldn't they see?

God had called him, and he had no choice but to obey.

Holt met Honeycutt in the foyer of the jail after checking his gun in a lock box near the elevator doors.

The big jailer looked nervously over his shoulder as he walked from the control booth, but the other jailers weren't paying much attention to him.

"What have you got?" Honeycutt asked.

Holt held up printouts. "I checked this several times. The name is Mark Turner, right?" He kept his voice low.

"That's what the girl said."

"All right, I ran a check on the name. Here's the girl's brother. Must be the one. Florida address, vagrancy and misdemeanor arrests."

"Sounds right."

"All right, this kid has no middle initial."

"So?"

"The first time I tried calling up his file, I got this." He handed Honeycutt the other printout. "Mark T. Turner."

Honeycutt studied the dot matrix lettering. "Alias Gargoyle?"

"Member of the Lucifer's Disciples motorcycle group."

"And a rap sheet a mile long."

"Never convicted of shit."

Honeycutt looked up from the paper, his mouth hanging open. "They got the wrong man." He dropped his hand to his side, the paper rustling as it brushed against his uniform. "It's real."

"That's shore as hell what it looks like," said Holt.

"Then they realized their mistake and instead of just letting him disappear. . . ."

"Yep. A motorcycle boy might just hightail it and never be heard from again. Happens all the time and people don't think too much of it. You never know when somebody's going to come looking for a wanderer, though. Better to have some kind of explanation ready. They put his body on a railroad track, the kind of fate you might expect an old boy with a history of drunk and disorderly to meet, passed out on the ties."

"Clean out your files of his presence and you've got the perfect crime," Honeycutt agreed.

"Nobody does it like cops do it," said Holt.

"How do we know which cops?"

"Good question. It's kind of hard to trust anybody."

"We could go straight to the sheriff."

"Yeah, he'll want this exposed. It'll look good come election time."

"State police, then?"

"How do we know some of them aren't in on it?"

"You're saying it's just me and you?"

"Looks that way, Chuck Wagon."

Honeycutt ran a hand over his face. "I've got a sick wife, Holt. If anything happens to me, who's gonna take care of her?"

"Somebody's got to do somethin'. 'Less you want this just to go on."

The jailer was silent for a moment, and his face grew solemn. He swallowed, thinking it all over. "That girl's brother was innocent."

"That's the problem with lynching," Holt said. "It's not an objective practice."

Honeycutt looked over his shoulder again, making sure he wasn't being observed from the booth.

"I'm in," he said. "I don't know what we're going to do, but you're right. We've got to do something."

Holt lit a fresh cigar. "Grab yourself a little sleep after shift change. I'll be by your house around nine. We'll play it by ear." He walked back to the check box and retrieved his gun, then moved to the exit door.

Honeycutt walked back into the booth and buzzed him out. Then he sat down and stared through the glassed partition, not seeing anything.

Chapter 16

Early the next morning, Jag drove Deb over to the newspaper office.

It was too early for the editors to be on hand, but they found Joan Frazier, the main keeper of the morgue, already at her desk. She always arrived well in advance of her assistant.

She was clipping copies of the morning's edition for filing.

"Are you the one that messed up my file on Melo Templeton?" she asked.

It was the first time Jag had seen her since he'd paid his night visit to the file cabinets. He nodded humbly.

"Try to watch how you put things back," she cautioned.

Her tone was only partially serious. She got up from her desk as Jag introduced her to Deb.

Joan's brow furrowed slightly. "What brings you in here this early?" she asked.

Jag nodded toward the small terminal in a corner of the room. "The courthouse computer can look up criminal records, can't it?" Jag asked.

Joan glanced at it over her shoulder. "It's tied in to all the public records. It's done with phone lines. If you had the equipment, you could do it from your house."

"Suppose I didn't have the equipment?"

"It could be done here."

"On election night I had to work at the computer. They had returns channeled through it. Would it be much different?"

"You could figure it out with a little help."

They walked over to the terminal, and Jag settled into

the swivel chair facing the screen.

The orange letters glowed on the black background, asking for a password.

"What do I log in?"

"Typist."

"What?"

"It works. Don't question it."

He typed in the word typist, then followed her instructions for tying in to the courthouse.

The unit in front of him dialed the phone number, the tones beeping in quick succession followed by a hiss like the sound of air escaping a cave as the link was established.

"Now, what do you want to check?" Joan asked.

"We want to check the record on a man named Mark Turner," Jag said. "This is different from the city police files, right?"

"Yeah, they have a separate computer for their records. It's based at city hall or something. We can't get into it from here. At least not with the access we have set up."

"This would have somebody who was arrested here in town, wouldn't it?" Jag asked.

"It should."

"How do I call it up?"

"Type in his name. Address if you have it. Last name first."

Jag hammered it in, then Deb gave him the Florida address.

A moment later the screen produced a brief listing on Mark Turner, arrested in Aimsley for public drunkenness 10-5-88. No other information was available.

"That means he hasn't been tried yet," Joan said. "The file is still open. Could be charges were dropped. If he's not convicted or he doesn't do anything else, that could sit there forever."

"How would this have gotten into the computer?"

"Probably punched in at the courthouse when he went for a bond hearing or whatever court proceedings they do. I'm not sure about all that. It could have been several days after he went through that they entered this into their records. They're backlogged over there just like we are. They're short-handed because of the economy just

174

like everybody."

Jag turned to Deb. "That might explain why it wasn't wiped out of this system when they started the cover-up," he said.

"Right. It was late being typed in. When they cleaned the police computer, they probably checked the court records too. It wasn't there yet, and they never looked back afterward to see if it had been added."

"Even cops don't commit perfect crimes," Jag said.

"What are y'all talking about?" Joan queried.

"A story. Hush, hush," Jag said.

"You'll need me again," Joan warned.

"That's why you're indispensable," Jag agreed.

They walked out the morgue door into the hallway.

"We know what they did. We know how they did it. We just don't know who, and we don't know how to get them," Deb said.

"Frustrating," Jag agreed.

His feelings were in turmoil. He'd been trying to keep his thoughts locked on the investigation alone, but he couldn't completely keep his mind off Debra.

"How can we do this? We'd have to crack the whole system," she said.

They walked along the corridor, their shoes echoing off the tiles. The early morning emptiness seemed almost symbolic.

"We have to keep bumming around and hoping for a break," Jag said.

"If we keep at it, they'll figure out we're after them. They'll kill us. Aren't there some law enforcement authorities we could go to?"

"With what? We've got nothing that's proof, nothing that would stand up in court. One court record is not enough. We can't prove the other records were wiped. We can't prove Mark's body was dumped on the railroad track."

She stopped walking, staring at him. "No one would believe us?"

"We're just a couple of kids," Jag said. "When you get right down to it. They'll laugh, and these guys will go right on doing what they've been doing."

"It's crazy. They won't hesitate to kill us. They've al-

175

ready killed people."

"It's a risk. We just have to watch our backs and try to find more pieces to the puzzle."

"Why are you willing to keep this up, Jag?"

He had to think about his answer. "Maybe because of last night. Maybe because I don't have anything else to lose. My career is going nowhere; my life is going nowhere. It's a make or break thing. If there's a chance for me to be anything as a reporter, this is it, and if there's a chance for you and me, if there's anything there besides an effort to soothe each other's pain, we've got to solve this first."

She looked at him, blinking, surprised. "A chance?"

He bowed his head. "Just a thought. This is a weird time, not the time to try and figure out—"

"I understand," she said. "It's a confusing world. I wasn't going to think about this either. Not now."

"It can wait," Jag said. "Like we said, we've been thrown together. It's intense. We need to concentrate on finding something out first."

He realized his heart was pounding at a more rapid beat. There was no real explanation for his feelings. He had entered into all of this seeking refuge from the pain of Caroline, but things had spiraled into something completely different.

He was drawn to Debra because of her strength as well as her vulnerability. It was nice to feel that she needed him even though she had come so far alone.

In a way, she allowed him to feel he had some purpose. If he could help her, regardless of the story that would result, he was more than just a naive little journalist who typed obits all the time.

What had he really done in his life otherwise? Spent four years in school reading books and writing papers? What did that really mean in the long run?

This investigation was a risk, but it could be a calculated one.

"We put ourselves on the line and hope for the best?" Debra asked.

"Yeah. We follow it through, and we find a way to protect ourselves."

"Like what?"

"We put our notes together, get a letter ready so that if anything happens to us, someone will have a record. We know your brother was here; we can prove that now. If somebody's got a letter in hand, and we die under strange circumstances, or disappear, it will get the ball rolling."

"Let's just hope it doesn't come to that," Deb said.

"Yeah, let's hope real hard."

"Tonight, then?"

"Yeah, after I get off work. We'll talk it through."

"Into the fire," Debra said.

"Right."

He held her and kissed her, enjoying the touch of her skin.

The houses on the east side of Aimsley were not run-down. Built inexpensively under federally subsidized programs, they had never been elegant, only functional.

Holt drove along the street, tapping his hands against the steering wheel as Honeycutt huddled on his side of the cab. The heater in the detective's pickup didn't have much effect.

Although Holt seemed lively, his eyes were sunken, and he did not appear to have slept. Stubble shadowed his face, but he was wearing a clean shirt.

He'd spent a couple of hours sifting files and going through computer material before picking up Honeycutt, who had dozed for a brief time before putting on civilian clothes and meeting Holt in front of his house.

When Holt parked the car in front of the house on Appleton Street, they both turned up their coat collars in preparation for the wind.

"We're gonna have a long winter," Holt said. "Long and cold."

"It's not supposed to be like this in Louisiana," Honeycutt said.

Side by side they moved up the walk and stood together on the front steps. Holt knocked, and about three minutes passed before Kevin Martin showed up wearing only a pair of faded blue jeans.

He was a weight lifter, and his bare shoulders were massive. His short, blond hair was messy from sleep, but his blue eyes were piercing.

"What's going on?" he asked with a yawn. He was about twenty-three and one of the newest men in the Aimsley Police Department.

Holt had met him only a time or two, passing at crime scenes which wound up on the jurisdictional lines between sheriff's office and police department.

"Semi-official," Holt said. "Mind if we come in?"

"Sure."

They walked into his living room. It was cluttered with crumpled beer cans and other fallout. Newspapers and pizza boxes were strewn across the couch, and several videotapes were piled on an end table.

A sound of movement from the bedroom indicated Martin was not alone. Honeycutt glanced over at Holt, who gave a nod.

"Friend in here?" Honeycutt asked.

"Uh, yeah."

Honeycutt walked down the hall and knocked on what looked like the bedroom door.

It cracked open to reveal a short girl wearing a red sweat shirt and sweat socks. Her blond hair fell to her waist.

"Is something wrong?" she asked.

"Nothing much," Honeycutt said, playing on her apparent fear. "We're associates of Mr. Martin's. If you wouldn't mind slipping on something, you and I can wait in our truck where it's warm while my friend has a little talk with Mr. Martin."

She looked past Honeycutt's bulk to the end of the hallway where she could see Martin. "Kevie?"

"Go ahead," he said. "Police business."

She closed the door a moment and emerged again wearing jeans and a denim jacket. Honeycutt realized she was only about nineteen. Impressed with police officers and uniforms no doubt.

He took her arm and guided her along the hallway.

"What's going on?" she asked.

"Police business, ma'am," Honeycutt repeated, doing his best Jack Webb.

Holt tossed him the truck keys as he led the girl through the front door.

178

When they were gone, Holt turned to Martin, who had folded his arms across his massive chest. The muscles rippled beneath his skin.

"What is this?" he asked. His words were emphatic. He had a certain amount of respect for elder officers, but he didn't intend to take any crap.

Holt put his cigar between his teeth and grinned. "Think back a few months," he said. "You're on patrol with another officer. It's training time or you'd be in a car alone."

"I spent a month cruising with other officers. That's how they break rookies in. We trade off with experienced officers."

"I know that. You know, it's amazing what kind of information is floating around in computers and files if you take the time to look. Some things just don't get purged. Isn't that the computer jargon? Purged? Sounds like what happens when you get a dose of castor oil. Anyway, you were riding with Glen Long the night I'm thinking about.

"He's a mean sumbitch, isn't he?" Holt observed.

"He's rough, yeah. You have to know him," Martin defended.

"People tell me that a lot. Anyway, this night I'm thinking about you go on a call downtown. Somebody's seen a drunk staggering around. Remember?"

"Common call. Those run together." His eyes were beginning to display his concern.

"This guy, real bum. You could tell when you spotted him."

"What's this all about?"

"I'm just looking into something, something you know about, a little about anyway."

His eyes grew much wider now. "I don't know what you're talking about."

Holt grinned and nodded. "That's the problem. You do know. When I get through with you, you'll fool around and call everybody you know to tell them I was here asking questions. I can't afford that."

He raised his foot and snapped a kick into Martin's right leg just below the kneecap.

With a groan, the kid sank to his left knee, clutching the injured spot with both hands.

"That won't do any major damage," Holt said. "That's just to let you know we're playing hard ball here, okay?"

"Shit, you've shattered my kneecap."

"I gave you a fucking bruise. Shut up or you're gonna be whining about your balls, and they bruise real easy. Take it from somebody who's been kicked there."

"What the hell do you want, man?"

Holt walked over and grabbed a handful of Martin's hair, lifting his head up so that they were staring into each other's face.

"Think of this as a learning experience. This is the way we used to interrogate prisoners."

"Let go, man."

The smoke from the cigar curled up between them in a gray haze. "I have to have your cooperation," Holt said. "You see, I know what's going on, and I know you've been let in on it. You're the new man and the inner circle filled you in, offered you a shot because you're the type."

"Shot at what?"

"The swamp, asshole. You're in on it up to your ears."

"Not me. They told me about it, but I haven't gone with them."

"Yet. Sounds like a good idea, doesn't it? Killing off some scum?"

"They're doing society a favor."

"Right. Forget about everything and just string 'em up."

"Well hell, the courts let them go."

"The courts have to because fucks like you screw things up. The wires got crossed on Mark Turner. Ring a bell? You ever think any of those people might be innocent? He was just a vagrant, and your friends killed him and made his death look like an accident."

"Innocent? Don't bullshit me. They said he was a motorcycle gang member."

"That's the *other* Mark Turner. You know who you helped kill? A medical student who went off the deep end when his girlfriend got killed. He was wandering the South to put his life back together. His only crime was being upset because somebody he loved died, and you were a part of it. Fuck you, does that bother you at all? Does that make you feel good, Kevie?

"You're a big tough cop, big hero, aren't you? Your

little girlfriends get off on your big arms and your uniform, and you see yourself as some kind of knight. You and your friends are above the law. Is that it? Is that why you feel so good about Mark Turner?"

"I didn't know, man."

"Tell that to the judge. He'll nod a little before he ships you to Angola. You know what they're gonna do down there when they find out you're an ex-cop?"

"I'm not going to Angola."

"Don't think so? By the time some ACLU lawyers representing the families of the dead criminals get all this into the press? Somebody's going down for it. Not the guys close to retirement. Not the ones who've got commendations and fast-draw trophies and feathers in their caps from big cases they cracked when they were good cops. And the state boys that are involved? You think they're going to send up a guy with twenty stolen vehicle recovery stickers on his unit?

"It's gonna be your shiny white ass that they throw in there. You think you're tough, but down there, there's fellows who don't have anything to do but work out. Your muscles ain't gonna mean shit when four or five of those guys get around you.

"It's nice rolling around with teenage tail, buddy. She give you blow jobs? Ever think about what it's like to give one."

"Give me a break, man."

He tried to twist away, and Holt gave him a thumb jab against a pressure point in his neck. "Like the break you gave Mark Turner?"

Martin rolled over in pain, and Holt shoved him onto his back and sat across his chest, placing his knees on the kid's arms.

"Now, if you were to cooperate with me in my little unofficial inquiry here, things might go a little easier on you when I crack this case. And I will because I'm not scared of any of your friends. Not any from my department, not from yours, not from the state. Why? 'Cause I ain't got shit to lose."

Martin was panting, trying to get a breath that Holt wouldn't allow. He pressed his legs against the kid's sides, refusing to allow his ribcage to expand.

181

"What do you want me to do?"

"I want names. Everyone you know."

"I just know a few."

"That's better than none. I want a place too. Where is the swamp?"

"I don't know. They haven't told me that yet."

"All right, let's remember that you're keeping this to yourself. You give this away, I'll kill you, and you know that's right."

"Yeah." It was a croak.

"If I don't kill you, I will see that you go down to Angola if you squeak at all."

"Okay, man. You've got me."

"Now let's go with those names."

The heater had turned the interior of the car stuffy, and the smell of exhaust fumes filled the air. The cold air that rushed in when Holt opened the door came as a relief for Honeycutt.

"You can go back in there and see your friend now," Holt told the girl. "Does your mama know where you are?"

"She doesn't care," the girl said.

"Neither does he," Holt muttered under his breath as he climbed into the front seat to take her place.

"What'd you get?" Honeycutt asked.

"Names."

"You're not worried about him talking?"

"He'll talk. It'll just take him a while. I gave him a pretty good scare."

"Damn, Holt, you're gonna get us killed."

"We're fine. We just have to be conscious of the time. We don't have long to work."

"What about the reporter and Turner's sister?"

"Let them keep doing what they're doing for a while. They might be able to help us, stir somethin' up."

"They could be in danger."

"It's a dangerous life."

"These names you've got. What do we do with them?"

"See what we can get on them. He only knew city people involved."

"Who do we concentrate on?"

"Scott Early, Idal Taylor, Winston Clark and Matt LaFleur. Which one of those would be a ringleader, do you think?"

"LaFleur," Honeycutt said without hesitation.

"See. We agree. This is almost too easy," Holt said.

He adjusted his cigar in his teeth and shoved the gearshift to jerk the truck forward.

Orson Hart's family had lived in the house at the edge of the woods for fifty years. His sister had been born in one of the rooms, his mother had passed away in another, and over the years many people had visited. The place had been renovated and remodeled and repaired a dozen ways, but it was still home. To him anyway.

Susie didn't come to visit much since she and her husband had moved to Dallas. That left Orson and his daddy to share the old place. It was too big for the two of them and a bit farther from town than Orson preferred, but neither of them wanted to sell. The place was too full of memories for both of them.

Orson was forty. He'd been a postal delivery man for fifteen years, and he'd grown accustomed to his life.

He rose early, went to the post office and collected his deliveries, then made his route. He was always through by noon, and he made it back to the house a little before one for lunch with the old man.

Walter Hart was seventy-one, and his age was beginning to show on him. His face was grizzled, and his hair, although not actually gray because of the oil he used to keep it slicked back, was thinning at the crown of his head. Unlike Orson, who was heavy-set, Pop was thin, gaunt now as age overtook him.

He always sat in the living room smoking his usual Marlboro when Orson came home. Orson felt guilty about purchasing cartons of cigarettes for the old man, but Walter was quick to point out he didn't have many years left. "Might as well make the time I've got enjoyable," he said. "No need to try to break nasty running habits when you're almost in the end zone."

Orson was afraid he was going to walk into the house

one afternoon and find the old man slumped over and unmoving. Since he was on the route, there was no one for Pop to call for help if he got ill. The nearest neighbors were too far off, probably the Rand fellow in the big house on the other side of the wood, too far for anyone to do any good even if the old man made contact.

Orson had recorded the thoughts about that a dozen times in his diary. After lunch, that was his habit. He'd never married, had never met the right woman, so he passed his time in quiet ways.

For a time he'd tried stamp collecting. It seemed a natural hobby for him except that it failed to excite him the way it did the other people in the stamp club the postmaster sponsored. He'd gone to their meetings awhile, almost hoping to meet a nice woman; but nothing had panned out, and he'd tired of talking about cancellation dates and first day of issue stamps. It was just too much like a carry over of work.

About five years ago, he'd taken to keeping the diary. He wrote in spiral notebooks he bought at Eckerd's Drug beside the post office. He usually got the kinds sectioned for five subjects. They lasted longer, and he wrote quotes he liked—either his own or those from William Blake or Walt Whitman—on the colored dividers.

Nobody knew he kept the diaries, just as no one had an idea he read the poetry in the textbooks left over from Susie's college days. He'd found them in the attic one day while storing some of his mother's things, and he'd been inspired to try his hand at some poems of his own.

He'd soon learned he wasn't suited for dealing with meter and rhyme, but he did like setting his thoughts on paper. It made him feel almost like a schoolboy again, sitting by his window and looking out at the forest as he scribbled things about the day's work, about his mother or Susie or about his father's declining days.

He made notations about people like Joyce Garrison, the window clerk he never had the nerve to ask out. With his near-bald head and wire-rimmed glasses, he didn't feel attractive enough for love. Once maybe, but not now.

Sometimes at night, when he couldn't sleep, he'd get up and scribble more, laments about unrealized dreams or thoughts about his school days.

He'd filled up pages recalling Jenny Lawson, the sweetheart of his senior year, his date to the homecoming dance who'd left him by that summer. She'd married a fellow from Bossier City and eventually had four children.

Somehow setting down the little lagging pains from the past helped him deal with the regrets.

He walked into the house, thinking about what he might write this afternoon.

Lunch was from McDonalds, a couple of McDLTs. His father liked them because they included tomatoes. The old man loved tomatoes.

Orson walked over to the table where Pop was sitting with the *Aimsley Daily Clarion* spread out in front of him.

"How's it going, Pop?"

"Not bad." His voice was coarse and low, his throat tortured by the cigarettes.

"Anything going on?" Orson asked. He didn't get the paper until evening when his father had finished reading every line.

"Paper don't have anything in it," said the old man.

His father's hobby was criticizing the paper's quality, finding fault even though he'd be lost if it ever failed to arrive.

"Got people missing nearby. A trailer not more than a mile from here."

"They'll probably turn up."

He opened the containers that kept the lettuce and tomato away from the hot meat to prevent wilting until time to eat them and began putting the sandwiches together.

Pop stuffed some French fries into his mouth and shook his head. "Whatever's out in those woods got 'em," he said.

For a while now Pop had been seeing things in the forest. He claimed that while he sat on the back porch during the day he sometimes saw things, manlike creatures, stomping around amid the trees.

He didn't have any other hallucinations, but Orson still grew concerned every time the old man started claiming he'd sighted the mormos.

His father had always been a strong, level-headed man. It hurt to hear him discuss such odd visions.

"There's nothing out there, Pop."

"Oh, yes there is. Mark my words. There's something.

185

We didn't used to think they were real, but I know better now. I probably better load up my huntin' rifle."

"It's old, Pop. It probably won't even shoot."

"Well, we need to do something. For protection. You hear?"

Orson shoved the hamburger across the table. "Eat up, Pop. You need your strength. Don't worry about the monsters. They'll go away."

Chapter 17

Jag grabbed a sandwich on the way to work and was eating it at his desk when Breech found him.

He'd just stuffed a large bite into his mouth, and a fragment of lettuce saturated with mayonnaise dripped out the corner of his mouth.

"Sorry to disturb your lunch," Breech said. "Try not to get any of that into the computer."

"Sorry," Jag mumbled through the food.

Breech ignored the remark. "I'm about to go to lunch myself. I'm working a split shift, so you need to man the phones for a while. Everybody's gone. Walden's out, and Nora is off doing whatever Nora does. Just take messages, Jag. If you get a hold of something you can't handle, I'm on a beeper. Just page me. Don't get in over your head on anything."

"I'll keep an eye on things," Jag promised.

Breech walked back to his desk and spotted a stack of papers. Picking them up, he walked back to Jag.

"Take care of these obits too," he said, dropping them on Jag's desk.

A half hour later Jag had finished his sandwich and the obits, and the newsroom was quiet except for the almost inaudible hum of the computers. Even the police scanner was silent.

Jag sat at his desk rereading the obituaries in order to spot any overlooked mistakes that might draw Breech's ire. It also helped to relieve the boredom.

He didn't want to think of Caroline. Debra kept infiltrating his thoughts. He was frightened of his feelings for her. She would go away when this was over, if they survived it all. She

187

had no reason to stay here, and she had work and friends in Atlanta.

Perhaps he could follow her back to Georgia. He had no reason to linger at the *Clarion*.

He wasn't sure if pursuing her would be wise, or if she would want him to follow her, but it couldn't hurt just to think about it.

It kept his mind off of other things like being murdered by rogue police officers.

An hour later Nora Winters came in, her black dress flapping about her as she hurried toward her desk, cigarette bounding out one corner of her mouth. Her longish black hair was wavy and hung in tangles from the wind.

"Jag, be a dear," she said. "Get me a cup of coffee and then keep the fucking phones off my back while I write this story."

She handled the city beat and had probably been out giving councilmen hell. She frequently nailed them on oversights or other questionable conduct, so the city stayed in some sort of controversy if she was given half a chance.

Jag got up and fetched her coffee, glad to have something to do. When he got back, the phone at the editor's station was ringing. He delivered Nora's coffee and then snatched the receiver from its cradle, settling into Breech's chair as he answered.

"Is this the newspaper?" the caller asked.

"Yes it is," Jag replied.

"The *Daily Clarion*?" It was an old man's voice.

"Yes, sir."

"I've been reading that paper forever," said the voice.

"Yes," Jag said. "What can I do for you, sir?"

"I want to know when you're gonna do a story on the momo."

"What, the swamp monsters?"

"Yeah."

"I don't know if we have any plans for anything like that," Jag said, glancing at Nora and rolling his eyes.

"Well, you ought to. I've seen them."

"Yes, sir."

"I have. Out in the woods behind my house. My son thinks I'm crazy, but it's true."

"Where do you live?" Jag asked.

"South of town. Out near the swamps."

"That's where the people disappeared?"

188

"They lived in a trailer down the road from me."

"My boss said there were legends about the mormo living out there."

"It's true, boy. They've always been there."

"What are they?"

"Swamp men. They're wild."

"What do they look like?" Jag asked.

"They're covered with this stuff, green, brown, gray. They look like the swamp."

Camouflage jumpsuits perhaps? Jag picked up a pad and began to scribble. "When do you see these things? Mr. . . ."

"Hart. Walter Hart. They come out in the evenings. I've seen them other times."

"Have they ever tried to bother you?" Jag asked.

"They've looked at me. They've never attacked."

"But the legend is that they are cannibals."

"That's the legend," said Hart. "Eat people so that there's hardly nothing left for anybody to find."

That cut into Jag's thoughts. "You mean they'd leave no trace or remains that were badly mutilated."

"Well, of course they would, mostly. Not always."

"Do you ever see anybody else in your woods, Mr. Hart?"

"Regular people?"

"Yes."

"Ever' once in a while you see hunters, guys riding horses sometimes. They're friends of this Nicholas Rand. You know him? Fellow that owns these woods. I don't hunt anymore myself. Not safe with all these momo things out here." The statement almost made Jag laugh, but in spite of the old man's craziness, he experienced an eerie feeling, as if there might some truth in the words, truth that somehow had a bearing on the investigation.

He got the old man's address and phone number before hanging up. As he got up from the desk, he noticed Nora had paused from her typing.

"What are you up to?" she asked.

"Holding down the fort."

"Breech giving you shit?"

He nodded. "Pretty much."

"Don't take any crap off him."

"I try not to."

"Stick with it all, Jag. It gets better around here after a few months."

189

"I've been here a few months."

"Time. You'll get better assignments. Once they decide they're not going to scare you off, they stop trying to fuck you around."

He held up his notebook. "Speaking of that, you ever hear of a guy named Walter Hart?"

"Pop Hart? He's an old guy that lives down in the swamp. He calls us all the time to tell us things he's seen on television. Everybody here has taken his calls at one time or another. His son's a postman. When the son's not watching him, Pop gets on the phone. I hate to think what the guy's phone bill will be like if Pop ever discovers 1-900 numbers."

"Hours on the party line?"

"No doubt. What'd he tell you about today?"

"He's seeing swamp men."

"Bayou bigfoots?"

"Something like that."

"That's new even for him."

"What does he report, UFOs?"

"He's always up to something. No telling. Don't put any stock in what he says."

"Right." Jag tore the notes off his pad and folded them before slipping them into his pocket.

Debra found Father Larson in the church rectory when she returned. He sat back in his desk chair and offered her his warm smile. A pile of correspondence lay in front of him, but he didn't seem to mind being distracted.

"Would you like coffee, Debra?"

She smiled back. "No thanks. My nerves are frayed enough without the caffeine."

"Any satisfaction about your brother?"

"We think we know some things. We just have to find a way to prove them. It could be dangerous."

"The Lord will protect you," the priest assured.

"I hope so. We'll need it."

He laced his fingers together in front of him. "What is it you have to prove?"

"Do you know much about local legends, Father?"

"Like what?"

"The swamp?"

"I'm familiar with many of the stories told in these parts. I

190

grew up in Avoyelles Parish. There's a great deal of oral tradition. Is there some particular swamp?"

"This one has to do with the disappearance of prisoners."

He raised his eyebrows. "Ah." He was silent for a moment.

"Do you know anything?" she asked.

"A few years ago I did some counseling with some prisoners. They spoke of it, but I was under the impression that went back a number of years. I didn't think it was something that existed today."

"How far back?"

He twisted his lips. "I suppose the forties or fifties. My impression, I guess. Those were different times. Times before so much attention was given to individual rights. Criminals were treated much more severely back then, I believe. It *was* a little before my time."

Deb smiled. "Before all our times."

"You suspect something like that happened to your brother?"

"Possibly. Very possibly."

The wrinkle that formed across his forehead indicated genuine concern. "That's distressing, and it could be dangerous for you."

"I know, Father. My friend and I are trying to be cautious."

"I will keep you in my prayers," he said, his slight Cajun accent deepening to its true intonation. Debra had hardly noticed it before. She decided he was sincere.

At his urging, she promised to keep in touch with him and to come by and see him again.

As she bid him her farewell, she hoped the prayers would do some good.

Terry Nielson had a face that made him look as mean as an alligator poacher. He didn't look bad; he bordered on handsome, but there was something in his expression and the intensity of his eyes.

In contrast, his manner was gentle and polite, at least for a cop.

The positive side of the misconception was that the intense look served its purpose in scaring criminals he was shaking down and getting waitresses to bring his meals on time.

He was sitting in a corner booth at a Shoney's having a steak when Holt and Honeycutt found him.

191

"We want to talk to you about an aggravated 34:14," Holt said, sliding into a seat across from him.

"34:14s are bad," the city detective said. "Especially when they're aggravated." He grinned and extended his hand across the table to shake Holt's. "What have you been up to, bud?"

"Not much of anything. You know Honeycutt here, one of our jailers?"

Honeycutt sat down and shook Nielson's hand also.

"You like being a detective?" Holt asked.

Nielson had only been off the line for a few months. He looked a little out of place in his white shirt, black pants and necktie.

"I can't complain," he said. "Lot more seldom that I have to deal with bullshit."

"There's plenty of it around," said Holt.

"What are you up to? I know you're not out soliciting jokes for your 'Humor and the Badge' collection."

"You do make a good detective." Holt placed his hands flat on the table. "We've got a problem, Terry."

Nielson put down his steak knife. The sudden turn toward the serious had his attention. "What?"

"You're one of the few people I can trust, and I need you."

"I don't understand."

"My department, your department, the State Police Troop, people from all of them seem to be in on it."

"What is it? Some kind of drug deal? Extortion?"

Holt leaned across the table and lowered his voice. "Worse. We think they're killing prisoners."

Nielson leaned back in his chair with a smile. "I thought you were serious for a minute there. We've all heard that rumor. That was a hundred years ago. Hell, they probably did everywhere back then. Times have changed."

"Not completely. Nothing ever gets better. I can't prove it yet, not totally, but it's happening. I know some of the people involved."

"How'd you get names?" he asked, now knowing his friend truly believed the rumors.

"Scared them out of a rookie who's in on it. He'll keep his mouth shut for a while because they'd probably kill him if they knew he talked to me. He may be bright enough to figure that out. We don't have forever on this, though."

"Who have they killed?"

"They usually concentrate on people who are guilty but

can't be convicted. They fucked up and killed an innocent guy recently."

Nielson closed his eyes and pressed a fist against his forehead. "Why'd you want to tell me this?" he asked. "My life is going good. I've made detective. I'm supposed to get married in two months. I don't need this."

"Neither do we," Honeycutt muttered.

"I told you because I thought it was something you'd want to know," Holt said. "We're old fishing buddies. We've talked. You're just like me; you didn't become a cop like some guys do, because they like wearing the uniforms and picking up a little authority."

"Don't start with any lofty crap, man. I'm a cop because that's what I do for a living."

"You could be a carpenter, and you wouldn't want to find out the people were putting up shoddy buildings that would hurt innocent people."

"You don't talk like that, Holt."

"I can when I want to. We both know this ain't right. Something's got to be done. If it's not, it'll happen again."

"Holt, I'm up to my armpits in cases. This is something for the state police criminal investigation division."

"If they try to investigate, everybody will hear them coming a mile off. It's our gig, not anybody else's."

"Hell, aren't you close to pension?"

"Not close enough to make me keep quiet about this kind of thing. This is bad for all of us, bad for any man that ever put in his years on the force. It's not a matter of justice. It's a matter of subverting the whole process. Cops are becoming outlaws, and that doesn't preserve society. Maybe the guys they've killed have been scum, but all this does is help the breakdown even further. This makes the labor of every decent cop in vain."

Nielson shook his head and threw up his arms. "Get off the soap box, Holt. I'll help you."

"You sure?"

"If it'll shut you up."

"Knew I could count on you. Welcome aboard."

Jag got off a little early and paid a visit by the morgue to rifle Joan's desk, finding a key to the map cabinet.

There were all kinds of sheets rolled into neat cylinders. He picked through them until he found a parish map that looked as if it might be useful. Tucking it under his coat, he made his way to the back door without being detected.

Fifteen minutes later, he had the map spread on his coffee table.

"I started thinking about this after I talked to the old man," Jag said, running his hand across the map.

Deb looked over his shoulder at the blue lines that marked the boundaries and other important features of Riverland Parish.

Jag tapped the southern portion of the map. "All of this down here is swamp. That's where the old man that I talked to lives."

"You really think there are wild men out there?"

"I don't know about that, but I'm sure this had to be the swamp area everybody talks about. This is the place where the shallow graves would be. Besides, he's seen men on horseback and that sort of thing."

"Why would they put Mark way up in Bristol Springs if this is their killing and hiding spot?"

"Distraction? They must have had some reason for wanting his body found. Whatever it was, it was placed a long way from their burial ground. Because they *didn't* want the burial ground found."

"What do you think we should do?"

"Maybe we need to check out this Nicholas Rand."

"Is that our first step?"

"No. We'll save that, look into it if there's some indication that he's in on this. First we go talk to this old man. What he's probably seen are cops in green uniforms passing by his house, and his mind has done the rest with legends he's heard.

"If we can find one body, one person that can be identified as a missing prisoner, we'll have something tangible," Jag said.

"You think the old man can help us?"

"Willis mentioned shallow graves. If they are shallow and the old man even knows the basic vicinity, we'll find something."

"When do you want to go out there?"

"First thing in the morning." Jag drew invisible quotation marks in the air with his fingers. "This could be the break we've been looking for."

Chapter 18

The night was settled, still and silent beneath the glow of the moon. Fog covered the world, swirling up through the silver-tinted darkness like the trail of a djinn.

Kyle was dozing when the grunts from the creatures awakened him. He opened his eyes, and in the moonlight he could see them circled around him, wisps of smoke puffing from their nostrils in the cold night air.

Their breathing was harsh, rasping through their throats like a death rattle. He blinked his eyes several times, trying to read something in their expressions, but that was impossible. They were beasts. Their faces showed only snarls.

The only place he could find any sign was in their eyes which peered at him with anger.

"What do you want?" he asked, afraid his sobs were going to start again.

One of the creatures grabbed his arm and dragged him from the nest of leaves.

Stumbling as he got to his feet, he followed the thing over to a tree. There Kyle was pressed back against the bark, and slowly the other creatures began to circle around him in some kind of ritualistic pose.

Kyle looked back at them, fighting his tears even as he felt the sobs quivering in his chest.

Moving forward, two of the creatures began to rip at his clothes, tearing first his shirt and then his jeans away. Next his shoes were removed so that he stood before them completely naked.

The night air bit against his skin, chilling him once more and turning everything to gooseflesh. He began to shiver, but he dared not curl his arms around himself. He let them hang limply at his sides, praying the monsters weren't about to devour him the way they had Corey.

They continued to move around him, circling him in some kind of dance or inbred ceremony.

He closed his eyes, trying not to concentrate on what was happening, but as their grunts continued, he was forced to open his eyes again.

One of the larger ones was standing amid the others, holding a small oak limb which had been gnawed to a sharp point.

Kyle's eyes locked on it as the creature walked forward, raising the instrument carefully in the air. Moans of fear escaped Kyle's throat as he waited for the branch to be driven through his abdomen.

Instead the creature paused at his chest, touching his flesh with the point. Tiny needles of pain shot through him as the stick was dragged through his skin, cutting a thin line deeply into the flesh.

He cried out again and was ignored as several of the creatures swarmed around him to hold his arms in place to keep him from thrashing.

His head twisted from side to side to side as the mutilation continued. He felt the stick forming a circle in his skin, and then within the circle the creatures began to make criss-crossing furrows.

Kyle thought at first it was just an effort to rip him open to make his internal organs accessible. Then he realized the monster was drawing some kind of arcane symbol, carving scars into him.

Blood began to ooze through the open cuts, running down across his stomach like streams of bright red paint dripping from an artist's brush.

His mind began to spin at the thought of what was happening as much as at the sight of his own body being ripped open. His head dipped to one side, but a hand closed around his chin and tilted his face upward again.

The creature in front of him stepped back as if to admire its work, and a loud cry issued through its lips.

The noise lifted through the trees, spreading out through the darkness on the wind.

It seemed to be a cue to the other monsters. They began to stoop to the ground, scooping bits of dirt, mud and clay to smear over Kyle's exposed flesh.

He prayed for a new unconsciousness as they covered him, smearing him with leaves and moss and whatever debris lay around. As he felt himself being decorated, a new fear seized him. Something seemed to be funneling through him, some kind of energy or force. It moved up through his muscles, encircling his very being.

Whatever it was, he realized it was touching his soul, sinking into his mind. His thoughts began to blur. Memory faded. This dark, cold feeling was taking control.

His vision altered, suddenly picking up more in the darkness, and he became more aware of smells and sound in the night.

He tried to think, to make some kind of comparison, but the ability to accomplish that task somehow eluded him.

New strength began to flow through his muscles, power that he had never felt before. He flexed his hands and felt the new response of his reflexes.

All of the fear was gone as his thoughts registered the fact that the pulp was no longer just smeared over him. It had melded with his skin, becoming his pelt.

His mind toyed with that only for a second before accepting it as reality.

Thoughts continued to swirl, giving themselves over to impulse and instinct. Soon only one feeling held his attention. It rose through his consciousness, seeming to throb as it seized control of him.

Hunger.

He felt the hunger.

And he knew it was time to feed.

Pop Hart walked out onto the back porch of his house, listening to the wind whip through the pine branches as he fired a cigarette to life.

Orson had gone to bed, but the old man could not rest. As he dragged the tobacco smoke deep into his lungs, his eyes scanned the shadows that clustered in the forest. He searched for any movement not created by the wind, wondering if the dark figure that had loomed there before had returned.

Nothing emerged from the darkness now. It was all still, and quiet, considering. Not even the sounds of beasts broke the stillness.

He turned and walked back through the sliding glass door into the living room, pushing it closed behind him and sliding the latch into place. Stopping beside the couch, he put out his cigarette in the ashtray there. He thought about trying to go to sleep again and thought better of it.

Dropping down into his armchair, he picked up the remote control and switched on the television. There were only a couple of stations because cable was not available. Reception was limited to what the antenna would pull down.

He had to settle for *Late Night with David Letterman*. It wasn't his kind of show. Pop actually didn't understand the jokes.

Letterman was interviewing Cher tonight. Pop hadn't seen her movies, and it had been a long time since her old television series. He didn't really concentrate on what they were saying, but the sound of their voices kept him company.

He had just started to get drowsy when the static started appearing. At first it was just a few flecks of snow, but soon it developed into horizontal streaks that stretched across the screen accompanied by coarse growls of interference.

With a growl of his own, Pop pulled himself out of his chair. Another limb had fallen on the wire, he guessed.

He walked as quickly as his slippered feet would carry him into the kitchen where he pulled a broom from the rack on the pantry door.

Then he made his way back through the den and out the back door. The wind had picked up, and it bit through the thin fabric of his bathrobe as he moved around the house to the side where the antenna was set in concrete.

Cursing, he began to swat at the branch that dangled from the flat wire stretching down from the antenna.

He became intent on what he was doing, trying to reach the branch that was just out of reach of the broom.

His curses rose on the wind, a loud flurry of expletives.

The racket awoke Orson. He lifted his head off the pillow, groggy and confused. He couldn't figure out where the curses were coming from.

Slowly he sat up, rubbing his eyes for a moment. The room was dim gray, kept from blackness only by the faint moonglow that crept through the curtained windows.

"Dammit, son of a bitch come loose!"

What was Pop doing? Orson scratched his head and swung his feet over the edge of the bed, preparing to stand.

They emerged from the edges of the room, seeming to fade out of the shadows. They must have been there since he'd awakened, but he hadn't noticed.

Now they came forward.

He jumped backward, pressing himself against the headboard of the bed. He had dismissed his father's warnings of the last few years. Now they were too real.

He could see their outlines, could hear their guttural voices. He knew they were the momo the old man had been whispering about.

In an unconscious effort, he pulled the sheet up from the pillow, clutching it against his chest as they converged on him. Before he could resist, the creatures gripped his arms and the calves of his legs, lifting him onto the center of the bed.

They held him there, four of them pressing downward with their weight as he twisted about and bounced from the mattress, arching his back to get free.

Their strength was too great, and he was quickly exhausted, gasping for air as the fifth creature moved toward him.

The moss and leaves tangled across its body seemed fresher than those on the others. The stench of dirt and decaying flesh was not as strong.

As the creature bent over Orson's prostrate form, a sound like weeping issued from its lips, just before it sank its teeth into his flesh.

The postman's cry drowned out all other noises.

Hearing the scream, Pop turned his attention from the antenna and looked back over his shoulder. The cry had come from inside.

With the broom now raised like a weapon, he hurried back around the corner. He'd left the back door open.

Dear God, he had left Orson unprotected. He had to get to his gun.

He ran as fast as his withered form could move through the back door, navigating around the furniture in the living room and down the front hall to Orson's room.

The scene that met his eyes when he burst through the bedroom door was a nightmare. He felt his heart tearing itself apart as his brain locked on the monsters kneeling over Orson's lifeless form.

They paused, their glowing yellow eyes peering toward the door and the source of their interruption. Blood and flesh dripped from their jaws. They looked up at the old man, and their sounds and snarls seemed to be akin to laughter.

Dawn Larson passed the endless hours of her husband's absence in various ways. She watched television broadcast on the satellite dish he had installed; she did crochet like her mother had taught her, producing useless pot holders that would up in drawers; she read thick paperback novels about romances in exotic lands; she talked on the phone with friends; she played with her cat.

None of these activities took the edge off the loneliness. She did not have a job. Gus preferred it that way, because when he was home from his job as a truck driver, he wanted her to be home as well and not off on some kind of shift work.

He didn't understand what it was like spending hours alone in this dream house he had built back in the woods. He liked living out in the quiet where there was nobody to bother them.

It was not unlike the suburban houses her friends lived in, but it was isolated and depressing. There was nothing around her at night except darkness.

She sometimes thought it would drive her insane to

200

spend another minute alone, not because of fear, but because of the same feeling that made hardened criminals hate solitary confinement.

Some days went by in which she had no human contact except for the people on television. She knew the local newscasters by name and in a way thought of them as friends.

She didn't think at twenty-seven this was the kind of life she'd wanted, and she'd been considering getting out more, but she didn't have any idea of where she wanted to go.

Some of the girls tried to get her to hit the night spots with them. They disapproved of the way Gus dominated her, but she couldn't bring herself to go out with them. Going out, even with a group of girls, would be too much like running around on Gus. No matter how he treated her — and she suspected he might have women on the road — she could not compromise herself and be unfaithful to him.

Sitting in her living room tonight, she was battling another round of insomnia. When night and day had little difference, sleep was sometimes a problem.

She had dressed for bed in the pink nightgown that Gus liked because it fell to mid-thigh. Dawn had always been one of the most beautiful girls in Aimsley, and that hadn't changed.

She was slender with the golden-blond hair of a homecoming queen. She didn't look much different now than she had when she'd been crowned ten years before.

She'd just learned the world was not as full of promise as she'd once believed.

As the late movie droned on, she spotted the cat walking under the coffee table, its tail pointing high like an arrow.

Bending down, she lifted it into her arms, pressing it gently against her breasts as she blew into its face.

"Now, now, you don't want to slink around here like a witch's familiar," she said. "You're a good cat."

She brushed her cheek against its fur, making a purring sound to match the sounds the cat made.

"Good baby," she said. "Nice baby."

She walked around the room, rubbing the cat's ears and

stroking its back. The warmth of it, its very presence, helped some, not enough but some.

At the back window she paused to stare out at the darkness. The curtains were not drawn. They were never drawn because there was nothing behind the house but forest, no danger of anyone being out there to look in.

Because the light was on behind her, she saw only her own reflection in the glass; still young, beautiful, but trapped, sealed into her little prison here.

She heaved a heavy sigh and spun around, preparing to walk back toward the couch.

The shattering of the glass also shattered the silence in the room. For a split second she had no idea of what was happening.

Shards pelted against her back and went spinning past her face as well. One sliver sliced a thin cut along her cheek. The cat jumped from her arms, a loud shriek escaping from its lungs as it raced across the room. Before she could run, Dawn felt hands gripping her, thick, massive hands.

The stench that reached her nostrils made her gag, but it did not slow her struggles as she kicked and screamed.

No one except the beasts heard her cry. She was dragged backward, over the jagged glass which ripped furrows through her gown and into her back.

She felt the teeth at almost the same instant. They sank into her neck, severing arteries and veins so that her blood began to spray in a wild spurting cascade.

The glass ripped across her buttocks and down the backs of her thighs, drawing red lines in her calves and tearing open her ankles before she finally cleared the window.

She did not fall to the ground because there were too many arms to catch her, like some hideous dance number in which the leading lady fell back into the grasp of a nightmarish chorus.

The hands closed on her, pulling at her limbs until they separated from her torso.

Her husband had wanted to own her and protect her. Now she was dying, devoured, consumed while he was far away.

Alone.

The car sputtered and croaked as Peter Brenton pulled it over onto the side of the roadway. It was only a couple of years old, but he'd had trouble with the monstrosity of a sedan ever since he'd driven it off the dealer's lot.

The only reason he needed the damned thing instead of a compact was for appearances in his insurance work, and he'd wound up shelling out far more than it was worth in impressing clients.

It couldn't even get him home from Baton Rouge without problems. It had begun to utter mechanical complaints as he'd travelled through Bunkie, and as he'd angled off toward Aimsley from the Rapides Parish line, he'd noticed the thumping under the hood growing steadily worse.

Now it was giving out here in south Riverland Parish where there was nothing. Signs along the roadway periodically warned: "Drive Carefully: Substandard Surface." It was the middle of nowhere if ever such a place existed.

Climbing from the car, he cursed under his breath as he began to roll up the sleeves of his white sports shirt. He'd already loosened the tie because the collar itched at the base of his neatly trimmed beard.

With a loud grunt, he lifted the hood of the car and slipped the bar that held it up into place. In the darkness he could make out little detail in the engine. There were no belts slipped out of place or hoses dangling to offer an immediate answer for the source of the problem.

He turned around and leaned back against the grill. "Wonderful." There might not be another car along here for hours. Maybe not even before daylight.

With another curse, he walked back and climbed in behind the wheel, jabbing the button for the hazard flashers with his thumb. It was pointless to try to walk anywhere, so he might as well just sit until somebody showed up.

Shoving the key back into the ignition, he turned the switch backward to prompt the flow of power so that he could at least listen to the radio. It would drain the battery, but that didn't really matter. He was going to have to have the car towed anyway. At least he wouldn't have to go crazy with boredom in the meantime.

Still swearing, he began to spin the tuning knob, trying to find something interesting on the FM dial.

When he finally settled on the soft rock station out of Aimsley with a DJ named Gibb spinning the easy listening tunes, he turned up the volume and tilted his head against the backrest, closing his eyes in hopes of dozing.

Maybe a trucker would spot his flashers or something. Otherwise when daylight came along he'd figure out what to do.

He was about half asleep when the fog began to settle. It seemed to ease down and nestle in the highway corridor, filling emptiness with its white ethereal body.

With his eyes closed and the music filling the car's interior, Brenton did not notice the figures slowly emerging from the mist.

For a moment they stood at the edge of the forest. Then they parted and began to encircle the car, the yellow light of the flashers illuminating the fog and casting a fire-like glow across their hideous faces.

The jolt of the car awakened Brenton. He shook his head a moment and then stared through the windshield.

The creature was crouched on the hood, its face and hands pressed against the glass where the mud from its body was smeared. Its breath clouded the window.

Brenton kicked about, trying to quickly lock all the doors.

He wasn't fast enough.

The back door on the driver's side, the one he'd opened to toss his briefcase into the back seat, was yanked open.

A second creature slipped in behind him, its arms stretching forward to encircle him and pin him to the front seat. An instant later the hands slid up to his throat, closing and crushing his windpipe.

He began to wheeze and grunt, unable to draw breath.

At that instant the monster on the hood slammed into the windshield, the impact spreading a network of cracks across the glass. Then the driver's door was yanked open, and more hands reached in, tugging Brenton from the car.

His mind was fading fast with the lack of oxygen. Together the creatures carried him into the forest, pausing only when they were several hundred feet from the roadway.

There they dropped him and squatted over his body, tearing into him slowly for their devouring.

On the road, the car's flashers continued their silent effort, orange eyes blinking through the fog, almost invisible to the eye.

The music from the radio continued, but it was faint.

In the forest there was no sound. Brenton was unable to cry out with his crushed throat.

If he had shouted, there would have been no one to hear him.

Chapter 19

The dawn was hazy with the fog that hung like thick smoke over the roadway, but Jag maintained a high speed in spite of the low visibility as he travelled south.

He had reasoned that a postman would have to be up early, so they were taking a chance that Pop had already risen to see his son off and would be awake.

"If he is a crazy old man," Deb said, "how are we going to pick out the information we need from him?"

"We'll do what we can," Jag said. He was staring through the fog, trying to make sure he stayed on the right side of the road.

He had only a general idea of how to find the house, so it was a perfect morning for what they were up to.

"If we can figure out what he's really seen, maybe it'll be beneficial," Jag said. "At least when we're finished, we'll probably know if this is where the killings take place."

He noticed flashing lights ahead, off to his left. He glanced at the parked car as he passed, but he could make out only its outline in the fog.

Locating the house was not easy, but finally, with effort, they spotted a mailbox. Jag had to pull up almost directly beside it to read the Hart name, but the letters were carefully etched into place. Of course a postman would make sure his address was legible.

Jag turned the car down the gravel road beside the box, and the headlight beams cut a path through the fog to the house.

As he pulled to a stop beside the pickup out front, they climbed from the car. The house was dark. At least no light showed in any of the windows visible from the front. Together they walked up the creaking front steps, and Jag pounded his fist against the facing of the screen door.

It brought no response.

On the third try he and Deb looked at each other.

"Maybe the son's already gone," she said.

"I was thinking that was his truck," Jag said. "I didn't expect the old man to own a vehicle."

"What should we do?"

"Let's wake him up."

They walked back down the front steps and moved around the corner of the house.

From there, light was visible. It spilled through a rear window and shone on the ground at the back of the house.

"Maybe he hangs out in a back room and didn't hear the knock," Jag said.

He led the way around the back corner. The patio came into view, streaks of mud marring its smooth stone surface.

The glass door was open wide.

"Something's wrong," Deb said.

They stopped in their tracks, uncertain of how to proceed.

Smears of mud and other dark lines streaked the glass as if children had attacked it while at play. Jag eased his glasses up the bridge of his nose as he stared at the marks.

"Blood?" he wondered aloud.

Deb gripped his arm. "It looks like it."

"I guess we'd better check inside. Somebody could be hurt."

Moving together, like children approaching a vacant house they'd been warned was haunted, they entered the glass door.

Inside they found the room had been ransacked, or vandalized. Mud was smeared across the walls, and thick footprints covered the carpet.

They were scanning the plunder when they saw the arm resting on the floor between the overturned coffee table and the couch. The hand was intact. The rest of it was stripped almost completely of flesh. Only a few tatters clung to the bones, and the ruined streams of tendon and cartilage streamed away from the shoulder where it had been ripped from the socket.

The first inclination was to run, but they were frozen by

the shock of the scene. They stood gripping each other even more tightly.

Jag eased his hands loose from hers and walked over to kneel beside the limb.

"How did it happen?" Deb asked.

"Well, it was ripped out," Jag said.

"Don't touch it."

"Don't worry." His voice was very weak.

He pointed toward the remaining flesh. "It's been gnawed," he said.

"Gnawed?"

Jag looked up at her. "There are teeth marks. Have you ever picked up a piece of meat and bitten into it and then looked at your teeth imprint?"

Slowly, reluctantly, Deb nodded.

"That's what this looks like."

"Jesus and the saints protect us."

He straightened up from his crouch.

"Jag, I'm scared."

"Me too."

"What if they're still here?"

"I don't think so. This place looks like they've cleared out." He took his glasses off and rubbed his eyes. "We need to check the rest of the house."

Reluctantly, Deb agreed.

They moved together again, shivering in unison, still like frightened children.

A demolished table near their feet caught Jag's attention, and he picked up a leg of it to use as a weapon.

Then they proceeded down the hallway.

Finding a light switch, Jag flipped it on. The luminance chased the darkness from the corridor, and they continued forward. He held the weapon high and ready.

About halfway down the hall a small flight of steps led upward.

"It's a split level," Deb observed.

They crept up the steps slowly. With each move, they looked cautiously from side to side, the fear growing worse from the play of imagination.

The shape came hurling out of a doorway without warning. The shriek was like nothing Jag had ever heard, and he began to swing the table leg wildly, ripping a deep furrow in

208

the paneling. Then he turned his attention to the floor where the shape was rushing forward.

The club thudded downward, striking the carpet.

He swung again.

Missed.

Swung.

Missed.

The raccoon darted on past him, past Deb, and disappeared down the steps without looking back.

"They're like little bandits," Deb said in a nervous burst.

"I think that was another hand it had in its mouth," Jag said.

"I didn't think they were scavengers," Deb said.

The unreality of the carnage they were discovering made the words sound facetious, but she spoke seriously.

They eased on along the corridor until they were standing in the doorway of the last bedroom on the hall.

He had never known it before, but Jag was certain that the sick, sweet smell meeting his nostrils was the smell of death.

The faint post-dawn light that slithered through the part in the curtain revealed the messy scene on the bed.

Intestines draped across the posts at the foot of the bed like stretches of yarn left behind by playful kittens. A splatter of internal organs stained the wall behind the bed, and blood was spread across the sheets, the floor and had sprayed onto the ceiling. The carcass at the center of the bed was like something from a medical examiner's lab or worse, a taxidermy shop.

They turned away together, fighting vomit and tears.

"He was eaten alive," Deb said.

Before he spoke, Jag had to struggle with a heave, just barely winning the battle to keep his stomach from turning inside out.

"Truth in legend. The old man said the momo, and he had to be right. Nothing human could do this."

Deb began to weep. "This is what happened to Mark. They let these things, whatever did this, have him and then let the train destroy his body to hide it."

"I know," Jag said, holding her, clutching her tightly and drawing strength even as he tried to offer comfort. If she were not here, he would be running now, probably wetting his pants as well, but together they had courage.

"I think I'd better look around that room," Jag said.

"Why?"

"I don't know. They're going to realize this fellow hasn't shown up for work pretty soon, and somebody will be out here. We don't have much time, and we definitely don't want to talk to the police."

Leaving her in the hallway, he slipped through the doorway, trying to divert his eyes from the horror show on the bed. He raised one sleeve to his face, using it to shield his nostrils as much as possible from the smell. He then stepped around the muddy patches on the carpet and tried to look for signs that might stand out amid the carnage.

He pushed aside the pile of clothes that the man had apparently worn the day before and hung on a chair at bedtime. He pulled back the curtains also and discovered the small balcony. He didn't open the door. He just looked out and saw the table and chair that sat there.

Turning, he glanced around the room, again avoiding the sight on the bed. He moved past the dresser and noticed the notebook then. He almost didn't pick it up thinking it to be something related to the postman's work, but on an impulse he flipped the cover open and saw the faint pencil script across the blue-lined paper.

His mind began to click. Diaries could reveal all sorts of things. He picked up the spiral and then moved across the room to the closet. Placing his hand in his pocket, he opened the door with the cloth to cut down on the fingerprints he was leaving everywhere.

The search of the closet turned up the box of other notebooks. He hoisted it into his arms after wiping the table leg and discarding it.

"What have you got?" Deb asked when he stepped back into the hallway. Her expression indicated her fear that he had confiscated body parts for some unknown reason.

"Diaries," he assured.

"What do we want with those?"

"They may indicate when the old man first started seeing the creatures. They may tell all kinds of things." He led the way back down the hallway and out of the house.

"Let's get out of here," she said. "Those things may be around still. And they may be hungry."

210

They half ran, half walked back around to the front of the house and climbed into the car.

Jag was back on the highway when they spotted the black Z-28. Its lights blazed through the fog. Speeding up behind Jag's car, it stayed on his bumper as if hovering there.

"Who is it?" Deb asked.

"Don't know. Not a cop car."

He pressed down on the gas pedal, urging the car's speed to climb. He pulled a little ahead of the Camaro, but it closed on him again in a few seconds.

Jag gripped the wheel, half-prepared for impact.

It didn't come.

After a few more seconds, the car pulled into the oncoming lane and sped past. Jag never got a chance to see the face of the man in the driver's seat. Once the red tail lights had disappeared into the fog, both Jag and Deb sighed with relief.

"Maybe it was just a guy in a hurry," Jag said.

"I never got a good look at him."

"Me either. I don't guess the momo can drive cars."

"I doubt it."

"This is strange, really strange. I don't know where we're going to look for answers, though. I'd never heard anything about these things until the other day. They're supposed to be the Cajun's answer to bigfoot, but that doesn't tell us much."

Deb turned in her seat, bracing one hand against the dash as she looked over at Jag. "I talked to a priest the other day. He was Cajun, I think. His accent was kind of strange. Maybe he'd know. Maybe he'd have answers."

"Maybe he sat on his grandfather's knee and listened to tales about momo," Jag agreed. "Where'd you find him?"

"At the cathedral."

"I'll head there now. Maybe he'll be up for an early mass or something."

Deb reached into the back seat and pulled out one of the notebooks. "I guess I'd better see if there's anything in these. We've removed evidence from a crime scene. We might as well try to benefit from it."

The fog was just beginning to dissipate when Jag pulled to a stop in front of the cathedral. He parked in a no parking zone and led the way into the sanctuary.

Father Larson was standing at the front of the room near the altar, talking with a custodian dressed in a gray uniform. When he saw Jag and Deb and detected the urgency in their faces, he dismissed the man and walked toward them.

"What's wrong?" he asked.

"Father, Jag Walker," Deb said.

They shook hands.

Deb hesitated a moment, a bit uncomfortable with the next question. "We were wondering if you'd ever heard of momo," Deb said.

"Does this have something to do with your brother?"

"Maybe. It could be coming together."

He crossed his arms and began to pinch his chin. "So you think mythical beast-men might have something to do with his disappearance."

"Can we speak to you in confidence?" Deb asked.

He nodded.

"We just found two mutilated bodies. Something devoured them. Isn't that what momo does?"

He paled slightly, the only indication that the revelation phased him. "According to the legend." He lifted his arm. "Let's sit down."

They stepped back to the pews. Jag and Deb settled onto one of them, and the priest sat down in front of them, turning sideways on the seat and resting his arm on the backrest.

"I have some theories about where the stories began," the priest said. "I'll tell you those after I've gone over the basics. Not many people talk about these things anymore. They're somewhat repulsive even as fairy tales go."

He adjusted his weight on the seat. "Where to begin? You know how the Cajuns got to Louisiana? They came from Nova Scotia."

"We studied *Evangeline* in poetry class," Jag said. "Some of it escapes me."

"I'm from Georgia," Deb said.

"It was in the 1700s. The era of the French and Indian War. The ancestors of the Cajuns were accused of being sympathetic to the French. There were supposedly alliances with Indian tribes as well. Some said they aided Indians by directing them to English settlements.

212

"Anyway, the British drove the Cajuns, the Acadians out of their land. Lot of 'em wound up here in Louisiana because it had been a French settlement before. Everybody wasn't nice here in those days. What I was told was that there were outlaws that terrorized the Cajun settlements.

"A lot of the Cajuns fought back and ran 'em off. Unfortunately some of the rougher ones didn't scare. They killed some wives in one settlement, and this group of men got together and caught these fellas."

"Vigilantes?" Jag asked.

"There wasn't a lot of law back then," Father Larson replied.

"Kind of seems to match what's going on today," Jag observed.

"Some," Deb agreed.

"When they caught them, they took them into the bayous, and they performed this ritual. No one knows where they learned it. Probably brought it from the old country. I have theories, but most of all you have to understand this ritual was designed to take their humanity away from them."

"How did it work?"

"That's where some of my speculation comes in. A lot of ancient cultures hold belief in bizarre spirits. This kind of matches up with some of the European groups."

"Druids?" Deb asked.

"Among others. I've read about it in *The Golden Bough*. It's a book about folklore. It details many cultures in which they dress someone up in leaves or corn shucks or whatever for a fertility rite.

"Now, the Cajun legend goes that when a man has the momo mark put on him, it makes him wild. He becomes a creature of the trees. He rips off all his clothes and makes a covering for himself out of leaves and moss and whatever he can find. Then he lives like an animal."

"The mark? What is the mark?" Jag asked.

"Some kind of arcane occult symbol, I'm sure," the priest said. "Something that draws an evil spirit or demon or channels some other kind of evil energy. You see, I think the word momo is a Cajun variation of Mormo. That's from the Greek. The name is for the king of the ghouls. He was a consort of Hecate, and that falls into line. What is momo, or Mormo, the mormo but ghouls? Humans who

213

feed on other humans."

"Where does it come from? This force?" Jag asked.

"We live in a fallen world, Mr. Walker. The Holy Bible tells us that Satan is the prince of the air. His powers and his minions are many."

"You believe this could be *real?*"

The priest rubbed his face slightly. "When I was a little boy, all of this stuff terrified me. My grandfather used to tell me the stories, and I'd hide under the covers at night. Then in daylight I was always fascinated. I read books about all of it, and one of the things I studied was werewolves."

"The full moon? Wolfbane, silver?" Jag suggested.

"That's Hollywood's version," said the priest. "The actual legend is little more intense. It holds that men *chose* to be werewolves. It gave them opportunity for total abandon.

"The ritual called for a man to carve a symbol into his chest, smear some kind of salve on his body and put on a special belt. I found this in a book by Montague Summers, and the similarities struck me."

"The makeshift fur, the symbol . . ." Jag ventured.

"Exactly. the notion of wild abandon, not that far removed from the thought of removing someone's humanity from him."

"I guess it would become a question of whether you'd cursed a criminal or set him free," Deb said.

"It did back then. The monsters got out of hand. They began to raid the settlements. And they devoured people."

"For food?" Deb asked.

"It wasn't just for food," the priest said. "No cannibalistic culture has ever performed its rituals for food. There was always some other motive. Power or something more."

"What are you getting at?" Jag asked.

"Sexual in a way, Mr. Walker. Sexual ritual. Sex makes two people one. It is a union. You cannot do more toward that end than consuming another individual completely. What a wonderful thing for evil, to take an act of love and procreation and turn it into something vile and deadly."

"That's horrible," Deb said.

"It's just an analysis. Probably of the subconscious of the people who made up the legends if none of this is true."

"The mormo got out of hand," Jag said.

"As the legends go. After so many raids on the villages,

the men went after them. They took their guns and went into the forest, and they hunted them."

"Gun shots killed them?"

"They remained physical beings even though the evil gave them increased strength. Some say eating the flesh increased their power, but the guns tore into them. Apparently many were killed. Those that weren't were driven deep into the bayous. After that they were seen only on occasion, just a few of them.

"Enough to keep people telling stories."

Jag looked over at Deb. "The original vigilantes turned their criminals into these things."

Her mouth dropped open. "You don't think, even if this is real, that they could have repeated such a thing."

"Recreated the ritual?" Jag asked.

"I don't know if I could do that," the priest said. "And I've studied it extensively."

"In books," Jag said. "That's not where it would be, is it? That's the kind of thing that's handed down."

Father Larson nodded. "I suppose there's still some people down south of us that would know the way it's done. Down in the bottom lands."

"Guys the cops might find and put to work?"

"The cops. Or whoever's behind this."

"Who would know how to do it. Where would we find him?"

The priest didn't have to hesitate. "In one of the little towns down through the swamps, Bellesport, an old man named Jean Quebedeaux. Ask for him at the cafe. If he's still alive. He's what you'd call a witch man in English."

"Could be history is repeating itself," Jag said. "If they did recreate these things, they've gone wild like they did before. They're killing people in their homes."

"Maybe we should get the police," Father Larson suggested.

"No," Jag said. "We don't know which ones we can trust. We have to find out what this old man knows. Pray for us, Father. If you want to do something, do that, but don't talk to the police. Not yet. They're dangerous."

Chapter 20

The meeting was hastily called.

LaFleur met Scarecrow and Rand in the gun room again, his hat in his hands once more. Holding the brim, he turned it around and around. He felt as though each of the guns on display was pointed at him.

"How bad is it?" Rand asked.

"Most of it's cleaned up," Scarecrow said.

"How many dead?"

"Four." Scarecrow grunted the word.

"It's going to be hard to cover up, but I think we can do it," LeFleur said.

"You've been to the sites?" Rand asked.

"Me and a couple of guys," said LaFleur. "The car we found is no problem. We'll just ditch it somewhere. We can mostly handle the two houses that were hit. One house was a mess. The guy was a postman, but so far no calls have come in on him not showing up for work. It may be a day or two before someone gets that worried. They'll go down as mysterious disappearances. Cops can cover tracks well because we know what other cops look for."

"It will draw attention to our area," Rand observed, rubbing one hand across his beard.

"We have other problems," LaFleur said.

"Such as?"

"These kids are poking around. Scarecrow spotted them outside the postman's house. We think they've got other people asking questions too."

"Who?"

"We're not sure, but there are rumblings."

"How close are these kids?" Rand asked.

"We've had an eye on them off and on. They've talked to Melo Templeton's mother."

"How did they know?"

"They were digging for connections. The guy works for the fucking newspaper. No telling what he can come up with."

Rand sat in his armchair, his eyes slowly moving from LaFleur's face to Scarecrow's. "What should we do?"

"Maybe a little scare," LaFleur suggested. "If that doesn't work, something else is a possibility."

Rand raised his eyes. "Expound."

"The kid got into trouble the other day. It was a pretty brutal beating he gave a guy. It involved a woman, and the victim was married. Charges were dropped."

Fire seemed to flare somewhere deep inside Nicholas Rand's eyes. "So he has committed a crime for which he has never been punished."

"Not as serious as we usually look for, but I had a medical check run. He broke the man's jaw. So the answer is, yes. He meets the criteria."

"He is a rather formidable young man, then?"

"He's a big kid. Nervous like, from what we can tell, not your average fighter, but yeah, he could be."

"Worthy of the chase?"

"The guy he beat up was a pretty tough ol' boy."

"Did he have a history of that kind of behavior?"

"No. There was a woman involved like I said. He snapped is all."

"A crime of passion," Rand said.

"Yeah."

"He's been helping this young lady?"

"She's staying at his house."

Rand raised his eyebrows. "Then her safety might motivate him?"

"Yeah. But do you want to endanger her? Her brother was the one we made the mistake about."

Rand gripped the arms of his chair so tightly that his knuckles colored white. "It was not a terrible mistake. He would have become like the other killers that roam America. He was on that path. We stopped him before it got to

217

that, before he harmed someone else's loved ones."

LaFleur did not argue. He'd learned the man's thought patterns and didn't challenge his thinking. Rand made it possible to wipe out a lot of scum. If he had an occasional twisted thought, that couldn't be held against him.

"What is the status of this young man's family?"

"He has parents somewhere. We could still make it look like an accident again."

"True. Perhaps it is a good idea. We silence him, make it look like an accident and then cover our tracks. If there are people making inquiries, we will give it time to quiet down before we hunt again."

"How long?" LaFleur asked.

"A few months. Talk will die down, the mormo will settle down, and we can resume."

"Right," LaFleur said. "No one will believe for very long that cops are bad guys."

"And," Rand said, "no one will believe that the woods are filled with monsters."

In daylight, the mormo slept, nestling amidst the pouches in the thicket that formed their beds. The growl of their breathing rose above them, a rough and tangled sound of disharmony.

They were content for now, satisfied.

There were more than a dozen of them, all masses of tangled gray moss and brown leaves mixed with mud.

They were waiting now, waiting for darkness when they could hunt again.

That was what they lived for.

Holt and Nielson sifted through the stack of computer printouts one more time. They had been up all night going over the information Holt had compiled on his first effort. Cross checks had helped confirm Holt's original postulation, but they still had little idea of where to look for further evidence.

"We can't keep shaking down other cops. Intimidation's not going to work for long," Neilson argued.

"It'll have its moments," said Holt.

218

"What do you suggest?"

"We go talk to my boy, Kevin, again, let him know he's up shit creek. We show him this stuff and tell him that we're going to blow the top off of it and he's going down with the rest of them. He'll start shaking in his boots and spill it. We get him to tell us when and where they'll be doing their thing again."

"You think he'll go for it?"

"He will or we'll be sinking *his* ass in a shallow grave," Holt said.

Nielson thought it over, "Sounds good."

Jag's car rattled in protest as he urged it down the highway, but he did not let up on his speed. An urgency had seized him.

His mind was having difficulty processing everything that was going on. He had seen the work of monsters, had heard things beyond belief and knew that all of it was real. That was almost too much on top of everything else he had endured in the last few days.

In a week's time his life had been turned upside down. One minute he'd been a miserable reporter in a bad relationship. Suddenly he was in a whirlwind of madness.

Debra was the only thing akin to solidarity that he had to hold on to. They had not had time to talk about the business of a relationship, but he found himself contemplating what might await them when all of this was over.

There would be time then for finding out. Debra was not talking much now, not with her mind tied in knots by the circumstances. He glanced over at her and noticed the intensity with which she stared out at the highway. She had stopped thumbing through Orson's diaries.

He could not blame her. Her world was as confused as his. Her brother had been killed, and she had been tumbled into the same nightmare as Jag.

Ahead of them, the small town came into view, first with speed limit signs, then with a white-on-green marker of the corporation limits of Bellesport.

They cruised in past a rundown-looking service station and remained on the highway which also served as the town's Main Street. The car rolled past a closed dress shop and an antique store that looked dusty. Antique stores always seemed dusty to Jag.

The diner was near the center of town. A sign in front of it proclaimed it The Blue Bonnet Cafe.

He pulled into one of the angled parking slots. An old and battered parking meter stood at the curb as if it were a greeter for the chamber of commerce. Jag shoved some change into it, and they moved on through the front door of the cafe.

It was cleaner than Jag expected, and the warmth was a pleasant contrast to the outside chill. He'd imagined grease, but the place had a quaint style with the red-and-white-checkered table cloths over the unvarnished wooden tables.

A counter with round stools ran in front of the grill, and several local people were sitting around eating early lunches and carrying on conversations in Cajun French. It was amazing what a difference a trip of a few miles could make.

Jag and Deb took seats at the bar.

The waitress behind the counter was rotund, a round-faced woman with a faint mustache on her upper lip.

"Catfish is the special today, fried and filleted. All the trimmings, three dollars." Her voice was crisp with the French-accented Cajun dialect.

To her regular customers she probably spoke in French all the time.

They ordered two plates of catfish, and the woman turned and shouted back through the window into the kitchen.

"Comin' up, Evelle" came her answer.

The smell of the fish frying drifted back to them in a few minutes, rich with the seasoning of the batter.

"You from out of town, *chere?*" Evelle asked.

"Aimsley," Jag said.

"Sightseeing?"

"Looking for someone."

"Ain't many someones aroun' here."

"We were told we'd find an old man named Jean Quebedeaux down this way."

She laughed. "You could say that. If you want to look at his headstone. He's dead. Since last spring."

Jag looked over at Deb, but he could tell by her eyes she had no answers either.

They chatted with Evelle until their food came. It was well prepared. The chef obviously took pride in his work. The clientele was a captive audience; they would be in every day whether the food was good or bad, but it was good anyway.

The breading on the fish was crisp, and the hush puppies had just a taste of sugar in them, making them something more than just fried balls of cornbread.

Jag and Deb consumed the food quickly, enjoying the taste as they continued to talk with Evelle, Jag's questions gradually drawing out information about the town.

She talked about her girlhood in Bellesport, how things had been at the Catholic school and how much she had enjoyed the orange soda pop at the picture show.

Jag maneuvered the conversation for a while until he could say: "Look, I'm a writer. I was told Mr. Quebedeaux could tell me something about Cajun myths and that sort of thing. Cajun bayou magic."

"Hoodoo? You're still a little far north for that."

"No not voodoo. Cajun myth, the mormo, er momo, that sort of thing."

The woman rubbed her chin. "Onlyest one I can think of that would know about this is old Mama Bordelon. She and Mr. Quebedeaux knew each other real well."

"How so?"

The fat woman leaned on the counter, smiling at Jag and Deb. "I ain't so crazy," she said. "You're a writer. You looking for them 'cause a all the talk there is about Satanism. I see Geraldo and Scott Ross."

"What do you mean?"

"You think they're like that, and you want ta play it up. They ain't no Satanists. They ain't really witches. In fancy language, you'd say they were practitioners of herbal medicine. See, I ain't stupid."

"Whatever you say," Jag said. "Where would we find Mama Bordelon. Am I going to have to look for a headstone for her too?"

"No, She's about a hundred and five, but she's still drawing air in her lungs."

Jag placed a folded ten dollar bill on the counter.

221

"Where?"

"She's got a shack."

"Of course she does," Jag said with a smile.

"You go on down the highway to the edge of town. Then you take a left on the first dirt road, and you follow it back around to the second curve. You'll see another road there. It'll take you back to her place. In the swamp."

The surface of the gravel road seemed as though it had been bombed. Ruts and potholes riddled it, creating an obstacle course for Jag's tires.

"Not many people go to visit her," he observed as he twisted the wheel from side to side, avoiding as much of the ruin as possible.

Occasionally the wheels still bounced across the uneven surface sending shocklike jolts through the car.

"Do you think were on a wild goose chase?" Deb asked.

"There's something to this," Jag said. "You saw how those bodies were torn up."

"I'm going to be seeing that in my nightmares for a long time," she agreed. "That was worse than the pictures of my brother, and I never thought I'd ever say that."

The road twisted around in a S curve, and Jag spotted the turn they had been told about. The road consisted of dirt overgrown with grass and was dappled with even more potholes.

"We should have brought a jeep," Jag said.

"Or an ATV," Deb suggested, bracing herself in her seat to cut down on the bouncing.

Finally the road played out, and they climbed from the car to follow a foot trail. Cypress trees, their tentacle branches draped with Spanish moss, lined the path like gnarled guardians.

Jag kept an eye on them lest they come to life and grab. If they were going to interview a witch woman about wild swamp men, anything was possible.

The wind whistled through the trees, as if it were making cat calls at the same time it threw out its chill. Finally they pushed through a cluster of branches and spied the house.

"Looks just like I expected," Deb said, eyeing the old gray shack.

"At least she doesn't have a black cat on the porch," Jag said as they started toward the front door.

"Maybe she ate it," Deb remarked.

They walked up the rickety steps and across the creaking planks of the front porch.

Jag pounded on the door.

The house was quiet, perhaps deserted.

"Another dead end," Deb said.

They were about to turn and head back to the car when the hinges on the door began to squeak.

"I knew it was going to do that," Deb said.

They turned back to face the withered crone who was peering out through the rusty screen.

Her hair was long, twisted tangles of gray, framing a face that was so weathered and wrinkled that it appeared like a mask. Her hands were like the branches of the cypress trees.

They clutched a thin shawl around her stooped shoulders, the fingers trembling.

Her dark eyes seemed to float in their sockets, making Jag think at first that they were unseeing. Still, she focused on him when he spoke to introduce himself.

"What do you want?" she asked in a voice that was stronger and clearer than he expected.

He glanced at Deb for support, and she nodded. There was no need to play games here.

"We want to know about the mormo," he said. "We think they're still alive."

The old woman laughed, her voice rising into a cackle which lasted several seconds.

"So you've see the swamp men, have you, boy?"

"Not the men," Deb said. "Just their work."

"Damn."

The profanity was unexpected. It seemed odd and out of character for the old woman.

She observed the shock in their faces. "I watch a lot of television," she explained.

"Way out here?" Jag asked.

"There's a satellite dish out back. Only way you can get anything around here. My grandson put it in for me."

223

"So much for the traditional image," Deb whispered.

They followed her into the dimly lit living room. It was cramped and stuffy from the space heater that sat near one wall. The color television was on, but she had turned down the sound before opening the front door.

She returned to her armchair, and her cat, not black but a grayish color, jumped back into her lap.

"Now, what did you see that made you think the mormo were around."

"Two dead men," Jag said. "Their bodies were torn up."

"Could have been animals again. They had a panther killing people up in Bristol Springs, didn't they? I didn't even think there were still any in these parts."

"This was not a typical animal attack," Jag said.

The tone of his voice took the old woman's attention. She studied him a moment before nodding. "You really ain't just sightseers," she said. "You're serious."

"It's real," Deb said. "We looked you up because we need to know what the truth is."

"You know the story, abut how the Cajuns came down here from Nova Scotia?"

"We know that part," Jag said. "The mormo, are they really swamp men, or are they werewolves or what?"

"The story goes that they're men turned into monsters, but they aren't supposed to be around anymore. You're talking about hundreds of years ago."

"Has anybody ever seen one?" Jag asked.

"Not to my knowledge. There's hunters that claim to have seen things in the distances and movements in the shadows, nothing more."

She shifted about in her chair, her withered face betraying pain as she searched for comfort. "My brother went out one night when we were young. He took his dogs and his pistol for coon hunting. They were trotting along through the forest when the wind shifted, and they caught this foul smell.

"He smelled it, and the dogs did too; and they started to whine and whimper and tuck their tails in. Then they heard this awful howl. He said the dogs tried to climb up into his arms. He forgot all about having a gun. They all ran, tore up the country getting back to the house. Next day he went back and looked and didn't find a trace of anything. Could have been a bear, I guess. Or a panther."

"There's supposed to be a ritual to create them," Jag said. "Would you know how to perform it?"

The old woman sighed as she shook her head. "Oh, nooooo," she whispered. "That's bad magic. Not the kind of thing I'm into."

"Who would know how to do it?" Jag asked.

"The last family in these parts, the last one this far north, would be the Celestine Broussard family."

"They're still around?" Jag asked.

"Most of 'em are dead or moved off. Celestine died a couple of years back. He was a deputy for a long time, then lost his job. He went a little crazy after that. Poached a lot. He had one boy, rough boy. Became a bounty hunter."

"He's still around?"

"You'd probably find him up your way."

Jag leaned toward her. Her slow method of speaking was irritating, and she didn't volunteer anything without it being dragged out of her.

"Where could he be found. What's his name?"

"He lived here up to a few years back. Went to work as a body guard for a rich man that moved in up in Riverland Parish."

"Names?" Jag urged. "Do you know names?"

"The boy, he's not a boy anymore; he'd be in his thirties. He just goes by Scarecrow. I don't recall his real name."

"Who'd he go to work for?"

"What was his name? He used to be in the oil business. Moved over here and got a hold of a sugar came plantation."

Deb's eyes widened, but Jag was staring into the old woman's features.

"What's his name? Where was it.".

"South part of the parish. Name was Grant. No, Rand, Nicholas Rand."

Jag took out his notebook to scribble down the information. He leaned back in his chair with a sigh of relief. They'd finally plucked what the old woman knew.

"How'd you know this?" he asked.

"I'm a witch woman."

After a few more minutes of small talk, he and Debra were outside again, ducking their heads against the wind as they followed the narrow path back to the car.

"Have you ever heard of Nicholas Rand?" she asked.

"He's been mentioned. I don't know him."

"I saw his name in the diaries. The postman wrote about the oil man moving in."

They reached the car and climbed into the front seat.

"So he lives near the forest?" Jag asked.

"Evidently."

"And the last man who knew how to create the mormo went to work for him a couple of years ago."

"We're on to something."

"Pulp dialogue," Jag said.

"But it fits."

Jag adjusted his glasses on the bridge of his nose before starting the car. "I guess the next order of business is to check up on Mr. Nicholas Rand, then."

"Back to the newspaper?"

"They're expecting me there anyway. We'll run it down between obits."

Chapter 21

Holt and Nielson found Kevin Martin working out in a gym over on Nelson Street. It was the place most of the cops used on their off days, especially the ones dedicated to building their physiques.

The guy who owned the place was supposed to be an expert in designing individual fitness programs.

Today the gym was almost deserted except for a couple of girls in black leotards working out in the front exercise area and a few guys with bulging muscles sweating over some tension equipment.

Kevin was on a bench press in a corner of the weight room, isolated from the other patrons. Wisps of air were seeping through his teeth as he strained his arms against the weights. The sweat shone on his face and arms, covering him like an oil.

Nielson approached him from one side while Holt came up on the other so that they could both look down into his face.

When he saw them, the bar slipped from his hands, letting the weights clang down with a loud crack of metal.

"What do you guys want?" he demanded.

Holt toyed with the match stick in his mouth as he let a grin spread across his features.

"Just to talk," he said.

"I don't want trouble with you, man."

Holt continued to smile, and his voice took on a friendly, reassuring tone. "You're gonna have more trouble than you know what to do with unless you come clean, shithead."

"I don't know anything else."

Holt put one foot on the edge of the bench and leaned forward, resting one arm on his knee. "You'd better find something out quick. Y'all are goin' down, unless you have something worthwhile."

The sweat that poured off the kid's forehead didn't seem to be coming from his exertion. "What do you want me to do?"

"Spill it all."

"I don't have anything else to give you. All I know is we went out in the woods and did some hunting. I don't even know where it was. I didn't drive."

"Who's behind it?"

"I don't know."

"When do they hunt again?"

The kid hesitated, licking his lips. His eyes avoided contact with Holt.

"What is it?" Holt demanded.

"There are rumblings. It could happen again soon. That's all I know. Really. I don't know any specifics."

"Find out," Holt instructed. "And don't get any ideas about telling your friends what we're up to. If anything happens to us, there are people who will find out, and your name is all over everything."

"Shit."

"You play with fire, you get fucked," Holt said.

"These guys will kill me if they think I'm tipping somebody off."

"You think that's scary? What about being an ex-cop in Angola? How you think you'll fare in prison? You want to be somebody's wife, I'll bring you a dress on visitor's day."

Holt removed his foot and turned, setting a pace that let Nielson catch up with him before he reached the exit.

"Think it'll work?" Nielson asked, once they reached the parking lot.

"It'll flush somebody out if it doesn't do anything else. Who knows? He may be scared enough to do us some good."

Jag had an assignment waiting for him when he got to the office. He had to cover an afternoon meeting of the city council, at least two hours' work. He gave Deb the keys to his car, deciding to walk the few blocks from the newspaper office to the city hall.

She drove over to the cathedral to look for Father Larson. He was in the rectory typing. He turned from the machine and stood up when she walked through the door.

"My secretary is ill, and the diocese hasn't sent me a temporary yet," he explained. "How goes it with your quest?"

"We turned up some information," she said. "The man you mentioned had died. We found a witch woman who helped us out."

"You know more about the mormo and the gris gris?" he asked, motioning for her to sit.

"Some about the mormo. Rhetoric. I don't understand it."

"You're treading in a very dangerous matter," the priest said. "I've been worried about you. I feel as if I'm letting you dabble in all this."

"You're not responsible, Father. I'm on my own. Jag is trying. He's concientious. I owe him a lot, more than I could ever repay, but I can't go to the police."

"I understand."

"Father, the old woman told us there might still be someone alive who could perform the ritual," Deb said. "The ritual to create the mormo."

"Interesting."

Deb looked into the priest's eyes. "How can this be happening? How can it be real?"

He pursed his lips for a moment. "It is difficult to believe. We live in some ways in a secular time, a time where we no longer believe old legends, where the mystical seems to be only the stuff of literature.

"It's easy to play games with crystals, I suppose, or listen to accounts of channeled entities, but those have become more like parlor games. Some take them seriously; the rest of us, with a grain of salt. Yet there are evidences strange things have gone on in the past.

"The Bible, the Hebrew Kabbalah, the Koran, all speak of odd and mysterious creatures. Demons, djinn, many things lurk in the realms around us. Just as they exist, power exists, power that men have sought for eons to manipulate. And man is imperfect, susceptible to such things.

"Magic serves many purposes. And make no mistake; it is real, and evil is real."

Debra listened intently, her gaze on the priest's as he spoke.

"When magic is toyed with, when men reach out to the forces of darkness, things are created. If they are indeed real, that's what makes the mormo.

"I mentioned the gris gris. Do you know what that is?"

"I haven't heard it before."

"Cajun black magic. The old witch woman might not speak about it, but it's known among the Cajuns. And if the one you spoke of knows it, then the mormo are to be feared."

"What can combat them, Father? They've killed people."

"Only the blessings of God can truly ward off evil. I will pray for you, that the Lord will protect you."

"I hope so, Father. I certainly hope so."

The thing that had been Kyle curled in the mass of leaves amid the other slumbering mormo.

Snatches of thought patterns tried to form in his brain, but something constantly shattered them, keeping him from remembering, keeping him from understanding.

The force controlled his mind now, controlled his very being even as the fragments of his personality tried to fight through the evil and recapture his soul.

Finally he rolled over, wrapping his arms around his head and snoring loudly. Night would come again, and with it the feeding.

That was enough. That was all he needed.

Clods of dirt piled up slowly on the last of the remains that had been found that morning. When he had finished, Scarecrow leaned on the shovel and wiped his face with the sleeve of his shirt. He was sweating in spite of the chill air and the overcast sky which blocked even the warmth of the sun.

Walking back to the house, he washed the shovel blade before returning the tool to the storage shed. He realized the prickly feeling at the back of his neck was fear. He looked back over his shoulder, making sure nothing was watching him.

The forest seemed still, but he couldn't shake the feeling that something was there, looking at him, trailing his every move. He knew it was only in his head, but he also knew the source of the anxiety was based in reality.

He was worried because the mormo had become unpredictable. No one had ever known what they did back in the depths of the forest, but they had never seemed a threat. They had always lurked back somewhere in the trees, waiting, always there when the prisoners ran too far.

Never had they ventured from their pocket of the forest, however. Not until now. They were growing bold. Last night had been some kind of frenzy. They had swarmed out of hiding, assaulting everything they came into contact with.

The rituals he had learned from his father had never offered any advice on what to do in that case. He had no idea of how to regain control of them or how to protect his charges if things got out of hand again.

Even the bulge of the pistol tucked into the waistband of his pants at the small of his back did not inspire the feeling of security it usually produced.

He wasn't sure what it would take to make him feel safe again. Nicholas was determined to make one more round of the hunt. Scarecrow couldn't help but wonder what would happen when the hunters, as well as the hunted, flowed into the woods.

The mormo were no longer confined to the farthest reaches of the swamp. They were moving forward, and they might be out there somewhere waiting to pounce on one of the hunters, not just one of the prey. The mormo did not differentiate between the police and the criminals.

So far there had never been any trouble in that realm because the hunters either killed the prisoners before they could travel very far back into the forest, or turned back once they heard the screams that told them the mormo had caught their prey.

The mormo could be anywhere now. He just hoped the guns the vigilantes carried would be enough to ward them off if they did attack.

Legend said guns worked. Scarecrow wondered about the truth of that.

He realized he was standing there, staring at the forest. Pointless.

He turned and rounded the corner of the shed, starting toward the house.

The cat was near the back of the small building, or at least what was left of the cat. It had been ripped apart. Fur was strewn about on the ground in little white tufts, and blood had soaked into the soil, freezing to the ground in a moist, sticky mass of red and black.

Scarecrow looked down at it grimly. They had been here, had devoured the cat sometime during the night from the look of the remains.

He would have to keep Serena from seeing this. The sight of the body in the woods had been hard on her. Losing her kitty would reactivate all of that emotion she had contained.

The girl had suffered most for all of this. It was not his place to question her father, but Scarecrow knew it was true.

For all of Rand's efforts to protect his daughter, he had wound up causing more damage.

Too bad. She was a beautiful girl. A waste to have her rotting here in this remote corner of the world.

With no change in his expression, the big man walked back to the door of the shed and retrieved the spade for one more shallow grave. Without thinking, he glanced toward the forest, checking to see if anything there was watching.

Except for the light play of the breeze, everything seemed still.

For the moment.

Chapter 22

Jag spent most of the city council meeting thinking about Deb and occasionally about the investigation and the story he would eventually write about it. He was convinced that would happen, that he would ultimately recount all of this business. If he lived.

He wasn't sure how he would explain the mormo, but he knew he'd have a hell of a report to make.

Then he and Deb could make plans. If he survived this, he'd be able to get attention for some better jobs.

In part it was fantasy, but he couldn't help himself. Things looked better, more possibilities than he'd experienced in a long time.

He found it hard to concentrate on the arguments of the city board. He was only able to keep track of their comments because each board member had a nametag in front of his seat.

They were concerned about natural gas wells on city property. Jag could not have been more bored, and it would take him at least an hour to come up with something for a story that would satisfy Breech.

Finally the meeting adjourned. He took only enough time to ask the board president what had actually happened. Scribbling down the reply that explained the final board action on permits, he slipped out the door and headed back to the *Clarion* office.

The short walk was long enough to let the weather numb his face with chill. He stomped into the back door of the newspaper building, shivering beneath his coat. As he walked up the hallway toward the newsroom, he slipped the coat off; but the heat in the building was malfunctioning again, and he didn't feel immediate warmth.

He was about halfway up the hall when a guy from the personnel office tried to interrogate him about entering through the employee entrance.

"I work here," Jag said in a fuck-you tone that got the guy out of his way.

He was in the newsroom and behind his terminal a few seconds later. A stack of new obits awaited, along with printouts of the ones he'd done the previous day. They had been bloodied by a red felt-tipped marker, almost every line slashed at some point because of a style error or typo.

He stuffed them into his drawer, called up a computer page on his terminal and began to recount the events of the meeting.

A half-hour later, Deb showed up and sat at the vacant desk beside his while he continued to work.

A few people glanced at her, but nothing was said.

He put the -30- at the bottom of his story for effect and shipped it off. The first real assignment he'd had in weeks, and it had come just when he had something more important to do!

"Just a little longer," he whispered to Deb before homing in on the obits.

He was a third of the way finished with them when Breech shouted to him across the newsroom. With a sigh he got up from his chair and walked over to the editor's terminal.

For about ten minutes they debated arbitrary points of sentence structure and meaning, Breech opting for his own way in each case. Finally Jag figured out how the game was played and started agreeing with him in order to get the ordeal over.

Satisfied at last, Breech dismissed him.

Jag finished the obits in record time, his fingers tapping across the keys in a rapid-fire output that he knew would net him a new stack of red-marked hard copies tomorrow.

With a nod toward Deb, he got up from his chair, and they walked around the corner into the morgue.

The sign Joan put on her desk when she was out for coffee was posted. They moved into the file area.

Nora was sitting on the reading table, a wad of clippings spread out in her lap. A cigarette smoldered between her fingers, a wobbling column of ash threatening to spill off.

She looked up when she heard their footsteps.

"Busy?" Jag asked.

"Trying to be. What are you up to? You two slip in here to grope? I could get out."

"We're looking something up," Jag said. "For a story maybe."

"You still on this mysterious case of yours, Jag?"

"Could be."

He moved past her and started to go through the file cabinets. After checking under a couple of headings, he slammed a drawer, uttering a curse.

"What are you looking for?" Nora asked. "Maybe I can help. I've had more experience with this guessing system."

"Information on Nicholas Rand."

"What's he do?"

"He owns a sugar plantation south of town," Deb said.

"Business profiles," she said, collecting her clippings and departing.

Jag opened the drawer and found the folder. "Thanks," he said.

He and Deb sat down with the small selection of clippings and began to go through them. There was one feature from a Sunday edition with a picture of Rand: *Oilman turns to sweeter pursuits.*

They read the article together. It was little more than an account of how Rand had given up the oil business to come to Louisiana. He had grown tired of the cutthroat world of Texas oil even before the oil crunch had come, the story explained. After the death of his wife, he'd decided to try his hand at something different.

"Sugar cane was about as far from crude oil as he could get," the story stated. It was upbeat in nature, a human interest piece concentrating on the drastic change in his career.

In the photograph, he appeared a friendly, jovial type.

The other items in the file were brief, no more than notices of Rand appearing at civic events. Those had been around the time of his arrival and had tapered off quickly.

"Looks like he came into town, accepted the initial attention and then dropped out of sight as soon as he could," Deb said.

Jag put the papers back into the file. "I agree."

"Seems to fit with the scenario we're both conjuring," said Deb. "The question is why? Why get this Cajun gris gris bounty hunter and hook up with a vigilante band of cops?"

"I don't know, but Rand seems to be the catalyst for everything. He recruited some cops, reorganized something similar to the old Cajun vigilante bands and somehow created a group of mormo."

"Then set out exacting a vengeance on criminals who slipped through the criminal justice system, with a few mistakes thrown in," Deb said.

"We're getting closer. We seem to be anyway."

"Where do we go from here?"

Jag shrugged. "Maybe we should go back to Honeycutt. He didn't turn us in before. Maybe with this much evidence we can get him to do something."

"Can you get out of here right now?" Deb asked.

"I guess so. Breech won't miss me."

After a quick detour into the newsroom to get his overcoat, Jag met Deb in the parking lot. They climbed into her Volvo and were on the street as a light rain began to fall from the gray late-afternoon sky.

"Louisiana winter. I thought they were mild," Deb said.

"This is worse than we usually get," Jag said. "It's usually rainy, but not this cold. Of course, when it gets bad, it's bad. I think the weather service said ice storms are possible."

"Georgia looks better every time I think about it."

She drove slowly over the wet streets, reaching the highway just as the sky got dark. The traffic was light in spite of the after-work hour. They met white rows of headlights, but few cars were headed their way.

The flashers appeared in the rearview just as they were preparing to turn into Honeycutt's neighborhood.

"I didn't do anything wrong, did I?" she asked.

"Not that I noticed." Jag turned and looked back through the rear glass. A brown sedan was behind them, the red light a beacon on the dash.

"It's an unmarked car," Jag said.

"Not a good sign."

"Not at all. Fuck him."

"You got it." She jerked the wheel hard to the left, skidding across the oncoming lane in front of a pickup truck.

The truck braked hard, sliding sideways in the lane and missing the Volvo by only inches.

Deb steered into the perimeter of a service station, missing the pumps and a VW as the Volvo moved across the lot and out a side exit.

That put them on a narrow residential street that was lined with thick, old oak trees. It was a twisting stretch of connected curves. She had to fight to keep control on the wet asphalt. The car went swishing through the turns, wanting desperately to fishtail.

Jag pressed his hands against the dash to steady himself. "You do this well," he said.

"Driving the Atlanta perimeter at rush hour during a rainstorm, I have experience."

The car rounded another curve, and she yanked the wheel again, spinning the vehicle onto a side street.

"Any idea where we are?" she asked.

"You run into trouble back here," Jag said. "These residential streets in this section weren't designed on a grid pattern."

"Surely they'll be careful what they do to us back here, though. People look out their windows."

"They've covered up everything else."

"Good point."

The sedan appeared again, the red light still flashing.

"Two of them in the front seat," Jag said.

Deb turned onto another side street, a boulevard, giving the car gas when it straightened out. They shot along the narrow stretch, swerving through a break in the median when it came into view.

The turn was sharp, and the wheels jumped the curb, then leveled out with a rumble.

The sedan slid past the turn and skidded to a stop before heading back.

The Volvo's advantage was only a matter of feet, and that disappeared a second later when the headlights of a shiny black pickup appeared.

It was in the center of their lane, barreling forward.

237

Deb gritted her teeth and yanked the wheel hard to the right, sending the car over the curb onto the sidewalk.

A mailbox scraped along the driver's side as the car curved through a front yard. She kept it steady, moving in front of two more houses.

The truck was left to make an abrupt U-turn.

"At least someone knows something's going on now," Deb said. "There are ruts in those lawns to prove it."

"That may not do us any good," Jag said.

"That's what I'm worried about."

She put the pedal close to the floor. The vibrations that rattled through the car were like an earthquake.

"I didn't shop well for a car chase, did I?" Deb asked.

"Who could have known?"

The car bounced back onto the street, and she set a course along the curving roadway. As they rounded a sharp bend, the sedan sped out from another side street, slamming into the Volvo's front fender.

The impact knocked the car sideways. It angled off the roadway, slamming through a white wooden guard rail. Beyond was an embankment, and the car went sliding down it. Deb fought the wheel, but there was no traction for the tires. The car piled on downward into a ditch that was filled with rainwater.

The water began to bubble into the car quickly, seeping up through the floorboard.

The ditch was not deep enough to submerge the car, but Jag quickly cranked his window open.

"We've got to get out of here," he shouted.

Unlatching her seat belt, Deb accepted his help in sliding through the open window.

A group of men had already started down the embankment. None of them wore uniforms, but they held weapons.

Jag pushed himself through the window behind Deb, stepping into water up to his thighs. It was chilling, sending numbing cold through him.

Taking Deb's arm, he prepared to rush them through the darkness, but the sound of a shotgun pump halted him. Running wouldn't get them very far if the men sprayed the darkness with buckshot.

Stopping side by side, he and Deb raised their hands,

praying they wouldn't be shot on the spot.

"Come on out of there," someone called.

Jag reached over and took Deb's hand so that they could steady each other. It was difficult to maintain balance while walking through water. Slowly, they began to slosh out of the water toward the flashlights that were shining in their eyes.

Rand stood at the window of his upstairs study, watching the caravan of headlights move up through the darkness along the winding driveway.

They had succeeded, judging by the number of vehicles. They moved to a stop at the parking apron, and he watched people begin to climb out.

From one car they pulled the reporter and the girl. Their hands were cuffed behind them, and they staggered about, disoriented.

They were young, fresh-looking in a way, but he fought back the sympathy that tried to rise. They were enemies, roadblocks to his mission, to that divinely ordained retribution he was exacting from as many animals as possible.

"What's going on?"

Startled, he looked around at Serena. He hadn't heard her open the door. His thoughts had been too intense.

"Nothing," he said.

She walked to the window anyway and looked out. "Who are they?"

"It's nothing for you to worry about."

"You're hurting people."

He took her in his arms. "You don't understand. There are many bad people out there, people like the ones who hurt your mother."

"You told me they had been taken care of."

"The courts tie the hands of the law, and somebody has to do something. We have to make sure things like that don't happen to other people."

She pulled away from him and shook her head, her frown displaying more hurt and dismay than anger.

"This is wrong, Daddy. I don't know all of what's going on here, but it's wrong."

"It's what has to be done," he said, his voice tense and

angry.

"Why? Mama is gone. We're not helping her this way."

He hated when the fights came, hated because he couldn't avoid them and because he couldn't control himself. He never wanted to raise his voice to Serena. All he ever wanted to convey to her was how much he loved her.

Before he could speak again, she had turned and moved back to the door. He attempted to follow her, but she moved swiftly down the hall, disappearing into her room.

He thought about going to the door and knocking, speaking to her softly through it, but then he heard the voices downstairs. His presence was required. It was essential.

He walked toward the stairs instead.

LaFleur and Scarecrow were standing in the entrance hall with Deb and Jag between them. The other cops had been dismissed.

The lower part of Jag's coat was dripping water, as were his slacks and Deb's jeans.

"They ran into a ditch," LaFleur said through a snarl.

"We couldn't really expect them to come peacefully, could we?" Rand asked. "You took care of the car?"

"We winched it out with Nick's pickup. No traffic passed."

"Where did you deposit their vehicle?"

"We ran it through the posts at the end of Bayou Sweet. If anybody finds it, they'll think the bodies washed out. Then they'll spend a few days dragging downstream."

"Well done." A deep chuckle rattled in the big man's throat.

"Do you want to go ahead with this tonight?"

"Oh, no. We need to invite our friends. These two can be missing a day or two without hurting anything. I'd hate to begin the hunt tonight. They're tired, not up to it."

Scarecrow heaved a sigh.

"You don't like that?" Rand asked.

"Just concerned about the mormo," the bounty hunter said.

"Their frenzy is over, I'm sure."

240

Scarecrow did not speak again, but his manner was restless.

A broad smile had crossed Rand's face. He stood in front of Jag and Deb, his eyes wide, studying them.

"Mr. Walker and Miss Blane I believe. Welcome. Sergeant LaFleur, if you will remove their handcuffs? I don't think they're necessary any longer."

As the cuffs were sprung, both of them lifted their arms in front of them to massage the red rings formed on their wrists.

"Scarecrow, if you will, show them upstairs. Let them get cleaned up. I think the young lady could wear some of Serena's things. Mr. Walker, I believe, will be large enough to fit into something of yours."

Scarecrow grunted and motioned them through the hallway and across the living room to the stairs.

At the end of the upstairs hall, he directed them into a pair of guest rooms. There was a connecting bathroom already stocked with fresh towels and unopened bars of soap.

As the outer door closed, a jangle of keys rattled from Scarecrow's pocket, and as soon as the latch clicked, the tumblers could be heard slipping into place. A prison had been created.

"Not bad accommodations," Jag said, walking through the narrow bathroom.

"We're privileged, I guess," Deb said.

He embraced her, holding her close as his eyes closed.

"What are we going to do?" she asked.

"We've got to try to figure a way out of here, before his hunt, or whatever it is, begins."

"This is what happened to Mark."

"Evidently."

"You think we can escape?"

"It'll be tough, especially with Scarecrow there. Still, it'll probably be easier than running the gauntlet against a bunch of armed cops and taking our chances with those wild men."

"I can't believe this is happening. I mean, how can it be real?"

"It's a nightmare, but everything we've found out is proving correct. That cop, LaFleur, he's the one you dealt with when you first got into town."

"Yes. They've probably had an eye on us the whole time."

The door to one of the rooms rattled. They walked from the bathroom to find Scarecrow standing in the doorway. He had a simple blue dress for Deb and jeans and a black shirt for Jag. He tossed them on the bed and departed without speaking.

"Nice guy," Jag said.

They took turns using the shower, then dressed and sat on the foot of the bed in one of the rooms, waiting for something to happen.

Jag tried the windows, but they were sealed shut, apparently welded since they had metal frames which would make breaking out impossible.

They jumped with each creak of the house, with each sound or vibration that duplicated a footfall.

A half hour passed before Scarecrow returned. The sound of the key in the lock startled them. He entered a moment later, gesturing for them to come with him.

They walked from the room and moved in front of him around the gallery railing and down a hallway on the opposite side.

Rand was sitting in a wing chair when they entered his study, a glass of wine gripped in one hand.

"Welcome." He smiled, seeming like a jovial uncle. "What can I get you to drink?" He rose from his chair and walked over to the bar. "I'm having muscadine wine," he said. "You Louisianians have forgotten what a fine product the muscadine makes." He lifted a bottle and replenished his glass.

"I'd never had this before Scarecrow introduced me to it. He's been very helpful in the things he's shown me."

Jag offered him an expression so stoic it looked as if his face had turned to stone.

"What would you like?" Rand repeated.

"To get the hell out of here," Jag said.

Rand only chuckled and poured two more glasses of wine.

"You know it's impossible for you to leave," he said. "Accept my hospitality. Please."

They picked up the glasses and followed him into the

242

sitting area of the study.

"You have attempted to interfere with my program," he said. "There is no way I can allow you to live." His words were slow and matter of fact, as if it all seemed perfectly simple to him.

"You murdered my brother," Deb blurted. Tears were streaming down her cheeks. "You killed him and mangled his body to cover it up."

"It was a mistake," Rand said. "Unfortunate but unavoidable. We checked on it. His name, Turner, matched up with another fellow. A hardened criminal."

"He was my half brother. You mean he died because he never changed his name?"

"It is unfortunate as I said. A mistake. There was another Mark Turner with a criminal record, a very bad man." Rand lifted his glass to his lips for another sip.

With the dark beard and the strange look that sizzled in his eyes, he seemed like a James Bond villain, yet he was real, Jag kept reminding himself. This was no film or dream no matter how much he wished it to be.

"Now you're going to kill us because we got in your way?" he asked.

"Once again, it is unfortunate, but the business we are attending to here is too essential to turn away from."

Jag pushed his glasses into place. "Isn't this all a bit melodramatic."

"That's the stuff of life, Mr. Walker."

"You bastard." Deb spat the words at him.

"Mr. Walker, Miss Blane, my wife was brutally raped and murdered. By scum, vermin. I was devastated. I could not understand it until I looked up to the heavens and understood that God wanted something from me. He wanted me to be his instrument. It is my task to purge humanity of the animals that prey on the good people. Someone has to restore the balance. You must understand that."

"You think those . . . things out there are instruments of God?" Jag asked.

"They are monsters, nothing more. They chose to be animals in life. All I have done is help them to be what they chose. They were animals of the worst kind, so we let them be monsters.

243

"We turned them out to be less than human because they were less than human to begin with. We selected only those of the worst caliber, leaving them to prey on their own kind.

"The first we selected were those three who killed my wife. Scarecrow hunted them down for me, trapped them and brought them here, to the swampland, where we could do our duty. Just as God leaves sinners to the hands of demons, there is a purpose for the ones who carry the mark of Mormo."

"There are more than just three of them, aren't there?" Jag asked.

"Now there are. We have selected others if we thought they deserved a punishment worse than the hunt. You were checking on Melo Templeton. He's out there somewhere. He was a vicious beast, so now he roams the forest as a beast, feeding on garbage when he can get it and the flesh of others like himself. When it's provided."

"Have any of these people who hang around you mentioned that you're mad?" Jag asked.

Another chuckle. "Mad? What an odd word. I am mad, mad about all of the creatures that are allowed to walk free. If I am crazy to want to establish some vestige of justice, that is as it must be. My allies must be crazy as well. Like me they see the need for this task. The policemen have watched criminals walk free. They have formed a band to work with me, reactivating an ancient society of vigilantes who saw the need to take on the outlaws who threaten order and society."

"You've modeled your group after the Cajun vigilantes that originally created the mormo," Deb said.

"You two have done your homework," Rand said, laughing again, a knowing laugh of one sharing in a joke. "Yes, that was the original basis. It was created to rid the villages of vermin. It was recreated in Aimsley in the sixties when things began to go awry with the judicial system. It was nothing extreme in those days, just a group of cops who did what had to be done. They took the same name as the vigilantes, Le Circle."

"A lot of them would be retired by now," Jag said.

"Right, but there are good men on the force still, and when Scarecrow and I learned of the Circle, we used

244

those retired men to recruit among the ranks, selecting those who could serve as hunters, as well as working within the system to cover our tracks. Twelve good men and true, if you will."

"People doctoring computer records and juggling other things around?" Deb asked. "All of that's criminal activity."

"No. It is not that at all. It is protecting society. The killers and the rapists and the others who are allowed to walk free, they are the criminals. The courts that free them are evil, and their rulings are not binding under the guidelines of true justice."

Jag shook his head. "You do all this without any trials, without any thought for real justice or mercy. It's wrong. It's dangerous. You've killed an innocent man for your game, maybe more than one. You're going to kill us. You're doing what you hate in the others."

"Don't question me," Rand said. "Think of the people who have been spared pain because of my actions. Think of the old women who were not raped in their homes because we took their would-be attackers off the street. Think of the people who are alive because killers were executed before they could kill again.

"And you, Mr. Walker. You brutalized a man while out of your head, and nothing was done to you. You should have been charged with aggravated assault, yet you walked free. How are we to know you won't snap again?"

"I've asked myself that," Jag said. "I've thought about it a lot, and I've wondered about myself. I think civilization is a thin line, but we can't operate a society the way you want. We'd have policemen gunning down jay walkers."

"We are not here to debate philosophy," Rand said. "I had you brought here to make you understand why you have to die."

He stepped to the window and looked out at the night, one arm folded behind him in perfect poise.

Jag leaned toward Deb. "He's completely out of it," he whispered. "He's off in a different world."

She nodded agreement. "I don't think it's quite real to him."

Jag looked around for signs of Scarecrow, but the guard had left them alone. There would be no escape from this study anyway.

"These other people must know," Deb said.

"I don't think they care," Jag said. "The bad cops get their chance to destroy criminals, and anybody else who works for him gets their money."

"Please, don't mumble about me," Rand said. "We're here to talk. You won't be killed before dawn. The hunt in darkness would be no challenge for our hunters. The mormo are more active at night and would devour you before you took a step. No sport for you or for the hunters.

"We believe in giving you a chance and them a chance. That's your trial. If your souls are truly innocent, God will deliver you. There is the sense of fairness in it all that you were asking about. God will provide an exit for the innocent. For the damned He will offer no grace."

"That's not what I was taught in Sunday school," Jag said. "I thought God was very loving, forgiving."

"It is a revelation I have received," Rand said.

He rose abruptly from his chair, terminating further conversation which might require him to defend his position.

"Dinner should be ready by now," he said. "Come, join me."

Chapter 23

Kevin was late finishing the paperwork from his shift because he'd had to handle an eighteen-wheeler accident. The trailer had been carrying a variety of items, some of which could be volatile if mixed together, so he'd had to radio in a state trooper with hazardous material training.

They'd sent H.D. Springer, the most arrogant son of a bitch in the entire Louisiana state police system. The central region had the reputation for being bastards, anyway.

He'd pushed Kevin through all of the inspections and other bullshit required, oblivious of the fact that traffic was stacking up like crazy. He'd also left Kevin with a pile of forms that had to be filled out, even though there had been no chemical problem.

That left him at a typewriter well after the others on his shift were gone.

He was in the locker room changing when Ed Clemmon wandered in. Kevin recognized him as one of the Circle. He'd seen him at a meeting.

He knew more than he'd told Holt. He was saving some information for bargaining. Holt had scared him, but not badly enough to keep him from thinking about saving his own skin.

For a moment he entertained an idea of trying to pry out information that he could pass on to Holt to help avoid prosecution. He couldn't quit thinking about taking a rap for all of this mess.

It had seemed like a good idea, and good fun the times he'd gone along. It had been a hoot to watch tough-assed bad boys get the look of fear in their eyes and piss their pants when they realized the cops weren't playing by the

247

rules anymore.

He'd laughed as loud as any of them when they'd watched the criminals struggle for footing as they turned and ran ass in hand into the woods, not knowing what waited for them there.

He hadn't believed that shit the first time, the word that there were monsters out there. He'd thought they'd meant something like the sasquatch. Then they'd told him these things were worse than that.

When he'd seen the remains of a corpse one of those creatures had worked on, he had become a believer.

He'd had a queasy feeling then about what they were doing, but he'd figured he would get used to it. He'd become accustomed to killing animals after his first hunting trip, and they'd told him it was the same thing: They were hunting human animals.

He'd never dreamed someone would get on to it. Hell, the cops were running the show. Cops didn't investigate cops. He'd heard that all through college about how the fraternity took care of its own.

Now there were other cops breathing down his neck, and he was dirty, as dirty as any of them. The only way to get clean was to violate the fraternity.

He'd been agonizing over the notion for a while now. It wasn't something that made him feel proud, but he knew he would do it when the time came, knew he would do it because he had to for his own survival.

"Have you gotten word yet?" Ed asked, walking over to him as he prepared to change out of his uniform.

"Heard what?"

"There's a hunt going down."

He stopped undressing and looked at Ed across the locker door. "When?"

"Your three days off have started, haven't they?"

"Yeah. Tonight."

"You'll be able to go. They're going out at dawn probably. LaFleur said get the people together. It's kind of a rush thing, not the usual hunting party. I mean, you know, the guys from other areas might not make it in."

"Who are we gettin' rid of?"

"Some kid the word is. He attacked a man or some-

248

thing, and they never even pressed charges."

Kevin nodded. "I'll plan on being there. We just meet out at the place around daylight?"

"That's it."

"I guess I'll see you later, then."

"Yeah. Later on." He slapped Kevin on the back before moving on.

Kevin turned back to his locker and quickly began changing his clothes.

For his own ass he had to get word to Holt. He definitely wanted to save his own ass.

Dinner was crawfish étoufée. Rand had purchased the crawfish in season from a farm in Avoyelles Parish and had them frozen for later. The dish was prepared in New Orleans style and served over steaming rice.

"I've come to love the Cajun dining in this state," Rand said. "It's another good thing about living here." His voice was bright and warm. He was trying to act the polite host.

Jag only picked at the food with his fork while Deb simply pushed her plate away and sat with her arms folded.

Rand tried for a while to eat without noticing their stares. Finally he put down his fork and glared back at them.

"You might as well be in your rooms if you're not going to join me," he said.

Jag took his napkin from his lap and dropped it on the table to indicate his agreement with the suggestion.

Rand slammed his fist down on the table and called out Scarecrow's name.

A moment later the grim angel-of-death figure walked through the doorway.

"Take them upstairs," Rand said with disgust.

Scarecrow nodded, indicating they should get to their feet. They rose in compliance and met him at the door.

"Wait a minute," Rand said.

Scarecrow looked back at him.

"Put them in the study. I want to speak to them again

before you retire them for the night."

The bounty hunter ushered them from the room, offering no words at all since they already knew the way to the sitting room.

They stayed alone there for another half hour, kicking around ideas for escape as their fear mounted. Jag kept running his hands through his hair as he paced the floor.

Deb handled her fear in a more compressed manner, curling in a chair and folding her arms around herself.

"We're going to die here, aren't we?" she asked.

"Looks like it from here," Jag said. "Unless we can come up with something."

"There's no way out of those rooms," Deb said. "Once they nail us back there, we can write it off."

The door creaked open, and they both jumped. Mutual sighs of relief rushed through their lips as they saw the dark-haired girl walk into the room.

She looked at them timidly for a moment, then tried to smile.

"I'm sorry about what's happening," she said.

Deb got up and walked toward her. "Do you have any idea what's going on here?" Deb asked her.

Her eyes fixed on Deb hesitantly for a moment, then she nodded slightly and rushed forward, throwing her arms around Deb in a tight embrace. She was crying by the time her face made it to Deb's shoulder.

"I'm trapped here too," she said. "Ever since my mama died."

Deb embraced her, touching her hair and gently trying to comfort her. "You're Rand's daughter?"

"I am. I've been here all the time this has been going on."

"My God," Deb whispered.

"I don't know about all of it," Serena said. "Just some, what I could figure out."

"It's all right," Deb said, soothing. "It'll be okay."

"I don't want you to be hurt," Serena said. "He's brought you here to hurt you, and I know you're innocent."

Deb looked over the girl's shoulder, making eye contact with Jag. He nodded that he understood. They might have a way out of this mess after all.

"It's been so long since I've seen anyone besides the people around here," Serena said. "Ages since I've seen another woman close to my age."

"I know it must be rough," Deb said. "I lost my mama too."

"He wants to protect me. All he's done, he's done to keep me safe, but he's killing me here. All the other things too."

"This all happened after your mother died?" Deb asked.

"Gradually. He wasn't always like he is now. After mama died, he started hunting the men that did it, and he met Scarecrow. While all that was going on, he started reading these books. He got them in New Orleans in some old shop in the French Quarter."

"Did they have to do with the mormo?" Jag asked.

She pulled back from Deb, rubbing her eyes. "I don't know about that."

"So did he find the books first or Scarecrow first?" Jag asked.

"I'm not sure, but he got really into these books. They were bad. They were banned. The Catholic church has this list of books, and these were on it. They were written by a man named Matthew Laird.

"He was a priest at one time, working in some parish in South Louisiana. He fell in love with a young girl, and they excommunicated him."

"I've never heard of him," Jag said.

"His stuff is very strange," Serena said. "I've been reading about him. He went to the French Quarter after they ran him out of his parish. He tried for a while to minister there as a street preacher, but he gave in, wound up living in a brothel. He wrote his books there after he contracted venereal disease.

"His mind was all messed up with rituals and philosophies that twisted the teachings of the Church."

"Your father's concept of divine guidance is based on *that?*" Deb said.

"Yes."

"A twisted combination," Deb said to Jag.

"I guess that's what it would take to create something as

251

bizarre as what's going on here," he said. "A crazed philosopher, a grieving millionaire, renegade cops and Cajun swamp men."

"If we live through this, I don't think I'll ever sleep again," Deb said.

LaFleur stood behind the house, his cigarette glowing with each nervous puff. He continuously scanned the forest's darkness.

He'd never been wild about the notion of dealing with the swamp men. He'd thought they had been joking about them at first. Now he knew better. He'd seen what they could do.

He was worried because of what had happened the previous night. It hadn't been easy to clean up, and there were going to be more questions asked.

He always had to clean up the messes, and he was growing weary of it. He'd had the job of placing the body on the railroad track, and he'd had to tie up loose ends many times, watchdogging computer records as well as he could and always looking over his shoulder.

While they did a lot of good, he was not thrilled about what was coming now.

No question that the kids had to be killed. They'd been able to learn too much, but the boy was a reporter. He'd be missed, and putting down questions about him was going to be a real challenge.

Still, there was a woman involved. That made the cover-up easier. Everybody knew men did crazy things where women were concerned. Dropping everything to run off with a woman as cute as this one was wouldn't be hard to belive.

He'd watched her during the moving process. She reminded him of his wife, cute, soft, warm eyes. Probably had a stubborn streak like Sandy as well. They were all alike really, weren't they?

Men doing strange things because of women? True.

He'd thought of Sandy while he was with the women he'd met after her departure. As he'd bedded them, he'd wanted to cry out: "You may not want my loving, Sandy, but this little bitch does, and she's enjoying the hell out of it."

Much of what he'd done with Le Circle had been because of her too, indirectly. He'd been thinking of her, thinking that he wished she knew what he was up to, that he was doing something important and valuable.

Somehow he felt it would impress her, thrill her because he was so tough and bold.

Maybe joining the Circle had been a bad call. What had they accomplished other than a few deaths? Innocent people were being killed by these monsters Rand had created. And this girl, Deb, who could blame her for wanting to find her brother's killers?

Maybe they didn't have to kill her. Maybe there were some other things she could do, interesting things. The things Sandy wouldn't do even when they were married.

Hell, if it meant staying alive, there was no telling what she might be persuaded to do.

Kevin got no answer when he dialed Holt's house. He stood by the pay phone, swearing as the night wind assaulted him. He let a few minutes pass before trying again and got only the answer of the constant ringing.

Jamming the receiver back into its hook, he turned up the collar of his jacket and stuffed his hands into his pockets. He didn't want to try Nielson yet. It was Holt he wanted to talk to, Holt he wanted to bargain with. Holt had issued the threats, and it was Holt he wanted to guarantee his immunity when things broke apart.

He could let a little time pass waiting for Holt. That wouldn't be a problem.

Deb had coaxed Serena over to a chair.

"I'm so sorry about all this," Serena said.

"It's not your fault," Deb whispered. "Your father is a very disturbed man."

"He's my daddy."

"I know that. I know how I felt about my daddy. He was the strongest man in the world."

Jag hovered quietly near the wall, watching without interrupting.

"He hasn't always been this way," Serena said. "Really."

"I know," Deb said. "Sometimes things happen and people can't deal with them. Your father has been trying to find justice somehow for the death of your mother, but he's gotten out of hand. He doesn't even understand that he's turned around. He's doing things that hurt people. He killed my brother, and my brother never hurt anybody. He was disturbed himself because he lost the girl he loved."

"I'm so sorry."

Deb gripped the girl's arms. "Serena, listen to me. You've got to help us. There isn't much time, and we need your help."

"What can I do?"

"Your father is going to kill us. You have to help us get away."

"I don't know. I've never been able to get out of here myself."

"We just need an opportunity, after they lock us back in our rooms or whatever. Somehow we've got to get out of this house before morning."

"I have to think. I have to get an idea." She closed her eyes tightly. "Will you take me with you?"

"That'll be too dangerous right now," Deb said. "But if we can get out of here, we can come back for you. If we can get out of here, everything that your father has been doing is over. Jag is a reporter. His story will blow this wide open."

"Will they take me away from Daddy?"

"You'll probably still be able to see him. You'll have an opportunity to get out and see other people, go to school. Meet guys."

"I don't want you to be hurt."

"Then help us. Please."

The study door opened, and Rand walked in, anger filling his face as soon as he saw Serena.

"What are you doing here?" he demanded.

Serena jumped up from the chair. "Please don't hurt them, Daddy."

"What have they been telling you?"

"Nothing. Really."

He turned to Scarecrow, who stood behind him. "Take her back to her room."

With a nod, the Cajun took her arm and led her through the doorway. She looked fleetingly at Deb, but she offered no resistance.

Rand walked toward them when she was gone, a smile gracing his features. "Were you trying to turn her against me?" he asked.

"We were trying to tell her the truth," Deb said.

"Your truth. She's not ready to know the whole truth, about how evil the world is. About how bad things are."

"What if she knew her father was part of the evil?" Deb asked.

"You'll never understand."

"What? That your concept of God is based on the ramblings of a man whose brain was eaten away by venereal disease?"

Without warning he brought his hand back across Deb's face. Her head jerked to one side with a hard snap, but she did not fall. She twisted her face back to stare at him defiantly even as her lips colored slightly with a drop of blood.

Jag was moving, about to take a swing, but she stepped toward him, blocking his path.

If he attacked Rand it could only make more problems. Better to let things settle a little.

She rested her hand on Jag's shoulder, whispering, "Let it go."

Jag was tense, his anger evident in every muscle. She kept her hand on his shoulder to stay him.

"You've obviously heard the wrong things about Father Laird. I don't think we have anything more to talk about," Rand said.

He turned and walked from the room. A few moments later, Scarecrow returned and ushered them down the hallway to their rooms.

Holt sat in Honeycutt's kitchen with Nielson, finishing

a second cup of coffee while the jailer checked on his wife.

Both men were tired, and they had no more leads to follow for the night; but they remained, talking about old cases and things that had happened to them, both good and bad.

Home for both of them meant loneliness, so rest could wait.

The floor creaked as Honeycutt walked back into the room. His face was lined with fatigue, and a look of worry had nestled behind his eyes.

"How's she doing?" Holt asked.

"Not good," the jailer said. "She's having trouble breathing. I think I need to take her to the hospital. Can you guys give her a hand?"

"Sure," Holt said, answering for both of them. "We'd be glad to."

"Let me get her dressed, and then if you could help me drive her over, I'd appreciate it."

Kevin dialed Holt's number again at a pay phone in the foyer of the diner where he'd stopped for supper. He checked his watch as he waited for an answer.

It was past nine. He wondered where Holt could be. In a little while he'd try the other numbers. There was still plenty of time if the hunt didn't begin until dawn. Plenty of time.

They sat on the floor in Deb's room, staring at each other.

The thought of dying hung between them in the air as if it were more than a thought, as if it were some hard, tangible symbol they could both view.

"What do we do if she doesn't come?" Jag asked.

"I'm thinking."

"We can't really count on being missed."

"I know."

"If we do get out of here, what do we do? Those things are out there."

256

"I know. If we don't get away, we're going to be up against those creatures while there are cops chasing us too."

"If she helps us out of here, we're still dead meat," Jag observed.

"Are you saying we shouldn't even try?"

He shook his head, his manner resigned. "We've got to try. It's just that the odds don't seem very good."

"If we don't get out, they'll keep on doing this. The man's insane, and he's got everybody backing him up."

"Okay," Jag said. "On the event that Serena comes for us, we have to get out of the house. We don't know how many cops are involved in this, but we can bet several are lurking around outside."

"We get past them any way we can," Deb agreed.

"Scarecrow?"

"He's big."

"No doubt tough as well."

"Can you . . . ?"

Jag laughed. "I was out of my head when my little incident occurred. I'm no regular fighter, and I'm sure he knows what he's doing."

"We'd better come up with some kind of weapon before we leave."

"Then we get past everybody in the house," Jag said. "We're outside."

"We avoid the woods."

"At all costs. That's the way they'd send us on the hunt. The mormo are out there somewhere."

"So we head for the highway, try to flag down a motorist."

"That's our best shot."

"They'll have people posted elsewhere too," Deb said.

"Probably. They don't want us to get away. They can't afford for us to get away."

The reality of the statement brought them back to the stagnant feeling, the stalemate of emotion. They looked into each other's eyes, studying each other's terror.

Eventually Jag moved over and put his arm around Deb. She rested her head on his shoulder.

257

"It won't work the way we've planned it," Deb said.

"I know," Jag agreed. "You want to try anyway if Serena shows up?"

"Of course. We'll do down fighting."

Sitting in his living room, Kevin tossed another beer aside and tried calling Holt's number one last time.

"Fuck it," he said, hanging up after fifteen rings.

He checked the number and dialed Nielson.

Hung up.

Tried Honeycutt.

Cursed again, a string of profanities this time since there was no answer. He was sitting here ready to solve their case for them, and they were nowhere to be found.

Climbing from his chair, he rattled the couch where Christine, the waitress he'd picked up at the restaurant, was sleeping.

He had jumped her as soon as they'd hit the front door, grinding her into the shag rug in the living room.

She hadn't protested, had helped him by squirming quickly out of her uniform, hungry for the touch of his hands and the feel of his lean muscles next to her. He had that effect on most women.

She looked up at him sleepily now and smiled as he gazed down at her. She wasn't beautiful, was a little flabby around the middle, and he didn't care for the way she frizzed her platinum blond hair—it wasn't her natural color anyway—but she wasn't bad. She was soft and willing, and she took his mind off his problems.

He had a pretty good buzz from the beer he'd downed while trying to get Holt on the telephone, but that didn't matter. He was up to the occasion.

He dropped down on top of her, pressing his face against hers in a hard kiss as she tugged the thin blanket from between them.

Holt could wait.

With the rise of the moon, the mormo slowly began to emerge from their nestings, grunting and sniffing at the breeze.

The fresh, cold air of the night energized them.

The wind that whipped through the trees was sharp and cold, and it seemed to gain speed with each gust. They ignored that, milling around each other in preparation for the stalking.

Their feedings had gone unpunished, so they could hunt the night again. They could move a little farther from their domain.

The men had been there to push them back before, and the internal fear held them in check; yet now they were able to venture outward. They did not have to accept the puny meals offered by the small animals that lived in the forest, animals hard to find in winter.

They did not have to wait for the few stragglers who drifted their way.

They could go out and search for food. Human food, the food they desired the most.

Chapter 24

Serena sat on the edge of her bed, her pillow clutched against her.

She had to act, yet she didn't know what to do. She'd been trapped here by her father's fears for too long. She wanted to get up, walk out there and set Jag and Deb free.

They were nice people — good people — at least that was her first impression of them. For so long there had been no one except the workers, the tutor, the people who came to see Daddy.

Now here were two people who, under other circumstances, could have been her friends — friends like she'd had in Texas.

Deb was pretty, and she was strong. When she questioned Serena, her voice had been firm in spite of the predicament she was in.

Deb could have been Serena's big sister. Someone to talk to, to be close to.

For a moment a scenario played in her mind. Deb *was* her big sister, and they sat in a bedroom far away from here, not in some isolated mansion but in a bright suburban home. There were teddy bears and lace pillows, and they talked.

Deb offered advice about prom dates and proper fashion, and they laughed and hugged each other.

The scene brought her sadness, however, because it was so far removed from where she really was.

She had no strength. She needed strength like Deb had. The courage required to come here looking for her brother's killers had been immense.

Serena needed that kind of courage. She had to summon it from within herself if she was to be able to slip out of this room and find some way to free Deb and Jag.

Slowly, she eased her weight off the bed.

"The journey of a thousand miles . . ." she thought.

Gently she placed the pillow back into place before walking to the door. With great care she gripped the knob and turned it slightly, easing the door back only a crack so that she could peer out along the hallway.

A fairly young man was sitting in a chair near the doors of Deb and Jag's rooms.

He looked incredibly bored as he thumbed through a gun magazine that had probably been brought up from her father's study to help him pass the time.

She watched him silently for a moment. He was not as formidable as Scarecrow, but she knew if he was involved in this business, he was dangerous.

She didn't feel confident enough to seduce him with feminine charm. She'd been told she was beautiful, but she didn't have the experience with handling men.

The alternative of hitting him with something also seemed out of the question. She wasn't experienced with violence, either.

That left her wits, not honed as much as she might have hoped, but the only option that seemed viable: hit him straight on with the fact she was Mr. Rand's daughter.

She drew a deep breath and stepped from her room, walking briskly down the hall.

The cop looked up at her when she reached him, a little surprised by her presence if not by the haughty air she presented. The way his eyes played over her suggested she might have found success in tempting him.

Instead she put a stern expression on her face. "I need you to open the door," she said.

He half grinned as if the suggestion amused him. "We got people locked up in there."

"I know that. I need to tell them something. My father said it was all right for me to talk to them. They're not dangerous, you know."

"Anybody's dangerous in a desperate situation. They could take you hostage."

"I've talked to them. They won't hurt me."

261

"Miss Rand, you'll be better off back in your room. I don't think you really understand what's going on around here."

"I know what my daddy does. My mother was the one those animals killed."

"I just don't think it's a good idea."

Mentally forcing herself to maintain control, Serena kept up her offensive. "Why don't I just go talk to Daddy about it," she suggested.

Finally the cop sighed and threw up his hands. She could tell he was aware things were strange around the Rand mansion. Who was he to question what she was allowed to do?

Reaching into his pocket, he pulled out his key ring. "You want me to leave you in there? If they hurt you, it'll be my ass on the line."

"They won't hurt me," Serena said, keeping her voice arrogant and firm. "They know better." She implied that he should know better than to question her as well.

Reluctantly he slipped the key into the lock and twisted until it clicked, then he pushed the door slightly inward.

She slipped past him without lowering her guard, pushing the door into place behind her.

Once it was shut, she sighed with quick relief.

Jag and Deb were already on their feet, moving toward her.

"We've got to figure something out," Serena said. "I got past him once, but when he opens the door to let me out, I don't know what we're going to do."

"Who else is out there?" Jag asked.

"Just one cop on this floor right now," Serena answered.

Deb looked over at him. "Think you could break his jaw, slugger?"

"A cop? With serious physical training and all that? I doubt it."

They looked around the room for something heavy enough to hit him with. Nothing turned up.

"Could you get him away from the door?" Deb asked.

"I had a hard enough time keeping myself together to get in here."

"She could go out and bring him back in here," Jag said.

"And?"

A bright look crossed his features. "The commode tank lid."

A check revealed that it was removable and made of suitably heavy porcelain to crack a skull.

"This place wasn't built like a prison," Jag observed.

"Thank God," Deb said.

They nodded, indicating Serena should return to the door.

"What should I tell him?"

Jag caught Deb's arm. "Maybe you should do it?"

"What?"

He didn't have to speak it.

"I can't handle that," she said.

"You'd be better than I would," Serena said.

"You're both beautiful," Jag said. "Trust me on this."

"Then, it's both of us," Deb said.

"An offer he can't refuse," Jag agreed. "He's a man. Even if he's suspicious, we know which head is going to win out."

Jag lifted the lid, testing first the weight of it and then his ability to swing it downward.

"Are we up to this?" Deb asked.

"Better than we're up to dying," Jag said.

Pausing for a moment before the mirror, Deb made an effort to smooth her hair.

"You first," she said to Serena.

"This is crazy," Serena whispered. "I've never done anything like this."

They moved to the door, and she knocked on it softly.

"What?" the cop barked from outside.

"It's Serena. Could you open up?"

The keys rattled for a moment, and then cautiously the door opened a crack so that he could look in.

Serena smiled at him.

"What?" He remained gruff.

Serena tried to seem seductive, but she couldn't speak.

Deb eased behind Serena so that she was visible through the crack.

"She got your attention for me," Deb said softly. "I don't want to die."

The cop shook his head. "I'm sorry."

Deb opened her eyes wide. "Isn't there anything I could do?"

263

He shook his head, but still he looked at her, unable to keep his eyes from checking her out.

Serena stepped back, leaving the space between Deb and the cop open.

Absently he let the door drift open a little farther.

Deb didn't have to feign the nervousness that made her seem awkward in his eyes. The vulnerability seemed to entice him. He was around twenty-five and thin almost to the point of being lanky, his nose somewhat sharp.

"You couldn't help me?" Deb asked.

"Where's your friend?"

"He went in his own room. He was crying."

"I don't know," the cop said.

"Come on," Deb urged. "You didn't become a cop to have young women turned over to killers, did you?"

He bowed his head for a moment, showing what was perhaps his ounce of decency. "I guess not."

Swallowing nervously, he stepped through the door and closed it, cautiously looking around. Reaching under his coat, he drew out a small revolver before walking toward the bathroom door.

Deb drew a quick breath and held it as he pushed it open.

The bathroom was empty.

Satisfied, he pulled the door shut and used his key to lock it.

"Okay," he said. "Maybe I could do something for you,"

Deb could tell by the look in his eyes he was lying. He'd overcome that ounce of decency in exchange for a nice roll with her. Even if his friends were going to kill her, no need for him to let her go to waste. She wanted to spit in his face.

He had no way of helping, and he knew it.

And now the damned door was locked. Jag had been smart enough to move back into his own room, but now there was no way for him to get in here and put the toilet lid to use.

She felt like a high school girl who'd made a promise she didn't want to keep.

Coyly she reached up and touched her hair, her thoughts racing to turn up some avenue that would lead out of this mess. Things had been bleak before, and now she was going to be molested before they killed her.

"What's your name?" she asked. That would delay things a millisecond or so.

"Doyle."

"My name is Debra."

"Nice to make your acquaintance."

He looked toward Serena. "Sit down over there."

She moved to an armchair against the wall by the door, obviously terrified.

Deb felt her heartbeat quicken. She'd never known this kind of fear before, had never been confronted with something quite like this.

She took a step backward as Doyle began to advance on her. There was no exit, no way to run as he slipped his arms around her waist and began to kiss her neck.

His kisses quickly became more like bites, like he was gnawing her. She closed her eyes, praying for deliverance just as his hands began to move across her body.

He started urging her toward the bed, not ceasing his activities even as he inched her across the floor. She clenched her teeth, trying to regain control of her breath. His hands groped her, clutching at her breasts and ass before moving to the dress belt. Lifting her hands, she took his shoulders and pushed him back, spinning him and easing him onto the bed.

"Just lie back," she whispered.

He fell onto the mattress, his legs hanging over the end of the bed. She knelt there, placing her hands on his thighs and rubbing gently through the cloth of his jeans.

Again closing her eyes, she rested her face against one of his legs. "I'm so glad you're going to help me," she breathed.

Doyle only grunted.

She continued to caress, listening to his breathing as he rested his head back, enjoying her touch. Slowly, she let her fingers glide up the large silver buckle of his belt. She let a soft purr issue from her throat as she lifted her head from his leg and began to fumble with the buckle.

He was content, eyes closed, slight grin.

She slammed her head down into his groin, aiming her forehead for a central spot with as much force as she could manage.

In an aerobics class once, one of her male instructors had given her some tips for taking care of herself. He'd told her about kicks as foremost defense, but he'd also shown her how to use other tricks. He'd explained what the human skull could do.

He'd also recounted a fight he'd had in which someone had kicked him in the balls. The reaction he'd described was much like that Doyle was displaying now. His moan was quick and accompanied by a rush of wind escaping his lips.

He drew his knees up to his chest and rolled onto his side, mumbling, "Oh, God."

Serena was sitting paralyzed in the chair.

"Come on," Deb called to her. "We don't have much time."

She scrambled onto Doyle, digging for the keys. He tried to resist, but he didn't have much strength left. She'd hit him right.

About then Jag began hammering on the bathroom door with the toilet lid. The wood cracked in one spot just before Deb moved to it.

"It's okay," she said as she slipped the key into the lock. "We've got it under control."

The door opened as soon as she released the latch, and Jag burst through it, gripping her in his arms when he saw she was all right.

Doyle was struggling to get up from the bed. When he realized it, Jag moved over to him and pulled the bed-spread up around the man, wrapping him in it and shoving him onto the floor.

"Groin?" Jag asked.

"Worked better than a toilet seat."

"You must have got him good. I got kicked there once in a basketball game, and it didn't mess me up that bad."

Through the blanket they heard the man retching.

"I gave it my best," Deb agreed.

Together, they moved to the door, slipping it open after peeping into the hall.

"I want to go with you," Serena said. "Take me away from here."

"It's too dangerous out there," Deb said. "You'll be fine here until we get help. Okay? We'll send back for you."

Reluctantly the girl nodded. "Okay."

Leaving her there, Deb followed Jag into the hall. They moved along the gallery and found a narrow stairway which seemed to be the service entrance.

They travelled down the stairs two at a time, being careful to move as quietly as possible. When they reached the bottom, they were in the kitchen.

It was deserted now and quiet. They rushed across the tiled floor to the rear entrance.

Deb prayed it wasn't locked.

It opened.

Outside the wind was harsh, showing little mercy. Both of them began to shiver since they had no jackets.

"It never gets this cold in Louisiana," Jag complained.

As if in answer to his complaint, a new burst of wind slammed into them.

The night sky was covered in clouds.

"Do you think it could snow here?" Deb asked.

"Hardly ever." He looked up at the sky. "Better chance of freezing rain."

"If we were in for some, it'd be right in line with what's been happening," Deb said.

"Let's see if we can get to the highway and flag down a motorist before we have to worry about that," Jag suggested.

They began to move along beside the rear wall of the house, agreeing to trace a route around it and make their way across the front grounds, cutting onto the driveway once they were past a few of the curves that put it out of the view of the house.

Deb felt her heart pounding again. She imagined eyes watching them from everywhere; the eyes of their captors, the eyes of the mormo, who were waiting to rip them open and devour them.

A few days ago her biggest worry had been locating Mark. Now he was dead, and she was fighting to stay alive.

Jag reached back to take her hand as they rushed along the side of the house, ducking past windows and stumbling over uneven ground. Before long the sound of their breathing was coarse. Their lungs labored, churning the cold night air, turning it into shadelike wisps from their nostrils.

Plotting a course through the shadows, they traversed the front lawn and moved along beside the driveway, dodging in and out of trees.

As they had planned, they moved to the edge of the driveway once it curved from the view of the house.

Slowing their pace slightly to let their bodies recuperate, they jogged along the uneven ground, stopping at the halfway point to catch their breath.

Leaning against a tree, both panted, sounding like hounds after a foxhunt, Deb thought.

"Do we just go out there and look for headlights?" Deb asked.

"I vote we try."

After a moment more of trying to catch breaths they could not fully regain, the started again, walking more than running now. Beneath the shrouded sky, with the wind tearing at them, that was the best they could manage.

They travelled through the trees and around the bends, avoiding holes and other obstacles.

Twenty minutes passed before they began to near the highway. It was in sight, a dim clearing. No sign of cars, but it was undeniably the road.

For the last few feet they moved onto the driveway, jogging again toward its mouth.

A feeling of elation began to flood through Deb. They had survived. They had made it when it didn't seem possible; they'd laughed at death.

The gleam from the shadows was almost undiscernible, yet in the slowing down, Deb began to realize there was something there in the darkness, something not hidden but still almost invisible.

She halted and grabbed Jag's arm, and then he saw it too, a car parked on the roadside, parallel to the driveway.

It became even more apparent a moment later when the interior light flashed on as the door opened.

The guy who stepped out was a large burly man with thick black hair. The sound of the mechanism of his pump shotgun carried on the wind, a loud grinding of metal that had a very final sound. He stood against the door of the car, resting the barrel of the gun on the vehicle's roof.

"Y'all weren't planning on leaving before the hunt, were you?" he asked in a slow Southern drawl

* * *

Kevin got rid of the waitress after he'd screwed her a third time. She was tired and almost lifeless, and his anxiety had returned. There wouldn't be any waitresses in prison.

After getting dressed, he tried Holt's phone, then Neilson's, and got no answer.

"Shit."

Where could they be? A heart-stopping thought caught him. What if they had turned up information of their own and didn't need him. They could be somewhere getting organized right now, ready for a raid.

He'd better get to the sheriff's office and offer some kind of assistance. That was his only hope.

He tugged on his cowboy boots, got his coat and rushed out to his truck.

Damned cold. He slid behind the wheel and cranked the engine to get the heat going. He turned the radio on for the hell of it, even though he knew there'd be no news of a raid at this hour.

It was past midnight.

Between songs on the country and western station, KTKL-FM, he did get a weather broadcast. If it started raining, it could be expected to sleet or to turn or freezing rain.

He'd never understood the difference between the two, but he knew ice storms were a real bitch. You hardly got cold weather in Louisiana, but when you did, it made up for the mild winters when you could wear short sleeves in Feburary.

He hoped he wouldn't have to go out with these guys on any raids tonight. The weather was going to be hell.

Chapter 25

Nielson stood beside Holt in the hospital corridor. They were drinking bitter coffee from the vending machine and fighting off their weariness. Both of them wanted to go home and sleep, but they didn't feel comfortable leaving Honeycutt alone.

His wife was probably dying. She had no more strength to fight the disease that had eaten away so much of her insides. They didn't want to leave him with that coming. He didn't have anybody else to turn to. She had some family nearby, but they hadn't made it to the hospital yet.

If she passed away, he would need someone to be there, and since they had spent a great deal of time with him in the last few days, it seemed significant that they be nearby.

Leaning against the handrailing, they made small talk about sports, fishing, women, and police work.

The minutes seemed to drag by, as if the second hand were going in slow motion. To kill the boredom, they walked down the hall to the waiting room labeled a solarium because of its large picture windows.

Now, with the blackness outside, the glass only reflected a mirror image of the room itself.

Stepping close to the pane, Holt could look out. He could see street lights and the traffic signals along Sanders Street. Off to his left the small blue lights of the Med Evac heliport glowed, the hue they created somehow eerie in the winter night.

"It's a shame," Holt said. "Nobody in this wonderful business of crime fighting can stay married; and you get somebody who manages to make it work and something else fucks things up."

"God works in strange ways."

"I guess He does. I wish I understood Him. And the devil. We see a lot of that son of a bitch."

"I don't think a lot about evil when I make an arrest," Nielson said. "I guess it's there."

"It's there," Holt agreed. "Inside us all. I'll guarantee you." He looked up toward the sky. "It could get nasty out there," he said.

"It's been a hell of a winter already. It started getting cold in November. That's early for around here."

"Letting us know what was ahead. Omens. The world is full of omens, but you never really learn to look for them."

The cop, Idal Taylor, had a walkie talkie on the front seat of his car. He used it to summon help, so within a matter of minutes, LaFleur and Scarecrow joined him where he was holding Jag and Deb.

"We can't leave them in the house," LaFleur said. "That's obvious."

Scarecrow only nodded in agreement.

"The shack isn't safe," LaFleur reminded. "It didn't work for those two kids."

"If they die too soon, they die too soon," Scarecrow said.

"Who takes them out there?" LaFleur asked. "It's not exactly a safe walk either."

Scarecrow's twist of his head indicated they would all go together.

The hesitancy lasted only a few seconds before Taylor lifted his shotgun and led the way, gun ready in case anything appeared.

Scarecrow and LaFleur were both carrying large flashlights which they shone through the darkness, the bright beams blazing the path around the house and into the forest.

Jag and Deb walked side by side, keeping their hands on their heads as instructed. LaFleur walked behind them with a revolver pointed at their backs.

As they entered the trees, the wind seemed to pick up its speed. The chill grew worse, and the darkness seemed to be alive with motion.

271

LaFleur occasionally swept the flashlight around, checking the nearby trees for signs of life. A few times the beam caught the eyes of small animals, producing a startling glow in the darkness. On each occasion, the party froze, and guns were trained in the direction of the eyes until everyone was satisfied they were seeing raccoons and not mormo.

Each stop served to heighten the terror that was throbbing within Jag and Deb, pulsing through them with each quickening heartbeat.

When the small cabin came into view in the beam of the flashlights, they both swallowed. In a way it was like viewing their own tombstones.

With a ring of keys, Scarecrow approached the door and unlocked a padlock which appeared new. The door rattled on its hinges, and Jag realized it fit loosely in the frame.

It had been damaged recently.

LaFleur opened it, stepping back for them to enter the small front room first. Then he followed them inside and pulled out a cigarette lighter which he used to light a Coleman lantern that hung from a peg beside the door.

A few wooden chairs and a bench were the only furnishings. Jag realized it was a place where people waited for death.

Taking Jag's shoulder, LaFleur shoved him toward a support beam that angled toward the ceiling. The cop then pulled a pair of handcuffs from his belt and locked Jag's hands over his head so that he hung from the beam, his toes barely touching the floor.

Deb was shoved onto one of the rough-hewn benches, where she sat rubbing her arms against the chill which seemed even worse in the interior of the building.

"Who stays with them?" LaFleur asked.

Scarecrow's gaze indicated he wanted LaFleur to stay.

The policeman did not disagree, even though he was not excited about the idea. He took Taylor's shotgun and selected a ladder-back chair near the door which allowed him to keep an eye on Jag and Deb while watching the door at the same time.

Scarecrow pulled it closed as he left, but the wind whistled through the cracks, spitting icy breath into the room.

Kevin found only one dispatcher sitting at the console at the sheriff's office. It was Broussard, a fat guy with a pock-marked face and curly black hair that always managed to look greasy.

As he leaned back in his swivel chair, the button on his shirt threatened to burst across his stomach.

"I'm trying to find Detective Holt," Kevin said.

"Who are you?"

"I'm from the city police. It's kind of important."

"It's the middle of the night."

"I know that. I just need to see him."

"He's at the hospital."

"What?" Kevin's heart felt like it was trying to climb up through his esophagus. Had they already found something and taken someone to the hospital?

"Guy from the jail's wife got sick. Holt is with him. He called in a while back to let us know about the guard since we work with him."

"What's the room number?"

"She's in ICU."

"Thanks," Kevin said, turning and rushing for the door.

His time was being eaten up. It was getting close to two A.M. now. Everything was going to fall apart. If somebody got killed before he could get Holt, he'd be in trouble sure as hell. The fact that he'd been trying to do something didn't mean anything.

He got back to his truck in the parking lot and piled in behind the wheel, scrambling to get the engine going again.

Fortunately the hospital was only a few blocks from the sheriff's office. He shoved the gas down and spun his tires, leaving a streak along the concrete as he pulled onto the street.

"I can't believe what you did," Nicholas Rand said, staring down at Serena as she sat in the armchair in his study. "They are my enemies. They would destroy all that I've tried to do here. Don't you see that? Have you no respect for your mother's memory?"

273

She did not cry, or at least she was able to withold her sobs, thus depriving her father of the satisfaction of breaking her spirit. She could not control the tears that oozed out the corners of her eyes and streaked down her cheeks, however.

She sat and listened to his assaults and determined she would defy him, defy his imprisonment. Even if Jag and Deb died tonight, she would escape here, get out of this place and find some way to have a normal life.

Finally, his anger at her spent, Nicholas left Serena sitting and slammed the door behind him, locking it into place.

Rising from the chair, she walked over to the window, pressing her face against the glass and cupping her hands around her eyes so she could see outside. She could see the forest, but only faintly, no sign of Deb, Jag or their captors.

That didn't really matter, though. She'd wandered the woods enough times in spite of the constant warning from her father and from Scarecrow. She knew where they had taken her new friends. She knew, and she could go to them. They would need her help again, and this time maybe they would take her away with them. She prayed that would be the case.

A cigarette dangled from LaFleur's lips as he sat in a chair near the door. The shotgun lay across his lap, and he kept looking at Jag with a disgusted expression on his face. He didn't have a high opinion of Jag as a human being. It showed.

Slowly his gaze played over from Jag to Deb. The short skirt had slid up her legs, leaving her knees and thighs exposed far more than she was comfortable with, but she didn't move to straighten the hem because she didn't want to give him the satisfaction of making her nervous.

He stared at her legs for a few moments, then looked up to her face. "What the hell does a girl like you see in a shithead like this?"

She didn't reply.

Easing up from his chair, LaFleur walked over to Jag, standing in front of him while cradling the shotgun across

274

his arm.

"What's she like? You nail her? You're the kind of shit that probably fucks my wife nowadays."

Jag looked at him. He had nothing really to say in reply to that, and it seemed to make LaFleur angry.

With a sweeping backhand slap, he struck Jag's face, knocking the reporter's head to one side. "Give you an idea of what you did to that poor bastard you attacked," LaFleur said.

The blow jarred Jag, and a trickle of blood began to slide down his chin from the corner of his mouth.

Deb stood up and started to move toward them, her voice spewing protest. LaFleur turned quickly and pointed toward the chair. "Sit down," he demanded. "Now."

Such anger and hatred sounded in his tone that she complied, frightened, still wanting to help Jag but uncertain of what to do.

"Did that hurt, pussy?" LaFleur asked. He rolled his fingers into a fist and struck Jag in the face just below his left eye.

Jag sagged against the cuffs at his wrists, and his head rolled as if it were about to topple. Still he remained conscious.

"You're quite a man," Jag managed through his bloody lips. "A real big man, LaFleur."

That made the cop madder, and he slammed the end of the shotgun into Jag's stomach. Jag bent forward as far as his body would give, and a new trail of spittle and blood flowed through his lips.

LaFleur was preparing to strike him again when Deb launched herself from the chair, slamming into the cop's back. Her shoulder struck him in the center of his spine, forcing air from his lungs and knocking him off balance.

The shotgun slipped from his grasp and landed at his feet. He tried to stoop for it, but Deb piled onto his shoulders, wrapping her arms around his throat and trying to squeeze. Backing around, he reached up to grab her. It was difficult for him, but he managed to grab a handful of her hair and pull.

The pain was not severe, but it brought tears to her eyes. She gritted her teeth to keep from giving in, but he pulled harder. When her grip eased, he bent forward,

275

gaining the leverage he needed to flip her over his shoulder.

She rolled onto the floor, surprisingly not hitting badly. She started to scramble away from him, angling toward the shotgun. Jag tried to kick it in her direction, but the cuffs did not allow him to stretch far enough to do any good.

And then LaFleur had her ankle. He yanked back hard, the force plopping Deb down onto her stomach.

She began kicking as LaFleur climbed up her, gripping tightly along her legs until he had rolled her over and straddled her waist, using his weight to pin her down.

"Leave her alone, you son of a bitch!" Jag screamed.

LaFleur backhanded her once and started to do so again. She lifted her arms to ward off the blow. When he swung, she grabbed his forearm, holding as tightly as she could manage.

He began to shake it in an attempt to disentangle himself, a string of curses spewing from his lips until he was able to bring his other arm around and strike her on the side of her head.

She let go of his arm while she continued to struggle beneath his weight, twisting her body from side to side and hammering her fists into his abdomen.

He cursed again, grabbing her shoulders and pulling upward. She spat in his face, and he slammed her back against the floor.

Deb jerked her head to the side just in time to avoid having her skull strike the floor. Her shoulders took the impact. The pain shot through her, and she was lifted again as he prepared another attack.

Before he could push downward once more, she threw her arms around his waist, gripping her left wrists with her right hand in a lock that gave her a slight advantage. She continued to twist and kick wildly, an effort to dislodge LaFleur's weight. In response, he grabbed new handfuls of her hair, pulling hard. His face was a contorted mass of anger.

Her grip loosened, but she noticed the bulge beneath his jacket.

LaFleur's eyes widened with realization at the same instant she pulled the seam of the coat open and yanked out

276

the small pistol.

Pulling back from him, she pressed the pistol up into his throat.

"Get off me," she demanded. "Now."

He slipped backward without arguing, lifting his weight so that she could slide from beneath him.

She pulled herself to her knees, keeping the gun aimed in his direction. She held it between both hands in an effort to keep it steady.

"All right, you bastard, let Jag go."

"You've got to be kidding."

She looked quickly at the mechanism of the gun, determining its function. She raised it a little higher. "Move."

Slowly, letting her know he wasn't intimidated by the weapon, he walked over to Jag.

"Slowly," she said, when the cop pulled the keys from his pocket.

"Yeah, yeah." He unlocked the bracelets.

Jag sighed as the tension was released. He didn't fall, but he staggered for a moment until his footing was firm. He rubbed at his wrists, then lifted his hand to his cheek where the flesh was swelling into a dark purple bulge. It was the color of Bic ink.

LaFleur stood by, acting impatient as Deb kept the gun on him.

Jag breathed heavily as he started to make his way over to Deb. On his second step, he lost his balance because a wave sloshed in his head. As he stood there like a surfer facing a wipeout, LaFleur moved, grasping Jag's shoulder and shoving him forward into Deb.

She stumbled backward and took Jag down with her, and then LaFleur was after the shotgun.

Deb screamed as the pistol slid out of her hand.

Rolling quickly off her, Jag grabbed for LaFleur, catching him by the belt before the cop reached the shotgun.

LaFleur spun around and punched Jag in the face again. The blow connected high on Jag's cheek, but it didn't crack his jaw or knock him unconscious. He drove a fist into LaFleur's ribs, angering the cop more than hurting him.

LaFleur's hands closed on Jag's shoulders and shoved him back toward the wall beside the door. As he slammed into the wall, Jag tried to get a grip on LaFleur. They went spinning around the room and then crashed to the floor.

LaFleur swung at him again, striking Jag's chest this time. He then grabbed Jag's collar, hitting him again in the face, then again.

Deb scrambled across the floor for the pistol and twisted around to aim it in the direction of the men.

"Stop it!" she shouted.

LaFleur ignored her.

She tried to point at him, find a way not to hit Jag. She knew her aim would not be that sure. She jumped forward, landing on her stomach, and angled the gun up in the only sure way to miss Jag.

In a split second, LaFleur realized what was happening. As he let go of Jag, the cop's mouth dropped open in shock while he looked down at Deb.

Before he could react to strike her, she pulled the trigger.

The explosion splattered his groin open in a gaping spray of crimson. He cried out as he fell to the floor, the blood gushing from the jagged crater between his legs.

His hands pressed against the wound, but blood leaked out through his fingers. He thrashed; then his body quivered. He gasped for air, and his eyes rolled back in his head. In an instant, his face was covered with perspiration.

Deb turned her eyes from his death throes and slid across the floor toward Jag, kneeling beside him.

"Jag? Jag?"

He opened his eyes. He was bleeding and bruised, but he sat up without hesitation. "Just watch to see if any clear liquids start oozing out of my nose," he said. "I think that means my brain is melting."

She helped him to his feet, and he walked over and picked up the shotgun, weighing it carefully in his hands.

"Can you handle it?" Deb asked.

"I guess I'll have to. You keep the pistol."

"You sure?"

"Yes."

They looked down at LaFleur, who was now still.

"What do we do?" Deb asked.

"Stay here and wait for daylight?" Jag asked.

"Will that work?"

Something struck the side of the building. A second later something else scraped along the outer wall as inhuman grunts issued through the thin planks.

"Something tells me it won't," Jag said.

Kevin's truck screeched into the driveway in front of the hospital. A security guard tried to tell him he could not park there, until he showed his badge.

With a nod the guard let him pass, and he walked into the lobby. The entrance desk was empty, so he had no way to get room information.

He moved up the hallway until he spotted a nurse. She was fat and fifty with a nasty disposition that was readable on her face.

He cornered her and asked where he could find Mrs. Honeycutt.

She told she was too busy to check that kind of business for him. She suggested he come back in the morning.

"Fuck that," he said. "I've got to find some people that are with her."

He let his size intimidate the woman until she went to a phone and checked with the nursing stations, finding the information he needed.

"ICU," she said.

He didn't bother thanking her as he headed for the elevator.

It seemed to take forever for it to wheeze up to the desired floor. He was ready to bounce off the walls when the doors finally opened.

He rushed out into the hallway and almost failed to notice Holt and Nielson standing in the waiting room.

Out of the corner of his eye he did spot Holt, however, and shoved his way into the room.

Both Holt and Nielson knew something was up when they saw him and his frantic nature.

"What's going on?" Holt queried.

"It's happening. A new hunt." He swallowed to catch his breath. "They're getting ready for it tonight."

"Who have they got?" Holt asked. "Who are they going

279

to hunt?"

Kevin swallowed again, trying to get his breath. "The reporter and his girlfriend."

"Holy shit," Holt swore. "Where are they?"

"South part of the parish. In the woods beyond Nicholas Rand's sugar plantation."

"It'll take forever to get out there," Nielson said.

Holt looked back to the window. "I don't think it will," he said.

"You've got to be kidding," Nielson said. "It's too damned windy."

Three minutes later they were in the ambulance office where the helicopter pilot had been eating a late night sandwich. He was a thin, dark-haired man with a sharp nose and large ears. Montgomery was stenciled over his uniform pocket.

He was startled when Holt came barreling into the room, and he shook his head repeatedly at Holt's request.

"Can't do it," he said in a deep Southern drawl. "Can't do it 'cause there's a storm blowin' up. Been listenin' to it on the Weather Channel. We're in for some sleet. Bad. I been thinkin' 'bout goin' on home. Can't take the bird up."

"You can get us there before the storm hits," Holt insisted. "People could get killed. We can't radio for help because we don't know who the bad guys are. We'll never get there in time with ground units. We have to catch them in the act."

"I'm sure it's important, but I can't do anything for you. I got regulations. I got that chopper to think about. It's not my property, and I'm responsible for it. Besides, it's to pick up people that are hurt or sick, not run errands for the sheriff's department."

"Let me give you something to think about," Holt said. He pulled his .357 from his holster and leveled it at Montgomery's head. "If you don't get that fucking plane warmed up, your equipment's gonna be blown to hell. You understand how that works?"

Montgomery swallowed. "I think I follow you," he said.

"No, I'll follow you," Holt said. "Let's get up to the roof."

Chapter 26

Scarecrow tried a third time to reach LaFleur by radio and finally put down the handset with a shake of his head.

"Something's wrong," he said.

"They could have escaped?" Rand asked.

"Possibly, or the mormo could have attacked the cabin."

"We've got to know."

"If they did escape, they won't get far," Scarecrow said. "That was the idea of putting them out there."

"No, we can't take the risk of leaving things to themselves," Rand said. "If they've escaped, then the hunt has begun."

"We've only got a half-dozen people here," Scarecrow said. "A lot of people aren't comin' 'til mornin'."

"Use what you have," Rand said. "I want them found."

Scarecrow did not offer further protest. He worked for the man. He did what he was told.

He made a quick check of his Magnum, then went over to a rifle case and selected a .30-.30.

Then he headed into the sitting room where the cops who had already arrived were waiting.

There were eight of them, and they all looked ready to get started. Dressed in heavy jackets, they had lanterns and guns on hand.

"It's time to get going," Scarecrow said. "The prey has made a premature escape."

Serena had slipped from the upstairs room and had been kneeling outside the door when her father gave

281

Scarecrow his orders.

Before Scarecrow exited the room, she had rushed back along the hallway and made her way up to her own room, where she collected a heavy overcoat.

Shrugging it on, she made her way down the back stairs. In the kitchen she picked up a flashlight before leaving the house into the night wind.

The sky above her seemed to be moving now. Soon the storm would come. She could sense it. She had to find Deb and Jag before then. She had to warn them the men were coming for them.

If she could, she had to help them escape the mormo as well.

If there was any way to escape the mormo.

As Serena was entering the edge of the forest, Deb and Jag were crawling through a window at the end of the cabin opposite the noises.

As they made their exit, they heard the snorts and grunts of the mormo, mingling with their occasional cries.

"They're out for another feeding," Jag said.

Deb nodded. "Let's hope they'll stay busy at that house for a while."

"Maybe the cop's body will appease them," Jag said.

"I doubt it," Deb said. "They aren't scavengers. They prefer to kill their meat themselves."

She followed Jag on a path through the trees, illuminated by the lantern they had taken from LaFleur.

Attached to Jag's belt was the walkie talkie. At the moment there was no chatter on it, although they had heard Scarecrow's voice crackle over the airwaves moments ago. They had decided not to respond, hoping he would think the weather was interfering. That was more likely to buy them time than trying to imitate LaFleur's voice.

They'd held on to the device because it might be handy in keeping track of what the others were doing tonight.

The best course now seemed to be to work their way through the forest to the highway or to the first sign of civilization they happened upon.

They prayed they would encounter no mormo on their way, knowing the possibility of unhampered flight was unlikely.

The wind continued to pierce them, sending shivers through their muscles. Deb knew they would not be able to survive the cold for long the way they were dressed, especially if the storm came.

The only optimism she could muster was the notion that the ice storm might send the mormo back to wherever they dwelled when they were not stalking people.

She followed Jag through the trees, making suggestions that allowed them to double back past the cabin.

Curiosity urged them to train the light toward the area where the mormo obviously crouched, but fear prevented them; the light beam might bring the monsters crashing down on them.

Instead they crept past, their shoulders hunched as they tried to ignore the grunts that carried on the wind.

Scarecrow led the men on horseback. He felt like he'd suddenly become a western sheriff leading a posse. In a way he wasn't far removed from that.

He had his six-shooter on his hip and his men at his back, and though the sharp beam of the Everready lantern was a technology not found on the wild frontier, it was a small technicality.

The cops cradled their rifles across their arms, ready for sighting fleeing prey or taking on the monsters if they were ambushed.

Scarecrow had taken the time to explain the danger before they had mounted up. In spite of his hatred of talking, sparing words at this point could cost lives.

With a tight grip on the reins of his mount, he plotted a course carefully through the trees, avoiding the low-hanging branches and other obstacles that might knock his men from their horses.

He planned to check the cabin first and get an idea of what had happened. If they did not find the corpses of LaFleur and the others being devoured, he would make a plan to search for the reporter and his girlfriend. They could not have gone far. Not on foot. Not in this cold.

The horses would give them an advantage. Besides, the kids were not experienced survivors. They would be clumsy prey, easily caught.

He guided his mount around a fallen log and coaxed it onward until the glow of the cabin came into view. He urged the animal forward with a kick to its side. With a snort the horse picked up speed, carrying Scarecrow out a little ahead of the others.

He dismounted in a fluid motion and gripped the reins in one gloved hand while holding the rifle ready in the other.

The door of the house was closed, but he sensed something was wrong. In a quick motion he twisted his reins around the branch of a small bush and gripped the rifle with both hands.

He'd approached houses where desperate men were holed up enough times to know he needed to be fully prepared for whatever awaited.

He paused while the men behind him approached, dismounting themselves. He held up a hand momentarily to let them know to be silent. Then he started for the door, one boot in front of the other, finger on the trigger of the rifle.

His intention was to kick the door in. It was rickety from the previous damage and would splinter easily.

If the kids were hiding in there, he was confident that he could outgun them. Even if they were armed, they would hesitate to fire at a human being, and a split second would be all he needed.

He was lifting his foot for the kick when the door crashed outward, ripping off the frame.

Scarecrow stepped back just in time as it flattened to the ground. A single mormo stood in the doorway, its arms raised high as its mouth gaped open in a bellow of anger.

Fragments of flesh dangled from its lips where saliva dripped down in strings.

Scarecrow squeezed off two quick shots, the bullets ripping into the creature's chest just left of center.

The explosion of its flesh and dark blood confirmed the hope that its heart had been ruptured, but that did not stop the flurry of bullets that came a second later from the policemen behind Scarecrow.

If he had not already moved to one side to avoid the

door, the barrage would have torn into him as well.

Instead, they riddled the monster, jerking its body about in a slow motion dance that lasted several seconds before the thing finally toppled to the ground.

Scarecrow kept his gun trained on the doorway for several seconds after that, waiting for more monsters. They never came, so he walked slowly through the opening.

He turned his head away from LaFleur's body. The thing had been eating him, but the gunshot wound was still apparent.

He backed from the house and nodded to the others.

"The kids must have gotten away."

"Which way?"

"Toward the highway. That's where they were tryin' to go before."

He climbed back onto his horse and led the way. He didn't speak to the other men. He wasn't worried about finding the kids. The dead mormo worried him more.

It was not one of those he had helped create. It was an old creature. He could detect that somehow its appearance, or perhaps he could sense it through whatever power of magic possessed.

If he had not created the monster, where had it come from? There could be more of the things out here than he could ever imagine. That was frightening.

The helicopter chopped uneasily through the air, the billowing wind swaying it from side to side as it cut its way through the dark sky.

"This is crazy," the pilot protested. "I need to set her down. The wind is bad enough, but if we get the freezing rain, you don't want to even think about what it's going to do to the prop."

"You don't want to think about what I'm going to do to your ass if you don't get us where we want to go," Holt warned. He was sitting in the seat beside the pilot while Nielson and Kevin scrunched together in the back.

The bird was not built for comfort, but it was designed for speed; so it whirred above the city, the lights below becoming quick white blurs.

Holt kept tapping his fingers absently against the glass

285

beside him. The sound was cloaked by the noise of the rotors above them, but his impatience could not be muffled. It was like a cloud that floated around him.

He had been pursuing this matter incessantly. It had given him some meaning in the last few days, and it was on the verge of coming to a head.

He didn't relish the idea of exposing corruption among other police officers, and he knew this was going to make things hard on everybody; but deep down he anticipated a feeling of fulfillment, some kind of accomplishment in a job that was so infrequently rewarding.

Reaching beneath his jacket, he rechecked his service revolver, making sure it wasn't going to fail him. Then he fumbled for a cigarette and was admonished by the pilot not to smoke.

"Just fly the fucking plane," Holt demanded, "or helicopter or whatever it is. Get us there, dammit. Just get us there."

Chapter 27

It became apparent by the sounds that carried on the wind that the mormo were behind Jag and Deb, trailing them perhaps, definitely moving forward.

"They must smell us," Deb said.

"So they're stalking us," Jag said. "We survive a bunch of killer cops only to be eaten by Cajun bogeymen. When I had nightmares like this when I was a kid, my mother always told me it could never happen."

"Anything can happen, can't it?" Deb said through gasps for air. They stopped for a moment, leaning against a tree and clutching each other closely as they tried to find some kind of warmth.

"Anything," Jag agreed.

He looked back through the darkness, trying to catch sight of the monsters, but his gaze could not penetrate the night. He could see little beyond the cloud of his own breath. "They must not have been satisfied with LaFleur's corpse," he said.

"No, you were right before. They want a hot meal," Deb said.

They pulled away from the tree and began to run again, swatting their way through the brush and praying they would not stumble.

The air seemed to be growing colder. It chilled the sweat on their bodies, and cold knots formed in their throats.

Deb had heard something about breathing through the mouth to provide moisture while running, but in trying it found little relief.

Jag's legs ached. He'd been sitting at desks longer than he'd realized. Even at this young age, he wasn't as spry as he once was.

They moved down a slight knoll and slid across some wet

pinestraw before stopping again. Jag took the flashlight and bounced it from one direction to another, now uncertain of whether or not they were headed the right way.

"Where the hell is the highway?" he asked.

Deb raised a hand hesitantly, touching it to her lips for a moment as she prepared to make a suggestion.

The tree branches above them rattled then, and before they could look up, a pair of the creatures dropped down on them, grabbing at them and dragging them to the ground.

Deb screamed, her voice rising on the wind as her attacker's claws ripped at her back.

Jag drove the shotgun back against his assailant, loosening its grip just enough to gain freedom. He wheeled around and pressed the barrel into its gut before pulling the trigger.

The blast tore through the creature, sending a spray of blood, organs and shattered bone out through its back. It twitched for several seconds, its hands futilely clutching at its ruined abdomen until it could move no longer.

Jag twisted around and shoved the shotgun against the forehead of the thing holding Deb. Its yellow eyes blazed and its mouth opened in a guttural roar that was cut off when Jag squeezed the trigger again.

The head exploded in all directions, sending bloody fragments and brain matter in a shower onto nearby leaves and against Debra's face.

Pushing the dead creature away from her, Jag knelt at her side and used his sleeve to wipe the mess away as much as he could.

She was trembling, and he had to use his fingers to pick chunks of meat from her hair. She gagged but did not throw up, and he hugged her.

"We've got to keep moving," he said. "We were lucky this time." He own voice was trembling badly.

She gasped, fighting the terror. "I know," he said. "I know."

They found the pistol and got back to their feet, setting off again in the direction they hoped would lead to the roadway.

The helicopter's spotlight played back and forth across the

landscape, painting a huge white glob on the ground below.

Holt peered down through the glass intently.

"We've got to be getting close," he said. "The mansion is out along this highway. I remember driving past its entrance."

"We'll find it if we don't crash," the pilot said. He seemed to be fighting the controls, doing his best to keep them from being carried away by the wind.

Scarecrow urged his mount to move faster, wishing he'd taken the trouble to put on spurs. They did make a difference in moments like this.

He wanted to round up the kids and get this over so that he could get out of the night. Something was wrong about these monsters. They had grown too bold, and now ones that he could not recognize were turning up.

The first real fear he had known in a long time was gnawing inside him now. He had overcome the tendency to think twice about men pointing guns at him. He never worried about dying when he went after killers, but monsters worried him, especially when they were out of control.

He kept his lantern trained in front of him, watching to make sure there were no mormo crouched on the trail awaiting him.

The men behind him were cautious as well, riding with their guns angled upward. They constantly glanced into the trees in spite of the speed with which they were travelling.

The gunshots they had heard ahead of them had served as a warning. The things were out here, and they were dangerous.

Scarecrow half expected to discover the mormo feasting on Jag and Deb. He wasn't sure how he would react to that. It would put an end to the hunt, but it would only signal a continuation of the problems with the monsters.

He almost felt like sighing with relief when they came upon the bodies of the dead creatures.

The kids had survived some of the mormo, at least. He had no way of counting how many others must be pursuing them.

He motioned for the men to ignore the carcasses and guided them on through the trees. They had to be getting closer, either to the creatures or to their prey, or both.

He slowed the pace of his horse a bit. They would reach the mormo before they reached the kids, he reasoned. They had to be prepared for that.

Jag and Deb had to pause once again to rest. They could hear the thrashing of the leaves behind them now as the mormo pursued them, knocking branches about as they scurried along.

"They're going to catch us before we make the highway," Jag said.

"We have to fight them."

"The guns aren't going to hold out that long, not against so many of them."

They grabbed a few more breaths and then got up again, running with as much speed as they could muster. Both of them were lagging now, their legs churning far slower.

The shotgun kept growing heavier in Jag's grasp.

Within a few more steps, they were able to look forward and see the clearing of the roadway. Despite the exhaustion that was seizing them, they staggered toward it, supporting themselves against the trees, moving one step at a time.

Their faces were numb, their limbs aching, and their lungs felt tight and dry.

About a hundred yards from the roadway, they heard the mormos.

They turned and looked back at the trees behind them.

A half dozen of the creatures were spread out along the ground, crouching in preparation for an assault. Another handful of them were scattered about in the branches of the trees, squatting, jaws sagging open.

Jag lifted the shotgun. He would blast whichever of them moved first. Beside him, Deb gripped the pistol between her hands.

The monsters seemed to leer back at them as the wind whipped the trees about. It was as if they knew Jag and Deb stood no chance against all of them and were only waiting for their moment, the perfect moment, to attack.

Jag flexed his fingers on the shotgun. He was sweating in spite of the cold. Deb closed her eyes for a second, squinching them tightly and then opening them once more. She and Jag both jumped when the horses broke through the trees, Scarecrow in the lead.

The other men were a short distance behind them.

He spotted Jag and Deb first and pulled the reins back tightly on his horse. His rifle swung around toward Jag.

Then he saw the mormo and realized he was in the middle of them.

A split second later they struck, dragging his horse down and yanking him from the saddle. The ones in the trees began dropping on the men behind Scarecrow.

Shots rang out, but few found their marks as the creatures clawed at the men and knocked them to the ground, piling on top of them to rip them open.

Jag grabbed Deb's arm, and they whirled again, with the cries of the vigilantes ringing up through the trees behind them. They ran, dodging branches and leaping over obstructions.

They could not help the cops, but they could make the roadway.

They did not look back as they covered the remaining distance, and when they reached the shoulder of the road, they began to race along the soft gravel, praying a car would appear.

The rain started then, fine at first then heavier. In their frozen state, the drops hit like bullets.

Scarecrow's rifle was ripped from his hands, and he felt claws encircle his shoulders as the mormo yanked him across the ground.

He cursed under his breath as he felt teeth pierce the flesh of his left shoulder.

His right arm was pinned, so he had to struggle with his left in spite of the pain. He forced his fingers beneath his jacket and closed on the Magnum, adjusting the holster to an angle that pointed the weapon against his coat.

When he pulled the trigger, the blast tore out through his coat and through the intestines of the creature that was trying to chew his head off.

With a screech of pain the monster fell backward, black blood spewing out in a geyser.

Shaking free, Scarecrow drove his right elbow back into

the face of the other creature that was on him. It drove the thing back a few inches, and Scarecrow tugged the pistol from beneath his ruined jacket and squeezed off a shot which tore half the monster's neck away.

As it fell, he tugged the kerchief from around his neck and pressed it to the wound on his shoulder.

He looked over at the other men. They had not fared as well. They were engulfed by the crowd of creatures, screaming as they were devoured.

He could do nothing for them.

He cursed and spat on the dead things at his feet, then wheeled around and jogged forward. His horse had bolted only a few hundred yards, and he was able to coax it to him in spite of its fear.

Using his belt to hold the fabric over his wound in a makeshift tourniquet, he climbed back into the saddle and urged the horse on.

"I see people down there," Holt said, pointing toward the roadway. "On the shoulder."

The spotlight swerved over to pick up the forms.

"That had better be them," the pilot said. "I've got to set her down. The blades are going to ice up."

The rain was already hammering against the windshield.

"Do it," Holt said, his pistol yanked from the holster.

The wind buffeted the chopper, and the men inside were pitched about violently.

"Fucking shit," Holt screamed as he watched the approach of the ground.

In spite of the weather, the craft leveled off before touching down. The landing was rough, but it was not a crash. The passengers were jarred with their weight straining against their safety belts, but they survived with little more than scrapes.

Holt recovered first and yanked the belt buckle free. He jerked the door latch open quickly and piled out of the cabin.

The wind and rain hit him as soon as he was clear. He squinted, looking for a sign of the two people he had seen running. The storm was blinding. He looked back over his shoulder and shouted for the spotlight.

The pilot complied, and the white light began to bounce about, flashing on the falling ice as the beam swept the edge of the forest.

Holt still couldn't catch sight of the people.

"You people, we're here to help," he called out.

While keeping his finger on the trigger, he stowed his gun beneath his jacket to keep it dry and took a few more steps away from the helicopter door, ducking his head beneath the slowing propeller blades.

The hands took him from behind, dragging him backward to the cold, hard blacktop of the highway. His gun tangled in his coat as he attempted to pull it free, and he felt a sudden pressure against his throat.

He tried to struggle, then realized that his throat was gaping open. The claw that had swept under his chin had sliced down into his jugular.

He gagged as the blood filled his windpipe. Dizziness seized his brain, and he lay back against the asphalt. He knew he was dying, but his mind would not excuse him from his effort to free his gun so that he could fire at his attacker.

His attacker? As his hand tangled in the fabric of his coat, he rolled his eyes upward. His vision was blurred, and the cold icy rain pelted against his forehead and ran into his eyes. The creature was hideous, unbelievable. He had never seen anything like it.

It was a maddening black monster covered with leaves, something out of a campfire story like the ones he'd heard in Boy Scouts.

Boy Scouts, Jesus, is this my life running before me?

He coughed, his blood coursing out his throat. He tried to shout, to warn the others, but his voice was lost somewhere in the damage to his body.

His eyes drooped shut just before the monster bit half his face off, its teeth snagging the edge of his mouth to rip back the flesh of his cheek. The flesh gaped open over his teeth, the cold air touching his gums in a way that he'd never felt. Spit drooled through his teeth, and blood from somewhere poured down his throat, strangling him. He tried to cough it up and sent a spray of gore through his nostrils.

From the doorway of the helicopter, Nielson could barely make out the movement that was shrouded by the darkness and the storm. He shouted to Holt and got no answer. His own weapon was already drawn, and he prepared to slip from the craft to offer help.

He didn't plant his foot on the ground, however. Something struck him in the chest, and he was driven backward into the cabin. Slamming against the seat, he felt the muscles of his back strain. He tried to swing his gun forward, but something grasped his wrist, something dark and hideous, like a moss-covered claw.

With a yell, he turned his gaze from his wrist to peer into the gaping maw that hovered over his face.

The screaming stopped with his breathing, and before the others in the chopper could react, more creatures were piling in, falling over each other to get to the prey.

Jag and Deb crouched in the ditch beside the roadway. Through the rain, they could see the bright light in the interior of the helicopter.

Bright red blood splashed against the inside of the windshield as if it had been sloshed from a bucket.

A moment later the lights flickered out.

Debra turned her face away from it, eyes closed again. She leaned against Jag for support. They clung to each other for a long moment as the rain continued its assault.

"We've got to get away from here," Deb said.

"Where the hell do we go? With this storm, there won't be any cars out. My God, it's over with."

She felt Jag's muscles trembling, and his words were lost in the near sobs.

"What the hell are we going to do?" he asked. "What the hell are we going to do?"

His breathing was out of kilter, and he continued to shudder. He slipped his arm from around Deb and pressed his hands against his face.

"There's not any way out," he said. "Did you see all the blood?"

With his wet hair twisting away from his head and his eyes wide with fear and near-hysteria, he looked like a mental patient in a padded room.

"They're gonna fucking eat us," he said. "We're mormo food."

Steeling her own nerves, Debra grabbed his shoulders and shook him. She could understand what he was feeling, but she couldn't let him give in. Another second and she would be reacting in the same way. "Get hold of yourself," she warned. "We've got to find shelter or we'll die out here before the mormo get us."

He shook his head. "It's no use."

The cries of the men in the chopper rose above the noise of the storm.

"Is that what you want?" Deb asked. "They'll be after us in a minute."

"What's the use?"

The grunts of the feasting monsters continued. Their meal would be complete in a matter of seconds.

Deb's motion was quick. With her open palm, she slapped Jag hard across the cheek where he had not been bruised.

The jolt widened his eyes even farther, this time with surprise. He looked down at her, confused for a split second before reality took a hold of him again. He wiped flecks of frozen rain off his forehead and shook his head.

"I'm sorry . . ."

"Let's just get moving," Debra said.

They pulled themselves from the ditch and continued along the shoulder of the road. It was a challenge to keep their footing as the ice built up, coating the ground with a slippery sheet.

Within minutes their clothes were drenched, their hair littered with fragments of ice.

They leaned against each other for support and were near collapse when they looked forward to see the huge black horse blocking their path.

Serena rushed through the trees in search of some sign of Debra and Jag. She had found the cabin empty except for LaFleur's ruined corpse, and she was frantic.

Her friends might be dead also, torn apart by her father's monsters. The horrible torn body she had found in the forest kept rushing back to her thoughts. She kept seeing Debra ripped apart in that way, her arms and legs strewn about on the ground like discarded litter.

Serena pulled her coat up over her head to protect her hair from the cold rain and ran through the forest, disoriented.

The trees above her broke the fall of the ice, but as the frozen mess built up on the high branches, which were large, they began to crack and tumble down in shuddering crashes, the noise of the showering ice sounding like an avalanche.

She kept dodging the debris as she moved, trying to find some sign of other people.

Even spotting Scarecrow would be a blessing now. She despised him, but he would take her to safety; she was confident of that. And as the thought of LaFleur's body kept playing through her mind, even the captivity of her father's house began to seem lucrative.

She thought about heading back there herself and realized she did not know the way. In the darkness, nothing in the woods seemed familiar.

She began to try and get her bearings but could find no landmarks.

She stumbled and fell on a downed branch and was about to pull herself up when a loud crack sounded in the oak tree above her. The branch tumbled downward in a crystal spray of ice, landing across her back and pinning her against the cold ground.

She cried out, but the wind and the slicing hiss of the freezing rain drowned out her voice.

Wrenching her body from side to side, she tried to pull herself from beneath the thick branch, but it was too heavy, especially with the ice coating.

Digging her hands into the ground, she tried to pull herself forward without success.

She saw rather than heard the footsteps. Her view was mostly of the ground, but she saw them walking forward through the night, muddy, dark.

She closed her eyes when they stopped beside her.

The creature crouched, grunting as it touched her hair and ran a grime-covered hand across her skin.

Chapter 28

Jag looked up at Scarecrow seated in the saddle with his Magnum drawn. The big man seemed oblivious to the ice that slashed all around him, bouncing against his clothes and cutting into his face.

"Put down your guns," he said.

"Do we have to carry this on?" Jag asked. "It's over. Your monsters are out of control. You can't keep any of this a secret any longer."

"I have orders to bring you in," he said. It sounded like a line from a John Wayne movie, but there was no sound of humor in his voice.

"You're as crazy as your boss is," Jag said. "You're insane."

"Drop the guns." He began to swing his leg over the saddle to dismount.

"Do as he says," Jag said. He stooped, preparing to lay the shotgun on the ground, but as he bent forward, he eased his thumb through the trigger guard. He glanced up at the bounty hunter, who was stepping from the horse, one foot still in the stirrup.

Jag jerked his thumb back on the trigger, and the shotgun blast exploded in a loud roar like thunder.

Spooked, the horse reared onto its hind legs, pitching Scarecrow backward. He hit the rough edge of the highway, and his pistol went bouncing from his hand.

The shotgun was now empty, but Jag dove for him with it in his hand, using it as a club. He struck the big man across his wounded shoulder. This was not a time to risk mercy.

A deep cry of pain issued from Scarecrow's throat as he slugged Jag in the side of his head. Jag felt his ear go numb from the blow, but he scrambled on top of the big man and hammered the barrel of his gun at Scarecrow's cheek.

Scarecrow blocked the blow, catching hold of the barrel. He ignored the scorching heat of the metal, gripping the weapon tightly and pressing upward against Jag's efforts.

Jag drove a knee into the man's gut, yanking back on the gun at the same time. It slipped from both their grasps and went sailing back into the ditch behind them.

Scarecrow swung upward with his left hand, striking Jag across the chin. The force of the blow staggered Jag, and he rolled backward, off Scarecrow and onto the icy ground.

The big man was on his knees in an instant and then his feet. From somewhere beneath his jacket, he produced a hunting knife. Then he lifted one heavy boot to stomp down on Jag's chest.

Jag rolled before the crushing heel could strike him, and it ground harmlessly into the gravel. Scarecrow staggered and lifted the knife, ready to slash downward with it.

The gunshot roared over the sound of the storm, a loud crack that echoed through the forest.

The bullet swished harmlessly past Scarecrow but made him pause. He turned and looked toward Deb.

"Is that what you used on LaFleur?" he asked. "Give it to me before you hurt yourself. I don't intend to let you castrate me with that thing."

He extended his free hand toward her, taking his gaze off Jag. When he did, Jag rolled sideways, catching Scarecrow around the knees and toppling him.

They went down the side of the ditch together, rolling across the ice-coated clay and down into the soggy pit of the crevasse, the knife bouncing in Scarecrow's hand.

Deb ran after them, slipping on the way down and falling onto her side. The mud raked her hip, bruising her badly. She moaned as she slid on down into the muck beside Jag and Scarecrow.

The big man held Jag by the collar, shaking him back and forth with one hand and moving the knife toward his face.

Without hesitating, Debra pulled the gun up and fired again.

The bullet hit Scarecrow in his arm just below the shoulder. He dropped the knife and reached for the wound, holding the point of entry as he staggered around to stare at Deb. His eye was filled with a look of hatred.

Bracing herself on her knees, she fired again. The next bullet bit into his chest near the center. It was a lucky shot. It penetrated the muscle with a thud which popped a spurt of blood back through his shirt. He clutched at the opening briefly, looking as if he'd had a heart attack.

Then he dropped facedown into the slush and lay still.

For a moment, Deb only looked at him, wondering if he had been one of the ones who had killed her brother. Without changing her expression, she walked past his body and offered Jag her hand.

He accepted it, getting to his feet only with a great deal of effort. The pains of the evening were taking their toll on him, and the continued attack of the rain was not helping.

"We've got to get out of this weather!" she shouted. "We'll die of exposure!"

"Any suggestions?"

They struggled up the slippery slope of the ditch together. The horse stood there, pawing the ground nervously.

"We're going to have to go back to the mansion," she said. "We'll die out here otherwise. We can't go back into the forest for the mormo, and we can't take much more of this cold."

Jag didn't argue. The mansion could be reached by following the roadway, and anything was preferable to the forest.

Slowly they approached the horse. Confused by the storm, it snorted and trotted a few feet away before Jag could grip the reins which dangled below its mouth.

Deb approached it next, speaking to the horse and reaching out gently. It pawed the ground and twisted its head from side to side against the stinging rain, but she managed to grip the reins.

Petting it softly, she did her best to calm it before motioning Jag over.

With a struggle, he pulled himself onto the saddle, and Deb took his hand and dragged herself onto the horse behind him.

In his study, Rand paced. He walked from corner to corner, his fresh glass of wine untouched on the table beside his chair.

He could raise no one on the radio. He should have gone with them on the search.

In this storm anything could be happening. He reached into the pocket of his jacket and checked the small .38 revolver secreted there. It was loaded and ready to fire if the need arose.

Dropping to a seat in his chair, he folded his arms. Things were beyond his control. He did not like that. He had grown accustomed to having things as he wanted them to be, yet now his entire system was threatened; his daughter hated him for all he had done to protect her. It was horrible.

He listened to the brutal hammering of the rain against his windows and closed his eyes, trying to combat the thoughts that assaulted his brain.

He remembered his wife. So many happy times had filled their days together. How could she have died so brutally?

It had been fitting, what they had done to the animals who had attacked her. It was only what those subhuman bastards had deserved.

He had grinned with satisfaction as Scarecrow had carved the symbols into their flesh and the transformation had taken place. He had laughed at them as they ran into the forest and smeared themselves with mud. It was the very squalor they needed.

Now he found no satisfaction in recalling those moments or in watching the fear fill the eyes of the later prey turned out to them.

He had down so much to punish the evil. Why were things so wrong?

He had not wanted to kill the young people, but they had intruded. They had challenged his quest to fulfill his mission, and nothing could be allowed to interfere. Nothing.

An eye for an eye, many eyes for many eyes. The guilty had to be punished. They could not be allowed to escape their crimes. The smallest evil had to be sought out and destroyed to protect society.

300

If not, anarchy would prevail, and anarchy of murderers running wild in the streets.

He saw no irony in his vision, no flaw. It was the outsiders who ruined things, not any inconsistencies of his own thinking.

He had no idea that he was insane.

He leaned back in his chair, lifting his glass to his lips and letting the bitter wine slide across his tongue.

The lights went out with no warning. The darkness was immediate, falling over the house as if a blanket had suddenly dropped.

Rand made no move. He knew the outage was the result of the storm. Branches fell on power lines, or the buildup of ice itself weighted the lines until they snapped.

That explained the darkness well enough.

The crash of the downstairs window caused him to stand up, however. The storm was not that powerful, not the ice or the wind.

Fumbling through the darkness, he opened the door and started to inch his way along the hallway, his eyes adjusting slightly but not enough to give him much visibility.

It was too dark for that.

"Serena," he called out. No answer returned.

He kept his hand against the wall to steady himself and moved along the corridor, headed for Serena's room.

He had covered about half of the distance to the stairs when he heard the screams below. He listened, cringing. They were the cries of the servants.

The sounds of their dying chilled him, but he found some comfort. At least Serena's voice was not among them.

He continued along the corridor, making his way around the gallery. He kicked open the door to Serena's room and called her name.

Everything was still except for the whisper of the sleet outside.

Fumbling about he found the decorative, scented candle he had given her the previous Christmas and then some matches in her night stand. The candle was a thick blue cylinder which offered up a sweet smell when it blazed to life.

He held it high above his head, surveying the room. The bed was undisturbed, but the closet was open. He walked over to it, dragging the clothes quickly from one side to the other.

Her coat was missing.

The shock of that sent him stumbling backward to the bed. He almost dropped the candle as he sat there, gripped by the horrible realization that Serena had gone outside. Somewhere.

That could not be, not in this storm, not with the monsters out there. Not after everything he had done to protect her.

He raised one hand to his face, weeping as the candle flame continued to flicker its warm golden glow across his face.

After climbing from the horse, Jag and Deb approached the front door of the mansion. He held the small pistol now, feeling a little like James Bond. Deb followed him, her hands against his back as they moved. She was holding her breath and chewing her lower lip.

He reached forward cautiously and tried the knob. It was locked and turned only slightly. Without hesitation, he pointed the barrel down at the latch and fired. The bullet made a loud ringing sound as it tore open the lock. Jag shoved the door inward with his foot, the gun pointed forward to blow away anything that greeted him.

After a few seconds, he and Deb stepped inside, and for the first time since the storm had begun, they felt some relief.

Quickly Jag pushed the door shut and jammed a chair under it to hold it in place. Deb moved to his side again, hugging him tightly, her head on his shoulder. He could feel her body shuddering from the cold.

The warmth of the house felt good, but it would be some time before the chill that gripped them could be melted away. Their wet clothes clung to them, cold and clammy. A few more minutes in the storm and hypothermia would have set in to finish them.

"No sign of anyone," Jag said, scanning the darkened entryway.

"Rand must be around somewhere. And Serena."

As if on cue he appeared at the top of the stairs, a huge blue candle in one hand and a small revolver in the other. His smoking jacket was open, and the tail of it flagged behind him as he started down the stairs.

Jag swung the Walther up toward him, but Rand ignored the weapon. "Have you seen Serena?" he asked.

"She must be in here somewhere," Deb whispered.

"Not on the second floor." He looked around, his eyes now filled with anguish. "We have to go out and find her."

"You can't go out there," Jag said. "The storm is too bad, and the mormo are everywhere."

"I've got to find Serena." He started for the front door.

Jag tried to take his arm, but Rand shook him away, moving onward.

He did not make it to the door before the creatures burst through the kitchen entrance, three of them, bloody and wild.

They shoved back the swinging door and crouched at the edge of the room, growls sounding low in their chests as they raised their claws in erratic sweeps through the air.

Jag dropped to one knee and fired, striking one of the creatures in the shoulder. It seemed to ignore the wound and began to move in on Rand.

He lifted his revolver and fired, his shots popping in rapid succession.

The first went into a creature's eye, bursting it in a rush of blood and other milky matter that bubbled out of the socket. His second shot hit the creature Jag had shot. The bullet plowed through its forehead, dropping it in an instant. The third shot entered the remaining creature's chest, striking somewhere near the breastbone. It stumbled backward with the force of the bullet, tripping on the rug and slamming to the floor.

Rand stood sideways then, his feet placed firmly as he aimed the gun like a marksman. He fired twice more, the shots chewing open the creature's head.

Its muscles twitched only for a moment before it lay still.

Rand looked back at Jag then, his hand still clutching the candle. The flame flickered its light across his features, and the madness in his eyes seemed to glow.

Jag swallowed, expecting the next shot to be for him. He

303

did not blink. His gaze was locked on Rand's. For a handful of seconds, a silent war raged between them, anger and unspoken will colliding.

The sound of shattering glass ended the connection. They turned together, looking toward the window beside the front door which had just imploded.

The creature that had entered was large and hulking, its head the size of a watermelon, its arms long and thick. It had an apelike appearance, yet it moved with an agile swiftness toward the men.

Jag grabbed Rand's arm and pulled him sideways just before the creature dove for them. Towing Rand, Jag then raced down the corridor which led toward the back of the house. He followed Deb, who had already set a course in that direction.

They reached the end of the hallway and found a set of double doors. While Deb struggled to get them open, Jag moved over to a tall decorative mahogany shelf which was lined with pewter figurines and other knickknacks.

Slipping the Walther into his belt, he grabbed the case and shoved it over to block the hallway.

He stepped back from it as it crashed to the floor, the glass shattering as he moved back to the doorway. The oak structure of the case remained intact, forming an obstacle if not a barricade.

Rand had produced a ring of keys from his pocket and unlocked the study door. He pushed it inward and led the way into the room with his candle overhead.

The light spilled long shadows across the racks of guns, and the glass display cases reflected the orange glow back at him.

As Deb shoved the doors closed, Jag looked at the guns, mystified by the sheer numbers. They pointed in all directions, pistols, rifles, shotguns.

"Are all of these functioning?" Jag asked.

"Most of them," Rand answered.

Deb walked from the door over to Jag's side. "We'll need the most powerful ones," she said. "If there's an onslaught of those things . . ."

"We won't have time for careful aim," Jag said.

"How do I know I can trust you?" Rand asked.

"We haven't tried to kill you yet," Jag said. "We're all in this together."

"I suppose that's true."

Rand set his candle on the top of the cases and fished a ring of keys from his pocket. Despondently he opened one of the gun racks and selected a large and heavy weapon. Its long barrel seemed almost a parody.

"This is a .460 Weatherby Magnum," he said. "An elephant gun."

"That should slow them down," Jag said. He took the weapon and examined it carefully, trying to familiarize himself with it.

"If you manage to get it pointed in their general direction, it should work," Rand agreed as he opened a small wooden case and withdrew a box of ammunition for the weapon. "It fires a five hundred grain bullet." He took one from the box and held it up, a massive slug that looked like a miniature rocket.

A loud roar issued into the room then, followed by the thud of something crashing against the outside of the door.

"It knows where we are now," Deb said. Her voice had grown calm, resigned to whatever happened.

Jag was still shaking. He handed the rifle back to Rand for loading and leaned against one of the counters. His head was swimming, and his muscles trembled beneath his wet clothing. His skin felt slimy.

He touched the swelling on his face and then closed his eyes for a moment.

The creature slammed itself against the door again, but the wood held. After a few seconds of silence, it seemed apparent that the creature had lost interest.

Deb moved over to Jag's side. He leaned his head against her shoulder and let the air expel slowly from his lungs.

"We're in deep," he said.

She touched his cheek. "We'll make it. We're in an armory."

Rand finished with the rifle and placed it on the case in front of Jag.

"It'll have a tremendous kick," he warned. "And it will be loud, especially in this enclosed space."

He reached into his pocket and took another set of keys.

These he used to open another wooden case. He pulled out a small box and opened it.

The small black weapon slipped easily from the foam that held it into place, and he pulled the barrel out and screwed it on quickly.

"An Uzi?" Deb asked

"Fully automatic," Rand said as he jammed an ammunition clip into place.

He handed it to her.

"How do I . . . ?"

"Just point it and pull the trigger," he said. "That's all it'll take."

He opened one of the glass cases and selected a silver-plated .357 for himself, sliding a black scope into a prepared notch on the top of it.

"This is a laser sight," he said. He held it up, and a thin red beam shot out from the scope. "Wherever the red dot is, that's where the bullet goes," he explained.

With the guns ready, they paused for a moment, a silence settling over the room.

Against the window the whisper of the storm was still audible.

"Is it me, or does this feel a little like *Night of the Living Dead*?" Deb asked.

Jag laughed grimly. "Too much like it." He picked up the rifle, the weight of it unwieldy in his hands. He pressed it to his shoulder and sighted.

"It'll tear the hell out of whatever you shoot," Rand assured.

Jag put the gun down and rubbed his face with his hands. "So much killing," he said.

"It's a violent world, son."

"Does it have to be?"

"You were violent yourself."

"Lost my head. It was stupid of me. It's not something I'd do again."

"Are you sure. What if this one here were with someone else?"

Jag looked at Deb before he could stop himself, then averted his gaze. "I wouldn't like it, but I wouldn't get into a fight again."

306

"Maybe you are a little better than some animals."

"There has to be some hope," Jag said. "Redemption, mercy, aren't those things supposed to be important? What makes us human if it's not mercy?"

"Animals don't understand mercy."

"What does vengeance really achieve? Look what you've done."

Rand was preparing a reply when one of the large windows crashed inward. One of the creatures had made itself a cannon ball, slamming through the glass.

Jag lifted the rifle and aimed as well as he could, squeezing the trigger as the monster attempted to disentangle itself from the curtains.

The explosion kicked the butt of the gun back against Jag's shoulder, making it feel like it was dislocated. The sound roared through the room, a thunder so severe Jag's ears began to ring.

As he winced at the pain, he saw the bullet blast into the creature near its left shoulder. In a spray of blood, the arm was almost detached from the torso, and the thing went stumbling backward, clutching at the wound as a hideous growl issued from its lips. The limb dangled by a few threads of tendon.

Slumping back against the wall, it looked up at Jag. Fierce, glowing hatred burned in its eyes even as blood pumped everywhere. Dropping its mouth open, it tilted its head back and let out a deafening cry that echoed through the room.

As its mouth closed, a red dot appeared on its forehead, and in an instant the head was gone. Rand eyed the scene coldly as he held the .357 leveled in the creature's direction.

A flutter of movement appeared in the window a split second later.

This time Deb's weapon blazed, spitting a rapid shower of bullets into the creature framed in the opening. The monster dropped backward through the jagged glass with only a slight yelp.

Jag and Rand moved to the opening. The white covering of ice on the ground offered more visibility than would usually have been available.

The rain had thinned to light sleet which blew in and

307

stung their cheeks as they peered at the creatures below. Approximately twenty of them were crouched in a line about one hundred yards from the house. They were like a troop of hideous soldiers.

Deb moved to the other window, pulling back the curtain to look out.

"Where did so many of them come from?" Jag asked. "Did you create that many?"

"Only a handful," Rand said.

"The line never died out," Deb said, shaking her head. Again her voice was calm, resigned to their fate. "The priest said the men drove them back into the swamps, but they didn't kill them all. They've lived on, maybe even found a way to reproduce. The ones you made went back into the swamps and found the hidden ones."

"Like a lost tribe?" Jag said. "Like those in the Philippines."

"Exactly," Deb said. "They lived back there and were spotted only often enough to keep the legends alive. Until now. Congratulations, Mr. Rand. You've drawn them out. They've been cowering from people for hundreds of years. Now they're on a rampage. They're pissed, if you will."

The creatures all eyed the house as the wisps of their breath puffed in the cold night air. They ignored the ice that fell on them, crystalizing in their makeshift pelts.

"Evil perpetuates evil," Jag muttered. It was something he'd heard somewhere. Now it was something he understood.

Behind them, the creature at the door hurled its weight against the wood again. This time, the door inched inward slightly before snapping back into its frame.

"We're in trouble," Jag said. "Even with all the firepower. If we shoot one of them, the others will charge."

"I've always been prepared for a siege," said Rand.

Dipping into his pocket, he pulled out a switchblade and flicked open the blade.

"Keep an eye on them," he instructed.

Leaving Jag at the window, he walked to the center of the room. He looked up at the walls to get his bearings, then began to test the floor with his foot.

After a few steps, he found the spot he was looking for

and squatted over it, using the blade to slit the carpet. When it parted, he peeled it back and opened a slender metal door concealed beneath it.

A long metal box was secreted beneath the door.

Rand lifted it out and began to open it.

He was still fumbling with the latch when the creature at the door launched another assault.

This time the door splintered inward.

The monster stomped over the ruined wood and dove for Rand the moment it set eyes on him.

Encumbered with the box, he was unable to dodge the creature in time. It dragged one claw down his chest in a diagonal swipe. His shirt was ripped open, and the nails cut razorlike into his flesh.

He tried to pull away, but the grip the creature maintained on his shoulders did not let him get free.

Rand shoved the box he held into the thing's ribs without creating a response. Baring its yellowed teeth, the thing prepared to bite into his neck.

Jag moved forward with the rifle, dreading the kick and the noise of it.

From her vantage point, Deb cried out. "Jag, they're charging."

She moved to the open window and braced her arms against the frame to steady the Uzi.

Jag didn't look back even as he heard the rattle of the automatic weapon. He had to get Rand free.

Pressing the gun against the creature's head to avoid hitting Rand, he prepared to squeeze the trigger.

With a sudden sweep of its arm, the mormo knocked the barrel of the weapon aside before it fired. The deafening explosion came, but the bullet flew wild into the wall.

The angry eyes of the monster glared at Jag, and a hiss issued through its open mouth.

Rand was bleeding badly, so his struggles to pull away were weak and ineffectual.

"Jag, they're coming," Deb warned.

The Uzi was jarring as she fired it, yet she refused to let it go. Yellow flame blazed from the short barrel as she sprayed bullets into the night.

Jag attempted to work the mechanism on the rifle, but

something jammed. He struggled with it, unable to produce results.

Without letting go of Rand, the creature made another swipe at Jag, grabbing the end of the weapon in an effort to wrest it from his grasp.

The reporter felt the stock slide through his fingers; then the creature hurled the weapon across the room. It spun through the air and crashed into the gun cases, shattering the glass and sending a shower of it down onto the displayed pistols.

To keep the thing from ripping Rand's head off, Jag dove forward, sliding his arms around its chest and forcing it backward.

It let go of Rand, hammering its hands against Jag's back. Jag drove his fist into the side of the thing's head, trying to aim for the temple area. He was reminded of the bruises on his knuckles as he felt the pain crawl back up his arm.

Jerking himself upward before the creature could sink its teeth into him, he saw Rand weakly extending the .357 toward him. Jag reached for it as the creature grabbed at his throat. His fingers brushed the weapon without managing to close in a grip.

The mormo's hands began to tighten at his neck, stopping the flow of air. He gasped, twisting his head to try to free himself as he continued to extend his hand back for the pistol.

He still couldn't reach it, and he felt the creature's nails biting into his skin.

With a lurch, Rand rolled himself forward, sticking the gun into Jag's hand.

As he felt his face tingle from the lack of blood and air, Jag swung the gun around and shoved it into the thing's open mouth.

The complaining roar was muffled, first by the obstruction of the gun in the orifice, then by the noise of the shot that blew the back of the creature's head across the carpet.

It had all happened in a handful of seconds. At the window, Deb was still firing the machine gun, apparently keeping the things at bay.

Jag pulled himself up from the carcass, wiping blood

310

from his face as he moved over to Rand.

The wound on the man's chest was not as deep as Jag had thought, but it was bad enough. He pulled Rand's coat over it to stop some of the blood flow.

"The case," Rand croaked, pointing toward the metal box.

Jag picked it up and flipped the catches back so that the lid would open. The olive-colored cylinders inside seemed small and insignificant.

The racket of Deb's weapons ceased.

"I'm out of bullets!" she shouted.

"It's an anti-tank weapon," Rand croaked.

"This is a LAWS?" Jag asked.

"It's called a Dragon. A medium-range weapon — that's about a thousand meters. And it's made to penetrate armor. I got them on the black market. Use it."

Jag grabbed one of the cylinders, surprised by the light weight. It was about thirty pounds, but he'd expected it to weigh a ton. He scrambled over to the window, examining it as he moved.

"It's got a blow back," Rand warned. "Don't get behind it."

At the window, Jag lifted the Dragon to his shoulder, fumbling with it, bracing the end of it against the sill.

The first wave of creatures was less than twenty feet away. They had been lumbering about just out of range of Deb's fire.

He peered into the sight.

"It's got a night sight," Rand hissed.

Jag adjusted it, finding the view improved through the red viewfinder.

Now the mormo were headed toward the window, crouching cautiously yet covering the distance quickly.

Jag closed his fingers on the firing mechanism, still peering into the sight. It took a second to figure it out.

"Shoot it," Rand demanded. "There's a tracker built in it."

Jag activated the trigger, and the missile soared, almost whistling as it sailed through the air, a thin trail of white smoke billowing behind it.

The bright orange bulb burst open in the darkness, a blinding ball of heat.

Jag averted his gaze as the blaze engulfed the creatures.

311

The explosion tore into a couple who were clustered together, blowing them apart. Others were overwhelmed by the repercussions of the blast. They lumbered into each other as their bodies were consumed by flame. Some raced about, dropping only when they could move no farther.

Even as they were consumed, another crowd of the things rushed forward, heading for the house with reckless speed. They were mad with the thought of killing, driven to their task.

Not knowing how to reload or if he could reload the weapon, Jag dropped the used Dragon and picked up another, checking only to make sure Deb and Rand were clear of the rear of it.

Then he let a second salvo fly.

Like the first, it whizzed through the darkness, exploding in the midst of the encroachers. They flew apart wildly again, dragging their injured forms along the frozen ground or beating themselves wildly as flames ate away their pelts and flesh.

Jag reached back, grabbing the final Dragon from the scorched floor and balancing it against the windowsill. He was about to fire it when Deb shouted for him to hold.

The dance of the remaining creatures, the uninjured ones, had slowed. Behind them something was walking slowly forward, and they paused as they noticed it.

Jag leaned out the window, staring at the form that was becoming visible through the smoke.

It was a mormo, not very large, and it carried something, almost staggering with the weight. The other monsters parted, granting safe passage through their ranks. They seemed confused, but they did not molest the traveller.

"It's Serena!" Deb shouted. "The mormo is carrying her!"

"What?" Rand limped to the window, one arm clutched across his damaged chest.

He grabbed for the remaining Dragon, but Jag stayed his hand. The creature was not harming her; it moved onward, making its way amid the flames and the ruined bodies.

In its arms Serena was unconscious. Her clothes were dirty, but she had no visible signs of serious injuries. Her wet hair hung limply from her head, and her arms dangled away from her body; but her lungs were working.

"She's alive," Rand muttered.

Part of the mess that covered the creature's face had been brushed away just enough to reveal the flesh that had once been a human face.

"Is he one of the ones you made?" Deb asked. "He looks so young through all of that slush."

"We had some young men who disappeared," Rand said. He drew a couple of difficult breaths. "He must be one of them. They did make him into one of them."

"In prison they'd call it turning him out," Jag said. "They converted him into what they wanted him to be."

"But he saved her life," Debra said. "He's bringing her home."

"Mercy," Jag muttered. "Something inside him prevailed over it all, over all the evil." He pulled himself through the window and took a step forward as the creature approached.

It showed no signs of anger at him, no hatred. It simply moved forward and offered the girl. Jag accepted her weight and managed to hold her in spite of his exhaustion and the hysteria that threatened to seize him.

He looked into the creature's eyes and saw a glimmer of something that had once been human. Somehow that had fought its way through the evil and the magic.

The thing grunted to him, trying to speak, but it could not form words. Something was lost.

With a final effort, it formed something in its throat. "Kyle," it said in a slurred gasp.

"Your name is Kyle?" Jag asked.

The thing nodded sadly, then turned, its shoulders slumped as it walked back through the row of creatures behind it.

Jag felt the muscles in his legs tense as he prepared to spin around and head toward the window if necessary.

He didn't have to. The creatures only stared at him a moment, and then fell in line. It seemed enough of them had died. They had been driven away before, and now they were driven away again, back into their hiding somewhere in the depths of the swamp where they had dwelt so many years.

Dawn was melting slowly into the sky. The forest was like

a crystal palace. Ice coated the trees, each pine needle, each leaf.

The fury of the storm had, in a way, created something beautiful, peaceful beyond the flames. It was white and clean, glistening in the first hints of sunlight.

Jag staggered back to the house, easing the girl through the window with the help of Debra and Rand.

He let the cold morning air seep into his lungs.

Somewhere in the distance he could hear sirens, summoned at last by the noises that had filled the night.

Epilogue

Jag was at his desk when Deb walked into the newsroom. He stood up slowly, his body still a tangled network of aches. His eyes were clouded with exhaustion, and the bruise on his face had not begun to fade. A pair of sunshades rested atop a stack of notebooks at his side.

He hadn't seen her for several days. She was staying at a hotel now, since the questioning of them both had begun. She'd said it was probably best.

She looked better than he. Her hair was pulled back in a pony tail. Her skin was clean, and she wore fresh jeans and a bright red sweater.

She smiled as she held up the newspaper. The front page was still emblazoned with headlines on stories that bore Jag's byline. He had broken the story the day after the nightmare, dictating it to Breech between interviews with police officers and medical treatment.

Now followup stories were unraveling the twisted web of Rand's conspiracy for the public's scrutiny.

The news stories referred to the attacking animals without being specific about their origin.

Federal investigators had converged on Aimsley, digging into every law enforcement agency to ferret out information.

A number of officers had been linked to the vigilante group, most of them still alive. They were placed on suspension as the feds began to turn the screws.

Chief White and the sheriff tackled the public relations problem with the charisma that had carried them through all of their previous skirmishes.

"Are you a real reporter now?" Deb asked.

Jag took her arm, and they walked from the newsroom and down the hallway toward the back door.

"They haven't asked me to do obits in three days. I think they're worried I'm going to collapse before everything is tied up."

"I'm surprised you haven't. I've been sleeping since the cops quit questioning me."

"I'd like to. There just isn't time. Too much to put together. I've been talking to everybody. They tell me I'm lucky to be alive."

"Did you find the girlfriend of that boy?"

"The one who saved Serena? Yeah, her name is Ruth. She talked a lot about Kyle. I think she really loved him. He was a hood, but apparently a good-natured kid, relegated to a life of hell. It's still unbelievable."

"How is Serena?"

"One of the churches lined up a family for her to stay with for now, while her father awaits trial."

They stepped out in the chill wind and walked along the sidewalk toward the parking lot.

"What happens now?" Jag asked.

"Trials? Lots of trials? You'll be busy writing stories."

"That'll take care of itself." He hesitated, afraid. "I mean about us."

She looked down at the sidewalk as they moved. "We've been through a lot," she said. "Both of us. We were thrown together. We talked about that."

"I know but—"

She stopped and placed her hand against his lips.

"Let's take some time to sort things out. I have to deal with Mark's death now. God knows neither of us is going to escape nightmares for a long time. I've woken up screaming several times. A maid at the Clairmont thought I was being attacked one time."

She sighed heavily. "I need to go home, see if I still have a job. So many things."

"They're going to give me some time off as soon as these things are wrapped up."

"We'll see. You mean a lot to me, Jag."

"I—"

She stopped his words once more, knowing what he would say. "Give it time. You've been turned upside down

316

because of me. I don't know how I feel right now. I'm confused. And your career. You can write your own ticket right now. Think about that."

He tried to protest, tried to argue, but she only shook her head and smiled. "We'll see," was all she would say.

He watched her walk into the parking lot and unlock her car. She paused before slipping behind the wheel, waving to him with a flutter of her gloved fingers.

He stood on the sidewalk with the wind biting at him as the little Volvo backed from its parking space and eased from the lot into the traffic that carried it slowly away.

Everybody that gathered regularly at Dean's Barber Shop knew Walt Mendler was crazy. He was near eighty, and he'd been involved in hair-headed schemes all of his days.

He'd led hunts for Jean Lafitte's treasure, launched get-rich-quick schemes and was convinced every time the new sweepstakes mailers came around that Ed McMahon was going to pay him a million dollars.

On the hot summer afternoon when he came blustering into the little shop at the edge of Penn's Ferry, they all chuckled the way they always did when he showed up.

His eyes were side, and he swept his sweat-stained gray fedora off as he glared at all of them.

Dean, a silver haired Cajun, stood behind the barber's chair, combing Matt Luken's hair

"What's up there, Walt?" he asked.

"I was fishin' out there at the creek, and I saw 'im in the shadows. He was lookin' at me.

"Then the wind came up and I could smell 'im. Near made me vomit, he smelled so bad. Dead stuff it smelled like."

"What are you talking about?" Dean asked. "Who'd you see."

"Seven foot tall he musta been. It was him. Like I seen when I was a kid."

Dean laughed at the old man's intensity. "Who?"

"The swamp man. You musta heard of 'im, Dean. It was ole momo. Musta been looking for food."

317

BLOOD BEAST
(17-096, $3.95)

by Don D'Ammassa

No one knew where the gargoyle had come from. It was just an ugly stone creature high up on the walls of the old Sheffield Library. Little Jimmy Nicholson liked to go and stare at the gargoyle. It seemed to look straight at him, as if it knew his most secret desires. And he knew that it would give him everything he'd ever wanted. But first he had to do its bidding, no matter how evil.

LIFE BLOOD
(17-110, $3.95)

by Lee Duigon

Millboro, New Jersey was just the kind of place Dr. Winslow Emerson had in mind. A small township of Yuppie couples who spent little time at home. Children shuttled between an overburdened school system and every kind of after-school activity. A town ripe for the kind of evil Dr. Emerson specialized in. For Emerson was no ordinary doctor, and no ordinary mortal. He was a creature of ancient legend of mankind's darkest nightmare. And for the citizens of Millboro, he had arrived where they least expected it: in their own backyards.

DARK ADVENT
(17-088, $3.95)

by Brian Hodge

A plague of unknown origin swept through modern civilization almost overnight, destroying good and evil alike. Leaving only a handful of survivors to make their way through an empty landscape, and face the unknown horrors that lay hidden in a savage new world. In a deserted midwestern department store, a few people banded together for survival. Beyond their temporary haven, an evil was stirring. Soon all that would stand between the world and a reign of insanity was this unlikely fortress of humanity, armed with what could be found on a department store shelf and what courage they could muster to battle a monstrous, merciless scourge.

Available wherever paperbacks are sold, or order direct from the Publisher. Send cover price plus 50¢ per copy for mailing and handling to Pinnacle Books, Dept. 17-437, 475 Park Avenue South, New York, N.Y. 10016. Residents of New York, New Jersey and Pennsylvania must include sales tax. DO NOT SEND CASH.